ALSO BY

MAURIZIO DE GIOVANNI

I Will Have Vengeance:
The Winter of Commissario Ricciardi

BLOOD CURSE

Maurizio de Giovanni

BLOOD CURSE
THE SPRINGTIME
OF COMMISSARIO RICCIARDI

Translated from the Italian
by Antony Shugaar

Europa
editions

Europa Editions
214 West 29th Street
New York, N.Y. 10001
www.europaeditions.com
info@europaeditions.com

Copyright © 2008 Fandango libri s.r.l.
First Publication 2013 by Europa Editions

Translation by Antony Shugaar
Original title: *La condanna del sangue. La primavera del commissario Ricciardi*
Translation copyright © 2013 by Europa Editions

Library of Congress Cataloging in Publication Data is available
ISBN 978-1-60945-113-4

de Giovanni, Maurizio
Blood Curse

Book design by Emanuele Ragnisco
www.mekkanografici.com
Cover photo: Rina Franchetti
(Naples, December 23 1907) © GBB Archive Contrasto
Digital elaboration: Papirus

Prepress by Grafica Punto Print – Rome

Printed in the USA

To the little boy in the baby carriage: my father

I

Though no one could possibly know it, the last rains of winter had fallen that afternoon. The street surface reflected the dim glow of the hanging lamps, which dangled motionless in the now-still air. The only light still shining at that hour of the night came from the barbershop. Inside, there was a man polishing a mirror's brass surround.

Ciro Esposito possessed an iron sense of professional rectitude. He'd learned his trade as a child, sweeping up hair clippings by the ton from the floor of the barbershop that had once belonged to his grandfather, and later to his father. He was treated no better and no worse than the other employees—if anything, with an extra smack in the head or two if he was a second late in proffering the straight razor or a damp towel. But it had done him good. Now, as in the old days, his shop counted among its customers not only those from the Sanità neighborhood, but even those from the far-flung quarter of Capodimonte. He was on excellent terms with them; he understood clearly that men came to the barbershop as an escape from work and wife, and in some cases, from their political party, every bit as much as they did for the haircut and the shave. He had honed that very particular instinct that allows one to chat or to work in silence, and to always have something to say on whatever subject people liked to discuss.

He'd become quite the connoisseur on the topics of soccer, women, money and prices, honor and shame. He avoided politics, which had been such a minefield in recent years. A fruit-cart peddler happened to complain about the difficulty he'd been having obtaining supplies; four guys nobody'd ever seen in the neighborhood had demolished his cart, calling him a "defeatist swine." Ciro steered clear of gossip, too. No point in running risks. He was proud in his conviction that his barbershop constituted something of a social club, which is why he was especially worried that last month's incident might cast a shadow over his honorable establishment.

A man had committed suicide, right there in his shop. The man in question was a longtime customer, already a regular back when his father still ran the place. A companionable, jolly fellow, who never tired of complaining about his wife, his children, the money that he never seemed to have enough of. A civil servant; he couldn't remember what branch of government, if he'd ever known at all. Lately, the man had become gloomy and distracted, and he didn't talk the way he'd used to, nor did he laugh at Ciro's renowned jokes; his wife had left him, taking the children with her.

It had happened that, as Ciro was carefully trimming the man's left sideburn with his straight razor, he'd reached up and gripped Ciro's wrist and with a single, determined jerk of the arm, he'd cut his own throat, from ear to ear. It was pure luck that Ciro's shop assistant and two other customers had been there to witness it, or he'd never have been able to persuade the police and the investigating magistrate that it had been a suicide. He'd quickly scrubbed everything clean and the next day he kept the barbershop closed, careful not to breathe a word of what had happened. The dead man was from another part of town. That, at least, was helpful. In a city as superstitious as Naples, it didn't take much to get the wrong kind of reputation.

This is what Ciro Esposito was thinking about on this last night of winter, when he had finished cleaning and was getting ready to fasten and lock the two heavy wooden shutters that protected his shop's front door. He was the only shopkeeper on the Via Salvator Rosa who worked this late. But his workday wasn't over yet. A man, murmuring a greeting under his breath, walked into the shop.

Ciro recognized him; this was one of his oddest customers. Lean, of average height, taciturn. Thirtyish; swarthy, narrow-lipped. Nondescript in every way, except for his green and glassy eyes, and for the fact that he never wore a hat, not even in the dead of winter. What little he knew about him only heightened the discomfort he instinctively felt in his presence. These were not times in which one could afford to displease customers, especially regulars, but this one, in particular, was no walk in the park. The man said good evening, took a seat, and closed his eyes as though asleep, bolt upright in the chair, as if embalmed.

"Buona sera, Dottore," he said, using the classic term of respect for the college-educated. "What'll it be?"

"Just the hair, thanks. Not too short. A quick trim."

"Yessir, I'll have you out of here in just a moment. Make yourself comfortable."

The man leaned back. He looked around quickly and Ciro saw him stiffen in alarm, holding his breath for a brief instant. Was it Ciro's imagination, or had he looked at the chair on the far end of the room, the one belonging to the dead man? The barber decided he was becoming obsessed; he was starting to think that everyone who came in could see the bloodstains he'd so painstakingly scrubbed away.

With a sharp sweep of his hand, the customer brushed aside the stray shock of hair that dangled over his narrow nose. He looked even more ashen by the light of the electric lamps, as if there were something wrong with his liver; his dark complexion verged on the yellowish now. The man heaved a sigh and closed his eyes.

"Dottore, are you all right? May I get you a glass of water?"

"No, no. Just hurry, please."

Ciro started snipping away rapidly, starting with the hair on the back of the man's neck. He couldn't know what the customer, eyes shut tight, was trying so hard not to look at.

The customer could see a man, sitting at the far end of the room, head sunken between his shoulders, hands lying limp on his legs, a black cloth tied around his neck, his eyes fixed on the mirror on the wall. Just above where the cape was tied ran an enormous gash, like a smile scrawled by a child, out of which waves of blood were pumping rhythmically. From behind his clamped eyelids, the customer could sense the corpse slowly turning its head to look at him: the faint snap of the vertebrae in its neck, the damp slithering of the wound's twin lips.

"What I'd give to see how she likes it now, the slut. Now that she's deprived her children of their father."

The customer raised one hand to his temple. Ciro felt increasingly uneasy; there was no one on the streets at that time of night, and that good-for-nothing shop assistant of his had gone home long ago. What else could befall him? The scissors clipped away at an ever-faster pace. The man was holding his eyes shut tight, and the barber could see beads of sweat standing out on his forehead. Perhaps he had a fever.

"We're practically finished, Dotto'. Just two more minutes and we'll have you out of here."

From the far end of the room, the dead man was repeating his lament. In the street outside the wide-open door, silence reigned and springtime awaited. The air itself seemed to be holding its breath.

The customer could hear the scissors chattering away, like frenzied crab claws. He was determined not to listen. What do you expect to see, anyway? You won't see anything ever again. You won't see how that slut likes it, and you won't see anything else.

With a deep sigh, the barber untied the cape from around his customer's neck.

"There you go, Dotto'. You're all done."

After tossing a few coins onto the side table that served as a cash register, the man walked out in search of fresh air. He was having trouble breathing.

The humid evening embraced Luigi Alfredo Ricciardi, Commissario of Public Safety in the Mobile Squad of the Regia Questura, or Royal Police Headquarters, of Naples. The man who saw the dead.

Tonino Iodice had returned home from work to his wife, mother, and three children. It had been a terrible day. As he did every evening, he stopped in the atrium of the old apartment building in Via Montecalvario to don his mask, that of the weary but satisfied father and provider, a man whose business was thriving. He knew it was wrong, but it was for their own good. The last thing he wanted to do was to make them share his burden.

It fell to him to lie awake most of the night, staring at the ceiling and listening to the breathing of his sleeping family. Another day without disaster; who knows how much longer we'll be able to hold out. It fell to him to reckon and re-reckon his accounts, always the same sums of money, always the same days of the calendar, waiting with dread for his promissory note to come due, searching for the words he hoped to use to persuade the old woman to give him one last chance.

Tonino used to have a pizza pushcart and, now that he thought back on it, things hadn't been so bad. His mistake was that he hadn't appreciated it, that he'd wanted something better. He woke up every morning at five, made the dough, topped off the oil, set up the pushcart, dressed as warmly as he could if it was cold out, or else prepared to be assailed by the blast of brutal summer sunlight, and headed out into the city. Always the same streets, the same faces, the same customers.

Everyone loved Tonino; he belted out songs at the top of

his voice, and it was a fine voice he had. That's what his mother told him and his customers said so, too. He kidded all the lovely ladies, pretending he'd fallen for them head over heels, and they'd laugh and say, All right, all right, Toni', just give me some pizza and get outta here. He was the kind of guy who spread good cheer, with his little pushcart, his whistle, and his fine voice, and the policemen would look the other way, never asking him for his vendor's license or food permit; in fact, now and then they'd come by and he'd offer them a pizza, *pe' senza niente*, on the house. The months turned into years, and he'd married his pretty Concettina, who was even more cheerful and penniless than he was. Then came Mario, Giuseppe, and Lucietta, the three children in quick succession, as good-looking as their mother, as boisterous and loud as their father, but as ravenously hungry as the two of them put together. Soon the pushcart wasn't bringing in enough to make ends meet.

That was when Tonino made up his mind that, unless he made an effort, unless he reached out for something better, they'd all soon be on the road to hunger. And, even though no one dared to say it outright, everyone was feeling poorer these days. More and more, people were filling their bellies with whatever they could scrape together at home. His customers were dwindling, and with the eight-day pizza plan—eat today and pay next week—many ate on credit, and then dropped out of sight.

That's when it occurred to him that rich people could still afford to go out to eat, and that rich people wanted to sit down to enjoy their meal, to listen to the parking attendant serenade them on his mandolin, to eat, drink, and make merry. The old blacksmith and farrier in Vicolo San Tommaso was about to retire, and he was giving up his place. Two long tables and one small one would fit in the space—maybe he could even fit in a second small table. To start out, he'd make the pizzas and

Concetta could wait tables; then, when business picked up, Mario, the eldest, could pitch in.

Having gathered together his mother's savings and borrowed every last lira he could from his other family members and friends, he was still short by a considerable sum. He'd sold his pizza cart, so there was certainly no turning back. And so a friend of his told him there was an old woman in the Sanità quarter who was willing to lend money long term, at a low rate of interest.

He went to see her and he talked her into it. He was good at talking people into things, and better still at persuading old women. He'd gotten the money he needed, and now six months had gone by since his pizzeria had opened for business.

Everyone he knew came to the grand opening—relatives, friends, and passing acquaintances. Not the old woman, though; she had told him she never liked to leave the house. Everyone came and everyone ate their fill, that day and the next. It would bring good luck, and he hadn't charged them a cent. The only problem was that after that the friends and relatives stopped coming around.

Tonino understood that envy wounds more than *scoppettate*, musketballs. That was what the old people said, and the old people knew what they were talking about. Sure, every now and then someone would pass by and stop in, but the pizzeria wasn't on a main thoroughfare. You had to know about it to get there—and no one seemed to know about it. As the days passed, and as the months hurried along after them, it dawned on Tonino that he'd been a fool: he'd spent too much money setting up and getting ready to open, money that he'd never see again. After three months, the old woman had extended the loan for two more, this time at a higher rate of interest. Then she'd given him one last extension, just one month this time, shouting him out of her apartment. She warned him that this was the final deadline. He would have to pay her what he owed.

Tonino swung open his own front door and Lucietta leapt into his arms, covering him with kisses; she was always the first to hear him come home. He hugged her tight and, with a smile stamped on his face, he strode in to face the rest of his family. He felt his heart tighten in his chest. The promissory note was coming due tomorrow, and for the last time. And he didn't even have half the money he owed.

II

S pringtime came to Naples on the fourteenth of April of the year nineteen thirty-one, just a few minutes after two in the morning.

It showed up late and it came the way it always does, with a gust of fresh wind from the south, following a cloudburst. The dogs were the first to detect it, in the courtyards of the Vomero farmhouses and in the alleys down by the waterfront; they lifted their muzzles and sniffed at the air and then, heaving a sigh, went back to sleep.

Its arrival went unremarked upon as the city got its last couple of hours' rest between the dead of night and early morning. There were no celebrations, no regrets. Springtime didn't demand a festive welcome, and required no applause. It occupied the streets and the piazzas. And it stood patiently outside the doors and shuttered windows, waiting.

Rituccia wasn't asleep; she was only pretending. Sometimes it worked. Sometimes he'd just stand there, looking at her, and then turn and go back up to the sleeping loft. Then she'd hear the creaking of the old bed, his body tossing and turning, followed by his sawing snore, a horrible sound that greeted her ears like a thing of beauty because it spared her such horror. Sometimes. Sometimes she was allowed to sleep.

But that night, the springtime had come knocking at the window, stirring his blood, blood curdled by the cheap wine from the tavern at the end of the *vicolo*, the dark, narrow

Neapolitan lane. Pretending to sleep wasn't going to do her any good. As always, when she felt her father's hands on her body, she thought of her mother. And she cursed her for being dead.

Carmela whimpered in her sleep; arthritis was a red-hot iron jolting and crushing her bones. She wasn't cold, the heavy blanket covered her snugly, and the walls were dry. If she'd been awake, rather than deep in a dreamless slumber, the old woman would have looked around proudly at the flowered wallpaper she'd recently had installed. If she'd been awake, she'd have mused that with all those flowers on her walls, she had bought herself a springtime of her own, and with the new season on its way, the flowers would be competing, out on her balcony and there in her apartment.

But Carmela would be denied the springtime. Not the flowers, though; she'd have those. It's just that she wouldn't see them.

Emma turned over on her side, careful not to awaken her husband, who lay sleeping to her left. Experience told her that when the movement of the soft woolen mattress roused him from sleep before he was ready, the selfish old man's thousand-odd afflictions became that much more exaggerated. She scrutinized his profile in the dim light; the glow of the streetlights filtered in through the silk curtains. Had she ever loved him? If she had, she certainly couldn't remember it now.

She smiled in the darkness, her cat eyes illuminated. Not another night, not another springtime without love. Her husband was sleeping with his mouth agape, his hairnet wrapped over his head, and his nightshirt buttoned snugly around his neck. God, how I hate him, she thought to herself.

Beyond the wooden planks that secured the door of the *basso*, the airless, windowless ground-floor hovel apartment,

Gaetano could hear the rats in the *vicolo*. During the day, the rats vanished down the drains of the new sewer system, except for the big sick ones, which the children hunted down and killed; but at night, and all the past week, he'd heard them scurrying past. Maybe it was the warm weather on its way. His mamma had finally dropped off to sleep. He'd listened to her muffled sobbing, close by his side, until just an hour ago; then the weariness of her long day had won out. Two hours of peace for her, maybe three, before she had to start all over again. But he wasn't sleeping; he was thinking about the decision they'd made. The decision they'd been forced to make. They couldn't go on like this. He closed his eyes and, as he did every night, waited for sunrise.

Attilio couldn't get to sleep. That night he'd been wonderful but, as usual, no one had noticed. He could feel the brooding frustration that was his frequent nightly companion poke at his stomach as he lay smoking a cigarette in the darkness. Unable to see, he let his gaze roam the walls; what did it matter, he thought, there was nothing to look at, nothing but poverty. Still, he knew, and he'd always known, that someday he'd be rich and famous, revered and adored. Like that conceited lout who had nothing that he didn't have in spades. It all starts with money. When you have money, the rest follows. Mamma had always told him that, ever since he was a little boy. Money before all else. Just one more week. Then he'd be done with dreary rooms in tawdry boardinghouses.

In the depths of her uneasy slumber, Filomena was dreaming. In her dream, she was standing outside her own front door and watching herself emerge from the house, bundled into a long black shawl, her face covered, as always, to conceal herself.

The door was emblazoned with a word, written in red paint in huge letters: WHORE. Just that one word, simple and straightforward, as though it were a last name. She saw her head droop in shame, guilty without guilt. Whore. No men, no love affairs, no lingering looks or smiles. A whore all the same. In her dream she felt the anguish, the fear that her son would see the word when he came home. Her fingers wet with tears, she tried to rub it off, but the harder she tried the bigger it grew, staining her hands red. Red with an age-old crime: the crime of being beautiful.

Enrica was sleeping on the first night of the new season. On the night table were her eyeglasses, a book, and a glass half-full of water. Her nightgown was folded on the armchair, under the frame with her embroidery.

In the black shade of dreams, an unfamiliar touch, a strange scent, and two eyes staring at her. Green eyes. In her dream, the young woman felt the arrival of spring, stirring her blood.

Just a dozen feet away, but so far he might as well have been on the surface of the moon, the man had fallen asleep. He'd eaten his dinner, then he'd listened to the radio as he watched her at her embroidery, through the window. Entering into someone else's life, as if it were his own. Touching objects with someone else's hands, laughing with someone else's mouth, imagining sounds and voices that he couldn't hear through the glass.

Then sleep—bringing a new sense of disquiet, a different anxiety under the skin—seemed like an affliction, but in fact it was the arrival of spring: blood searching for a way out. And at last, the darkness that contained the images of his greatest fears, the last remnant of his innocence.

In his dream, the man was a little boy again, and it was summertime; the heat scorched his skin. He was running head down through the vineyard next to the courtyard of his father's house, playing by himself, as always. In his dream, he could smell the scents of his own sweat and of the grapes. And then the scent of blood. The blood of the dead man sitting on the dirt in the shade, his legs stretched before him, his arms resting on the ground, his head lolling over onto one shoulder. The handle of the field knife protruding from his ribcage like a stump, an abortive third limb. As the man slept, he gasped in childlike astonishment.

Like before, the corpse lifted its head, and like before, it spoke to him; and the most horrific thing was that, like before, it seemed perfectly natural to him for the corpse to speak. In his dream, he turned and fled once again; and the man who the child had become uttered a lament through his slumbering lips. There was no chance of escape; a hundred, a thousand dead men would speak to him from unknown mouths; just as many times, they would look at him with empty eyes and reach out to him with broken fingers.

Outside the window, spring was waiting.

III

He liked strolling through the city in the early morning. The streets were almost empty, practically silent aside from the distant calls of early-stirring street vendors. Not making eye contact, not having to look down at the street to avoid showing his face, his eyes.

He knew he had a highly developed sense of smell. Not surprisingly, this wasn't a particularly good thing, because there were far more bad smells than there were good ones. Still, on a morning like this one, he could detect the perfume of the green hills, well hidden under the miasmas that rose from the stench-ridden city quarters, and winning out over the smell of the sea. It reminded him of the aromas of Fortino, the small town in Cilento where he was born and where, without knowing it, he'd been happy for the last time. It was the smell of nature, primal and luxuriant, embracing mankind like a mother.

A subtle pleasure, and a worry; he knew what awaited him. Springtime, Ricciardi mused as he walked toward Piazza Dante: it changed people's souls like so many leaves on the trees; stern, dark, lofty trees, strong and unyielding in their centuries-long wait, suddenly went crazy in that season, showing off garish blossoms. In much the same way, even the most stable people suddenly got the strangest ideas into their heads.

Though he had only just turned thirty, Ricciardi had seen, and saw on a daily basis, exactly what every single individual was capable of, however innocuous that person might appear at first glance. He had seen, and continued to see, far more than he wanted and more than he ever would have asked for; he saw pain; he saw grief.

Overwhelming grief, pain that repeats itself, over and over. The anger, bitterness, and even the strutting irony that came with death. He had learned that death by natural causes settled its accounts with life, amicably and conclusively. It left no lingering footprints in the days that followed, it snipped off all the threads and sutured the wounds, before heading off down the road bearing its load, wiping its bony hands on its black tunic. But that's not how violent death worked; it didn't have time. It had to leave in a hurry. In those cases, death staged a show, offering up the portrayal of the final pain and grief for the eyes of Ricciardi's very soul; it was heaped upon him, the sole spectator of the rotten theater of human evil. The Incident, he called it, or even better, the Deed. And the idea that death in its hasty departure hadn't had time to settle its accounts washed over him like a wave, demanding vengeance. Those who leave the world in this manner do so with a backward glance. And they left messages that Ricciardi gathered, listening to that last, obsessively repeated thought.

The first of the balconies overlooking Piazza Carità threw open their shutters, bringing it to life. As he walked toward police headquarters, it dawned on Ricciardi, the way it did every morning, that he'd never have a choice, that there was only one profession for which he was suited in life. He'd never have the strength to ignore the pain, to turn away from it, or travel the world scattering his money with a free hand. There's no escaping who you are. He knew that his distant relations couldn't understand why he, the only child of the late Barone di Malomonte, didn't take his place as the new Barone di Malomonte, capitalizing on the social advantages that would come so easily with that title. He knew that his Tata Rosa, the nanny who had raised him from his infancy and was now in her seventies, ardently wished to see him at peace, living an untroubled life. No one could explain his prolonged silences, his downcast gaze, the constant gloom that absorbed him.

But, as Ricciardi knew full well, it hadn't been his lot to choose; he was obliged to walk against the wind, buffeted by the last shifting gusts of grief of all the dead people he met along his path. So that he could complete the work that death hadn't had time to finish.

Or at least try to.

In the placid early morning air, Ricciardi walked into the building that housed police headquarters. The watchman at the front door, half-asleep in his guard booth, made an attempt to leap to his feet and salute him military-style, but he succeeded only in knocking over his chair with a sharp crack of wood that echoed across the courtyard. Irritated, he shot the spread index-and-pinkie sign of the cuckold toward the back of the commissario, who hadn't so much as waved in his direction.

Ricciardi wasn't well liked by the staff at headquarters, whether uniformed or administrative; and it wasn't because he was a bully or took a hard line. If anything, he was the one most likely to conceal the oversights or failings of others from the notice of the top brass. Rather, it was that no one could figure him out. His solitary, taciturn personality and behavior, the seeming absence of any weakness, and the complete lack of information about his private life did nothing to encourage camaraderie or fellowship. And then there was his extraordinary ability to solve cases, which had something of the uncanny; and there was nothing that struck more fear into the heart of that city's populace than the supernatural. The idea that working with Ricciardi brought bad luck became increasingly deep-rooted. It was becoming a matter of course for those assigned to one of his cases to be kept home by a convenient but debilitating head cold, or, even worse, for his presence to be blamed for mishaps that had nothing to do with him.

A self-perpetuating state of affairs: the greater the void Ricciardi created around himself, the happier other people were to steer clear of him. The commissario seemed not to be aware of this, much less bothered by it.

With his superiors, the deputy chief of police, and the police chief himself, things were no different. These weren't years in which one could easily afford to dispense with the services of such a talented individual. Increasingly, Rome had been interfering with the independence of police headquarters, and the police were expected to provide evidence of their successful investigations by tossing a guilty party to the press. The regime demanded that the image portrayed of Fascist life in the big cities convey safety and high hopes. Ricciardi, with his rapid and unorthodox way of cracking cases, was perfect.

But there was no denying that his presence created a sense of unease. He wasn't welcome, and so his merits were overlooked. He was denied the promotions and the opportunities that he objectively deserved. They might not be able to do without him, but they weren't about to reward him, either. For that matter, Ricciardi didn't seem to care about advancement in the least. He was constantly absorbed in his work, more a priest militant of justice than a civil servant, bent over his desk or striding through the seamiest quarters of the city, in the driving rain or the blistering heat of summer, frantically seeking the source of the suffocating grief and pain that engulfed him.

Within the barricade of mistrust that surrounded him, however, there was at least one person he could count on.

IV

rigadier Raffaele Maione sipped his coffee looking out from the balcony, enjoying the panoramic vista. Truth be told, the liquid in his demitasse wasn't proper coffee at all; he wasn't sure he could even remember what real coffee tasted like. For that matter, the word "balcony" didn't accurately describe the oversized windowsill with an undersized railing which the landlord of the building in Vico Concordia had installed some twenty years ago, without a permit. And last of all, the labyrinth of dark alleyways that stretched out as far as the eye could see, riddled with hunger and sordid dealings: only an absurd stretch of the imagination could justify calling it a vista.

But Maione possessed the requisite imagination, and the optimism, too. God, did he have optimism. And God alone knew how much he had needed it, to get through certain times in his life.

As the darkness gave way to the first light of dawn, Maione sniffed the air in the same way the dogs had sniffed it a few hours earlier. Today, there was a different smell in the air. Perhaps it had come at last; perhaps that interminable winter was finally over. Another springtime: the third without Luca.

There were times when he could hear his laughter. A fine laugh, disjointed and loud, a laugh that announced his arrival. Perhaps it was that very laugh that had been his undoing. He would never know. Maione looked at his hand, and then at his arm; it was dark-complected and big, solid and powerful in spite of his fifty years.

Unlike Luca: his boy had been blond like his mother and, like her, he laughed all the time. Except that Maione hadn't heard his Lucia laugh once since that day. Of course, life went on—and how could it stop, with five more children to bring up? But laughter: never again. On winter nights, when the children were asleep and time stood still, Luca would come home cheerful as ever to cradle his mother in his arms, to hoist her in the air laughing; or to tease his father, calling him a potbellied old timer, standing proud in his new uniform, a newly minted rookie on the police force.

On that still-chilly morning, springtime brought the brigadier the scent of his son's blood. And the memory of how Deputy Officer Ricciardi, that strange young policeman no one wanted to work with, had shut himself up in the cellar, alone with the corpse, for five endless minutes. And how Ricciardi, gripping Maione's arm and staring him straight in the eye, had brought him Luca's last message of love, couched in words of tenderness that he couldn't possibly have known. Even now, three years later, the love and horror he felt still made him shiver.

Since then he had been the commissario's trusty squire. He would brook no bad-mouthing of Ricciardi from anyone, not the slightest hint of mockery.

He was also the guardian of Ricciardi's very particular police procedure, which involved a preliminary solitary inspection of the scene of the crime. Maione would keep everyone else back as the commissario tuned in to whatever had happened there; Maione was also his confidant for what little Ricciardi was inclined to share, which was very little indeed. These confidences amounted to reasonings, spoken out loud, musings on the investigation underway, but through those musings Maione was able to guess at his character, simply by dint of his own experience. Each time it was as if this were Ricciardi's own personal crusade, his own loss, his own infamous wrong to be avenged, an injustice visited upon him in need of restitution. Ricciardi wasn't like the others, who investigated for money, advancement, or power; he'd met so many. No, Ricciardi wasn't like the others.

That morning it occurred to Maione that Ricciardi wasn't actually that much older than his own Luca: just ten or so years older, maybe a little more. But he seemed to be a hundred years old, and completely alone, like a condemned man.

As he squinted and ran a hand over his cheek, already rough just an hour after shaving, it suddenly occurred to Maione that it was precisely this very curse that had made it possible for the commissario to deliver his son's last words to him. Shivering, he went back inside. It was time to go to work.

V

S
he hated that place, and yet she couldn't live without it. As she was waiting, Emma reflected on this fact: she had tried more than once, but she couldn't live without it. She hated the horde of clamoring children. She hated the steep, narrow stairs that led up to the top floor, the tattered humanity that she met there: the poverty-stricken tenants of the building and the customers she encountered, who stood aside to let her pass.

She understood: she was as ashamed as they were. This is how she imagined a bordello, not that she'd ever been in one. Still, this is how she imagined them: places where being recognized could mean forever tarnishing a sterling reputation built up at the cost of great effort over the years.

And then there was the smell. Garlic, rancid food. And urine, as an aftertaste. Urine in the street, in the entryway, in the apartment. Sometimes she brought flowers, but they were viewed with suspicion, as if they concealed an implicit request for a discount. She only brought them so she could breathe in there, to ward off the smells. Of course, the woman was elderly, and the elderly can't control themselves. She was happy to be young and she had every intention of remaining young as long as she could. And pretty. And rich. And desired. Now that she had finally found true love, life was more beautiful than ever, and the future was radiantly bright. Everyone'd been saying it in recent years: the Italian nation's future was going to be an exceedingly bright one. So why shouldn't her own be? How long would she have to go on paying for a mistake made by others, though the penalty was visited upon her?

She needed one last blessing, one final authorization from fate. She was certain of her feelings, but she couldn't afford to make another mistake. Not anymore.

It was hot in the apartment. She had left her house wearing her heavy overcoat, a thick fur stole around her neck, and her charming aviator's cap with earflaps, declining the proffered car and chauffeur. She remembered the look in the man's eyes last time, a mixture of commiseration and distaste for the long wait surrounded by the dozens of street urchins who tried to scale the massive vehicle, as if it were a mountain made of steel. She unbuttoned her coat. She wished she could smoke, but the old woman didn't like it. Where was the old woman? How long would she have to wait, before she could finally begin her life?

Standing at his office window, Ricciardi was looking out onto Piazza Municipio. The street was still wet from last night's downpour, but now the sky was blue and cloudless. A faint breeze brought with it the smell of the sea.

The trees in the garden of the piazza down below were perfectly shaped to provide shade for the wrought-iron benches. The four green refreshment stands were beginning to collect customers, newspapers, and soft drinks.

A few carriages, four automobiles, a truck. In the distance, beyond the piazza, loomed the three smokestacks of the English cruise ship that had docked a few days ago. Overshadowing everything, the immense Maschio Angioino, the old Angevin fortress.

Few living beings. No dead people at all. Ricciardi permitted himself to take a deep breath, and he held it in. Slowly, he exhaled. He turned around to face his office, with the city behind him. Before him lay "Ricciardi's cell"—that's what the headquarters staff called his office.

Once again, the woman witnessed the ritual, her heart in her throat, the usual pounding in her ears. A million times she'd told herself it was a bunch of nonsense, and a million and one times she had found herself once again in the grip of those lovely and terrible sensations. Fate. She watched as fate took shape before her.

The old woman had been unlike any other. She used to laugh whenever her idle and bored girlfriends told her how they spent their loveless afternoons, chasing after the dream of a better tomorrow. She'd even gone with them once or twice, only to witness ridiculous playacting, theatrical witches with assistants who pretended to be ghosts and produced sepulchral voices from the Beyond. The problem was that the Beyond was a crawlspace behind a fake wall, not even all that well concealed behind a half-open curtain.

Then one day she'd met Attilio, after a play. She'd gone to the theater alone as usual, and that same, magical night, she'd had that chance encounter with the old woman. The old woman had approached her with her shuffling gait, and she had mistaken her for a panhandler. She'd ignored her, and was about to pass her by. But then the old woman seized her by the arm, staring at her in the darkness; she stopped, speechless. Then, with the same scratchy voice that she'd later listen to so eagerly, the old woman told her in no uncertain terms that she was unhappy because her heart was empty.

That phrase: an empty heart. How could she have known that that was exactly how she saw herself—a woman with an empty heart? Attilio had intervened, impetuous, so muscular and handsome, without warning, first under the portico of the theater and then out in the rain. He'd chased the old woman away coldly, with exaggerated indignation. But before leaving her, the old woman had whispered an address in her ear. And the young woman had gone there the next day. Since then, she'd returned at least a hundred times, returning unfailingly, to follow the paths that the old woman indicated, for help overcoming her doubts, to decide which direction to turn at the crossroads that had always made her hesitate. She couldn't so much as breathe without the old woman's help. She paid her the pittance she asked for, but she would have given twice, three times, a hundred times more. She was buying the strength to live.

This time, once again, it was her life that was at issue. She was expecting a definitive response, and she already knew the answer in her heart: this time she'd be able to feel she was alive, perhaps for the first time; this time she'd be able to choose love. She instinctively clamped her legs together at the thought of his hands. Her stockings rustled faintly and she felt ashamed, convinced as she was that the old woman could easily read her thoughts. But the old woman was laboriously sitting down at the card table, with great pain: her bones, of course. The smell of garlic and urine wafted over her, and she blinked slowly. The misshapen fingers reached out for the deck of greasy cards. She held her breath.

VI

There were no curtains or candles in the apartment. No concessions to theatrical effects, except for the modest flowers on the wallpaper. It was one of the first things she had noticed and it had caught her off guard when she first came to the place, short of breath from the steep stairs and the stale odors. A simple apartment, from what she'd been able to see: a single room adjoining a small kitchen, and a closed door.

With the usual startling quickness of her gnarled fingers, the old woman shuffled the deck, whispering something under her breath; Emma had never understood what she was saying and she never wanted to. After reciting her cryptic words, she spat on the cards—three times. Emma clearly remembered the disgust she'd felt the first time she saw her do it. She'd been tempted to leap to her feet and run out the door, but the power in those movements had rendered her helpless. The gobs of spit vanished immediately, wiped dry by those deft hands and by the cards themselves as they slid one over the other. Suddenly, with the elegance of a croupier in a gambling den, the old woman held out the deck so she could cut the cards. Emma heaved a sigh. Her hands were sweaty. The old woman took half the cards and laid them down on the stained table-cloth. With the rest of the cards she made eight small piles, arranging them in the shape of a cross, and then she looked Emma straight in the eye. After a long moment during which Emma, as always, felt as if she were sinking into a sea of petroleum, she pointed to the pile at the center of the cross. The old woman nodded, again without a word. Since she'd arrived in the apartment, not a single word had been uttered.

With the flash of motion that never failed to startle her, the old woman beat her fist down on the deck she'd pointed to, cawing out: *"Munacie', damme voce!"* Spirits, give tongue!

From the little balcony, two pigeons took flight, startled. In the street, four floors below, the chorus of urchin voices fell silent for a moment. Time stood still, as the woman once again witnessed an act of magic in which she believed implicitly and wholeheartedly. Now the old woman's eyes were closed and she was breathing hard, lips clamped shut, white hair gathered in a bun, head sunk between her shoulders, both fists clenched on the table. After a moment she relaxed, took a deep breath, and lifted the first card from the chosen deck.

The King of Coins.

Filomena Russo emerged from the *basso*, knotting her scarf around her neck; she was cold, and this year's winter seemed to go on forever. The icy wind battered her as she stopped to lock the deadbolt on the wooden door. She saw the word "whore" written in chalk. *Goddamn them*, she thought. *Damn them.*

The Vico del Fico was a blind alley, an inset halfway up one of the steep streets of the Spanish Quarter. At the entrance to the alley was a shrine to Our Lady of the Assumption, a few flowers placed there in hopes of response to prayers that had gone unanswered; then there was a little *piazzetta*, invisible from the street: five *bassi* teeming with life, surmounted by the tall, darkened windows of ancient, half-empty buildings. Sunlight for just a few hours a day; the rest of the time, shadow and damp reigned uncontested.

A tiny village in the heart of the city, and she was an outsider in that village.

Head down, lapels lifted to cover half her face. Her handkerchief covered the other half. The man's overcoat, old, worn and shapeless, shoes with cardboard soles. She carefully avoided puddles; otherwise, her feet would stay wet all day. And her feet were crucial. They had to support her during the long, exhausting workday in the fabric store on Via Toledo. She walked quickly, looking down at the ground and keeping close to the wall. She could feel the hostile eyes all over her, following her from the windows. She could feel hatred.

Luckily, that evening she'd be home before her son; she could erase the word on the door. It was chalk or whitewash, and it would come away with water. It had happened before: some lowlife had carved the word with a knife, and she'd had to scrape away at it for an hour. Gaetano had asked about it. Nothing, she'd told him. Nothing. They have nothing else to think about.

Behind her raised lapel, she smiled wryly. To call her a whore, she who hadn't felt the touch of a man's hand in two years, she who shrank from the eyes of everyone. To call her a whore, when she'd only had one man in her life, and one was all she'd ever have, because her Gennaro was dead and she'd never be able to stand anyone else's hands on her body.

At the corner of the *vicolo*, Don Luigi Costanzo stood waiting, as he did every morning. She would have liked to just avoid him, but the one time she'd taken a different route he had shown up that night and knocked on the door of the *basso*. He seized her by the arm, hurting her and hissing into her terrified face, Don't you ever try that again, I'll come and get you where you live. Gaetano watched from the shadows, a scream in his eyes but not on his lips. She had reassured him with a glance: Don't be afraid, my darling son, don't worry; this bastard will be out of here any second. Don Luigi was young, but people said that he'd already killed two men: an up-and-coming young *guappo* and the future capo of the quarter. He was married, with two children born in two years. So what did he want from her? You're driving me out of my mind; I have to have you. What are you talking about? What did I do to make you lose your head? When I've never even looked in your direction, when I live like a slave, working from dawn to dusk, to feed my boy, to let him earn a trade, so he can earn a living, so he can have a future?

And she had driven him out the door, threatening to scream, to bring shame upon him, to tell his young wife everything, or, worse, to inform his father-in-law, the true capo of the quarter. And he'd left. But before turning to leave, he'd smiled at the boy, the smile of a demon from hell. Why, what a handsome young man, he'd said. Tender flesh, just waiting for a knife. Filomena sobbed all night long.

The old woman turned over the second card in the pile. Seven of Swords. The old woman's hand, twisted like a centuries-old oak branch, trembled for a moment, and her eyebrows came together. Emma held her breath and didn't blink. Garlic, urine. The shouts of children in the street below. The morphology of fate.

Filomena picked up her pace, as much as her broken-down shoes and the wet cobblestones allowed. She did her best to avoid the man, but he took a few quick sidelong steps and blocked her path. She stopped, head lowered, her face concealed by the upturned lapels of her coat. He emitted a ridiculous sound, smacking his lips in imitation of a long kiss. She stood motionless, waiting. He pulled his hand from his pocket and reached out for her; she took a step back. Then he said, Filome', it's only a matter of time. A matter of time, she thought. He asked her, with a laugh: What are you doing, all covered up like that? It's like you're ashamed. Are you ashamed? She maneuvered around him and strode off briskly toward Via Toledo. Yes, she thought to herself, I'm ashamed.

Filomena Russo was ashamed of her worst defect, her curse. Filomena Russo was the most beautiful woman in the city.

The old woman turned over the third card: an Ace of Cups. Her lips clamped shut. A fly smacked against the windowpane and the sound rang out like a shot. Emma realized that her own hand was at her throat; she could feel her suddenly racing pulse. Her feet were like ice. Another card, the fourth one: the Five of Swords. The old woman's expression remained unchanged, but her hand trembled.

Over time, she'd learned to recognize the card that represented him, the man she loved: the Knight of Clubs. It had always turned up, from the very beginning, accompanied variously by cards that urged flight, change, life. Why was it failing to appear, this of all times, now that she had made up her mind?

The old woman turned over the last card in the deck, her last chance. It was neither a knight nor a king. It was the Queen of Coins. To her horror, Emma realized that a tear was running down the old woman's cheek.

Filomena waited for the first customer to enter the fabric shop where she worked. Standing on the street corner, bundled in her overcoat, with her handkerchief tied tightly around her head, she was indifferent to the wind. She'd have been glad to feel the warmth of the shop's large stove on her skin—it was certainly already lit by now—but she couldn't go in yet. She knew that Signor De Rosa, the shop owner, attached a great deal of importance to making sure the place was cozy from the minute it opened, convinced as he was that, that way, women chilled from the cold would gladly linger to make their choices, and therefore, to buy.

But she also knew that Signor De Rosa, in his fifties and already a grandfather, had been threatening her for some time now. Filome', out you'll go. If you don't come with me right away, I'll toss you out on your ear. But if you're willing, I'll make you rich, shower you with gifts and jewelry. Filome', you've bewitched me. You've driven me mad and now you have to heal me.

Speaking with his wife would have been pointless; Filomena's word against the word of a respected man, held in high regard for his seriousness and professionalism, and for his love for his family. In the best possible scenario, he'd throw her out, and she couldn't afford to lose her job, not as long as Gaetano was still an apprentice; she'd be forced to send him to do menial labor, and he'd be poor for the rest of his life. And Gaetano's well-being came before all other considerations. Standing erect at the street corner, all her beauty concealed in an old overcoat, Filomena Russo waited and wept silently.

VII

Ricciardi left his office at eight at night. He hadn't allowed himself many breaks during the day; around one that afternoon he'd stepped out to buy a pizza from a street vendor, attracted by the column of smoke rising from the oil pot which also served as a sort of sign. Tata Rosa would not only disapprove of his choice, she would have gone on muttering for hours: You don't think about your health. You might as well just shoot yourself in the head, she would have added. Better to just tell her he'd skipped lunch entirely.

It hadn't been a very good day. He'd spent it filling out forms, which were destined to go on moving from desk to desk ad infinitum. He often felt like a miserable accountant, unable even to grasp the few rigid formulas he used to reckon up the evil he encountered, an evil he struggled to express in rational terms. As if perversions, savage emotions, rage, and hatred could be put into words.

Not that there was any shortage of murders; what was missing now was action, the open air, movement. He never felt comfortable shut up inside four walls, even knowing what awaited him out there; that's the way it had always been. A leftover from his years at boarding school as an adolescent, most likely. People shunned him back then as they did now, driven away by the instinctive perception of some unnatural sorrow that he harbored within; even in a school full of cruel boys, ready to lash out at the slightest oddity, he went his solitary way, allowed safe passage and a wide berth. He couldn't remember being pained by the experience; all things considered, he'd been better off that way. When you're acquainted with the Deed, he thought, what are you going to tell a friend? Are you going to tell them what the dead tell you?

The hallway was dark. Almost everyone had gone home. That's how it always was: he was the first one there in the morning, the last one to leave at night.

He knew what he'd see and, sure enough, he saw them: standing side by side on the second step of the broad, empty staircase, arms linked like a couple of old friends: the cop and the robber, like in the children's game of that name.

In their way, they were an anomaly in the world of the Deed: it had been two years now, and Ricciardi could still see them, faintly luminescent in the half-light; maybe because of the magnitude of the surprise, or maybe because there were two of them. He remembered the event clearly. It had been one for the books: a small-time ex-con, arrested after a brawl, had grabbed for the holstered revolver of one of the two officers leading him to his cell and had fired a bullet into his own temple. A bad break: the bullet had shot straight through his head and continued on, killing the officer to his left as well.

As he walked past the pair, Ricciardi heard for what seemed like the thousandth time the words they kept repeating on an endless loop. The convict was saying, "I won't go back, I won't go back in there," the police officer, "Maria, Maria, oh, the pain." Not Maria the Virgin Mary—Maria his wife.

The right side of the jailbird's head, the one run through by the bullet, was destroyed: the gaping hole, the scorched skin all over his face, the eye socket vacated by the burst eyeball, brain matter splattered across his shoulder and chest. On the left side, only a small wound where the bullet had emerged to go hurtling into the head of the guard. The officer's right eye was a deep red, as if a gnat had wandered into it, when in fact it was tinged with the blood that had flooded his brain. Eyes downcast on the steps, seeing without looking, Ricciardi whispered along with the dead officer, barely moving his lips, "Maria, the pain," as though it were the punch line of a familiar joke. He walked quickly through the half-open front door, ignoring the hostile gaze of the watchman who had snapped a sharp salute. He needed some air.

Even at that time of night, when the shops and cafés were all closed, Via Toledo swarmed with both the living and the dead. It had officially been called Via Roma for sixty years now, but for the people of the city the street's name had never changed: it was Via Toledo when the occupying Spaniards built it, and it was Via Toledo now, as Ricciardi crossed it, brushing past the mendicants begging for bread, coins, attention. Whatever one wished to call it, the real name of that street was "borderline." A boundary dividing two populaces as different as night and day, pitted against each other in a tacit, unending war. Each of those who clutched at the hem of his overcoat considered himself heir to a uniquely unfortunate lot in life. And yet every one of the countless shades of passion could be traced back to two primal needs: procuring immortality through procreation and feeding oneself and one's family. Power and the abuse of power, honor and pride, comfort and envy: all of them the spawn of hunger and love.

Enrica ate her dinner while her father and brother-in-law argued. She was accustomed to the lengthy political diatribes that accompanied the evening meal: both she, the eldest daughter, and her mother and siblings had realized by now that there was no avoiding them, much less breaking in or changing the subject; so they might as well just eat their meal and let the two of them keep going at it after dinner, sitting over by the radio. That was the moment she awaited eagerly, all day long and perhaps even at night, as overbrimming with desire as she was in her dreams. She had become a skilled actress, able to feign interest in the argument underway when on the inside she was actually pursuing her own thoughts. She could hardly wait for dinner to be over and for everyone to troop off into the living room, leaving her to wash the dishes. It was a routine she liked: her stubborn, radiant, introverted, and sensitive nature had always made her a precise, orderly person. She was happiest when everything was in its place and everyone was doing their job, and the kitchen was her own personal domain. She didn't want anyone's help. She wanted to be left alone.

And besides, she had a date.

VIII

Ricciardi ate, and Tata Rosa watched him eat.

The same thing every evening. He would rather have come home to find she'd already retired for the night, since she was seventy years old and had been up since dawn. But she refused to relinquish her fundamental principle: she would not go to bed until she'd seen him eat every last bite. He would gladly have foregone the same narrow selection of dishes. She complained that she didn't how to cook anything different. All he wanted was to give his brain a rest. She spent the whole day charging the batteries of her complaints and waited for him to walk through the door to unleash them on him. It's idyllic, no doubt about it, mused Ricciardi as he chewed, without tasting it, a mouthful of spaghetti with basic, routine tomato sauce, the third time in six days it had been on the menu.

"It's a sad, miserable life you lead. Just look, you had your hair cut yesterday and you've already got your bangs in your eyes again. And look at you, you're pale, so pale that you look like a ghost." At this, Ricciardi grimaced wryly. "Tell me, do you ever see daylight? Today, for example, there was a scent in the air that blew down from the forest of Capodimonte, it was just lovely, but did you even think of taking a walk in the gardens in front of police headquarters? No, eh? I knew it. What's a poor old woman like me supposed to do? Am I supposed to close my eyes once and for all, condemned to the knowledge that I'm leaving you with no one to take care of you? Don't you want to find yourself a pretty *guagliona*, so you can put me in a hospice and let me die in peace?"

Ricciardi gravely nodded in agreement, occasionally looking up from his food to show his full appreciation of the disaster that had befallen his Tata, whose dreadful fate it was to have to look after him. He hadn't actually heard a single word she'd said. Still, he could have recited her litany word for word; he'd listened to it so many thousands of times over the years. He had other things on his mind, as usual, and he dealt with Tata Rosa the way you deal with the rain: you wait for it to end and do your best to stay dry. If he so much as dared to answer back, he'd have to spend the rest of the evening persuading his Tata that there was no life he'd rather live.

And besides, he had a date.

Enrica was washing the dishes. The whole family had moved into the living room, in that cheerful daily migration that carried noise and disorder away from her domain, giving her a chance to look around with a sense of satisfaction.

She wasn't pretty; you wouldn't bother to give her a second glance if you saw her walking down Via Santa Teresa on her way to Mass, or buying greens from the vegetable cart on the corner. Tall and swarthy, she wore myopic eyeglasses with tortoiseshell frames. She was twenty-four years old and she'd never had a boyfriend. She wasn't pretty, it's true, and she cared nothing about fashion; but there was a gracefulness about her, in the way she smiled, in her slow, careful movements, with her sure way of doing things, her left-handed precision.

She'd studied to be a schoolteacher, and she spent mornings tutoring children whose parents had given up all hope of keeping them in school; without raising her voice or resorting to punishment, she seemed to be capable of taming even the most feral little beasts. Her father and mother worried about her. They often talked anxiously about her lack of marriage prospects, but they'd given up trying to matchmake with the sons of friends. She had always declined these introductions, courteously but firmly.

Ricciardi had walked into his bedroom, hairnet on his head, hands in the pockets of his smoking jacket. The old oil lamp on the night table cast a yellow light on the few pieces of furniture: a chair, the small writing desk, the two-door armoire. He was standing next to the bed, his back to the window; his hands were clammy in the pockets, he was short of breath, his racing heartbeat pounded in his temples.

He heaved a long sigh, turned around, and took two steps forward.

Out of the corner of her eye, Enrica saw the glowing lamp behind the windowpanes on the opposite side of the narrow lane. Fifteen feet, no more; she'd done the calculation a thousand times. And about three feet higher up, at most. A seemingly infinite distance. She wouldn't have traded it for any other sensation on earth, that minute of waiting between when he lit the wick and when his silhouette came into view. It was like opening a window and waiting to feel the breeze blowing gently against your face, or being thirsty and lifting a glass of water to your lips. That backlit figure, with his arms folded or else at his sides, or perhaps with his hands in his pockets. Motionless. No gesture, no signal, no attempt to make contact aside from the simple fact that he was there, every night, at nine thirty. She wouldn't have missed it for anything in the world. And slowly, with her own particular slowness, she finished washing up with a series of gentle motions, then sat in the armchair near the kitchen balcony and took her embroidery frame in her lap, or else picked up the book she'd been reading. Enveloped in that gaze, she smiled and waited.

Ricciardi watched her embroider. As he watched her, he spoke to her, telling her about the things that most troubled him, and she helped help him to untangle his thoughts. It was strange, no question. Through the glass of the two windows, he watched the unhurried gestures he'd fallen in love with, more than a year ago. Her carriage, the way she read, the way she embroidered. Herself. He thought he'd never seen anything in all his life as lovely as the way that girl embroidered. And yet it was more than he could do to approach her; the man who remained impassive in the face of the most horrific crimes was terrorized by the idea. He had inadvertently found himself face-to-face with her a few months earlier at the vegetable vendor's cart, and he'd taken to his heels in the most undignified fashion, leaving a wake of broccoli behind him. She had watched him, tilting her head to one side in that way he know so well, her eyes half-closed behind her tortoiseshell spectacles. And the man who knew no fear had run for his life.

If only you knew, my love. If only you could imagine.

Fifteen feet away, the girl who was so good at waiting embroidered, stitch by stitch; and on the frame, beyond the sheet to be added to an optimistic trousseau, she saw a pair of green eyes, unknown to her and yet so familiar. She thought that if two roads are destined to meet, they will eventually, however many miles it takes. And she also thought back, with a hint of shame, to the visit she'd made just two days earlier at a girlfriend's insistence, to that strange place, a place she never would have imagined. She remembered the questions she'd asked and the answers she'd been given, without hesitation, as if they came from a book written sometime in a far-off future.

Embroidering and smiling with her head tilted to one side, Enrica was thinking about something Ricciardi could never have imagined.

She was thinking about the Knight of Clubs.

IX

The stage, the dust, the lights. This is what I want to feel, this is what I want to breathe. When I was small, I was poor, cold, and hungry; but I already knew they would cheer for me, that I would bowl them over, move them to tears. I've always been good-looking, I've always known how to tell a story, how to charm people with words. There's no one else like me; that's what my mother's always told me.

How she slaved away, my mother, to make sure that my enthusiasm never flagged, that I was always up for the challenge. I sang and I danced, at parties, at weddings. Surrounded by oafs and bumpkins incapable of appreciating what they were seeing. The magic of words, the magic of movements: those were my passions. The voice is an instrument. I know that I'm handsome. I've always been handsome. My mother was the first one to say so, and I've had plenty of confirmation since.

My beauty has also been my downfall, what's held me back. Women like me, and men seethe with jealousy. Mamma says that life is a theater; in her way, she's an actress herself. Son, she says to me, you can't even begin to imagine how many times I've pretended. But every time, I provide my own applause; I applaud the money that ends up in my pocket. Do as I do. Money: that's all the applause you'll need.

That's what Mamma says, but I have to disagree. The way I see it, if you're really good, then everyone should applaud for you; there can't be just one conceited wretch standing between you and the success you deserve. So I'm going to find a way to buy a theater troupe and, if necessary, even an entire theater.

And then we'll see.

Concetta Iodice stood peering out the small window that overlooked the *vicolo*. It was late, and Tonino should have been home an hour ago. The pizzeria had been closed for quite a while now. He had told her to go ahead and head home, because he had an errand to run. She would never have thought to question her husband's orders, but it had caused her some anxiety, some concern.

Precisely because of his cheerful nature, the *pizzaiolo* was an easy man to read. When something was off, Concetta and her elderly mother-in-law Assunta immediately became aware of it and exchanged a knowing look; for several days now, they'd both been detecting that same discordant note. They knew business wasn't as good as they'd hoped it would be, and that the loan that had been taken out in order to open the restaurant was sizable; maybe that's what was stirring trouble in the man's soul. Tonino no longer sang while he shaved, he trudged rather than walked up the stairs, he greeted his family as if he had something else on his mind, and the day before he'd smacked their eldest boy for calling his name aloud. Nothing like that had ever happened before.

Assunta joined Concetta at the window.

"The children are asleep. No sign of him?"

Without turning around, the woman screwed up her mouth and tossed her head. Anxiety gripped her chest, growing stronger by the second. Her mother-in-law placed a hand on her shoulder and she reached up and squeezed it gently. A shared love; a shared fear.

When she saw him turn the corner, she felt a surge of relief rise up inside her—but only for an instant. His dragging step, his slumped shoulders. He looked like an old man. She ran to the door and pulled it open; behind her, in the shadows, Assunta stood wringing her hands. His slow steps coming up the stairs, in the silence of the dark old building. The last flight of steps. Concetta searched the darkness for Tonino's eyes, both yearning and dreading to look into them.

Ashen, sweaty, his hair plastered to his forehead underneath his cap, Tonino was staring blankly ahead. He walked past his wife, gently squeezing her arm. The woman felt the warmth of his hand on her wrist.

"I don't feel well. A slight fever, maybe. I'm going to bed."

Concetta looked at the stretch of floor that her husband had just walked over. He'd left a footprint, as if his shoes were wet.

To look at them, you'd think they were two perfectly ordinary children. Like the children you'd see in the Spanish Quarter or on the streets down by the port, who moved in flocks, like birds, noisy and boisterous, the girls indistinguishable from the boys and all of them equally filthy, dressed in clothes that were equally tattered; not like the city's other children, insipid, dressed in sailor suits or junior fascist uniforms, marching military-style across Piazza Plebiscito. In contrast, these children had their heads shorn bald to fight lice and went barefoot, a rind tougher than leather on the soles of their feet, purplish and chilblained in winter, bound up crudely with threadbare rags.

Gaetano and Rituccia had grown up together. Even though their bodies were still years from the full bloom of adolescence—he was almost thirteen, she was twelve—it was enough to look into their eyes to guess their ages. Old. They were old because of what they remembered, because of what they had seen and continued to see.

They both had vague memories of a happier time, when his father and her mother were still alive, and they were just two more little birds in the flock that burst into flight every morning among the city *vicoli* that they called home. But that was a long time ago, when they used to sit absorbed in conversation on the steps of the church of Santa Maria delle Grazie, occasionally begging coins from the old women hurrying in for the midday Mass. Now, ever since Gaetano had begun his apprenticeship as a bricklayer, they were only rarely able to speak; they didn't need words, though, having mastered the ability to read new developments in each other's faces, detecting news from the crease in his furrowed brow or the angles of her downturned mouth. They conducted themselves like those old couples who know each other so well as to communicate only through gestures.

In the evening, before returning home, they sat together on the ground, under the porticoes of the Galleria Umberto Primo, just as they were doing right now. In silence, they tried to summon the courage to go home for the night.

Concetta Iodice had sat there, watching her husband sleep, without being able to get a wink of sleep herself. She was afraid that his fever might spike, that he might be really sick without her realizing it. That was something that had always terrified her; her father had gone that way, during the night, while she and her mother and her siblings were sleeping peacefully. That night he was there and the next morning he wasn't; he'd left behind that pitiful worn-out dressing gown with one eye half-open and the other shut, his blackish tongue lolling out of his open mouth. Sprawled out on the floor next to the bed; maybe he'd called for help and no one had heard him.

So Concetta sat there on the chair by the bed, watching Tonino Iodice, owner of the pizzeria and restaurant that bore his name, as he laboriously carried on the business of his troubled night's sleep. He tossed and turned, he moaned, he pulled up the bedclothes and threw them off again. His leaden face, the hair plastered to his sweaty brow, his lips twisted in a grimace. Perhaps he was dreaming. Concetta did her best to make out words, but all she could hear were moans and laments. She sighed and rose to her feet, doing her best not to make a sound. She took Tonino's jacket to put it away in the clothes cupboard. She smiled unconsciously, thinking of her husband's habitual messiness, of how often she'd had to pick up the articles of clothing he scattered around the house. A sheet of paper dropped out of one of his pockets. Concetta bent down and picked it up.

She couldn't read, but she understood that this was a promissory note, signed by Tonino. Standing out boldly, like an inky stamp from the post office, was a large red fingerprint. She snapped her head around toward her sleeping husband and looked with horror at his big hand, the hand of an honest laborer, the fingers dirty with caked blood.

X

Even with the door open, the light was faint. Silence: only the occasional creak of hinges, a window or two left open to let in fresh air. The knife blade glinted in a flash that no one saw, without so much as a moan.

Donna Vincenza went out into the *vicolo* very early each morning. She didn't like to keep a full chamber pot in the apartment until late, and she also enjoyed stepping out for a walk. The winter seemed to stretch on forever, and windows still had to remain locked tight to ward off the damp of night that seeped into her bones. She'd been walking with a hunched back for months now, looking even older than she actually was. That drunken lout husband of hers, in contrast, never stirred until the church bell rang; thankfully, it chimed so loud and so close that it made him leap out of bed and start the day with a sonorous oath.

She emerged from the narrow little door, tugging her shawl tight around her head. Chamber pot in hand, she walked past the locked door of Rachele's *basso*, and her thoughts ran to the poor woman who had died a year ago, leaving behind such a young orphan girl. Still, better her than me. She trundled along for a few more yards, toward the drain that topped the cesspit. She noticed that the front door of the whore's *basso* was ajar. That's odd, she thought. She knew that the little boy was the first to leave in the morning; he was an apprentice with some relative of theirs who was a builder. Then the whore went off to that shop in the Via Toledo, to ruin who knows what family.

The woman gave in to her curiosity and drew closer to the narrow aperture. She placed one hand on the doorjamb and the door creaked open. She looked inside and as soon as she got her breath back, she started screaming.

Brigadier Maione walked briskly. He wasn't late for work; in fact, he was early. He liked to take his time, make a pot of ersatz coffee, get the police officers set up, assign the staff their jobs for the day. Still, he walked briskly, because he wasn't the kind of person who liked to waste time, and because he was heavily built and he was walking downhill.

He didn't have far to walk. From Piazza Concordia he walked up a long *vicolo*, the Via Conte di Mola, and that took him straight to Via Toledo, just a minute's walk from police headquarters and the start of a new day, which he was already fully immersed in mentally. The buzz and bustle around him was that of the city awakening: a shutter or two creaking open, a woman singing, a small child wailing. Then there were the smells: dust, excrement, yesterday's food, horses.

The scream shattered the air he was breathing, along with every other memory and thought: Maione had a sharp ear, and he knew that that was a scream of terror, not a shout of anger or a roar of despair. The sound reverberated in his ears, and so far no rubberneckers had come out to their balconies. Maione was already racing toward the source of the sound, his hands clenched in fists. A policeman is a policeman. It had never occurred to him to tell himself, Raffae', just mind your own business.

It was a woman's voice, and it was coming from the Vico del Fico. He was the first one to reach the scene, where he found an elderly woman with a shawl on her head and her hand over her mouth, a shattered chamber pot beside rivulets of urine, the front door of a *basso* halfway open. With his eyes he followed the direction of the old woman's gaze, trying to register and record as many details as possible: door opened from within, unbolted; silence inside, no sign of movement. A partial footprint, possibly a man's shoe, between the floor and the street, black. Black: why black? Then he understood.

"Don't move, stay right here, Signo'. Did you see anyone leave?"

Donna Vincenza, still overwrought, shook her head no. On the second story a shutter swung open and slammed hard against the wall, and an elderly man stuck out his head.

"Vince', what's going on? Have you lost your mind, screaming like that so early in the morning? Who's down there . . ."

Maione raised his hand in one sharp movement and the man fell silent at the sight of him. His reaction was so prompt in fact that he closed the shutters on his fingers; this was followed by a muffled howl of pain, and then finally by the sound of bolts shooting home. The brigadier detected a flash of satisfaction in the old woman's eyes. That must have been her husband.

He stepped onto the threshold and waited a second for his eyes to adjust to the dark. He began to make out the outlines of things: a bed, a sleeping loft, an armoire, a table. Two chairs. One was empty; the other wasn't. Silence. A noise, or rather, something dripping, slowly. He took another step, and was able to distinguish the profile of the person who occupied the chair. A woman sat there bolt upright, motionless, facing the wall. Something about her posture made the hairs on his back stand on end. Absurdly, he asked: "May I come in?"

Slowly, the face turned toward him, entering the narrow blade of light that filtered in through the half-open door. He glimpsed a long, white neck, locks of hair as black as night. Temple, ear, forehead, a perfect nose. An eye, calm, steady, not a flutter of the long lashes. Even in the dim half-light, to the unsettling metronome of falling drops, Maione could see that this was no ordinary beauty. The profile was transformed into the full vision of a face caught in the morning light. Maione was breathless. When the woman had completed her movement, the brigadier saw what Donna Vincenza had seen just a few minutes earlier.

Filomena had been disfigured by a broad slash, running from her temple to her chin, across the right side of her face.

Another drop of blood fell from the wound onto the red-stained floor.

Maione let out the breath he'd long been holding, and along with it, a moan.

Teresa had gotten up early that morning: it was a habit that she had maintained from when she lived in the countryside, before she came to work as a servant in the city. She had often thought about going to see her father and her numerous siblings, who still lived in the single large room that was so icy in the winter and hot in the summer, and which still haunted her dreams. But then laziness won out, along with the faint fear that something or someone might keep her there, making her as poor and miserable as she has been before.

In order to placate her conscience, therefore, she sent money to her family now and then through a farmer who brought a load of vegetables into the city once a week. She told him to send them her greetings and tell them she was doing well. For the time being, she held tightly on to her job in the distinguished palazzo in Via Santa Lucia, down by the waterfront, in the midst of elegant carriages, fine clothing, and even automobiles, which she could see driving by from the balcony.

It was a good job. There were no children or elderly people to look after, many of the palazzo's fifteen bedrooms remained unused and closed off, and she herself, who was theoretically responsible for keeping them clean, entered them no more than twice a year. Moreover, Teresa enjoyed living in close contact with the gentry, watching the life they led. She wondered how it was possible to own all those fine things and not be happy. And yet it was very clear, even to her naïve eyes, that her employers lived in a constant state of misery.

The signora was much younger than the professor. She was remarkably beautiful, and she reminded Teresa of the Madonna dell'Arco with her jewelry, her dresses, her shoes; and, like the Madonna, she always had a look of sorrow on her face, sad eyes that stared off into the void. Teresa remembered a woman back home in her village who had lost a son to a fever: she had the same eyes as the signora.

The professor was never home, and when he was, he didn't say a word; he just sat and read. Teresa was afraid to look at him. He intimidated her with his white hair, tall man that he was, invariably elegant in the stiff collars that she starched for him, his golden cufflinks, his spats, his monocle on a fine gold chain. She'd never heard him speak to his wife. They seemed like strangers; once, she thought she'd overheard them quarreling as she was walking into the green parlor to bring them their coffee, but who could say, it might just have been the radio. They came together for meals, but he read at the table and she would stare into space. Occasionally, in the early hours of the morning, she'd seen the signora come home after spending the whole night out.

That morning she was doing the laundry. It was still early, and off in the distance the fishermen were hauling their boats onto the beach, shouting loudly one to another. It must have been six, perhaps even earlier. Suddenly, the professor appeared before her, in a state of disarray unlike anything she'd ever seen before: his hair was tousled, his collar was unbuttoned, and there was a shadow of whiskers on his normally impeccably clean-shaven cheeks. His staring eyes rolled frantically, and his monocle dangled from the breast pocket of his jacket like a broken pendant necklace. At this hour he should have still been asleep in his bedroom; he was never up before eight o'clock.

He walked up to her, grabbed her by the arm, and gripped it tightly.

"My wife. My wife. Has my wife come home?"

She shook her head, but the man did not release his grip.

"Listen to me, pay attention to what I'm telling you, what's your name, Teresa, right? All right, then, Teresa: my wife will be home before long. You mustn't say a word, you understand? You keep your mouth shut. I came home last night and you haven't seen me since. Understood? Keep your mouth shut!"

She nodded her head yes. She'd have done anything to get her arm free of that man's grip, that man who looked like a demon out of hell. A fisherman was singing; the slow morning waves murmured gently.

Still staring at her, the man let her go and, walking backward, exited the laundry room. Teresa's heart was pounding in her ears. The professor had vanished: perhaps she'd been dreaming; perhaps she'd never seen him. A powerful shiver ran through her body, and she lowered her eyes.

On the floor she saw the footprint left by the professor's shoe; it was black, as if from mud, or blood.

XI

Maione emerged from the *basso* door, holding the woman up, pressing his handkerchief, already sopping with blood, against her ravaged face. In less than a minute the usual crowd had gathered, the kind that the poorer quarters of the city bestow upon every event, be it a stroke of good fortune or a catastrophe. When it was the former, one always sensed envy in the air; when it was the latter— a far more common occurrence—there would be a sense of having dodged that bullet, and of chilly commiseration.

This time, however, Maione read in the eyes of the women lining the little piazza a vein of hostility, throbbing more powerfully than the awful wound he could feel through his handkerchief. The person he'd hauled out of the darkness was certainly not beloved by the quarter. The brigadier looked around him.

"Serves you right, whore!" he heard someone hiss behind him. He turned around, but he couldn't say which cruel mouth had uttered those words. The woman's eyes were stunned and glassy, as if she'd gone blind.

"What's your name?" Maione asked, but she didn't respond.

"Filomena's her name," the old woman he'd first met, the one who had screamed, replied on her behalf.

"Filomena what?" Maione asked her, giving her a hard cold stare. Her hostility and indifference were unmistakable.

"Filomena Russo, I think."

Had there been time, Maione would have smiled bitterly. In a place where people knew everything about each other, down to the number of hairs on their neighbor's ass, that "I think" sounded just as ridiculous as a toy horn at the Festa di Piedigrotta.

"Are any of the signora's friends here? Anyone who would be willing to see her to the hospital?"

Silence. A few of the women standing closest even took a step back. With a look of disgust, Maione pushed through the crowd and walked briskly in the direction of Piazza Carità, toward Pellegrini Hospital. But not before committing to memory several faces, the half-open door, the blood-smeared partial footprint.

Already gathered in front of the hospital was the usual crowd of fake invalids, those who tried to gain admission by playing on the sympathies of doctors, nurses, and attendants, all for a warm room and perhaps even a bite to eat before being sent back out onto the street. Maione, with his hand wrapped around Filomena's shoulder and his handkerchief over her face, pushed through the crowd with great determination, making his way toward the main entrance. Outside, the Pignasecca market was teeming with life and the air was full of the shouting of vendors competing for business.

The brigadier had tossed his overcoat around the woman's shoulders; she hadn't spoken a word along the way, nor had she moaned or complained. A couple of times she had winced, when the uneven ground had made Maione press her face a little harder. The pain must have been atrocious. He wondered who could have done such a horrible thing to such a lovely woman; and what motive there could be for her neighbors' hatred, in a place where one usually found solidarity and consolation.

The wound was on the side of the face that Maione was covering, so that one or two peddlers from the market snickered when they recognized him, Look, look, the brigadier with the girlfriend. He ignored them; he was starting to worry about all the blood the woman had lost. As he walked into the hospital lobby, he called out to the porter.

"Is Doctor Modo on duty?"

"Yes, Brigadie'. His shift is over in an hour. He's been here all night."

"Call him immediately. There's not a second to waste."

Doctor Bruno Modo was a surgeon and a medical examiner. He had trained as a military officer in the north, but as far as he was concerned, it was nothing compared to what he'd seen after that, when he witnessed the things people were capable of doing to each other without the justification of war. That is, granted that war is, in fact, any justification, he thought to himself with a hint of bitterness. It astonished him that he had failed to become jaded, that he still felt on his own skin the pain of the wounds he saw, the gushing blood of the miserable people who passed through his hands from morning till night. And he had failed to make a family of his own; it took too much courage to send a child out into this world. Thus as far as women were concerned, he found what he needed in one corner or another of the ravenously hungry city, then he paid and returned home content.

He watched the fascist era unfold from a distance, unwilling to tolerate a new power with such violent inclinations. He was unable to accept the idea of doing evil in the name of a greater good, and made no bones about making his opinions known. This had isolated him, depriving him of a social life and of the career that he would have otherwise deserved. But he had earned the respect of the people he worked with, and Ricciardi for one would never have accepted a murder case unless Doctor Modo's skilled hands had interrogated the victim's wounds.

That's why Maione sought him out, and why the doctor, in spite of having spent a grueling night stitching up heads cracked open in a drunken brawl, promptly forgot his exhaustion.

"Brigadier, what fair wind brings you my way, so early in the morning? Your boss with you?"

"No, Dotto', just me. While I was heading to headquarters I found this . . . this poor thing here."

Modo had already uncovered Filomena's face, turning it toward the light. She had obediently lifted her head from the policeman's shoulder without complaint.

"Madonna . . . who on earth could do such a thing . . . what a pity! Okay, Maione. Bring her into my examination room and I'll see what I can do. Thank you."

"No, thank you, Dotto'. Please, do me a favor: don't let the signora leave. I want to find out who was behind this. I'll be back later today."

Neither man failed to notice a flash in Filomena's eyes. What was it? Fear, anger. But also a hint of pride.

XII

By mid-morning, little by little as the southern wind grew stronger, a vague perfume began to spread; or rather, more than a perfume, it was an aftertaste, a sensation. It contained almond blossoms and peach buds, new grass, and sea foam from distant cliffs.

No one seemed to notice it, not yet, but some suddenly discovered that their blouse collar was loosened, their shirt cuffs were unbuttoned, or their cap was pushed back to the nape of their neck. And a faint sense of cheerfulness, like when one expects something good to happen but doesn't know what, or when something nice, however small, has happened to someone else: everyone's happy, though no one can say exactly why.

It was the spring: it danced on tiptoe; it pirouetted daintily, still young, full of joy, not yet aware of what it would bring, but eager to mix things up a bit. Without any ulterior motives; just for the fun of shuffling the cards.

And stirring people's blood.

Ricciardi looked up from his desk to regain a sense of reality. The murder of a tenor at the San Carlo opera house, a case he'd investigated the month before, had left him a bequest of miles of ink scrawled over acres of paper, in yellow and white triplicate, the same words and phrases repeated endlessly. He suspected that someone, somewhere, either upstairs or in Rome, was checking to see whether he would slip up and contradict himself. It was like being back in school again.

He glanced at his wristwatch and saw to his surprise that it had gotten to be mid-morning, already ten thirty, without his realizing it.

Focusing on particulars now, he realized that there was something missing from the monotonous cadence of his morning, and that was why he hadn't noticed the time. Maione. The brigadier with the awful ersatz coffee that he forced on him every morning at nine o'clock, marking the beginning of his day; what had become of Maione?

Before he could even complete the thought, he heard two hasty raps at the door.

"Avanti!"

The doorway was filled with the shape of a brigadier giving a loose military salute, with a somewhat frantic demeanor and an unmistakable bloodstain on his jacket's epaulette.

"Hey there, Maione. Good to see you. What on earth have you been up to this morning? And what's that stain? Are you hurt?"

Ricciardi had risen suddenly to his feet, causing his pen to roll across the form on the desk in front of him. His expression betrayed concern, and Maione felt a surge of pride and fondness; it wasn't every day that one detected a hint of emotion in his superior's eyes, as he knew very well.

"No, no, it's nothing, Commissa'. I just helped out a woman who . . . had an accident. I took her to the hospital. I'm sorry I'm late, please forgive me. You haven't had your ersatz coffee."

"Don't worry. There's nothing going on here. Everything's fine; the city was safe even without you, as Mascellone would put it." Mascellone—a jocular reference to Il Duce, or "Thunder Jaw," as Ricciardi liked to think of him.

"I'll go make it for you right away, then; that'll give me a chance to get cleaned up a little, too. By your leave."

As soon as he'd left the room, Ricciardi bent over to resume writing; but the form was destined to remain uncompleted, at least for that day. A mere instant later, in fact, the officer who guarded the entrance appeared at his door to inform the commissario that a body had been found in the Sanità quarter.

The mobile squad of the Royal Police Headquarters of Naples was mobile in name only. Ricciardi had always appreciated the irony of the unit's official title, accompanied as it was by the chronic shortage of working vehicles at its disposal.

Truth be told, they possessed not one but two automobiles: an old Fiat 501 from 1919 and a gleaming, almost new 509 A from 1927. He had personally laid eyes on them no more than twice, in his four years on the job. The former was always in for repairs, while the latter was assigned, along with its driver, to the crucial and urgent duty of accompanying the police chief's wife and daughter on their shopping trips.

And so, whenever something happened in a far-flung quarter of the city, as it just had, the squad became mobile on its own regulation boot-shod feet.

Ricciardi was among those who believed in the importance of a timely arrival. He knew well how much damage one or more rubberneckers could do to a crime scene, the delays that could be caused by people's desire to be eyewitnesses, to have something horrible to give an account of. Shoe prints, objects moved from one place to another, windows closed that had been open, or opened if they had been closed, and doors left wide open.

Thus, if there was one thing the commissario hated, it was to be the last one on the scene of the unfortunate event. Having to elbow his way through the crowd, being forced to answer a stream of pointless questions, dealing with wailing family members: all things that tended to double or triple in number if it was a poor neighborhood, and he knew, as one who lived on the border of the Sanità quarter, that it was a poor neighborhood par excellence. As he strode up the Via Toledo at the head of his squad, with Maione out of breath a step behind him and the two police officers bringing up the rear of the little procession, Ricciardi decided that every minute that passed was a minute wasted, and he picked up the pace, taking the same route he took every night on his way home from work. But this time, it wasn't dinner and a brightly lit window across the way that awaited him.

Once they were within sight of the little piazza above Materdei, it became clear to him that there would be no need to ask directions; all he'd have to do was follow the excited children who were running in the same direction. The spectacle must be more or less like it was in the jungle, as described in the books of Emilio Salgari, Italy's Kipling, with the hyenas and vultures guided by the scent of blood. The crowd swelled in front of a small apartment building. Maione and the two officers formed a human wedge, clearing a path for Ricciardi; though all they really needed to do was raise their voices and the crowd would have scattered. People in this part of town were none too eager to come into contact with the police, even incidentally.

When they arrived at the front door, the men came to a halt and silence fell over the crowd. Ricciardi looked around to see if anyone had something to say, some preliminary piece of information they cared to volunteer. More silence. Men, women, children: all stood mute. No one lowered their gaze, no one whispered. Heads uncovered, hats in hand; in their eyes, astonishment, curiosity, wonder, even irony—but no fear.

Ricciardi recognized his age-old enemy, the established authority in this quarter, an alternative to the one he himself represented. These people did not acknowledge his authority over them: they wouldn't hinder his investigation, but neither would they lift a finger to help him. They simply wanted him out of there, the sooner the better, so that they could go back to their own business, or to mourning their dead.

From upstairs came a prolonged lament; possibly a woman's voice. Ricciardi spoke, continuing to stare straight into the eyes of the people at the front of the crowd.

"Maione, have the officers keep watch at the front door. You come with me. If anyone has something to report, make sure that we get their name: we'll interview them at headquarters."

His words prompted no reaction from the crowd. An old man shuffled along with a slight rustling sound. A small child babbled in its mother's arms. In the middle of the small piazza, several doves flapped into the air.

Ricciardi turned, walked through the front entrance hall, and started up the stairs.

XIII

Step after step, the acid smell of urine and excrement blended with the sharp odor of garlic, onion, sweat.

Even before the advent of the Deed, Ricciardi had been made aware of another curse visited upon him: the damned odors. Sometimes they stunned him and other times they distracted him; they tangled up his thoughts the same way that the wind tousled the disobedient shock of hair he was constantly brushing away from his furrowed brow. Issuing from the dark corners of the uneven stairs he could feel unfamiliar eyes watching him. Though he couldn't quite see them, he sensed them, and he sensed their unfriendly curiosity. Behind him came Maione's heavy footfalls, confident and protective; Ricciardi considered the brigadier to be something of a human notebook, on which the images and words that they encountered in their investigation would remain impressed. All he needed to do later was leaf through Maione's memory to pull up sensations, voices, and facial expressions.

When they got to the third floor, they found an enormous woman standing in front of a half-open door, her greasy hair pulled back into a bun at the nape of her neck, her face flushed, her hands clutched together beneath her breasts, her fingers interlocked so tightly that her knuckles were white. She seemed accustomed to dealing with emergencies, but not the situation that had just befallen her. It was Maione who addressed her.

"And you are?"

"Nunzia Petrone, the building's porter. I'm the one who found her."

Not a trace of pride, awkwardness, or fear. A simple statement.

From inside, a ray of morning light cut like a blade through the dark shadows of the landing and Ricciardi clearly heard the lament that had already reached his ears down in the street a few minutes earlier.

"Who's in there?"

"Just my daughter, Antonietta. She's impaired."

That was all she said, as if that explained everything. Maione glanced over at Ricciardi, who nodded without meeting his gaze. Behind them, the usual small crowd had gathered, silently. Their necks craned upward, eyes darting to capture details worth recounting, to be exaggerated if necessary. The choke point of the staircase funneled the crowd into a line.

"Cesarano!" Maione bellowed. "What did I tell you? No one is to be allowed upstairs!"

The police officer's response echoed from the street below.

"And nobody went up, Brigadie'!"

"They're people who live in the building," the porter cut in.

"There's nothing to see here. Everyone go back to your apartments."

Nobody moved. The people at the front of the crowd looked away in a show of innocence.

"Fine, fine, I see how it is; Camarda, please take down the names of the signori and signore, so we know who to call down to headquarters for a chat."

He hadn't even finished reciting the magic spell before the crowd had dispersed. The sound of slamming doors boomed in the stairwell and the landing was empty again, with the exception of Nunzia the porter.

Maione turned to Ricciardi.

"Commissa', should I bring out the signora's daughter?"

*

The old, well-established procedure: Ricciardi goes in alone for the initial inspection, to relive the scene of the crime. Then Maione enters, making observations with a policeman's eye: the first survey, the position of the body, the condition of the windows and doors. Then witnesses are tracked down and questioned. Last of all, the magistrate is summoned, a decision is made about whether the revolting mess can be cleaned up, and everyone heads back to headquarters, to begin the hunt.

"No, let her stay. I'll go in."

Life is full of surprises, Maione thought to himself. He said yessir and stood aside to let his superior officer by.

Ricciardi pushed the door shut behind him. A small foyer, a coat rack with a hat shelf and a small bench, all hardwood: a piece of furniture that you'd hardly expect to see in a hovel apartment in the Sanità. The moan came from the only door that seemed to lead into a lighted room. Two steps forward: a small dining room.

A sofa and an armchair, upholstered in sky-blue satin with gold thread filigree, the seat cushions worn bare, small pieces of embroidered cloth draped over the place where one's head would go. A round table, three chairs—one in very poor repair—a carpet. He noticed a hole worn into the weave, at the farthest corner from the point of view of someone entering the room. Perennial anguish, pure pain. Garlic, urine: a place inhabited by the elderly. Daylight, blindingly bright, pouring in from the wide-open French doors leading to the balcony: not a single building blocking the view. A breeze stirred the curtain but did nothing to dissipate the smells. Too bad about that, thought Ricciardi.

The sickly sweet aftertaste: death was calling for attention.

A large fly was diving obstinately against the windowpane. Another step forward: now he could see what the armchair had been concealing. Crouched down on the floor behind the armchair, almost invisible to the eye, a girl was rocking back and forth, emitting a song that consisted of a single note. One or perhaps two yards farther on, just outside the shaft of sunlight that poured in from the balcony and near the fourth, overturned chair, there was a bundle of rags in a dark puddle, now almost dry, which extended from the black-and-white floor tiles to the edge of the carpet. The girl wasn't looking at the bundle; she was looking at the other corner of the room.

Ricciardi turned to look in the same direction. And he saw.

XIV

Ricciardi and the girl were both looking at the old woman. Not at the corpse; that was a dirty, abandoned thing, like the carpet on which it lay. They observed the image, erect in the shadowy corner, vivid in the colors of her last passion.

The commissario wasn't surprised. He'd understood right away that the girl had second sight.

It was a paradox: Ricciardi wasn't afraid of the dead; he was afraid of the Deed and those who had it inside them. Including himself.

Now he was watching the girl as she squatted on the floor: she was rocking back and forth rhythmically, moaning. Her eyes were focused, as if she saw something. Her brow was furrowed, as if she didn't understand. She was looking at death, not at a dead person. And she was crying, possibly in sorrow, or else in horror.

He focused his own attention on the image of the woman. She was like so many others, the kind of woman you'd see at the market, weighed down by years and suffering. A cotton print dress, the same outfit in summer and winter, a stained shawl. Diminutive, her hands twisted with arthritis, hunched over. Swollen legs, red with varicose veins, blue with bruises.

It was immediately obvious to Ricciardi that the murderer had beaten her to death. A red-hot fury, rather than a cold and calculated violence: a blind, stupid rage. The way her neck bent was unnatural, due to her shattered vertebrae; a profound hollow in her skull, on the right side, her eye crushed, the cheekbone staved in, the ear torn to shreds. A succession of blows, possibly from a club.

The other side of her body also seemed to be crushed in. Ricciardi glanced at the bundle of rags and saw what he had expected: she was lying on her right side. The murderer had taken out his rage on her corpse, perhaps by kicking it repeatedly. That would also explain the extent of the bloodstain across the floor, a trail nearly a yard long. We have a center forward on our hands, he thought. A talented soccer player.

He concentrated, blocking out the girl's whining lament and the sounds of movement and conversation coming from outside the door. The one intact eye had an almost sweet, tender expression: probably a cataract, a translucent, light-blue film. He cocked his head slightly to one side, to listen more carefully.

He didn't hear the surprise that almost always accompanied sudden death. He didn't hear violent hatred, blind rage, or the wrath of privation. He didn't hear the ripping of one being wrested away. What he heard, instead, was melancholy. And a certain obscene tenderness, a hint of pride. The faint, scratchy whisper from the old broken neck: "'O Padreterno nun è mercante ca pava 'o sabbato." God Almighty's not a shopkeeper who pays His debts on Saturday.

They stayed that way without moving for another minute: an odd little family, bound together by death, pain, and grief. The girl, with her singsong lullaby and her furrowed brow, a trickle of drool sliding out of the corner of her mouth. The man standing motionless, as if made of wax, just inside the dining room door, hands stuck in the pockets of his unbuttoned overcoat, his head tilted at a slight angle, a shock of hair cutting across his bare forehead. The ghost of the old woman with the broken neck, gazing at the consummated death with unusual emotion, repeating with a faint sigh an age-old proverb in dialect.

What finally broke the black enchantment that had made time stand still, slamming shut the gates of hell, was the large, stubborn fly, as it had one final and definitive collision with the balcony window, thus becoming the second corpse in the room.

XV

Teresa was dusting in one of the parlors. She asked herself why it was her daily duty to clean what was already clean, to tidy up what was already tidy, and why that enormous, perpetually closed-off palazzo should have so many drawing rooms and parlors when there were never any guests.

It seemed like the house of the dead; her employers lived their lives elsewhere, outside of it, and then came home to immerse themselves in the silence of the dark rooms and the lightless silver, as unlikely to glitter as if it were buried in a tomb.

The signora had returned from her long night out at about nine in the morning. Teresa had crossed paths with her in the hallway and whispered a *buongiorno* that went unheeded, as it always did; the dead can't hear. All the same, in that fleeting instant Teresa had noticed something different: the faint smile that had brightened her lovely features for the past month had disappeared from her face. This time, her expression was one of grief, loss, and resignation. She dragged her feet, her eyes empty, the tracks of tears discernible in her makeup.

She hadn't spoken a word to her; she hadn't asked Teresa about her husband, as she sometimes did. Teresa was relieved. She wasn't sure that she could have lied, as the professor had ordered her to do, to say that she hadn't seen him since the night before. Fortunately, Signora Emma had walked right past her without seeing her, as though she were in another dimension. Like a ghost.

Leaving a police officer to guard the door, Maione had responded to Ricciardi's call and was now searching the apartment with his superior officer. They had a good half hour before they the magistrate and the medical examiner they had summoned would show up.

Not that there was all that much to see. The victim, whose name was Carmela Calise, lived alone; she was unmarried, had no children, no known relatives. Two rooms, a tiny kitchen, and the lavatory on the landing, which was shared with three other families. Aside from the dining room where she had died, there was a bedroom with a squalid lining of bright floral wallpaper, from which emanated a strong odor of fresh paste. Maione thought to himself that if they hadn't killed her, the old woman would surely have died that very same night, asphyxiated in her sleep.

There were only a few simple pieces of furniture: the narrow bed pushed up against the wall, a crucifix, a chest of drawers, atop which stood a statuette of the Madonna with a crown of gilded plaster on her head and a rosary around her neck, a portrait of a man and a woman from bygone times, and a small flickering candle. Perhaps those were the parents, or perhaps a brother and his wife: memories now lost forever. A chair. A bedside rug on the gray-and-black checkerboard floor. They went back to the dining room where the expressionless porter woman was bent over her daughter, stroking her hair. The girl went on singing her lullaby, rocking back and forth, never taking her eyes off what only she and Ricciardi could see in the dark corner. Mechanically, the commissario followed her gaze.

"'O Padreterno nun è mercante ca pava 'o sabbato," repeated the image with the broken neck and croaking voice. God Almighty's not a shopkeeper who pays His debts on Saturday. The curtain stirred slightly in the breeze. From the street came the shouts of children playing.

Maione spoke to Nunzia.

"So then, you're the one who found her."

The woman looked up from her daughter, straightened up, and gave the commissario a look of fierce pride.

"Yes, that's what I told you before."

"So tell me exactly what happened."

"Every morning, when she wakes up, I bring Antonietta up here to spend the day with Donna Carmela. She's the only child that she keeps; she says that she keeps her company and isn't any trouble at all. Antonietta stays close to her and watches her work, and now and then Donna Carmela gives her a cookie or something else to eat. It makes me happy to know she's here, I got so much work to do. There's a whole apartment building to run. You have no idea how much work it is. I'm alone. My husband . . . in the war, he went north and never came home. The little girl was only one year old."

"So this morning you brought the girl here."

"Yes, it was nine thirty. I know because I'd finished up with the stairs and the landings and I hadn't started cooking yet. Before I went down to the pushcart to get some vegetables for the broth I wanted to make sure that my girl wouldn't be afraid to be left alone."

"So, you knocked on the door . . ."

"Who said I knocked? Donna Carmela's door was already open. She opens it first thing in the morning, when she comes home from seven o'clock Mass, and that's how she leaves it. This whole palazzo is one big family. We all know each other. There're no locked doors here. It's all safe as safe can be."

Maione and Ricciardi exchanged a quick glance, to highlight the unmistakable contradiction between the presence of that bundle and the trail of blood on the floor and the porter woman's claim.

Nunzia saw it too, and turned as red in the face as if they'd just insulted her.

"The miserable coward who did this isn't from the neighborhood. Take it from me, that way you'll save yourselves a lot of pointless work. Much less from this building. Donna Carmela was a saint, a genuine saint, and everyone loved her. She gave everyone a hand, she helped everyone. Damnation and eternal suffering be visited on the swine who did this."

Teeth clenched, almost in a hiss: the hatred poured out of the woman's mouth like a spurt of bile. Maione and Ricciardi, if only mentally, instinctively struck the woman off the list of suspects.

The brigadier proceeded with his questioning.

"So you went in."

"That's right, I wanted to say good morning to her and tell her I was leaving the girl. And what I found was this . . . this thing, on the floor. This act of slaughter, this disgrace."

"When was the last time that you saw her alive?"

"Late last night, it must have been ten o'clock. We went up, me and my daughter. We closed all the windows, put out the coal fire in the kitchen. It's what we do every night."

"And how did the signora seem to you? Nervous, worried . . . ? Did you notice anything out of the ordinary?"

"No, nothing. She said, 'See you tomorrow.' I went downstairs, and Antonietta came down about an hour later. That's all I know."

"Do you know whether the signora had had any, I don't know, any disagreements or disputes with anyone, any friction, as of late? Maybe she complained about something, or you overheard fighting . . ."

"No—what're you talking about? I told you once and I'll say it again, Donna Carmela was a saint and everyone loved her. No one would have dared. Not to mention she had gnarled hands and was very weak. She had that disease old people get . . ."

"Arthritis?"

"Yessir, that's exactly it. She got these pains. We could hear her moaning in her sleep in the summer, through the open window. Well, she's done suffering now," she said, looking down at the bundle of rags.

Maione turned to Ricciardi, to see whether he had anything to ask her.

"You said, 'My daughter stays close to her and watches her work.' What kind of work did she do, Donna Carmela?"

To their surprise, the woman blushed and looked down, suddenly abandoning the haughty demeanor she'd maintained up until that moment. There was a long silence. Maione broke in.

"Well, did you hear what the commissario asked you? Answer the question!"

The woman slowly looked up and answered the brigadier. Maione realized that throughout the conversation Nunzia had never once looked Ricciardi in the eye. Here we go again, he thought. The usual fear and revulsion.

"Donna Carmela . . . she was a saint. She helped her fellow man to work things out."

Ricciardi spoke in a low voice.

"How? How did Donna Carmela help her fellow man?"

Silence: Nunzia didn't answer. Sensing tension in the room, Antonietta had stopped her plaintive song, though she continued to rock back and forth, staring at the corner.

From the little piazza below came a joyful burst of noise from the boys; someone had scored a point, whatever game it was they were playing. In the air, a delicate scent of flowers was winning out over the smell of caked blood, but still not over the garlic and the urine.

Nunzia turned slowly to face Ricciardi, looking him straight in his glassy green eyes.

"Donna Carmela read the future. She read cards."

XVI

Rosa was seventy years old. Her memories stretched back into the distant past, times with other values. In the period in which she grew up—the period in which she still lived, at least in her mind—a woman consecrated herself to a family, even if that family wasn't her own. She had consecrated herself to the Ricciardi di Malomonte family, after they rescued her from a one-bedroom house in the countryside, where she lived with eleven siblings and parents who couldn't even remember her name. She had never felt the need for a husband or children of her own. Looking after little Luigi Alfredo satisfied her completely; the Baroness was unwell, and lacked the strength that a mother must possess. That's what she was there for, the energetic Tata Rosa, who had taken on this trust from her frail friend with the sorrowful green eyes, and she had upheld that responsibility for the rest of her life.

By now the young master was over thirty, and showed no sign of being ready to cast off the burden of solitude that he'd been bearing since he was a child. Her greatest worry was that she had so few years left; who would take her place alongside Luigi, who would watch over his fevers, who would feed him? She never missed the opportunity to ask him those questions, over and over again, but she never got an answer.

She loved him deeply, but she didn't understand him. She couldn't figure out his indifference to money, to people, to human emotions. No ties to his distant family, no attention to the administration of his property; if she hadn't been there to look after things with her scrupulous simplicity, those viper cousins of his would have devoured it all. He didn't care; all he cared about was his damned job. His evenings were spent shut up in his bedroom, listening to radio broadcasts of American tunes played by those black jazz musicians, or else reading.

A poor old woman wants to hear children's voices in the house again, she thought sadly. And she wants to be able to wait for the end with a faint sense of serenity.

She thought of the Baroness: the same green eyes, the same sad smile as her son, the same nervous hands. The same silence.

She wondered yet again whether she was really up to the task that that frail woman had entrusted to her.

Doctor Modo reached the scene of the crime around two in the afternoon, wiping his brow dry with his handkerchief, his instrument bag in the other hand and his hat under his arm.

"I can't understand why people always seem to get themselves murdered in ways and at times of the day designed to make me skip lunch. And really, am I the only medical examiner in this city?"

Maione went to meet the doctor as soon as he heard his unmistakable muttering in the stairway.

"Hello, Doc. Have you got any news for me?"

"What news do you want me to have, Brigadie'! A poor wretch works all night only to spend it with four imbeciles who decided to crack each others' heads open just to prove there's nothing inside, except maybe a signed photograph of that bald guy in jackboots up north in Rome. Then the minute he leaves to get some shut-eye, your police officer shows up, and here I am. Do you do these things to me on purpose, or what?"

"No, Dotto', for the love of all that's holy. I was asking, what about that . . . that lady that I brought for you to look at, this morning. The one with the . . . the cut, you know who I mean. How is she?"

"Ah, Signora Russo. How do you think she is, Brigadie' . . . they've ruined her for life. I sutured her the best I could, but that side of her face will always be disfigured. Her eyelid even droops now. It was a miserable job, a real ordeal. And she never made so much as a peep; just sat there, hands folded in her lap, looking straight ahead, not uttering a word. Except that at one point, a tear ran down her cheek."

"Did anyone come to see her, in the time you were there?"

"No, no, no one at all. She told me she had a son, a boy, but he has a job; he may not have heard yet. What a pity. It's such a crime: a truly beautiful woman. And her voice, Brigadie' . . . what a warm, gracious voice. Do you have any idea who could have done such a thing?"

"No, not yet; but I want to look into the matter. Did you detain her, like I asked?"

"Of course I did. Besides, with that wound of hers, she could contract a nasty case of septicemia in no time. If you'd seen the things I saw at the battle of the Carso . . . No, you'll find her right where you left her, at least until tonight. Hurry though; you know there's no overabundance of beds."

As they were speaking, Ricciardi had joined them.

"Here's our good doctor. Please, take your time. After all, your patient is in no hurry."

"Look who's here, Ricciardi, the prince of darkness himself. I should have known. When someone calls me outside of regular working hours, you're always to blame: the man without a life of his own. Just the kind of thing that happens to someone like me: someone like you. And here I was, so close to retirement."

"Sure, that'll be the day. I guarantee you'll be one of those old pains in the neck who are always buzzing around crime scenes after they retire, giving advice no one asked for."

"You've got my personality type pegged, at least. When I retire, I'm going to get everything off my chest, once and for all. That way they'll send me into internal exile on some beautiful sunny southern island teeming with women and I'll never have to look at your ugly mugs again as long as I live—no offense, Brigadie'."

Ricciardi and Modo had an odd, rough-edged friendship. The doctor was the only one who dared to address the commissario with the Italian informal "tu," and he was also the only one capable of grasping his wry sense of humor.

"Come along, doctor. Come meet the elderly signora who's been waiting for you all morning. But there's no hurry; believe me, she's not going anywhere."

XVII

Off to one side, Ricciardi watched the minuet that always took place in the wake of a murder. The stage setting varied, but the cast of characters was more or less the same: the medical examiner, a photographer, a couple of police officers, Maione, himself: each with a score and choreography all his own, treading carefully to avoid incursions into the others' territory, just trying to see his own work through to completion. Talking, commenting, sometimes even laughing: a job like any other.

Outside the door, behind the police officer responsible for isolating the crime scene, morbidly curious eyes scanned the front hall for details that could be exaggerated in the neighborhood tall tales that would enliven conversations between next-door neighbors, friends, and relatives in the days to come. The same old story. Every time.

Ricciardi distinguished between murders with evident motives and murders whose motives were concealed. The former type had all the evidence right in the first scene, visible at first glance: the man with a gun in his hand sprawled out on top of the woman's body, their faces disfigured by point-blank bullet wounds. The man splattered across the sidewalk, and up on the fourth floor the other man telling him to get up and take the rest of what he's got coming. The *guappo* lying on the ground, with the knife protruding from his jacket like the handle of an umbrella clamped under his arm, and the other man, being restrained by four bystanders, still spitting out all the hatred he feels for him. Unmistakable motive. No doubt at all; all that's left to take care of is a bit of cleaning and a small mountain of reports.

Concealed motive: the tenor found in his dressing room with his throat slit and a whole slew of people with excellent reasons for wanting him dead. The whore with her belly ripped open by a knife that's vanished into thin air, in a bedroom that dozens of people pass through over the course of a single day. The rich gentleman killed in a crowd during a neighborhood street celebration, and no one saw a thing.

A poor, harmless old woman, mused the commissario, a "saint," beloved by one and all, and then brutally clubbed and kicked to death: he had an unpleasant feeling that it wasn't going to be easy to get to the bottom of this murder, to find the motive.

Maione summoned Riccardi's attention; he was squatting down close to the carpet, being careful not to move or touch anything. Given his size, in that position he looked like an alabaster Buddha, which for some reason was dressed as a Neapolitan policeman.

"Look right here, Commissa': somebody stepped in the blood. You can see the footprints."

Ricciardi came over and looked carefully. Maione was right: he made out at least two footprints. One was broad and heavy, the other was fainter. A third footprint, farther back, broad and smeared. Maione went on, pointing to this last one.

"That's the foot that the bastard who kicked her rested his weight on. And he slipped on the blood, twice, see?" pointing to another spot in the blackish puddle.

"Here, on the other hand, and again right here, it's as if someone walked up on tiptoe. And neither the porter nor her daughter had any blood on their shoes; I checked myself. What did this guy do, dance a ballet?"

Ricciardi thought it over.

"They could have been made at different times. Someone who came in later, when the victim was already dead."

"Huh, what a lot of hustle and bustle . . . what is this, the central train station? And when would all this have happened, anyway, given that they saw her retire for bed last night and they found her dead at nine thirty this morning?"

From the bedroom came the voice of Cesarano, the other police officer.

"Commissario, Brigadier, come here!"

The policeman was standing next to the chest of drawers, holding a notebook in his hand. It was a school composition book, with a black cover and red deckle edges on the sheets. Ricciardi took it in his hand.

"It was here, under the sheets."

On every sheet in the notebook there was a number, possibly a date. A list of names, with numbers next to them, almost like a schedule. Also next to the names, in wobbly handwriting and large, slanting letters, were a number of ungrammatical words. Ricciardi read at random:

"9 Polverino, male, yung lover, not much money

10 Ascione

11 Imparato, femail, dead fatther, lots of money

12 Del Giudice, femail, husband beets her

14 La Cava, man, detts to be payd, no money, sausidge-maker

15 Pollio

17 S. di A., meet man of her dreems

18 Cozzolino, femail, poor boy frend, rich old man wants her. Ask for a lott."

Ricciardi looked over at Maione with a half-smile on his face.

"Good old Cesarano here found the book in which the saint wrote her customers' futures. Rates included. Let's go in the other room and see what the doctor has to tell us."

As they walked toward him, Modo looked at them and shook his head.

"She was definitely already dead after the first blow. Look right here: skull shattered, brain reduced to a pudding. I'll be able to tell you more once we get her to the hospital, but if you ask me, it shouldn't even have taken this much force. Osteoporosis had made her bones thin and brittle; even a good hard slap could have killed her. Why on earth are people such monsters?"

Ricciardi said nothing. He went on looking at the bundle of rags, which Modo had straightened as if it were a marionette, a small, roughly dressed mannequin, an old tattered doll.

Maione looked on, frowning slightly, as if he had been personally insulted.

"And after that? What happened after the first blow?"

"More of them followed: at least three, on the head, with the same blunt object, possibly a walking stick, an umbrella, I don't know. Then, as you've seen for yourself, they started kicking her around the room. She has several fractured ribs, possibly a broken spinal column—I don't know yet, I'll have to look into it. They really let her have it. I don't know how many of them there were. I'll have to determine whether the marks on her body are uniform. I need to take her to the hospital with me. I'll tell you tomorrow night."

"You'll tell me tomorrow morning. I know you. You're a bloodhound."

"I can't get it done by tomorrow morning!" the doctor objected. "I'm not some kind of superman! I need to get at least a little sleep; and if I want to get to sleep after a day like this, I'll need to get drunk, too. These are things that require time."

"Go on and protest, protest all you like; you'll pull it off all the same. You know all too well that the first twenty-four hours are the most crucial."

"If I'm ever reborn, I'm coming back as a policeman. That

way I can bully doctors around, too . . . all right, all right, I'll do what I can. Have her brought to the hospital; I'll go in myself in a couple of hours, and then we'll see."

Still grumbling, Doctor Modo left without saying good-bye to anyone. Maione touched his fingertips to the visor of his cap, and the police officers saluted. Ricciardi smiled wearily and said nothing. He turned toward the image with the broken neck, and she said to him: "'O Padreterno nun è mercante ca pava 'o sabbato." God Almighty's not a shopkeeper who pays His debts on Saturday. And as she said it she made a little gesture that he hadn't noticed before, a movement of the arm, as if she were moving something.

Ricciardi turned to look at the corpse and tried to reckon its location, before it was moved by Doctor Modo and even before the woman's attackers began kicking it. And he found himself staring at one side of the carpet, the one a bit farther away from the table and near the dismal old sofa.

He knelt down and scrutinized the floor: under the sofa there was a biscuit tin. He reached out his hand and carefully pulled it toward him; the lid was half-open. The words "Le Marie" were written on top. Maione walked over to him and looked him briefly in the eyes. Using his handkerchief, he opened the tin completely. It was full to the top.

Cash and promissory notes, all covered with caked blood.

XVIII

Along the street that ran from the bowels of the Sanità back to headquarters, walking briskly behind the bowed figure of the commissario, Maione looked around distractedly. He was well aware of the hostility that the good people of the heart of Naples were capable of unleashing, how quickly the complacent benevolence made up of smiles, bows, curtseys, and cap-doffings could transmute into the violence of furtive hands hurling cobblestones retrieved from the pavement at the detested cops.

He guarded Ricciardi, walking three feet behind him: not close enough to be intrusive, but not so far back that he couldn't get to him in time to shield him with his solid physique.

Usually, while they were walking, he would observe the bare nape of his neck, his tousled, unkempt hair; he mused on Ricciardi's absurd habit of going hatless, showing a scornful disregard for others, an indifference to his fellow man. In this city, "man without a hat" meant a man without money, like the nameless, family-less beggars who filled the porticoes by night and emptied wallets and handbags by day.

It was not lost on him, though it came as a surprise, that Ricciardi was neither an object of ridicule nor the recipient of sympathy, even from those who saw him but didn't know him; rather, he tended to fill people with dread, an emotion midway between disgust and outright fear that the brigadier would have had a hard time defining. Maione was a simple man, unable to discern nuances, which he could only vaguely guess at. He loved the commissario; he would have liked to see him less troubled, though he couldn't possibly imagine him being happy.

As they walked through the fresh breeze that blew down from the Capodimonte forest, leaving a new corpse behind them, Brigadier Raffaele Maione was unable to get the thought of Filomena Russo out of his head: the woman who from that morning on would have two different profiles.

He thought of the half-open door, of the strange silence shrouding the little piazzetta on Vico del Fico; of the pitiless eyes of the people who gathered in front of the *basso*; of the insult spat at the poor woman's back. Once again he saw the drop of blood fall in the darkness; the bloodstained half-footprint on the floor; the woman leaning against him on the walk to the hospital, decorously, with dignity, without fear.

And he saw the horrible cut gouged into her flesh, deep, clean, inflicted with neither hesitation nor shame, without conscience or remorse. And the faint scent of jasmine that had remained on his uniform jacket along with the bloodstain, a scent not unlike the one that was just beginning to waft through the air and which would soon burst out into the streets, triumphing once and for all over the winter.

But, more than anything else, Brigadier Raffaele Maione couldn't rid his mind of the perfect beauty of the healthy profile that he had glimpsed in the darkness of the room, or of the serene gaze staring into the middle distance.

In Ricciardi's office, back at headquarters, the shadows began to lengthen in the afternoon light. Maione sat down again after flipping the switch for the light hanging from the ceiling, which was missing a lampshade. It had broken a year earlier and had never been replaced.

"I told 'em a hundred times to replace that shade, Commissa'. They don't give a damn, and that's the truth. So help me God, I'll go down there now and slap them silly."

"Don't worry about it. Let it be. I don't need it anyway; I use my desk lamp. Let's keep going; no point in wasting time."

Between them, with its lid removed, was the biscuit tin they had found under the sofa. Scattered over the desk were promissory notes, IOUs, and letters promising payment. They had found them arranged by maturity date, bound together by ribbons tied in delicate bows. Each document was accompanied by a scrap of paper bearing the original sum and, where applicable, the extensions granted.

Maione, with the tip of his tongue protruding from his lips and his brow furrowed from the mental strain, was writing out columns of numbers on a sheet of paper as he diligently performed arithmetic operations.

"Some saint, eh, Commissa'? A lady who helps her fellow man in exchange for three percent monthly interest. A genuine saint. A martyr, to be exact."

"This is no laughing matter. With all these . . . clients, anyone could have killed her. Look at this, there must be about thirty of them. Still, I keep asking myself: why didn't they take the money?"

They both turned to look at the three wads of banknotes, stacked one on top of the other on the table. A substantial sum: more than you'd expect to find in a little hovel in a poor part of town, in the possession of an old and ignorant woman. More importantly, it was more than you'd expect to find left behind by a killer at the scene of a ferocious murder. Maione shrugged.

"Maybe he didn't realize it was there. Maybe he didn't see it—the box, I mean. The fear, the confusion. The anger, for that matter. He killed the Calise woman, then he took to his heels."

"No. You saw for yourself, the promissory notes and the bills are covered with blood. He rummaged through the tin, with blood on his hands; then he tossed it under the sofa. Was he looking for something? Did he find what he was looking for? And if he took what he was looking for, can we trace the crime back to him? He certainly didn't leave behind anything that concerned him. I have a feeling that none of the clients we have here"—he indicated the small pile of documents with a wave of his slender hand—"is the man who did the kicking. Let's keep checking, to be thorough. Let's finish our little census of the saint's faithful worshippers."

As night fell, moved to pity by the prolonged exertion of his mathematical calculations, Ricciardi told Maione, stricken by a splitting headache, to go home; he himself would stay on and complete the list of interest-paying chumps, all beneficiaries of the undeserved good fortune of their patron saint's untimely death.

When he was out in the open air, the brigadier heaved a deep sigh. Now the weather had definitely changed. He felt a growling in his stomach and realized he'd skipped lunch. But he also thought of Filomena Russo's profile, and of her wound.

Dinner could wait a little longer; he headed off toward Pellegrini Hospital.

Ricciardi emerged from headquarters two hours later, by which time the creatures of the day had dispersed, and the creatures of the night had installed themselves in the wide street that was his route home. His head down, his hands in his pockets; on his cuffs, an ink stain or two, evidence of the long reports to be completed whenever there was a murder.

As he walked among the eyes that followed him from the shadows of doorways or the mouths of *vicoli*, he paid no attention to the petty exchanges that broke off momentarily as he went by with his easy gait; nor did he pay attention to the bare-breasted women, who withdrew into the darkness of the cross streets as he passed only to reemerge immediately, offering themselves to anyone who felt the springtime pulsing in his veins, or who simply felt loneliness in his heart.

He walked with his head lowered, his mind filled with this new mystery, the suffering, the grief that demanded peace. Step by step, he glimpsed, by the swaying light of the lanterns that hung over the middle of the street, the trail of blood on the carpet, the miserable bundle of rags, the broken neck. That waxen figure, continuing to repeat an old proverb with the half of its shattered head that was still intact.

But he could also imagine the despair that the victim's seedy, hidden business must have been brought to dozens of families. Usury is vile, Ricciardi thought to himself: one of the most despicable crimes, because it takes trust and turns it against those who give it. And it sucks away work, hope, opportunities; it sucks away the future.

He smiled at the surface of the cobblestone street. What irony: the old woman practiced two professions; with one she offered hope, while with the other she took it away. She had lived off of one business and died because of the other. No differently than the mysterious and sordid humanity that now surrounded him in the darkness of the narrow recesses along Via Toledo, Carmela Calise had carved out a way of life, taking advantage of other people's trust.

In the end, those two professions weren't really all that different. The fortune-teller and the money lender both sucked trust and hope away, and made a desert of the human soul. But the question was the same one as always: did she or did she not have a right to live? Ricciardi knew the answer. And he had no doubts about it.

Maione walked into the women's ward of the hospital, panting slightly after hurrying up the stairs. As always, the vast, high-ceilinged room was crowded with people, even at that late hour: children crying, whole families gathered, chattering on loudly around the beds without the slightest regard for those who were trying to rest. Not a doctor or a nurse in sight.

Mopping his brow, his cap pushed back high on his head, the brigadier looked around him in search of Filomena Russo. He spotted her almost immediately because she was all alone, composed, dressed in black, in the same clothing she'd worn that morning. Maione remembered how that simple dress had been drenched in blood, the first time he'd seen it. And again he heard the thundering sound of the blood dripping in the darkness.

He moved toward her, walking down the aisle between the two rows of beds, well aware that as he passed the conversations would cease and the looks would suddenly turn hostile.

"Buonasera, Signora. How are you feeling?"

Filomena turned, very slowly, as she had that morning, more toward the sound of the voice than toward the person. The right half of her face was swathed in bandages, in the middle of which could clearly be seen a red line of blood: the disfiguring slash.

Her raven hair was encrusted with blood and sweat, her dress was dirty, her features betrayed weariness and pain. And yet, even in this condition, she was by far the most beautiful woman Maione had ever seen.

"Brigadier. I want to thank you. With all my heart."

That voice. Maione remembered how Doctor Modo had spoken admiringly of Filomena's tone of voice. As for him, he thought this must be what angels sound like: deep, sweet, vibrant, like the sound that lingers in the air after a church bell stops tolling. In a flash, the policemen could feel himself floating, from the hospital down to the water's edge.

After a long moment, he came to. With only one aim in mind, that of escaping the obligation to meet the gaze of that single eye, which was the color of the night, he said: "Come, Signora. Come with me. I'll see you home."

XIX

As he climbed the stairs, Ricciardi could hear the radio in his apartment bellowing out a dance song. My Tata is going deaf, he thought with tenderness. She's a bossy, indelicate, nitpicking ballbuster, a lousy cook with a rotten personality. But she's all the family I have.

He unlocked the door, fully aware that he could have head-butted it off its hinges without Rosa noticing a thing. He walked straight into the parlor and resolutely rotated the handle of the large, light-colored wood radio. He counted to three and then turned to face the door, at the exact instant in which his infuriated Tata appeared in the opening.

"Well, what's going on? So now I can't even listen to a little radio?"

"Of course you can, why shouldn't you? It's just that over at the National Museum, about a mile and a half from here, a bunch of mummies woke up and started dancing to the melodies of Cinico Angelini, and the museum director came in to complain at headquarters."

"Good boy, you've developed a sense of humor! You must have had a nice easy day, eh? Sitting there, as comfortable as can be, reading documents, while I, poor old woman that I am, and with all the pain I suffer, have to run around in circles to keep this house from falling to pieces."

"That's fine, you keep on doing that while I go splash some water on my face."

"All right, but hurry up, I'm serving dinner in ten minutes. It's late and you still haven't eaten your dinner."

A threat and a punishment, Ricciardi thought to himself. I already know what she's planning to inflict on me tonight. You can smell the stench of cauliflower all the way from Piazza Dante.

He went to his bedroom, doffed his overcoat and jacket, and gave in to the temptation to walk over to the window. A few yards away, the family on the third floor was finishing dinner. From his vantage point he could see half of the large kitchen and only a section of the table where the meal was taking place.

But even less of a view would have been enough for him. Right in his line of sight, as usual right at the end of the table to make sure that her left hand wouldn't bother a neighboring diner, Enrica sat eating. Around her were her siblings, her parents, and the man he presumed to be her brother-in-law because he had seen him hold her sister's hand.

He knew every detail: dishes, glasses, tablecloth and napkins, chairs. A year of mute devotion combined with the professional habit of memorizing every detail. He didn't even know her surname, but he didn't care. To the contrary, for once, he had been careful not to do any investigative work.

He liked her this way, with her timeless normality, outside of space: all calmness and gentleness, strength and quietude. Motionless, the one beacon in the fog of his unhappiness, the small, tranquil port to which he could return every night. When work kept him away, when an investigation dragged on or there was a report to complete, and he was deprived of the enchantment of that moment, a faint sense of uneasiness would take possession of him. He wouldn't find peace until he was able to return to the window once again.

Rosa bellowed his name from the kitchen. Angelini sketched out one last arabesque with his orchestra.

See you soon, my delicate love.

Maione said nothing. A hundred questions bore down on his stomach, but he remained silent.

Filomena walked along next to him at a distance of less than three feet. As hard as he tried, Maione couldn't get her to walk at his side. She kept just slightly behind the man in uniform, almost as if she didn't think herself deserving of the honor: almost as if she were ashamed.

"You must be in a lot of pain."

"No, not really. The doctor was very kind. He was gentle with me."

They walked along a little farther in silence. Maione looked down at the ground, while Filomena stared straight ahead of her. Without fear, without audacity, without pride. She held the bandage in place with her hand.

"Signora, you must understand. I have some questions I need to ask you."

"But why, Brigadie'? I haven't pressed charges and I certainly don't intend to."

"But . . . Signora, this is a crime, and I'm a policeman. I can't turn a blind eye to what happened."

Filomena slowed her pace, as if she were thinking over what Maione had just said.

"You just happened to come by. I wouldn't have called you. That is, you mustn't think that I'm not grateful. You did something for me that not even a brother would have done. The people in my quarter . . . I don't have many friends, as I'm sure you've guessed. I could have sat there bleeding for the rest of the day."

"Yes. I mean, no. I didn't do anything special. I took you to the hospital, and now I'm going to see you home. Still, I need to know."

Maione stopped walking. They were standing on the corner of the Piazza Carità, in the faint cone of light cast by a street lamp. Somewhere, a dog was barking.

"You've suffered a terrible wrong. Perhaps you don't real-ize it yet, but someday soon it will become clear to you. The way they slashed your face . . . you'll never be the same again, don't you understand that? What happened? Who did this?"

The light illuminated the wounded side of her face and the bloodstained bandages. The other half was in shadow and Maione couldn't have deciphered the expression. But even though he knew it was absurd, for an instant he could have sworn that she was smiling.

There, thought Tonino Iodice, *pizzaiolo*. I'm done sweeping up—not even a crumb on the floor. Everything looks as if no one had even eaten here, just as it was before. They've all gone home, to their wives, to their mothers. They laughed, they sang, they got drunk. They paid, too: just the right amount. Some of them will come back. I wonder when. Who knows—they may bring their friends.

If they liked what they ate, they'll come back again. And again and again. A bit of luck will finally come my way: my wife will look at me with love in her eyes, and my children will look up to me with respect. Because good luck brings money, and money brings respect. God gave me a little more time. If the old woman had lived, I wouldn't have had the time I needed. I'd have had to shut this place down, and it'd be good-bye freedom, good-bye children, good-bye wife. But she died. There was so much blood, by the holy virgin. There was so much blood.

I can't remember the stairs, I can't remember the street. It was God's will that no one should see me. And I'm sorry; I'm truly sorry. But now I have time. She's lying dead in her own blood and now I have time. I'll go on. And I'll wait.

I'll wait for the day they come to get me.

Ricciardi was back at the window, watching. Enrica had

swept up every last crumb, and the kitchen was just as it had been before, as if no one had even eaten there.

He watched her look around, swiveling her head, cocking it slightly to one side, drying her hands on the apron that she wore tied around her waist.

There: now she'll nod her head ever so slightly in approval and she'll sigh. She'll pick up her embroidery frame, turn on the lamp next to the easy chair, right there: just next to the window. She'll start stitching.

Ricciardi holds his breath, slowly closes his eyes, and then opens them again. His arms are folded across his chest and he's breathing slowly. Enrica threads the needle.

No one on earth will ever love you the way that I love you. Me, the man who never speaks to you. You don't see me, but I watch over you. That's what a man does when he loves a woman, in silence, the way I do.

On the stairs at police headquarters, the ghost of the police officer calls out to his wife, saying "Oh, the pain." In the dark fourth floor apartment in the Sanità, the figure of the murdered old woman repeats her proverb.

Ricciardi watches Enrica as she embroiders.

The dead seem alive and the living seem dead.

XX

Lucia Maione liked to sleep with the shutters open and the curtains pulled back. It was one of those things that she thought of as having "come after"; she wanted to be able to see the sky, the heavens, at all times.

They'd "come after" she'd lost her smile, her will to laugh, her love of the seaside. After. She split her life up into a "before" and an "after." Before and after the death of her son.

She could still hear Luca's voice when she came up the stairs, and she saw him in the faces of her other children; he would steal silently into her thoughts and laugh, whereas she no longer could. She had brought him into daylight, and he had extinguished that daylight for her.

Deputy Chief of Police Angelo Garzo had already taken his overcoat off the coat rack when Ponte, the clerk, appeared at the door. As soon as he saw that his boss was on his way out, he stopped on the threshold, hesitating; it was too late to turn back, but he knew what a short fuse the deputy chief of police had when it came to administrative matters that detained him as he was getting ready to leave.

They stood there, staring at each other, Garzo erect with his overcoat draped over his arm, and Ponte bent over in a half-bow. The deputy chief of police broke the spell.

"Speak up, damn it. What do you want? Can't you see I'm on my way out?"

Ponte blushed and bowed a little further.

"No, Dotto', forgive me. It's just that a woman has been murdered, in the Sanità quarter. I have the report for you right here, Commissario Ricciardi left it for me. He's on the case. You can certainly take a look at it tomorrow, Dottore, no problem."

Garzo huffed in irritation, tearing the folder the man was holding out of his hands.

"Well, of course, I should have known: Ricciardi. If there's trouble, you can be sure that Ricciardi's mixed up in it. Let's have a look; maybe there's someone important implicated in this thing and I'll make a fool of myself at the theater tonight if I don't know about it."

He quickly scanned the lines of the report and was visibly relieved. He shrugged his shoulders.

"Nothing here, nothing at all. Some poor woman, beaten to death. You're right, Ponte; it's nothing that can't wait until tomorrow. If anything comes up, I'll be at the theater. Buonanotte."

There weren't many people in the orchestra seats; the play had been running for a while now, and there were other attractions in the city. Marisa Cacciottoli di Roccamonfina sighed; she would rather have gone to see something else tonight. She looked over at her girlfriend sitting beside her in the box.

"How many more times are you going to want to come to see this show? At this point we might as well take a seat in the prompter's box; we know every line by heart. We're the talk of the town, today's top story. Yesterday, at Gambrinus, Alessandra Di Bartolo said to me, 'You know all about the theater, can you recommend anything interesting? Really, because I've heard that you and Emma never miss a show!' Just think: the two of you never miss a show! What do you think she meant by that?"

The woman she had just addressed was young and elegantly

coiffed and dressed. Her dark hair was cut short, as fashion dictated, her skin was ivory white, and her chin was just slightly pronounced, an indication of her determined, strong-willed personality.

She turned for an instant to look at Marisa, but without allowing her attention to be diverted from the stage.

"Listen, if you no longer wish to join me, say so clearly. I'll find someone else. You know, there are people who are willing to be seen in public places in my company. Also, you can go ahead and tell that dimwit Alessandra, along with all the other girls who gather at her house with the excuse of playing canasta but really just like to sling mud, to come and say it to my face if they are curious about me."

Marisa recoiled in the face of this vehement attack.

"Emma, we've been friends all our lives. Our poor mothers were friends before we were, and if we'd had children, they would have been friends too. But that's exactly why I feel I have to tell you that you're making a fool of yourself. I'm not telling you not to have your fun, I wouldn't dream of it. After all, you know what I'm capable of getting up to. But a little dis-cretion would not be a bad idea."

"Discretion? What on earth for? Who am I harming? I go to see a play that I've already seen before: what of it? Does that give those vipers permission to spit their venom in my direction?"

"First of all, you see this play two or three nights a week, and have done since it opened, at least one time out of three with yours truly, and I'm starting to become stupider than I really am what with trying to keep up with you. Next, you stay out all night more often than you sleep at home: don't try to deny it, because Luisa Cassini's husband ran into you twice in Via Santa Lucia, when you were coming home at eight in the morning and he was on his way to work."

She reached out and took her friend's hand, squeezing it tight.

"No kidding, Emma: I'm worried about you. You were always the strong one. The one who set an example for others. You have a distinguished husband who loves you: all right, so he's older than you, so what? Didn't you know that when you accepted him? No one says you can't have your own . . . amusements, but use some discretion! And then go home. Don't destroy a place in society that so many people envy you for."

In the darkness of the box, the eyes of Emma Serra di Arpaja welled up with tears.

"You don't understand, Marisa. It's too late to go back. Too late."

The orchestra began playing and the curtain rose to reveal the stage.

XXI

The next morning, as Ricciardi climbed the last flight of stairs at police headquarters, he was surprised to find Maione fast asleep in the chair outside his office door.

"Maione? What on earth are you doing here so early?"

The brigadier started and leapt to his feet, knocked over the chair, lost his hat, caught it in midair, cursed, picked the chair up again, snapped a military salute with cap in hand, thus smacking himself in the forehead with it; then he cursed again, put his cap on his head, and said, "Yezzir."

Ricciardi shook his head.

"I don't know what's come over you; one day you come in late, covered with blood, and the next day I actually find you fast asleep at headquarters at seven in the morning."

"No, Commissa', it's just that I wasn't sleeping well and so I thought, I wonder if the commissario ever finished up with all those numbers? I said to myself, I'll go see what he's up to and lend a hand, because I know him, until he finishes the job, he won't go home; I'll go down there, I thought to myself . . ."

"All right, all right, I understand. Make me my ersatz coffee, go on, and make a quart of it for yourself; that'll wake you up. And come see me as soon as you're done. We have a lot to do. I've been doing some thinking myself."

Ruggero Serra di Arpaja, illustrious jurist, university professor, central figure of Neapolitan high society, and one of the wealthiest aristocrats in the city, sat weeping in the satin-upholstered armchair in his bedroom. This is what happens, he thought, when you marry a much younger woman. When you have such a strong need to feel you are loved that you no longer know how to do without it. When you reach the age of fifty-five without realizing how much time has gone by. When you have no children. When you forget what it means to be alone in the world. When you have no friends, only esteemed colleagues.

He shivered at the thought of his own loneliness. It was as if he had suddenly found himself on a mountain peak, with no paths he could take to seek out help. And yet he truly needed it. He, a man who had studied so much, unfailingly advising his clients on how to extricate themselves from intricate legal traps, couldn't see a solution for himself.

And yet, he mused, he'd worked it out perfectly, a perfect example of premeditation. One contract, two jobs performed, one payment. What does one do, esteemed law students, when there is no way of determining whether the service contractually agreed upon has indeed been performed?

He noticed that the shoes he'd worn the day before had left marks on the carpet. He'd have to remember to tell the servant girl to scrub them out. Or perhaps, for once, he might have to do the scrubbing himself.

Rituccia was waiting for Gaetano, on the steps of the church of Santa Maria delle Grazie. Their place. She waited with her hands in her lap, neatly composed, like a grand lady who's just ordered tea. He'd told her that he would ask his foreman, the Mastro, permission to show up at the construction site a little late, so that he could speak with her. The way they used to. Because these days, what with him working and her keeping house, they practically never saw each other anymore.

Of course, they only needed to rendezvous for a minute,

outside the front doors of the adjoining *bassi* in which they lived, to tell each other everything that had happened. That was how well they knew each other; a glance, a half-word would be plenty. Even just a expression.

She saw him coming a long way away, with that distinctive, gangly stride that made him seem off-balance, something she'd teased him about so many times in the past. It always made him mad; Gaetano didn't know how to joke around. Rituccia shoved over on the step. He gave her a look.

"Again?"

She lowered her gaze. He clenched his fist and punched himself in the leg, with silent force. That's how he let out his rage.

"I'll kill him. This time, I'll kill him."

Rituccia said nothing. Without lifting her eyes from the ground, she reached out her hand and brushed her fingers across Gaetano's knee. They remained motionless in that position for a long time. He was breathing furiously, his eyes reddened in his swarthy face.

"What about you?" she asked, looking him in the eyes.

A moment passed, then Gaetano nodded his head yes and looked down at the step.

They stood there in silence. After a while, he spoke.

"There's a police officer. He was with her, last night."

Rituccia started in shock and seized his hand. Her glance betrayed a concern that verged on terror.

"There's nothing to worry about. He has the usual puppy-dog look. *Guappos*, police officers. The usual look."

Whereupon she smiled, reassured. She put her head on his shoulder.

XXII

Doctor Modo appeared in the doorway between the autopsy rooms and the waiting room, and there he found Ricciardi and Maione, just arrived from headquarters. The doctor was drying his hands with a handkerchief, his lab coat splattered with unmistakable stains.

He looked like a little boy about to run out into the street to play soccer.

"Oh, what nice visitors! Welcome, friends; have you come to take me out to breakfast?"

With a nice broad smile, satisfied.

Ricciardi looked him up and down.

"Yes, but please take off your butcher's uniform first. As it is, people turn away when we walk by and make hand gestures to ward off evil, and let me tell you, some of those gestures are hard to look at. The last thing we need is to show up for a stroll through Pignasecca market with Doctor Frankenstein."

"Here's the Ricciardi I love best: cheerful, optimistic, a lover of light reading. Have you tried reading Carolina Invernizio, or that author who goes by Liala? Or Pitigrilli; I see his books being carried around by all the idiots who passionately support your regime."

"My dear intellectual friend, for your information, I don't have time for reading—and I'm more optimistic than you are, since you see a future darker than the present. Come along, and I'll treat you to an espresso and a sfogliatella pastry, as promised."

Outside, Pignasecca market had already reached a fever pitch of activity. From the ramshackle stalls a roar of singsong voices touted the wonders of whatever merchandise happened to be available that day; rickety pushcarts pushed their way through the crowd; dozens of dark-skinned, half-naked street urchins, their heads shaved to ward off lice, darted from one vendor to another, trying to steal a bite to eat.

As the trio moved through the crowd, people obediently stepped aside, as if pushed away by a silent bow wave. Two policemen and a doctor—the latter a professional butcher of corpses. What could possibly bring worse luck?

They came to a café in Piazza Carità and sat down at a small table inside, near the plate glass window. The moving picture of the busy city outside suddenly became a silent one.

Ricciardi gestured to the waiter: three coffees and three pastries. "Well? Any news about how the Calise woman died? Don't tell me she died of consumption."

Modo snorted with a smile, lit a cigarette, and crossed his legs.

"You might show a little respect for the work that other people do, for a change. Between you and Brigadier Maione here, I haven't been able to leave that dump of a leper colony I work in for the past two days. If it weren't for the fact that I want to be at the hospital when someone sends you there, so that I can personally put you out of your misery, I would have already fled the country. To Spain, for instance, where they truly appreciate doctors; otherwise they line them up against a wall, give them a last cigarette, and good night, nurse!"

Maione broke in, ironically, feigning an afflicted tone. "Dotto', forgive us, it's just that the sight of all that lady's blood . . . It was too much for me, and you know I don't trust anyone else's work. After all, when you find a shop that provides good service, you go back. Am I right?"

"Go on, keep jerking me around, since that's become our

national pastime. Of all my faithful clients, luck had to send me the two most down-at-the-heels cops in all of Naples! Well, listen, I'm a gifted physician, understand? Your lady friend, for instance, Brigadie', I'd love to see what my colleagues who boast about their academic titles would have done with her face. I operate in the hospital for ideological reasons, not because I couldn't have any position I wanted in any one of the best private clinics!"

Ricciardi was baffled.

"Shop, lady friend, clinic . . . what are you two talking about? Who is this lady friend of Maione's?"

The brigadier's plump face had turned red as a watermelon.

"No, what lady friend? That woman I told you about yesterday, Commissa', the reason I had blood all over my jacket, remember? I don't know her; that is, I'd never met her before yesterday. I took her to the doctor, here, because she was badly hurt."

"Damned right, she was badly hurt! They've ruined her for life, is all! And she was a stunningly beautiful woman. Believe me, Ricciardi: a living cameo. An honest-to-God cameo, carved in mother-of-pearl. But why on earth has our good brigadier turned so red? Did someone slap him in the face? Or could it be he's in love?"

"Trust me, Maione has a wonderful family waiting for him at home; he's not a lonely dog like the two of us. So he's not going to fall in love anytime soon. Let's just say that a cop is a cop, on duty or off."

Maione looked up in silent gratitude for Ricciardi's help. But the commissario did not return his glance.

The doctor went on, stretching out his legs under the table and clasping both hands behind his head.

"A cop in springtime, then. And what about your springtime, Ricciardi? Any sign of it?"

"It's still cold out and you know it. Come on, now, enough

chitchat; it's getting late. Have you finished up with the Calise woman? What can you tell me?"

"What am I supposed to tell you? Why don't you just tell me what you want to know? You know that I can make the dead sit up and talk. They keep no secrets from me; if they want to tell me something, they just whisper it in my ear. Then it's up to me to decide whether to report it to you or keep it to myself."

Maione snickered at the efficacy of that macabre image. Once again, Ricciardi's expression remained unchanged.

"Are you trying to tell me that the dead speak to *you*?" he was tempted to say. You have no idea what that even means. You know that every morning two dead men greet me on the staircase down at headquarters? And the corpse that you sliced into tiny pieces this morning? It keeps repeating the same weird proverb to me out of its broken neck. And now you're trying to tell me that the dead speak to *you*?

"Take the Calise woman, for example. She was sick; a particularly nasty form of bone cancer. She had maybe six, eight months to live. Your murderer was wasting his strength. He just barely beat Mother Nature to it."

Six, maybe eight months, Riccciardi thought to himself. And you think that's so little? Spring, summer, and autumn. Flowers, the scent of new grass, the smell of the sea breaking against the cliffs; the first cool wind from the north, chestnuts roasting on street corners. A few flakes of snow, naked children plunging into the water, or with their noses lifted in the air to see what this or that cloud looks like. Rain on the street, the clang of horseshoes. Street vendors calling their wares. She might have lived to see another Christmas and hear the shepherds playing bagpipes in the piazzas and in people's houses.

Six, maybe eight months. Wasn't she entitled—the poor despicable usurer, the lying fortune-teller—to even an extra six, maybe eight minutes, in exchange for the two-bit illusions that she bestowed upon her customers, if life had decided to concede her that time?

". . . and her bones were like paper, like the wood of a worm-eaten piece of furniture. All that force wasn't even necessary. You know how much the corpse weighed? A hundred pounds."

"But what about the wounds? What kinds of wounds did you find, Bruno?"

"The wounds, you ask? Right parietal bone, crushed in, with loss of brain matter," the doctor began enumerating with his fingers, without putting down the cigarette in his hand, which he held cupped a manner uniquely his, "right ear shredded; three fractured vertebrae in the neck; at least two blows to the side of her body. Right cheekbone recessed, while the eye was literally popped. And then there's the kicking."

"What do you mean? More wounds?"

"Yes, Brigadie', numerous wounds. Fortunately by that point the poor thing had already been reduced to a bag of rags, already flown away to wherever it is she is now, into the absolute void, if you ask this old materialist physician. All of her ribs broken, and I mean every last one of them, with her lungs and stomach perforated, her spleen crushed, and so on. Name a traumatic lesion, and she had it. After a while I just got tired of transcribing what I found, if you can believe it. I got sick of the job altogether; so I stitched her up, closed the bag, and went outside to smoke. I needed a breath of fresh air."

They all sat in silence, looking out the plate glass window. It had suddenly become very pleasant to watch the street urchins running around, the women chatting, and the men ripping each other off, pretending they were making business deals. That was life, as it would be always. And life was preferable to death.

"But leaving aside the laundry list of wounds and fractures, did you come to any conclusions that might prove useful to us? About the mechanics of the thing perhaps?"

Modo scratched his whiskery cheek, with a sorrowful expression.

"Let's see: the woman died between ten PM and midnight, give or take a minute or two. The fatal blow, the first one, came from above, as you can see from the direction of the cranial fracture. The fact that it's on the right side could mean one of two things: either the person who dealt the blow was left-handed and was standing face-to-face with the victim, or else they were right-handed and the Calise woman had her back to them. I'd opt for the second hypothesis, because then the first kick fractured her neck and that landed here, at the base of the nape of the neck. Also, even though the bones were fragile for the reason I explained to you earlier, a remarkable amount of force was used. It's not certain, of course, but I'm inclined to think it was a man. Or else an enraged young woman."

"Any marks on the wounds? I don't know—imprints of rings, strange cuts. Sometimes that sort of thing happens."

"No, nothing like that. They were definitely wearing shoes. The wounds showed abrasions—cowhide, leather, stitched soles. Is my memory failing me or weren't there some nice clear footprints on the carpet? That's it," and he pointed out the window, "you should be looking for someone with stains on their shoes."

They looked out at the market again. Now, for some reason, the cruel expressions were more vivid than the smiles. As if the world outside were full of murderers seething with hatred, the soles of their shoes black with blood.

"And someone out there, my dear Ricciardi, and my dear Brigadier Maione, was carrying around a good deal of anger, which they vented on the poor little old woman who's been my guest for the past day or so. They showed no mercy, nor could they have imagined even for an instant that she could have survived. Of course, the unfortunate woman had no idea that she was dying. She can't have suffered; she just saw stars and then she was gone. Not a scream, not a breath. Whoever hit her must have had the fury of hell inside him. He wanted to get rid of it. He satisfied his urge and then put the thought out of his mind."

"No, he didn't just put the thought out of his mind, Bruno. He didn't. He'll have to think about what he did, over and over again. And he'll curse the moment that he decided to satisfy that urge. Trust me."

Ricciardi spoke in little more than a whisper, barely opening his mouth and staring into the blackness of his untouched demitasse of coffee as he leaned back against his chair, a shock of hair dangling over his forehead, his hands in the pockets of his unbuttoned overcoat. His green eyes were clear and he seemed to see beyond what was visible to others. And in fact, that's how it was.

As he whispered, the other two men shuddered.

XXIII

Attilio Romor took the stage midway through the first act. He was playing a handsome, superficial man, full of himself and convinced that he was God's own gift to the world. Aside from the superficiality, in real life he wasn't very different from the character he was playing, as far as his opinion of himself was concerned.

He made his entrance with a leap, in the middle of an amusing conversation between the male and female leads. He would say, "Here I am, my friends, at your service!" and then doff his hat with a broad gesture and a bright smile. The male lead, who was also the playwright and the director, would pretend to have been caught unawares and in his fright, would lurch forward, knocking over a chair.

Everyone was expected to laugh at this show of clumsiness; and in fact, they usually did. But when the female spectators, the clear majority of the audience, sat gazing in ecstasy at the handsome Attilio as though enchanted, the chair would tumble across the stage into an embarrassing silence. The playwright couldn't stand to have another actor steal the scene. And he took his revenge. God, how he took his revenge. Attilio felt persecuted at every turn: during rehearsals he made him act out the same silly scene dozens of times, and during the long weekly script meetings he forced him to read the women's roles, "to teach him the middle tones," as he liked to say in a high-pitched voice, humiliating him in front of the rest of the troupe.

Attilio knew he was the better actor; and he suspected that the other man knew it too, which is why he was punishing him. Not only the better actor but also far better-looking.

Long hair, raven black like the coat of a panther. Eyes the same color, strong jawline, tall, slim, broad-shouldered, with a deep voice. He could see the desire in the women's eyes, the passion throbbing in their breasts; he could see it in their mouths, which blossomed like flowers, in the pearls of sweat that moistened their lips.

That's how it had always been. Men at his throat, women at his feet. As a student he had been persecuted by his schoolmasters and the treachery of the other boys, while the schoolmistresses doted on him and the girls all fell in love with him. When he was on stage, the women in the audience followed him with glistening eyes, and the men glared at him with eyes full of hatred.

Ever since he was a little boy, his mother had warned him: be aware of your beauty, she told him, consoling him when he complained of other people's malevolence. It's your beauty, it makes them crazy with envy. Defend yourself, think of yourself only; look only to your own benefit, and all the better if it adds to those rascals' misery.

Jealousy dogged his every step. The jealousy of his many sweethearts, none of whom could lay claim to him; the jealousy of the colleagues from whom he stole scene after scene and the jealousy of the husbands whose wives he stole just as easily.

And since decisions in the theatrical world were made by men, Attilio found himself relegated to ridiculous minor roles. He wasn't blackballed, no; quite the contrary, he was rather in demand. All the impresarios of Neapolitan theater were happy to be able to count on an extra fifty or sixty adoring female audience members for every performance. But if the director of each theatrical troupe could find a way to humiliate him, he gladly did so at every opportunity.

And this one was proving to be worse than all of them. Upcoming playwright that he was, he was eager to follow in the footsteps of the most famous names in the theater; three years earlier his first play had been a spectacular hit, and he'd consolidated his reputation in the two seasons that followed. He was good at blending comedy and tragedy, winning the plaudits of his audiences and the venom of the critics, both signs of indisputable greatness. The playwright's sister and brother were members of the same troupe, and Attilio, who suspected he was hardly alone in his opinion, found them to be much more talented than the playwright himself. Whatever the truth might be, there was no denying that besides being damnably presumptuous, he was commanding and charismatic, and he knew how to write a hit play. Even though his perfidious treatment of actors was legendary, being a member of his troupe was nevertheless a ticket to fame and glory.

At first, he felt welcome. The Maestro, as the playwright loved to make people call him in spite of his tender years, showed utter indifference toward him, and the impresario had assured him that, when it came to the Maestro, there could be no clearer sign of admiration and esteem. The sister, an unsightly but gifted actress, smiled at him hungrily, even in her husband's presence. The younger brother mocked him often, though good-naturedly.

Then, predictably, he indulged in a short-lived but torrid affair with one of the troupe's ingénues. No gift for acting whatsoever, but lovely to look at. What a fool: how could he have failed to understand? What could someone so inept possibly be doing there, in a troupe so select that even the prompter was a seasoned actor with an excellent résumé? The answer was obvious: the Maestro himself had taken a fancy to her.

Everyone else knew about it, but no one had warned him: the women out of jealousy and the men out of envy.

By the time it dawned on him, the damage was done. He was forced to break it off with her, abruptly and without a word of explanation. Sure enough, the woman threw a fit during the dress rehearsal for the premiere. As he knelt before her, a bouquet of artificial flowers in one hand, rather than refusing him she burst into tears and spat right in his face, screaming like a madwoman and pouring out all the hatred and resentment she had inside her.

The Maestro savored the scene from the front row of the empty theater, for once happy to be a spectator and not an actor. After she stormed offstage, slamming the backdrop door behind her, he got to his feet without saying a word to anyone and withdrew to his dressing room.

From that day forward, the Maestro was his bitter enemy. It was as if his only goal was to tear Attilio down. It was a daunting challenge: self-confidence was the pillar of his very being as a youthful actor. But the Maestro could certainly make his life difficult: and so he did, at every single opportunity that presented itself.

After a certain amount of this treatment, all Attilio wanted to do was to leave; to hell with the ticket to fame and glory, and to hell with the chance of a lifetime. But the terms of the contract called for a huge penalty if he did, so he could ill afford to unleash the rancor he felt for that hateful, frustrated buffoon. And so, night after night, performance after performance, the battle of nerves went on. Before long, his part had degenerated into a comic role, so that when he joined the scene, the audience would snicker and guffaw at every line he spoke.

The Maestro was a genuine bastard, but in spite of everything, he was still a genius: even when he was reciting the same lines as ever, he knew how to shift the color and tension of the entire play which he had scripted. And so Attilio lived the nightmare of his own dissolution, of artistic defamation from which his reputation would never be redeemed.

It was during this period of ongoing frustration that he met a noblewoman, wealthy and beautiful, sufficiently impulsive for him to lure her into his web and do with her as he pleased. He saw her as his real ticket to freedom and fame. Seducing her was child's play. Yes, he could read women's eyes like a book, but he hadn't yet detected in those particular eyes the utter abandon and absolute submission he needed to change the course of his life.

He had made use of his usual weapons, judiciously alternating between tenderness and cruelty, passion and nonchalance: all that was needed to bind her to him. Now it was only a matter of time.

Amidst the idiotic laughter of the audience, marionettes whose strings the Maestro manipulated in the darkness of the orchestra seats, Attilio knew that the adoring eyes of Emma Serra di Arpaja were focused on him and him alone.

Concetta Iodice watched her husband. As she put away the dishes and trays and got ready to head home from the pizzeria, she wondered, for what seemed like the thousandth time, what could be the worries that manifested themselves so clearly in his face.

She observed his expression, the furrowed brow, the knit eyebrows. Money, she thought. It couldn't be anything but money. She knew that business hadn't been going well, and that they still owed a sizable sum to the usurer from the Sanità.

And that blood-smeared scrap of paper that had fallen out of his pocket the night before, when he'd come home with eyes that glistened with fever: what was it? She didn't understand what was happening, and she was afraid; but she couldn't get up the courage to ask Tonino about it. She thought that sooner or later, he would be the one to come to her, that he'd take her face in his hands, smiling, and tell her that everything was just fine.

But right now, at the end of that long day, that moment to her seemed too far in the future.

Ricciardi had a dream about his mother.

He could count on the fingers of one hand the number of times that had happened. When she had died, at the outbreak of the Great War, she was thirty-eight; he had been away at boarding school for seven years and he saw her twice a year, once at Christmas and then for ten days or so during the summer holidays. He didn't remember much about her other than that she was always sick, tiny, in a bed covered with pillows.

They had brought him in to say good-bye to her, when it was clear that she was not going to recover: left alone in the bedroom with her, he couldn't think of anything to say, and so he took her hand. He thought she was sleeping, but she squeezed his hand with surprising strength, almost hurting him. Then she loosened her grip, and she was gone. One moment she had been there, and the next she had crossed over.

By the age of fifteen he had already come face to face with the Deed many times. He could hardly turn away from the horror of those violent deaths; and he would see so many of them, too many, in his lifetime.

In his dream he was back in that gray room. Rosa and Maione were looking at him, and he was looking at his mother who lay there with her eyes closed. From the smell of flowers he thought that springtime must be at hand. He waited; he wasn't quite sure for what. Maybe just for his Mamma to wake up. Without warning, she spoke:

"'O Padreterno nun è mercante ca pava 'o sabbato." God Almighty's not a shopkeeper who pays His debts on Saturday.

She said it in a harsh, croaking voice. He realized that she had no teeth and that her long hair was streaked with white.

Suddenly his mother opened her eyes, which were large and green like his. She slowly turned her head, with a faint crackling of the vertebrae in her neck, a sound that in his dream rang out like a string of firecrackers exploding one by one. She stared at him, expressionless. Then she began weeping silently: no sobs, just tears steaming down her cheeks, soaking the bed-clothes.

He turned to look at Rosa and Maione; they were crying too. Everyone was crying. He asked Maione why he was crying and the brigadier replied that it's wrong to hurt your Mamma.

He turned to look at his mother again and asked: What can I do? What do you want me to do?

Green eyes, frantic. A tender smile.

"Study. Study hard. Read everything, get good grades. Be a good boy."

He felt the anguish of a little boy and the anxiety of the grown man he had become.

"What, Mamma? What should I study? I'm a grown-up now! They don't make me study anymore!"

From her deathbed, Marta Ricciardi di Malomonte reached out her slender hand, as if to assign a task.

Ricciardi turned to look at Maione, who handed him a notebook with a black cover. There was something familiar about it. He took it and then looked back at the bed. His mother was gone. In her place lay the old usurer, dead, her neck broken, a teardrop of black blood oozing slowly from her empty eye socket.

Outside, in the night, the breeze coming down from the forest of Capodimonte sought out new blood to agitate.

XXIV

Walking downhill from his home, Maione stopped at Vico del Fico. How could he help himself?

The thought of Filomena had found fertile soil in which to put down roots and germinate in the brigadier's pragmatic mind. Leaves, blossoms, and fruit, all bearing the same sad smile, those eyes with the night inside them, that bandage: like a beautiful coin caught under a carriage wheel.

Maione felt a dull ache. His innate sense of justice could not stand to see such an atrocity go unpunished. Whoever had dared to ruin that work of perfection, that creation of God, deserved to spend many years in a prison cell, meditating on what they had done.

Was he falling in love? If someone had so much as dared to ask him that, he would have flown into a rage. It was a policeman's duty when faced with a crime, whatever its nature, to investigate, delve into it, uncover the truth, and make arrests.

Still, he preferred not to admit to himself that, faced with any one of the countless other crimes that stained the city's streets every day, he wouldn't have spent a sleepless night staring at the ceiling, awaiting the first light of dawn with such overwhelming desire. And he wouldn't have left the house so early, even before the sound of a woman singing on her way to wash clothes at the fountain came wafting along on the first morning breeze.

Maione started walking down from Piazza Concordia, his pace just a little faster than usual; the difference was so slight, so slight as to be undetectable to the naked eye. But the two sad eyes that observed him from the crack between the shutters, which were just barely ajar, could see even what was invisible.

The door of the *basso* on Vico del Fico wasn't bolted; the slab of wood that served to shut out the night had already been removed. Gaetano, Filomena's son, had to be at the construction site where he worked as an apprentice by dawn. Maione stopped several feet short of the threshold, respectfully; he removed his cap, then after a moment's hesitation, clapped it back on his head. With his cap in place, he was the on-duty Brigadier Maione, whereas without it, he really wouldn't have known how to explain what he was doing there.

One story up, a window slammed shut decisively. He looked up but saw no one. The *vicolo* observed and sat in silent judgment. He took a step forward and knocked gently on the doorjamb.

Filomena had cleaned and disinfected her wound before getting dressed and preparing the bread and tomatoes that her son ate for lunch. She hadn't slept a wink all night: out of pain, anxiety, the thought of the tests she'd been through and those that still lay ahead for her. Out of remorse. The large ungainly silhouette that appeared in the doorframe brought her equal measures of uneasiness and security.

"Buongiorno, Brigadier. Please, come in," she whispered, serenely.

"Signora Filomena," said Maione, touching a finger to his visor and taking a single step forward, without entering the room. "How are you feeling? Doctor Modo said that you should go see him whenever you like, in case you'd like to have him change the dressings for you."

"*Grazie*, but no, Brigadie'. I can do it myself. If you only knew how many times my son hurt himself when he was little, playing in this *vicolo*. The mammas of the Spanish Quarter are all nurses of sorts."

Maione took off his cap and began turning it in his hands. There was something about Filomena's voice that always made him feel at fault. As if he were somehow partly to blame for the wound beneath her bandage.

"Signora, I know that this isn't a pleasant subject for you. But my line of work isn't like any other; if I see, if I learn about someone who has done something like . . . like this thing that happened to you, well, I told you before, it's my duty to investigate, to get to the bottom of it. I can understand that you're afraid, that if you talk and you say something that . . . if there's someone who could, you know, do something to you, to your son. I . . . you don't have to worry. I'd never do anything to put you in danger. But if someone's hurt you, they have to pay for what they've done."

Filomena listened, her eyes fixed on the eyes of the brigadier. He, on the other hand, had no idea where to look. In the still chilly air of that third morning of springtime, Maione was sweating as if he were climbing a volcano, surrounded by molten lava.

"Brigadier, I thank you. I told you before and I'll say it again: I don't want to press charges against anyone. Sometimes certain . . . situations develop that look like one thing but are really another. That's all I can tell you and that's all I have to say."

"But if . . . if you . . . I have to ask you, if you have . . . if you're in a relationship with someone, in short, how can I put this . . . Jealousy can make people lose their minds."

A silence fell that was as thick as the earth covering a grave. Far away, out in the world, a woman's voice was singing:

Dicitencello ch'è 'na rosa 'e maggio,
ch'aggio perduto 'o suonno e 'a fantasia
che 'a penso sempe, ch'è tutta 'a vita mia . . .

She sang the verse a second time:

Tell her that she's a rose of May
That I can't sleep or think
That I think of her always, that she's my life . . .

"No. No one, Brigadie'. There hasn't been another man since the day my husband died. It's been two years."

That voice. Confident, stern. And distant, too, as if she were speaking from the bottom of the sea. Maione shivered and felt as if he had just uttered a loud oath in the middle of the city's cathedral, just as the bishop was raising the consecrated host.

"Forgive me, Signora. It was never, never my intention to cast doubt on your good name. In that case, is there someone who wants you, who's threatening you? Tell me; point me in the right direction."

"Brigadier, you're going to be late for work, and so will I. I'm certain that you have much more important matters than mine to attend to. Don't worry; I'm not afraid. Nothing is going to happen to me. Nothing else."

Maione studied her in the dim light. There was an absurd amount of certainty in Filomena's scornful gaze, as if she had no doubts about what she was saying. He sighed and put his cap back on his head. He took a step back.

"That's fine, for now. If that's how you want it . . . but I'll have to keep coming back, until I'm sure that neither you nor your son are in any danger. If anything occurs to you, send for me. It only takes five minutes to get here from headquarters."

He turned to go and almost bumped into the woman whose scream had first caught his attention two days earlier, the same woman who had so effectively expressed her contempt for Filomena. This time she was holding a bowl and glaring at the brigadier.

"Donna Filome', it's Vincenza. May I come in? I brought you a cup of hot broth. Is there anything you need?"

Maione decided that sometimes bloodshed helps to change people. He waved a farewell and left.

The man who had just stepped out of the front door of the adjoining *basso* felt like his head was about to explode. He'd tied one on the night before. And the night before that. Cheap wine, smoke, bawdy songs, all to help him find the strength to sleep without *la schifezza*—the filthy mess—which always made him feel the next day the way he did this morning.

But a poor man who'd lost his wife, he thought to himself as he hurried toward the construction site where he worked, what's he supposed to do, stop living? Or should he go out and find another wife? And who would take him anyway, a man like him, with a small daughter, and penniless to boot?

Salvatore Finizio, first-class bricklayer, widower. A man who had nothing to smile about and very little to eat, who had to take care of his daughter, Rituccia, feed her and clothe her. And so if wine and weariness made him forget about poor dead Rachele every once in a while, was that such a sin? If God Almighty is truly God Almighty, He'll understand. And He'll forgive. Madonna, what a headache.

XXV

Ricciardi couldn't seem to get that dream out of his head. He could still hear his mother's voice, a voice that in reality he was unable to remember, telling him to be a good boy, to study. Study what?

Sitting at the desk in his office, he turned the heavy lead paperweight over and over in his hands, a piece of a mortar shell brought back from the front, a gift from the overseer on his estate in the country.

His papers, all those sheets and scraps that lay scattered over the wooden desktop. Instead of jotting down notes on little pieces of paper, he should have put his mind in order, should have procured himself a notebook and written in it. A notebook, like the appointment book that old Calise kept. God Almighty's not a shopkeeper who pays His debts on Saturday.

The flash of light that illuminated his mind was followed almost immediately by a clap of thunder, like in a rainstorm. Ricciardi sat there, astonished, with the chunk of lead in his hand, contemplating his own stupidity.

"Maione!"

He had raised the roll-up shutter halfway, just as he did every morning. He knew perfectly well that the other merchants on Via Toledo had their salesclerks open shop and didn't come in themselves until later. How conscientious Don Matteo De Rosa is, bravo! they'd say to each other behind his back, snickering. A salesclerk you were born and a salesclerk you remain, even now that you're the boss. They thought that he had no idea what they were saying, that he didn't realize, but he knew exactly what he was doing.

As he tidied up the rolls of cloth on their wooden poles, he took a quick look at his reflection in the mirror the customers used. Sure, he had a bit of a belly. And his hair was starting to go, slowly but surely. Not even all that slowly, come to think of it. But his mustache was dark and beautifully curled; and his handsome checkered vest with the gold watch chain made it clear to anyone who might wonder that Don Matteo De Rosa was the boss now.

He'd always known that he'd be in charge one day, even back when he was working for old Salvatore Iovine, the leading fabric merchant in Naples. Iovine was a man who had obtained everything he ever wanted from life—everything, that is, except a male heir. And Matteo had won the heart of Iovine's daughter Vera, a homely monster with a mustache a few hairs short of his but a fuller beard, a woman who was impossible to look at, even from a distance, but who had more suitors than Penelope, because of her immense wealth.

And so, when old Iovine died, spitting blood onto a scrap of beige fabric that was a masterpiece of the weaver's art, Matteo was left to run the business. Yes, it's true that the old man had left everything to his daughter. But he was the man of the family, wasn't he? So he said, let her stay at home in the dark, since even the sunlight was disgusted at the thought of touching her; he would look after the shop.

And everything had gone smoothly until Filomena. Just the thought of her name made his heart rejoice. Filomena.

She'd come in one morning, wearing a black dress made of rough, cheap cotton, a shawl over her head, as if she were covering up some astounding homeliness. Are you looking for a shop clerk? she inquired. Let me see what you look like, he replied. And with a sigh, she pulled back the shawl.

Matteo De Rosa lost his heart and his soul the instant he laid eyes on the face of Filomena Russo. He realized then and there that he'd never be able to rest until he got his hands on the body of that goddess descended to earth. So he hired her; of course he hired her. He told her: every morning at eight o'clock on the dot. And every morning at eight o'clock on the dot he was there, too, while the other salesclerks never arrived before eight thirty. They would often come in to find him flushed, his hair all mussed; he knew that she was a widow, a poor, desperate woman with a son to bring up. He couldn't understand why she refused his advances. All the other female sales assistants would have given their eyeteeth for the opportunity: the padrone's mistress, just think of the advantages. But not her.

He'd tried everything: gifts, money, threats. Nothing worked; she rejected it all. All he managed to do was to fill those moonlit eyes with showers of tears. The more she rejected him, the clearer it was to Matteo that he could not live without her. So he finally told her it was time to make up her mind: otherwise she'd have to find herself another job. That is, if she could find one at all; no one would hire a salesclerk fired from the famous De Rosa fabric shop. *Capisci*, Filomena? Choose Matteo or choose to starve, both you and your son. I'll expect your answer tomorrow morning.

And the next day, she wasn't at work. Her son, swarthy and feral, with cap in hand but eyes that showed no respect, came in to say that his mother wasn't well.

Matteo continued to go in early every morning to open the shop: just biding his time. And Filomena returned, with the same shawl covering her head that she had worn when she had come to the shop for the first time.

He took a step forward, holding his breath. What have you decided? he whispered.

Out in the street, a carriage went by, its iron-rimmed wheels thundering over the cobblestones. A street vendor's cry pierced the air.

Filomena recoiled into the semidarkness to avoid his touch, until she fetched up against the shelves behind her. Her shawl caught on a roll of cloth and fell away, uncovering her face.

At first Matteo thought the shadows were playing tricks on his eyes, and then he saw clearly.

There was a piece of antique furniture in the bedroom. In the challenging lives of a married couple who had brought six children into the world and had always struggled, it had been a luxury. A gift from Raffaele, back in the days when laughter was a more plentiful commodity than even conversation was now. A tribute to her femininity. It was as if a hundred years had gone by since then.

Lucia Maione was standing with a dustrag in her hand, looking at the little dressing table. It resembled a writing desk, the slightly curved legs surmounted by two small drawers and an inlaid tabletop. Above that, an oval adjustable mirror supported by two wooden posts. A useless piece of furniture, too fragile to support anything heavy; you couldn't have used it as a place to keep sheets or tablecloths, nor could you really have leaned your elbows on it while eating or studying. Only her two daughters occasionally played at it, making it home to a couple of rag dolls.

Lucia gazed and remembered.

She remembered her husband, stretched out on the bed, drinking in the sight of her as she brushed her hair in front of the mirror, his eyes filled with the joy of love. She remembered his adoring smile and her tenderly mocking response: What do you think you're watching, a moving picture? And he had replied: There aren't any actresses as pretty as you. What would I want to go to a picture show for?

A hundred years ago, life had given her a strong, cheerful

husband, and then six wonderful children. Laughter, hard work, quarrels, Sundays in the kitchen, every morning mountains of clothing to wash, down at the washhouse in the piazza, singing old Neapolitan songs as she scrubbed. Life had given her gifts. And life had taken away from her as well. She hadn't even been able to pick out Luca's clothes, to dress him one last time. He'd left the house one morning with a slice of bread in hand, as usual: Cheer up, Mamma. And that morning, too, he'd taken her in his arms and made her fly, whirling her around and leaving her breathless.

The last time she'd seen him alive. He wouldn't live to see that evening. He was my life. Why should it come as a surprise that I've stopped living?

Lucia took a step toward the vanity and ran an inquisitive finger over the tabletop. No, not a speck of dust. She'd become even more fussy about cleanliness and tidiness; her children knew it and they were careful. There was no dust, but there was no life either. The apartment seemed like a church; one could hardly tell that five other children still lived there. She understood that they weren't eager to spend time with their now close-lipped and irascible mamma. She was sorry, but there was nothing she could do about it. They would go outside to play, enlivening the street below, beloved by everyone in the neighborhood, including her: but from a distance.

No dust; but there was still a black cloth draped over the mirror, the only one still in place, three years later. When the period of mourning was over, she'd gotten rid of all the other signs of it, except for her black dress and the cloth draped over the mirror. She wondered why: just that mirror. She took the chair that completed the set, a chair that for years now had only been used as a stand for their dressing gowns at the foot of the bed, and scooted it over. She sat down. She tested the seat to make sure it was stable: she'd forgotten how comfortable it was. She moved it a little closer to the vanity, careful not to drag it across the hexagonal ceramic floor tiles. She sat there for a moment, perched between past and present; her heart was racing in her chest. Why? The sounds of the neighborhood entered through the open window: *Pesce, pesce, chi vo' pesce, è vivo ancora.* Fresh fish, who wants fish, fish still alive. She heaved a deep sigh, impulsively reached out her hand, and pulled the black cloth off the mirror.

Lucia had always been conscious of her beauty. Blonde, with beaming blue eyes, and a full-lipped, slightly pouting mouth. A narrow nose, just a little long, to give her face a touch of personality. Pretty. And she knew it. She'd stopped thinking about herself; who was this stranger looking in the mirror?

She looked at her eyes: a hard, slightly reddened gaze. Her mouth, thin-lipped. The new creases and wrinkles, at the corners of her eyes, running along her cheekbones: the signs of enduring, daily grief.

How old am I now? she wondered. Forty. Almost forty-one. And I look like an old woman of seventy. She looked around, bewildered. Invisible, the springtime danced in the shaft of sunlight that struck the mirror frame, turning it red. She heard Luca's voice; she thought of her husband, who had left for work that morning without turning to look up at the window from the street, something he'd always done, a hundred years ago.

She ran her fingers through her blonde hair. She turned her face slightly to one side and tried out a smile.

XXVI

By the time Ricciardi left headquarters and set out for the Sanità quarter, there could be no doubt that springtime had made its grand entrance. There was a note of cheerfulness in the air, a gentle wind blew in changing directions, with varying intensity, carrying off the ladies' little hats and the men's fedoras and bowlers, rumpling the occasional overcoat. A childlike wind, one that was capricious and playful, but had stopped biting.

The dominant scent was that of the sea; but mixed in with it were the smells of new green grass and leaves, which became stronger the closer he got to the forest and the verdure of the Villa Nazionale or the Orto Botanico, the botanical gardens. The scent of flowers hadn't yet emerged, but it hovered in the air, like a promise.

All up and down Via Toledo that morning, acquaintances had begun lingering for a chat. It wasn't hot out exactly, but at this point the season was clearly warming up.

In the *vicoli* there were snatches of song and voices calling, balconies thrown open to let in a bit of sunlight. Clotheslines strung tightly between one window and another shared sheets and shirts, moving lazily in the fresh breezes. People struck up conversations with a smile, for no special reason; here and there strolling vendors spoke in familiar, even intimate tones with the young ladies who leaned out their windows, lowering coins in baskets and hauling up fruit and vegetables, or soap, in exchange.

The street organs were churning away beautifully: *Amapola, dolcissima Amapola, Amore vuol dir gelosia*. From the little neighborhood marketplaces rose the tone-deaf symphony of the vendors: for once, their cacophonous rumba was a pleasure to hear. Although no one saw it, if you looked closely the springtime was dancing on tiptoes, leaping from one hat to another, from one of the trees that lined the street to the next, from balcony to balcony.

And with the newly diminished space between one person and another, coin purses vanished from pockets and handbags were whisked off café tables, here and there friendly conversations deteriorated into slapping fights, and now and then a knife blade glittered in the sunlight. But this too was part of springtime. The lines of sailors and construction workers outside the box office windows of the whorehouses grew longer: it was the new season casting its spell, stirring the blood. Young women could be seen weeping over their lost loves. And the springtime laughed mockingly at all the promises that would not be kept.

All these thoughts swirled through Ricciardi's wary mind as he walked toward the Sanità, followed by a taciturn Maione with downcast gaze. As they passed, a dark bow wave tinged with fear washed over the street, and then closed up behind them, giving way to the trickery of the first burst of fresh spring air once again.

They could have waited for the streetcar, crowding in with busy housewives and mothers, idle youths in search of a sweet smile, but Ricciardi preferred the open air; it helped him think. He wanted to take another look at the scene of the crime, get another whiff of what had happened there.

They marched past the one hundred construction sites of the perennially rising city: all those new apartment buildings with their thick white walls, tiny square windows, and no balconies. Grandiose mottos over the flat street doors, lettered in bronze or engraved in stone, commemorating dates and slogans down through the ages. Ricciardi had no particular love for these new architectural contours, and was always moved by the sight of ancient, noble arches and the delicate friezes that lightly ornamented the massive marble blocks.

The commissario's thoughts wandered to the countless other construction sites, from the new Vomero to the hilltop of Posillipo, from the burgeoning districts of Bagnoli that were springing up to provide housing for the steelworkers in the new mills, and out to San Giovanni. He mused that, as always, Naples was a city that got bigger without growing up. Like a little girl magically transformed into a grown woman overnight, still playful and childish, with an adolescent's sudden outbursts of anger.

As he passed close by the scaffoldings, the commissario glimpsed the figures of men who had fallen in the construction of the imposing palatial edifices dictated by Rome's new ambitions of grandeur. There had always been deaths on the job, even in the years when he'd first come to the city to study, when old buildings were being renovated or badly constructed walls were being reinforced. Ricciardi couldn't say exactly why, but he found it somehow more upsetting to think that people were dying needlessly in the service of ugliness.

He knew perfectly well that he would encounter two dead men along the street that ran from headquarters to Via Santa Teresa. At night, they were especially gloomy, standing there at the foot of the buildings from which they'd fallen, murmuring their last living thoughts; by day, he almost couldn't tell them apart from their old coworkers: one of them, however, had fallen face first, and the contorted mouth with which he continued to curse all the saints had been practically driven into his chest; the other one, a fair-haired boy wearing a sweater that was at least two sizes too large, had landed on his back; he stood hunched over in an unnatural posture. He was calling for his mamma.

Teresa could feel the atmosphere that the coming spring-time brought in through the open windows, and she was aware of the contrast with the stubborn winter that refused to abandon the dark rooms of the palazzo. Her peasant upbringing had made her attuned to the rhythm of the seasons, and her whole being was reborn at that time each year. Thus she found it all the more disheartening to have to face that gloom so thick you could cut it with a knife, as she walked through the magnificent hallways.

That morning, once again, the lady of the house had come home after spending the entire night out, then shut herself up in her bedroom. The professor hadn't emerged from his suite, and the tray with last night's dinner had been left untouched on the lacquered wooden console table outside his study. She had knocked gently when she brought it, but she'd been unable to understand his response. She thought she heard him sobbing.

If she could have said her piece, Teresa would have said that what they needed were children. She'd raised her own brothers and sisters; she'd held them in her arms two by two when she was still just a little girl herself, and she knew the joy children could bring. The house where she worked was a house without mothers, grim and unsmiling.

The door to the study suddenly swung open.

The man she saw looked nothing like the Ruggero Serra di Arpaja whose impressive learning and prestigious place in society carried so much weight. The stiff collar was askew, the tie dangled slack; the waistcoat was buttoned off-center, the unkempt hair revealed a receding hairline that was usually carefully concealed. And his eyes were the eyes of a madman, bloodshot and swollen, bulging out of their sockets. A madman who had wept through the night.

The professor stared at her in bewilderment, as if he'd never seen her before. He tried to speak, but nothing came out.

He coughed; he clutched at the handkerchief in the pocket of his rumpled trousers. He reeked of cognac.

"The newspaper," he said, "where's my newspaper?"

Teresa nodded in the direction of the console table where the breakfast tray with the daily paper had taken the place of the tray with his dinner. Ruggero grabbed the newspaper and started leafing through the pages, one by one. He was feverish, his breathing labored. Teresa stood petrified. The man stopped at one page and read without blinking. He'd even stopped breathing. He'd found the news report he was looking for.

He staggered as though he were about to faint and leaned on the tray to steady himself, knocking it to the floor in a crescendo of shattering glass and tinkling metal. Teresa leapt backward. Ruggero glanced at her, then went back to staring at the newspaper. He was weeping. The young woman wished she were somewhere else, anywhere but there. He let the newspaper fall to the ground, turned around, and went into his study, closing the door softly behind him. Teresa noticed that he was barefoot.

She was illiterate, so she ignored the newspaper. If she had been able to read, she would have seen the headline that had so upset the professor: Dead Woman in the Sanità: Was a Wooden Club the Murder Weapon?

XXVII

A few months earlier, Ricciardi's boss, Deputy Chief of Police Angelo Garzo, in a rather pathetic attempt to establish some sort of personal bond with his taciturn coworker, had lent him a slender volume with the garish yellow cover that in Italy was synonymous with detective novels. Garzo had told him that he'd enjoy it, that he'd take special pleasure in discovering that their line of work had even been accorded a certain literary dignity.

The commissario hadn't had the heart to dampen his superior officer's enthusiasm with a dose of his customary irony at the time; he also suspected that the thick-headed bureaucrat would miss the point, ignorant as Garzo was of any aspect of the policeman's profession that couldn't be performed from the comfort of a desk. No question about it: he'd only taken the book with the firm intention of keeping it at his desk for a few days and then returning it without comment.

But instead he had actually read the book, and he'd even enjoyed it: an action-packed story in which the good guys all had Italian names and the bad guys had American names, the women were blonde and emancipated, and the men were tough and tenderhearted. But he saw no connection to reality in it whatsoever.

In particular he remembered how he'd almost laughed out loud, reading by the light of the kerosene lamp in his bedroom, when the author had described how a police raid caught the lowlifes off guard in their lair. For him it would have sufficed to just once arrive at the scene of a crime without being heralded as well as followed by a chorusing fanfare of street urchins, announcing at the top of their lungs *"gli sbirri, gli sbirri,"*—"the cops, the cops"—with Maione trying to shoo them away, like an elephant swatting at flies; and along the way encountering old men sitting out on the street, standing up halfway and respectfully doffing their caps, as well as clusters of young men who scattered quickly, though not before looking their way with a gleam of defiance in their dark eyes.

It would suffice if just once he were able to arrest a wanted man without a crowd of people railing against him as if he were marching a saint off to his martyrdom; if just once the populace chose to ally itself with justice, instead of regarding criminals as their brothers and the police as their sworn enemy.

Catching criminals off guard, indeed.

That morning, too, as they arrived outside the building of the late Carmela Calise, the stench of rancor and hatred in the air was just as strong as the smell of garlic and the onset of springtime. Street urchins howling, shutters slamming shut as they went by, the bolts sliding home with an indignant click, malevolent glares from the dark *vicoli*. Ricciardi noticed it, as always, and as always he said nothing. Maione was also quiet that day; one of the urchins noticed and was so emboldened by the officer's silence that he tugged his jacket from behind. Without even slowing his pace, the brigadier kicked him in the chest like a mule and the boy flew through the air. Then he picked himself up and took to his heels, without so much as a peep.

Ricciardi watched his subordinate with a degree of concern. He sensed a strange tension in the brigadier, as if something were troubling him. He made a mental note to talk with him, taking care to be discreet.

When they arrived at the street door they found Nunzia Petrone, the porter woman, standing outside the entryway, at attention. Aside from the straw broom in her hand instead of an army-issue rifle, she resembled a noncommissioned infantry officer down to the last detail. Mustache included.

"Good morning. Did you forget something?"

Ricciardi turned to face the enormous woman without changing expression or removing his hands from his overcoat pockets. He leveled his fierce green eyes straight at hers. No doubt someone, perhaps one of the street urchins, had run ahead and alerted her to their arrival.

"Good morning to you. No, we didn't forget anything. And if we did, we don't need to report it to you."

He had addressed her in a low, firm voice that only she could hear. The woman stepped aside, looking down nervously as she did.

"Of course not, Commissa'. Come right in and do what you need to do. You know the way."

Ricciardi climbed the stairs, followed by Maione. The building seemed deserted. Not a voice could be heard, not even the sound of singing echoing in the courtyard.

They came to a halt in front of the Calise woman's locked door. Maione pulled the key out of his pocket, opened the door, and stood aside to let the commissario enter the apartment.

The room was cool and shady, and shafts of sunlight filtered in through the shutters. Dust swirled in the sunbeams. Still the same rancid odor of garlic and old urine mixed with the sickly sweet smell of the caked blood on the carpet. In the far corner, the old dead woman with her broken neck greeted Ricciardi, reiterating her proverb.

"'O Padreterno nun è mercante ca pava 'o sabbato." God Almighty's not a shopkeeper who pays His debts on Saturday.

Indeed, thought the commissario. He paid you on a Tuesday. And he wasn't scrimping on the interest, though this time you'd probably have been willing to do without it altogether.

Maione walked over to the window and opened it, letting in a gust of sparkling, sweet-smelling air.

"The season is certainly on its way, Commissa'. There'll be hot weather before long."

Waves of heat blasted out of the oven. Tonino Iodice had just tossed a shovelful of wood shavings and sawdust into the faint flames dancing over the logs, stirring a burst of sparks in response. Of all the things he did during his workday as a *pizzaiolo*, this act had always brought him a special happiness. Simple soul that he was, it reminded him of a tiny model of the festival of Piedigrotta, with the beautiful fireworks bursting into the dark sky over the water, creating blossoms of light as the children clapped their hands and jumped up and down.

Back when he had the pushcart and fried his pizza in a large kettle full of boiling oil, there were no flames: only dangerous splashes of oil that could even blind a person. The searing waves of heat in the summer, the steep hillside streets that became slippery when it rained, having to cry his wares at the top of his voice, even when he was burning with fever in the winter chill.

And yet he regretted—oh, how he regretted—having abandoned that hard life with its daily battles. In all those years of making do with his state of dignified poverty, he had never found himself looking over his shoulder with terror in his heart; and he'd never had to conceal anything from his family.

That morning, once again, before opening the restaurant and starting to mix the water, yeast, and flour together to make the dough, he had rushed to buy the newspaper; and he'd hungrily pored over the article, without skipping the long, difficult words that he didn't understand and which therefore struck him as especially menacing: *brutality, cervical vertebrae, contusions from a blunt object.*

Even in the violent heat that blasted out of the oven, Tonino shivered. He felt as though he were looking at the flames of hell as the wood burned rapidly. He imagined himself in the midst of those flames, burning in torment for the rest of eternity. When he ran his hand over his face, it was damp with tears and sweat.

He looked around him. The dining room was still empty, clean and awaiting the diners who'd be arriving shortly. His dream: how much had it cost? And how much more would it cost him and his family?

He thought about the moment when he'd see them come in through the front door. The looks he'd get from the diners, from the passersby in the street. He would rather die than dishonor his children. He put both hands up to cover his face. From the other side of the dining room, his wife watched him with her heart in her mouth.

XXVIII

The little bedroom where Carmela Calise had dreamed of the springtime she'd never see was cold and immersed in darkness. Maione reflected on how quickly a home could lose its life, just as soon as it became uninhabited.

Sometimes he would return, days later, to a place where no one lived anymore and he'd still encounter a vibration in the air, the feeling of whoever had lived in the place, as if they had just gone away temporarily. Other times, however, just a day after the murder, he'd walk into an apartment and find it inert, devoid of life, devoid of breath.

He didn't like digging through dead people's possessions. He hated sticking his nose into that little temple, a chapel that still housed a surviving thought or an old emotion. It made him feel like an intruder.

He carefully measured his gestures: a mark of respect for the departed. He'd have to rummage through the drawers and armoires, lift up carpets and tablecloths, move dishes and pans; that was his job. But no one could make him do it disrespectfully.

He thought of Doctor Modo, who would have to rummage through much worse places in search of clues, but the thought did not console him.

Not far from him, standing on the threshold, his back to the spacious room where Carmela Calise had received her diverse clientele, Ricciardi watched Maione conduct his search and listened to the old proverb uttered incessantly by the lips of the dead woman. Pay, pay. Money owed and payments due, still, even as she was making her way out of this life.

Who could say what it was that made a person look back over their shoulder from the dark bourn of death, anchoring their last thought in the things of this world: money, sex, hunger, love. It was understandable enough for a suicide, Ricciardi thought; but someone who had been murdered? He had never picked up a thought of fear, expectation, or even simple curiosity with regard to the something or the nothingness that awaited them.

"No, Commissa'. There was nothing but the notebook that Cesarano found. No other notes. And there are no dates in it."

"Look in the bed."

Maione walked over to the lumpy, narrow mattress supported by an old wooden bedframe. With slow, careful movements, as if he were preparing the bed for a night's sleep, he uncovered it, pulling aside the bedspread and the clean but threadbare sheet. Underneath, the mattress was stained yellow.

"She was an old woman, poor thing," Maione said, almost apologetically, looking at the commissario with a melancholy smile. Then he lifted the mattress. Beneath it, in the middle of the broad plank that served as the main support, the two men spotted a small bundle wrapped in a handkerchief. Maione picked it up. Ricciardi drew closer.

Inside were several banknotes: one hundred thirty lire, a tidy sum. And a scrap of paper; written on it, in the dead woman's unsteady handwriting: Nunzia.

The sea breeze came in through the open window. The curtains flapped lazily.

Emma Serra di Arpaja suppressed the urge to vomit; the odor filling the room seemed rank with rotting fish and putrefied seaweed.

Stretched out on the sofa, she looked up at the frescoed

ceiling. The days when she still loved that house were long ago; she remembered events, not emotions, much less passionate ones.

These days, she spent almost all her time out of the house, and when she was in the palazzo in Via Santa Lucia, she shut herself up in her own suite of rooms. That is, until it was time for the pantomime they staged for the benefit of the domestic help, when she'd walk into the chilly bedroom to sleep alongside the stranger she'd married. Except for those nights when she decided not to come home at all, offering no explanations to anyone, least of all him.

Sometimes she thought of her husband as an obstacle, a barrier separating her from happiness. Other times, she simply saw him as an unhappy man, aging in a state of melancholy. It was easy for Marisa Cacciottoli and the other serpents that surrounded her to say that he was a man with an enviable position in society, a figure of considerable prestige. She didn't give a good goddamn about his prestige or his position.

If she'd never met Attilio, she thought, sooner or later she might have resigned herself to an empty life like the ones led by the matrons and wives of her milieu. Charity balls, canasta, the opera, gossip. At rare intervals, a swarthy sunburnt lover, either one of the fishermen that sang along the beach of Via Partenope or one of the starving factory workers of Bagnoli, just to have the mental strength to face a future no different from the past.

But instead, it was her fate to find love.

Every morning she woke up she counted the minutes until she'd see him at the theater, or in one of the out-of-the-way places that they chose to meet in from one night to the next, how long it would be until she felt his hands upon her, his body atop hers. For some time now, she had understood that without him, without his divine perfection, she might as well be without air to breathe. She had lost, once and for all, the ability to resign herself to her fate.

She choked back a sob at the thought. Now what could she do? Her mind flew to the old woman. Damned old buzzard. Absurdly, the faces of Attilio and the Calise woman were bound closely together in her mind.

Day by day, her belief had grown stronger that her life now depended on him: she couldn't go on living without Attilio. But if she wanted to live with him, she would need the tarot cards.

In the rotating succession of kings, aces, and queens, the old woman read what was fated for every single day of her life. They'll steal your scarf at the theater, and sure enough, it would vanish. You'll trip over a beggar, and there she was, sprawled on the pavement with a sprained ankle. Someone will give you a bouquet of flowers on the street, and that's exactly what happened. Your car will hit a pushcart, and it promptly transpired. A thousand confirmations had turned her into a slave: she no longer dared to do anything unless Carmela Calise, with her tarot cards, had ordered her to.

It was she who had told Emma that it would be in that theater crowded with coarse and vulgar people: that was where she would find her true love.

And that's what happened.

First Attilio had smiled at her, and then he had approached her on the way out of the theater. Of course, she had noticed him onstage. And how could she have overlooked his masculine beauty? That memory brought a smile to her lips; her heart raced at the mere thought of it. And she had lost herself in those eyes, eyes that reminded her of a starry night. She had rushed to see the old woman and had told her every detail, whereupon the old woman had gazed at her, expressionless, as if she didn't understand. Maybe she really didn't understand; maybe she was merely an intermediary between her and some kind soul in the world beyond who had decided to reach out and save her.

Then came days spent living, living and nothing else. Heaven and then hell, locked up in her prison cell, staring at the ceiling. And never again after that day had she allowed her husband to lay a finger on her. In her soul, she was Attilio's woman, and there was not a single aspect of her previous life that she missed. No more lying. She had taken care of everything, selling jewelry and other possessions. They had only one concern, and that was being happy.

Only one thing was missing: for the old woman to tell her yes. The damned witch. Emma thought back once more to the terrible moment a few days earlier. To the blind fury she had felt rising up inside her. To the terrible condition imposed upon her: that she should never see Attilio again, not even on the stage. And now, what could she do? Now that she could no longer go back?

XXIX

Nunzia came to a halt at the threshold of the front door. Her fierce gaze wavered, wandering left and right. Her hands still clutched the straw broom.

Behind her, Maione reached out and gripped her arm with a firm hand. She snapped out of it and walked forward into the apartment.

Ricciardi was sitting at the rickety table, waiting for her. He was staring straight ahead, his mind and his heart flooded with melancholy, his ears filled with the proverb repeated over and over again by the ghostly figure of Carmela, in the corner of the room. He preferred to question people in the presence of the victim's ghost: it gave him strength and reinforced his determination in his quest for the truth.

"Sit down," he said to the woman. She stepped forward, pulled out a chair, carefully checked to see that it was sturdy, and sat down.

Both Ricciardi and Maione registered that detail, remembering that one of the chairs had a broken leg. Not that it told them all that much, but it did prove the porter woman was used to sitting at that table.

Outside, four floors below, the boys had resumed playing: their shouts accompanied the game of soccer they were playing with a ball cobbled together out of rags and newspapers.

"You're going to have to tell us about your relations with the Calise woman. The truth this time: not the usual claptrap."

Nunzia blinked her eyes. The firm tone, the deep voice, and

most of all, those queer, icy green eyes unsettled her. Maione took the broom and propped it in the corner.

"What do you want me to tell you, Commissa'? She was one of the tenants here. I told you before, my little girl liked spending time with her; it was convenient for me to have someone keep an eye on her while I worked. Then, in the evening . . ."

" . . . you'd come up to get her, yes, you told me that before. And would you pay her, for watching your girl?"

Nunzia emitted a nervous little laugh.

"No, Commissa', how could I pay her? Here, aside from the little one-room place on the ground floor and a few pennies every month, I don't get a cent; we have to struggle to make ends meet. There was no way I could have paid Donna Carmela."

"So money never changed hands between the two of you?"

A brief hesitation. Her eyes darted from right to left.

"No, I already told you. What money are you taking about?"

Ricciardi sat in silence. He went on staring the woman in the eye. Maione stood next to her chair, towering over her. On the windowsill, there was a fluttering of wings. A pigeon perhaps.

After nearly a minute, Ricciardi spoke again.

"What kind of person was she, the Calise woman? You knew her well, better than anyone else did. Maione here has asked around, and it seems that no one had any contact with her at all—the usual story. But you saw her every day. Did she have a family? What were her habits? Tell me all about her."

As Nunzia felt the viselike grip relax, she was visibly relieved. She decided to show herself to be as cooperative as possible. She shifted in the chair, causing the wood to creak loudly as she moved her enormous posterior.

"She was a saint, Donna Carmela. That's what I told you the other day and I'll say it again now, and anyone who says otherwise doesn't deserve to go on living. I swear it on the head of my poor sick girl, on her very soul, innocent angel that she is."

"Sure, a saint and an angel, I get it. Which would make this a little patch of heaven. Tell me about the Calise woman's life, and kindly refrain from changing the subject."

"Well, she didn't have any family in Naples. She wasn't married, and she never mentioned any brothers or sisters. She was from some small town, I don't even know the name. Once or twice a girl came here. Donna Carmela told me that she was a distant relation, but then I never saw her again. She never even told me the girl's name. She had a gift, this ability to fore-tell the future, and she used it to help people. She did so much good."

Maione broke in.

"And all this good she did for her fellow man, she did it free of charge, is that right? Out of the goodness of her heart."

Petrone looked up at the brigadier, offense showing in her eyes.

"What harm was there if people chose to give her a small gift out of gratitude? She never asked for money; she'd say, if you want to give me a token of appreciation, I thank you for it. People were satisfied with that arrangement."

Ricciardi raised an eyebrow and looked around the room.

"And just what did she do with these gifts? This place hardly seems luxurious to me. What did she do with the money?"

"How am I supposed to know, Commissa'? It's not like I could read Donna Carmela's mind."

"You couldn't read her mind, that's fine, but you knew what she thought and what she felt, you told us that yourself. Or at least, your daughter did. So I'd imagine a little something filtered back to you, didn't it?"

The woman sat up straight in her chair.

"No, never, Commissa'. Perish the thought. I loved Donna Carmela. *Per senza niente.* No strings attached."

Ricciardi and Maione looked at each other. This was going nowhere. The commissario sighed and once again fixed his transparent gaze on Nunzia, looking her in the eye.

"Petrone, let's be perfectly clear. We have all the evidence we need to prove that you were doing business with the deceased. We know that she not only read cards, but was also a loan shark. And that she gave you money."

This time it was the woman's turn to sit in silence, caught once again in the grip like a vise.

After what seemed like an endless pause, Nunzia spoke in a low, hard voice, meeting Ricciardi's eyes.

"No proof. You got no proof. Talk. It's all just empty talk."

Without taking his eyes off her, Ricciardi nodded a signal to Maione, who dropped the little bundle he'd found under the mattress onto the tabletop. Written on the bundle was one word: Nunzia.

Attilio Romor knew he wasn't particularly bright and could often be distracted. But he knew he truly excelled in the few areas he was competent in. One of those areas, the most important, was women.

When he could have possessed Emma, he'd made her wait, letting her desire swell within her. Gradually dismantling all her self-confidence, methodically testing her resistance, sapping her will, until she was finally putty in his hands.

A hundred, a thousand times he had read slavish devotion in her gaze, had felt the irresistible yearning grow within her, the desire to become his possession, something he owned. By now he knew with absolute certainty that he had become the center of her world, that he was the only reason she woke up in the morning. He couldn't be wrong about this. No, not at all.

As he went on carefully combing his pomaded hair, he smiled at the image that he saw reflected in the mirror; Emma would soon beg him to find a way for them to be together forever. She would provide him with prosperity, comfort, and finally, revenge. All he had to do was play his cards right, and wait.

XXX

Filomena walked uphill from the Via Toledo in the direction of the Vico del Fico. She had her shawl wrapped over her head, downcast eyes, and her face covered as usual. She walked briskly, skirting close to the walls.

The wide overcoat concealed her shape. Old shoes, an ankle-length skirt.

The usual masquerade, her suit of armor to protect her from the eyes of her predators: if you lack claws, hide.

She raised her head for just an instant as she came up to the last few yards of pavement separating her from the Via Toledo, and there he was, loitering at the corner: Don Luigi Costanzo, the picture of elegance as always in his light-colored suit, his hat pushed back on his forehead to reveal his swarthy brow, his mustache. Leaning back, shoulders resting against the wall, one hand in his pocket, the other at his side, holding a cigarette.

In the distance, Filomena saw two construction workers walk by, bowing so low before the *guappo* as they passed that they were practically crawling on the ground. Fear and power. She didn't want to be afraid anymore.

As she slowed her pace, she thought of Gaetano. He'd been at the construction site for two hours already, carrying bucketfuls of gravel, balancing his way across wooden planks perched sixty feet above the street. She trembled at the thought of the risks he took, but work was work and in those difficult times, one didn't have a choice. She felt a surge of anger that sprang from her frustration at having to see her son, still just a little boy, being forced to fight for scraps of food.

As she walked with her eyes on the ground, she regretted not being the whore they said she was. They would have lived better, she and her son. Perhaps in luxury, the luxury that came with a lover. She'd be respected, too. Money brings respect. She'd no longer be a whore; she could be a lady instead, with silk dresses and a fashionable haircut. Perhaps even a house to live in. Warm blankets to ward off the cold. Real mattresses. And Gaetano, smart boy that he was, could go to school.

How many nights, when the wind rattled the door, trying to make its way into the *basso*, or the heat almost suffocated them and rats scurried past, the masters of the *vicolo*, had she choked back her doubts and her tears?

But some people are born to do that sort of thing. She, on the other hand, had been born with a beauty that made it impossible for other people to believe that she lived only to care for her son, to make ends meet, and to hold on to the memory of a husband carried away by a coughing fit and a burst of blood.

She had almost come to where Don Luigi was standing. He saw her, flicked away his cigarette, and took a step forward to bar the path. The usual confident smile, the same piercing eyes.

"There you are, Filome'. How are you? Did you miss me? I was out of town a few days for business, in Sorrento. But I thought about you the whole time I was gone, you, the most beautiful girl in all Naples. So, have you given it some thought? I'll come see you. Tonight. Send the boy out to sleep in the street; after all, as you can see, the cold weather is gone. Spring is here."

Filomena had slowed to a halt. She held her head low, gripping the shawl that covered her face. Time stood still.

Annoyed that her reply was slow in coming, Don Luigi reached out suddenly and jerked the shawl off her face.

"Look me in the eye, why don't you, when I'm talking to you."

Filomena lifted her head and stared straight at him, tears flooding her eyes. The *guappo*'s smile froze on his lips and he took a step back, as if he'd just been slapped in the face. His shoulders collided with the wall; his hat fell to the pavement and rolled a short distance downhill. He lifted one trembling hand to his mouth and uttered a wail, the sound a frightened woman might make. His power was gone; fear had just moved house.

Filomena slowly drew her shawl back over her head and continued on her way. A young man walked behind her and looked curiously at Don Luigi, still shrinking back against the wall, one hand covering his mouth.

He didn't bow.

Ricciardi and Maione watched Nunzia cry, waiting patiently for her to finish. In their line of work it was common for people to break down in tears.

When confronted with the ragged bundle that had been found underneath Carmela's mattress, the porter woman had been, in her own way, a spectacle to behold. At first, there was only a faint trembling of the lip, which then spread to her shoulders. Then a tiny whine, almost a whistle, like a far-off train. When enough pressure had built up inside her, as in an overheating boiler, she threw herself face-first onto the table, racked by sobs, her skin covered with bright red splotches. Beneath her, the chair creaked in helpless despair.

The two policemen looked at each other and waited for the rainstorm to end.

Sniffing, the woman raised her head from the table. She looked at Maione, hoping for a handkerchief, a friendly hand, or at least a look of compassion, but he just stared at her, expressionless. So she shifted her gaze to Ricciardi, meeting those green-glass eyes in which she felt as though she were drowning.

"She gave me a little help, sometimes, Donna Carmela did. She loved my Antonietta, the poor child. And she'd give her a little present now and then, just a trifle—pennies for candy."

Maione took the wad of cash from his other pocket.

"Well, mamma mia, that daughter of yours sure eats a lot of candy! Guess that's why she's such a little roly-poly. Looky here, ten, twenty, fifty . . . one hundred thirty lire. How much candy is that, two cartloads?"

The woman glanced around her, her narrowed eyes seeking help. She'd walked into a trap and she knew it, but she wasn't ready to give up the fight.

Ricciardi sat waiting, as patient as a spider at the center of its web. It was only a matter of time. Soon they'd have Nunzia with her back to the wall, and that's when she'd lift the veil on another part of the story. He'd never thought for a second that she was responsible for the old woman's murder; if anything, now that he knew she'd been giving the porter woman money, he was all the more certain that it hadn't been Nunzia. Money: a strong motive, both to kill and to mourn. This woman's grief was genuine. She'd suffered a terrible loss.

From her corner, the old woman with the broken neck croaked out her proverb about accounts due and accounts payable. In his mind Ricciardi asked her: Did the person who killed you owe you money? Was he or she angry, desperate, offended? Or perhaps in love? As hideous as she'd been, deformed by her arthritis, she'd been able to stir such powerful emotions in someone as to be killed the way she was killed, murdered with such ferocity.

Ricciardi had always thought that hunger and love, or at least perversions of these two powerful drives, were at the root of most crimes. He could sense their presence in the air, around the dead people who called out for justice, and around the hatred of the living who survived them. Which had been behind the terrible blows that had ravaged Carmela Calise: hunger, or love? Or possibly both?

Nunzia straightened her back, once again assuming a proud expression. The chair beneath her creaked briefly.

"Who said the money was for me? A person can write whatever they want on a handkerchief. If you ask me, you don't have a scrap of evidence and you're just going around looking for someone to pin the blame on."

This reaction was also a familiar one, both to Ricciardi and Maione. The final whiplash: the last spark of rebellion.

"Exactly, Petrone. You're quite right; what a smart woman you are. We have no evidence and we just need someone, anyone, to pin this murder on. Otherwise, what'll we tell our bosses? All we have in hand is this handkerchief with the money for the candy. So you know what we're going to do? We're going to haul you off to jail. We're going to say you were blackmailing the Calise. And that's all there is to it."

Without changing his tone of voice, without changing his expression.

"You mean you'd actually have the nerve to do such a thing? You'd have that much nerve? What about my daughter?"

Ricciardi shrugged.

"There are excellent orphanages. She'll be well provided for."

Nunzia ran a hand over her face.

"All right, Commissa'. I'll tell you everything I know."

XXXI

It had all started years earlier, five years, perhaps, when her daughter was still a little girl. The old woman, crippled by the pain of arthritis, could no longer take on the small seamstressing jobs that had allowed her to make ends meet in her poverty. One summer evening, as they sat side by side down in the street, seeking refuge from the crushing heat and trading tales of woe, Carmela had told Nunzia that when she was a little girl she'd learned to read tarot cards. Her mother had taught her, and she in turn had learned from her grandmother, and on and on, back through the generations to the earliest mists of time, when the sirens sang on the shoals of Mergellina. She couldn't remember which of the two of them had first had the idea to devise a nice little con.

In those days, not far away, there lived the widow of a merchant who was obsessed with her deceased relatives. The local children liked to howl beneath her windows for fun, and one morning she confided to Nunzia—whom she regularly ran into at the vegetable cart—that she would give anything to talk to her husband just one more time. Anything—she'd give anything.

The two women came to an understanding. Nunzia told the widow that she knew a woman who was capable of telling her anything that those in the great beyond wanted her to know with tarot cards. After many years of listening to her confidences, Nunzia knew the things the woman most wanted to hear, and sure enough, Carmela told her all of them. A little at a time. First five, then seven, and finally ten lire per séance.

When the widow died, overjoyed to be rejoining the devoted and loving soul of her husband, who had forgiven her for all her betrayals, the respected corporation of Nunzia and Carmela already boasted a dozen or so loyal customers. And word was spreading fast.

Here's how it worked. A person would hear about Carmela. They'd show up one day and the old woman would say that she was busy just then and couldn't find time to see them until the following week. She would take first name, last name, address, and reason for calling: love, health, or money. At that point, Nunzia would swing into action. Thanks to her dense network of porter women, hairdressers who made house calls, and gossipmongering women street vendors, by week's end she was ready to provide Carmela with all the information she needed to ply her prospective new client with delectable scraps of news from beyond, for five lire apiece.

After all, the Petrone woman said, what harm were they doing? People came in sad and walked out happy. In a way, really, they were a couple of benefactors.

By now the name of Carmela Calise had gotten around and she had more paying customers than she could handle. The two women had also begun to supplement reality, giving fate a little push every now and then, just to make the oracular responses of the tarot cards that much more believable. A panhandler, a meeting with a man, a minor accident. Negligible things, apparently random incidents that constituted, for those who chose to view them this way, major confirmations. That part was Nunzia's business, with the occasional paid assistance of chance extras who took the money and asked no questions. Nunzia's investigations weren't always necessary; in some cases the old woman excused her from performing this particular duty because, she told her, there were people who supplied her directly with all the information she needed. Sometimes people just needed to get things off their chests.

It was all going splendidly. There was more than enough money to improve their quality of life without attracting too much attention. So much money, in fact, that they both wondered what they were going to do with it all. And in Naples, everyone knows that there's only one thing to do when you have too much cash: you lend it out at interest.

The carousel had started spinning about a year and a half ago: a woman who needed to put together a trousseau for her daughter, an office clerk whose wife was ill, a merchant who was having business troubles. If any of them had failed to repay the principal and interest due in full, everyone would have heard about it. The backbiting would have left their good names in tatters. It was the most effective form of debt collection imaginable.

A neat, efficient little operation: two complementary lines of business that whirred along beautifully, side by side. There'd never been the slightest problem. Until now.

No, she had no idea what Carmela did with the money. The old woman had always been particularly reticent on that subject and had never confided in her. She herself had put every penny into an account in her daughter's name, held at the bank on Via Toledo, depositing a little at a time to avoid arousing suspicion. When Nunzia asked her, Carmela had replied, with resignation in her voice, that, in the end, the two women weren't as different as they might seem.

Nor did she have the faintest idea as to who might have killed her. Carmela, with her tarot cards, constituted a threat to no one. She never hounded her debtors to get her money back. She gave them plenty of time and wiggle room. She was always happy to grant extensions—for a small added fee, of course. She couldn't think of anyone who could have murdered her. And then, the brutal *way* she was murdered? Unthinkable.

"Well then," said Ricciardi, tapping his finger on the cover of the black notebook that lay on the table in front of him, "you'll be able to provide me with a surname, address, and story to go with all the names that are written down in here, whether they belong to the clients of the tarot card business or victims of your loan-sharking scheme. Names to go with their dreams—dreams that you nursed and tended, cultivated for a fee."

Nunzia lowered her gaze under the commissario's moral condemnation.

"Yes. For everyone."

"All right. So, Maione: you have a seat here with Signora Petrone and take down the addresses and names of everyone the Calise woman saw on her last day, the day before her body was discovered. Tomorrow I want you to have them all come in to see me in my office, one by one, and we'll check them out. And if that doesn't give us anything to work with, then we'll just start working backward. Until we find the right dream, the sick dream we're looking for. The one that killed this old woman. I'm going home now. I have a headache."

XXXII

That night, Ricciardi felt more than his usual need for some semblance of a normal life. He yearned for simple, ordinary, measured gestures. Contact with the stuff of everyday life: chairs, tables, utensils, food. Healthy glances, normal expressions.

He'd had his fill that day of weeping, feelings of hatred, death. He couldn't wait to be at his window.

He reassured Rosa, who wasn't used to him coming home so early. He told her that he had a grueling day ahead of him, and he just wanted to get a little extra rest.

He ate quickly, read for a while, listened to the radio: grand symphonies that as if by magic restored his peace of mind. With his eyes closed, he imagined cinematic couples in ball gowns and tuxedos twirling over a glistening marble floor, following trajectories known only to them, without ever so much as grazing each other. The ladies with their dazzled eyes lost in the faces of their preux chevaliers; one hand raised, fingers intertwined with those of their partners, the other hand holding their skirts.

As he sat in his dark-red leather easy chair, by the dim, diffuse light of the table lamp, he thought of himself and the lives of other people as a grand ball in which the dancers brush up against each other as they move, alone or as couples, each moving to their own rhythm. Every so often, as they danced, there would be a collision, and someone would fall. And it fell to someone else, someone specially assigned to the task, to help the fallen to their feet and punish whoever had caused the accident. It was an ugly job, but someone had to do it.

At the usual time, perhaps a few minutes early, he found himself standing by the window, in his bedroom illuminated by the yellow light of the old kerosene lamp that had once belonged to his mother. In the dining room of the apartment across the way, the evening meal was coming to an end. The diners were rising from their seats, to return to their own occupations after the interlude of conviviality. A few lingered behind, over coffee, a slice of cake for the little ones.

Ricciardi imagined that genuine love, the kind of love that didn't pollute the soul, could easily become the driving force of one's life. As he watched that family, he intuitively understood their feelings for each other. A distracted caress, a smile, an affectionate hair-tousling. Gestures that were normal and, at the same time, extraordinary. In short, a family.

He was capable of articulating in any of a number of ways the grief he felt at losing something he'd never actually possessed. He had only the vaguest of memories when it came to his ailing mother; he couldn't remember her caresses, or the warmth of her embrace. He could only dream of her.

Across the way, the woman under whose spell he had fallen remained the mistress of the dining room and kitchen, as she was every night. She had started to wash the dishes. He watched her familiar actions the way one listens to a beloved record heard thousands of times before, predicting each move, studying her gait.

In his thoughts, he had become accustomed to calling her *"amore mio."* Words that he would never actually utter in her presence; in all likelihood, he would never speak to her. All I could offer you is my grief and pain, he thought: the terrible burden of the cross I bear.

He'd never dare to stand by the front door of her building or ask Rosa to find out about her, much less discuss her with one of the neighborhood gossips. Incredible, considering that he made his living investigating the lives of others.

It didn't bother him too much, though. He preferred to imagine, dream, and watch from afar. The one time he'd run into her on the street he'd turned and fled; and if the same thing happened again, he'd just turn and run away again.

As he admired the woman's precise, measured gestures and her luminous normality, Ricciardi thought about Carmela Calise and Nunzia Petrone, peddlers of illusions. What an awful crime it was to trick people into thinking that they could achieve the unachievable. The porter woman had said that people were sad when they came and happy when they left. But what kind of happiness could such a deception bring them? You, with your slow, certain motions, would never let a con artist sully your dreams with her false playacting. Your dreams must be like you: moderate, delicate, and peaceful. You'd never go to a fortune-teller to have them interpreted.

Even more than kissing you and holding you in my arms, I'd like to be in your dreams. And I'd like to keep them safe for you.

It was late by the time Maione left the Calise woman's apartment. He carried with him the list of all those she had seen on the last day of her life. Names, dreams, addresses. Their personal traits, their families, what had driven them to beg the woman for her pronouncements, paying for each word in cold hard cash.

The brigadier didn't understand. He couldn't see the point of paying someone such exorbitant fees for reading tarot cards. Were these people rich? Perhaps there were some on that list who earned their money by the sweat of their brow. He walked on, shaking his head: the Petrone woman had rattled off all the information, names and numbers, displaying an extraordinary talent for investigation. If it'd been up to him he would have enlisted her on the spot, with the rank of private first class at the very least. Among the names, there was even one that struck him as important, one he'd make a point of mentioning to the commissario: not the sort of person who would be happy to be summoned to police headquarters. They'd deal with that tomorrow; right now he had other business to take care of.

He walked uphill through the Spanish Quarter, huffing and puffing because he was overweight and it was a steep climb. As he went, the usual dumb show of greetings and cap-doffings, always at a respectful distance. He'd decided to pay a call to someone. He wasn't thinking of dropping by Filomena's to see how she was doing or ask if there was anything she needed, though perhaps he would do that the following morning. Nor was he thinking of going home; it was still early and, though he was unwilling to admit it even to himself, the idea didn't appeal to him.

He clambered up the hill, passing under the Corso Vittorio Emanuele, the Bourbon-era road that encircled the old city. Behind Vicolo di San Nicola da Tolentino, at the back of a blind alley that came to an end in the tall dry grasses and shrubs of the countryside, there was a small apartment building. A steep, narrow staircase led up to a garret apartment, its windowsills heaped high with pigeon guano. It was the home of a person who had been very helpful to Maione on more than one occasion.

Panting again, he knocked on the door, which was falling off its hinges. A deep but gracious voice asked who it was, and Maione said his name. The door swung upon.

"Brigadier, what an honor! If I'd known you were coming to pay me a visit, I'd have put on some makeup and changed my underwear!"

Bambinella almost defied description. Her black hair was gathered in a bun, with a few stray locks falling out around her ears. She wore dangly earrings and her face was heavily made up. A garish nightgown parted to reveal a lace negligee underneath. Fishnet stockings, high heels. A faint five o'clock shadow could be seen on her cheeks, under a thick layer of face powder.

"Come on, let me in. It's taken ten years off my life just to get up here."

"You can't be serious. A big strong handsome man like you, all worn out from a little climb? Come right in, make yourself comfortable. Can I offer you a cup of ersatz coffee, a little rosolio cordial?"

"A glass of water. I need to talk to you, and I'm in a hurry."

Maione had met Bambinella a couple of years ago, when he'd taken part in a raid on a underground bordello in Via San Ferdinando, one of those low-cost operations where older women and country girls peddled their services without proper license or certification. Among the array of homely, handicapped, and elderly "signorinas," this Latin beauty with her almond-shaped eyes had seemed out of place; and in fact, when the police demanded identification, the "defect" emerged.

Maione was forced to intervene because Bambinella, whose real name could not be ascertained, managed to lure three of his men to her in rapid succession, practically scratching the third man's eyes out with her claws.

During the night that followed, which Bambinella spent in a cell as a guest of police headquarters, she never stopped sobbing, talking, and shouting in an unbroken stream of abuse. In the end, Maione took it upon himself to order Bambinella's release. In part because, technically speaking, Bambinella couldn't be called a "lady" of the evening.

As he listened to Bambinella's seemingly endless chain of delirium, the policeman came to the conclusion that the ladyboy, or *femminiello*, to use the Neapolitan term, possessed a great deal of useful information. And that the debt of gratitude he created by releasing her might well be more than amply repaid.

Since then, Maione had cashed in his chips with Bambinella more than once, sparingly but always to good effect. A number of case-cracking details were provided right in the garret where Bambinella continued to run her discreet little business. Maione looked the other way, and Bambinella whispered in his ear.

XXXIII

The sea had started slapping against the rocks off Via Caracciolo around seven o'clock that night. Now the waves, whipped up even higher by the buffeting wind, were splashing so high that the spray could be seen from the balconies along Via Generale Orsini in Santa Lucia.

Ruggero Serra di Arpaja stepped out onto the balcony to feel on his face the first breaths of spring wafting up from the sea. They seemed somehow threatening, and brought him none of the comfort he had hoped for.

It wouldn't be long now; he knew that. He didn't have a clear idea of what was going to happen, but at any rate he wouldn't have to wait long to find out. The newspaper described those details that he knew about, but seemed to have left out others.

He had no particular confidence in the abilities of the state police, nor in the skills of the corps of magistrates; he'd had daily dealings with them both for more years than he cared to remember and he had always pictured them in his mind as a large, ungainly beast, slow-moving and incapable of reaching its objective.

In recent years, moreover, the machinery of justice had been even further hindered by politics, which slowed the grinding of its gears and altered its course to suit its own goals.

But now, everything he had built was teetering on the brink. For the thousandth time he thought through the various potential outcomes with the anguish of a trapped rat. The memory surged up inside him on a wave of nausea that he managed to ward off by shutting his eyes: blood. It was one thing to talk about it dispassionately in his study with the guilty individuals whom he defended, the scum of the earth, no doubt, but wealthy, and willing to pay for their freedom. It was quite another thing to find yourself surrounded by it.

All that blood. He instinctively looked down at his bare feet; it dawned on him that since he'd come home that day and removed his blood-spattered shoes, he'd never put on another pair. He had to get rid of those shoes, and he had to take care of it himself; there was no one else he could trust.

He sighed in the sweet breeze. His greatest anguish, the anguish that clutched at his throat until he was unable to breathe, didn't stem from the thought of what might happen to him. His anxiety came from the thought of what Emma might do. And if he wanted to know the answer, he would have to screw his courage to the sticking place, leave the apartment, and go to the theater. That very night.

A dog barked somewhere out in the countryside. Bambinella was sitting in a Chinese-style chair and had assumed the pose of a prim young lady, knees together and hands resting in her lap.

"Well now, Brigadie', what brings you here? Have you finally decided to try something different? It goes without saying, for you, it'd be on the house."

"Listen, Bambine', there are still plenty of normal things I haven't tried yet; so why would I get a yen for 'something different'? You know I'm here for the usual reason: work."

The *femminiello* let out a refined snort.

"Oh, Madonna mia, what a bore! Work, work, and more work. Go on and take a half hour off once in a while! A handsome man like you, so masculine, and with all that hair! Oh dear—but you could probably use a little more on your head, couldn't you?"

"Hey now, don't get cute with me or I'll run you in, all right? My hair's no business of yours, and besides, it's right where it ought to be. Why don't you worry about your own hair? Your face is turning dark blue."

"Eh, I know, Brigadie', I have the kind of beard that's always showing. But I still have to make myself up for the night, and you can rest assured that when I'm done you won't be able to see a thing. So how are things with you? I heard from some of my girlfriends in the Sanità that you're trying to find out who murdered Donna Carmela, the one who reads the cards, am I right?"

Maione spread his arms wide.

"What a city! It makes me sick. Someone sneezes at the train station and someone out at the Vomero says bless you! Yes, we're looking into it. Do you know anything?"

"No, Brigadie', I really can't help you on that one. Aside from the fact that that's not my part of town, with all the stinking, penniless lowlifes that live there, I haven't heard anything about it. All I know is that she was doing a little loan-sharking in her spare time. Did you know that?"

"Yes, that's something we already knew. What else can you tell us?"

"She really was good at reading cards. A little girlfriend and colleague of mine from Via Santa Teresa went to talk to her because she was worried about her boyfriend, who'd told her he was working the night shift on a construction site in Giugliano and couldn't see her in the evenings The old woman read her cards and told her"—and here Bambinella made her voice even deeper and squinted, as if she were peering into a crystal ball—"'Check your facts, because that man's not going to Giugliano. He's going to a bordello on Viale Elena.' And sure enough she goes to that very same bordello and she sees him, coming out arm-in-arm with a whore! It took three people to hold her back; she was going at them with a straight razor, ready to slice both their faces. That old woman was good at what she did. But who could have killed her? That's something I really can't tell you."

Maione shook his head, awestruck.

"No doubt about it—people really are stupid. How could anyone be so gullible? Calise was a fraud. She'd gather information about people, the way I'm doing right now with you, and then tell people their present and their future. And she took anyone willing to listen for all the money she could squeeze out of them."

Bambinella looked down at her lacquered fingernails with a sigh.

"Brigadie', sometimes people just need something to believe in. Don't you ever feel that need yourself?"

Maione looked out the window, where the countryside was gradually turning to greet the spring. The evening carried chirping cicadas in its arms and you could hear the tall grass rustling. Believe in something? He immediately thought of Lucia, laughing in the sunshine on the rocky beach at Mergellina, twenty-five years earlier.

"Sure, Bambine', I see your point. A person has to believe in something, to make it through this life. But I'm here for another reason. The other night a woman in the Spanish Quarter, on Vico del Fico, was cut, badly. Her face was slashed."

"Yes, I know. Filomena la Bella. There's been a lot of talk about her. The virgin whore."

Maione squinted.

"What do you mean, the virgin whore? What is that supposed to mean?"

Bambinella giggled, lifting one hand to cover her mouth in an affected manner.

"It's just a figure of speech. That's what I call those women who get a reputation for being a whore without ever doing anything wrong. The fact is that when people gossip, they say just the opposite of the truth. It happens all the time, Brigadie'."

"In this case, what's the truth of the matter?"

"Well, let me start by saying that everything I'm about to tell you I know through one of my closest girlfriends, who was her late husband's cousin—because this woman is a widow, in case you didn't know."

Maione nodded his head yes.

"And she has a twelve-year-old son, if I'm not mistaken."

"Almost thirteen, I think. A quiet boy, dark-skinned like his father. I saw him a couple of times, when I went with Irma, the cousin I mentioned, to pay a call on them. You can't imagine they way they looked at the two of us, there in the *vicolo*," Bambinella said, giggling again behind her hand. "There was this one old bag looking down at us from right above the *basso*, dressed in black; she looked like one of the witches of Benevento, with a face that you couldn't even begin to imagine."

Maione remembered Donna Vincenza, with her compressed lips and the hissed insult she spat at Filomena.

"Actually, I'm pretty sure I can imagine it, trust me. Go on."

"Well, the Lord Almighty gave Filomena Russo the gift of beauty. If you've ever seen her, even now that her face has been slashed, you know what I'm talking about. She's the most beautiful woman in Naples, and possibly on earth. That is, she used to be. Poor thing."

"What do you mean, poor thing? Because someone slashed her face?"

"No, Brigadie': because she was born beautiful. That was the curse of her life. You have to understand that when a woman is that beautiful, it's best if she's also born with a whore's heart. If she has the heart of a whore, then she can enjoy a life of luxury, she and her children, her mother and father, the whole family. She'll let herself be kept, she'll show off and conceal that thing she's got between her legs, lucky her;

while the men, miserable shits that they are—no offense meant to you, Brigadie'—get a whiff of her scent and run after her like dogs in the street. But if you're like Filomena, and you don't have the heart of a whore, then you just have to live your life in hiding, if you want to live in peace. And no one will let you live in peace anyway."

"And just who is it who won't let her live in peace?"

Bambinella looked Maione right in the eye, for a moment that seemed to last for a long time.

"Lately, the *guappo*, Don Luigi Costanzo. And also the merchant who owns the fabric store where she works. She told us about it the last time we went to see her. One of them was threatening to hurt her son, the other one wanted to turn her out onto the street."

Maione clenched his fists. This wasn't lost on Bambinella, who went on with her story.

"Of course, now I sincerely doubt anyone will be bothering her anymore."

"And in your opinion, who could it have been?"

The *femminiello* shook her head.

"Take it from someone who works with beauty and tortured love: when someone becomes infatuated with a beautiful person, they might kill them, but they'd never disfigure them. It was neither of those two, Brigadie'. I don't believe it. But I really couldn't tell you the name of the lunatic who destroyed that splendid beauty."

"So why do they call her a whore, if she's such a respectable woman?"

"Because women refuse to admit that another woman might be superior to them in some way. They think that if men lose their heads, it must be over a certain something else—not just what they see alone. If you only knew how many times the same thing had happened to me—and continues to happen!"

Maione stood up and moved toward the door.

"Thank you, Bambine'. If you find out anything else, please send for me. And stay out of trouble; I don't want to spend the rest of my life fixing your problems. You're not my son."

Bambinella smiled fetchingly, but with a hint of sadness in her eyes.

"Sure, Brigadie', I'll be a good girl. But there's something I want to say to you. Beauty can make you lose your head. A beautiful face can do it, but so can a beautiful soul. You have a wonderful family; don't let yourself get sucked into anything. If you don't mind my telling you so."

Maione stood stock still in the doorway.

"Well, I do mind. This is strictly a professional matter, as far as I'm concerned. Take care of yourself."

And he left and hurried home.

XXXIV

The following morning was the fourth since the first gust of new spring air had swept through the narrow lanes just off the waterfront. The air was growing warmer by the hour, overcoats had vanished almost entirely, and straw hats were starting to appear here and there.

Inside the apartments that now had their windows open, jackets and skirts that had lain forgotten all through the long winter were being brought out of hiding; and people were singing and quarreling loudly, to the greedy delight of the old gossips eavesdropping from their balconies.

Out on the street, the breeze, fortified with the scent of the sea, was having fun lifting hats off heads and snapping branches. Men and women who for months had walked past each other without so much as a glance now eyed one another intently, exchanging silent messages concealed behind a smile. Slumbering feelings, sluggish from the cold, began to reawaken: attraction, tenderness, envy, and jealousy.

Along the streets of the city center, where the smell of horse manure had intensified, street vendors hawked their wares with reinvigorated spirit. The air was filled with promises, and among them twirled the invisible springtime.

The sun was shining, the air was soft and fragrant, and perhaps all was not lost.

Attilio filled his lungs with the faint breeze that was coming in through his bedroom window. For the first time in days he went back to thinking that he might be able to steer his life in the direction he had hoped.

Not that things had gone better than usual at the theater the night before; quite the opposite. That damned pompous ass had been, if possible, even more cutting and abusive than was his wont. He had even come up an offensive moniker for his character: the "fop." Just one more way to undercut him, to belittle his talent. And, as if that weren't enough, the box remained empty.

He shuddered at the thought that he might not even be able to take refuge in Emma's adoring eyes if the audience laughed at him.

That man had been there at the stage door, come to make him a deal, and his heart had raced in his chest, in spite of the fact that he had nothing to fear. Still, he'd turned his offer down, contemptuously. Let no one think that Attilio Romor could be bought.

And yet, that encounter had made him realize something: that there might be another way. And he was determined not to let that opportunity slip through his fingers.

He stretched his arms, making his pectoral muscles pop underneath his sleeveless T-shirt and suspenders. He shot a dazzling smile at the woman lingering over the laundry she was hanging out on the balcony across the way. Let her enjoy herself too. The sun was shining and the future was bright.

Ricciardi was reading over the list of the last people to see the Calise woman alive. A message from beyond, written in the dead woman's own hand. Not the only message he had received from her. *'O Padreterno nun è mercante ca pava 'o sabbato.* God Almighty's not a shopkeeper who pays his debts on Saturday.

He took his time, studying the shaky handwriting of the names.

Passarelli: male, muther.
Colombo, female, new, love.
Ridolfi, joolery, wife.
Emma.
Iodice, pay.

It had been a quiet day for her. Some of the pages of the black notebook with red trim contained as many as ten names, and the average was six or seven. Perhaps one of those sessions had gone on longer than usual. Perhaps the old woman had read her own fate in the cards.

Ricciardi loved cold air and would throw open the windows to let the spring breeze in as early as possible. The smell of salt air wafted up from the large market piazza, bringing with it the voices and songs of the new season.

Maione stood gazing out the window, rapt in thought. That morning he felt a pain inside him, though he couldn't have said exactly what it was. Bambinella's words came back to him, stirring a vague sense of remorse. Impressed into his brain was the recent memory of Filomena's still-bandaged face and her sad smile. When she had found the shaggy-haired brigadier on her doorstep that morning, she had said to him: Brigadie', you're making me get used to hearing you say hello. Maione had replied: Then get used to it, Filome'.

"Maione, what are you doing, dreaming on your feet?"

"Commissa', it's nothing. I just haven't slept well for the past couple of nights. Maybe because it's getting warmer. Now we'll have a lot more work on our hands, same as every year. That's how it always is in the spring. No?"

Ricciardi nodded, with a sigh.

"That's what experience tells us. Let's hope for the best. Now then, tell me all about your date."

Maione opened his eyes wide and went on the defensive.

"What date, Commissa'! I just stop by to say hello, to see how she's doing with the wound. There's nothing personal between us, for heaven's sake. I just drop by to see if she needs anything, but I'd never dream of . . ."

Ricciardi looked at him with a certain intensity.

"What on earth are you talking about? I mean the chat you had with the Petrone woman to decipher this list. Listen to me, Raffaele: I'm not somebody who pries into other people's business, except when it's my duty. But there is one thing I want to say to you: I was there for your . . . that terrible moment for you and your family. I met your wife and your children. I remember Luca. Believe me when I tell you that what you have at home can't be bought at any store on earth."

Maione looked down at the floor.

"Why would you say such a thing to me, Commissa'? What did I make you think? I'm a lucky man, and I know it. It's just that ever since . . . since that thing you mentioned, we don't talk anymore. Me and Lucia. That is to say, it's not like we don't talk at all. It's just that she's always somewhere else. Even the kids look at her funny. She doesn't say anything. She just looks straight ahead of her; who knows what she's looking at."

"What about you? Don't you reach out to her? Don't you talk to her?"

Maione smiled sadly.

"I have, Commissa'. I still do. But it's like talking to a wall. Sometimes I act like a lunatic, walking around the apartment talking to myself. It's as if the two of us could only talk to each other through Luca. Luca's memory. And we never say his name."

Ricciardi looked at him.

"It's not as if I can tell you how things work in a family. You know I don't have a family of my own, and I never did, not even as a child. I grew up with my Tata, and I live with her still. I love her, but I can't call her a family. You know what I think? I think it's easy to stick together when everything's going well. The hard thing is when you have to climb over the mountains, and it's cold out, and the wind is howling. Maybe that's when everyone should huddle a little closer together, to try to find a little warmth. Take it from someone who lives out in the cold. And who doesn't have anyone who can give him warmth."

Maione stared at Ricciardi in astonishment. He'd never heard him talk so long, and certainly not on topics having to do not with an investigation, but with himself, his life, and his family. Maione knew that he wasn't married—or, rather, that it was as if Ricciardi were married to his own solitude.

"Commissario, there are times when I think that the love between me and Lucia died the day my son died. What does she think, that she's the only one who's grieving and suffering, just because she was his mamma? That I don't see him standing in front of me every day, with that smirk on his face, telling me, 'Ciao, Brigadier Potbelly, what do you expect me to do now, snap you a military salute?' And that I don't see him in my arms every time I close my eyes? He's seven years old and he wants to see my service pistol. There are times when I can't breathe at all, my heart is aching so bad. But my pain doesn't matter: all that matters is her grief as a mother."

Ricciardi shook his head.

"I couldn't say, Raffaele. You might be right. Still, if you ask me, it's not a contest to see who suffers most, me or you. Sometimes grief and pain can bring people together. Maybe you just need to try to talk a little, at night. I can feel that chill I was telling you about at night, especially. And when it comes . . . I look out the window, and I get some fresh air. I listen to a little music on the radio. And I go to bed, hoping for dreamless sleep."

A street organ starting playing in the piazza, two floors beneath his office window. *Amapola, dolcissima Amapola.* A flock of doves took flight, filling the air with wings. A bit farther off, from the port, came the loud cry of a seagull. Maione looked out to sea and imagined his son. Ricciardi looked out to sea and imagined Enrica.

"Anyway, if you ever want to talk to someone, I'm right here. Now then, let's take a look at this list."

XXXV

As he works with his hands, his mind sees it all again: the blood, the body on the floor, the biscuit tin, him rummaging through it, looking for his promissory note among all the others, the note he had signed when he still believed in his dream.

He works with his hands, kneading, rolling out, gently slapping the dough, his heart filled with anguish, the real significance of things. Of his children, his wife, his mother, my poor little old darling mother. His dishonor, the rumors, the heads turning as they walk past.

As he works with his hands, only with his hands, the heat of the oven scorches the hairs on his arms, the fire crackles and mutters promises of hell; but not his eyes, his eyes scurry from the dining room to the front door, to the tops of the hats going by in the street, to the glances of people out walking in the air of rebirth.

If only this spring had never come. If only he'd never given up his pushcart.

Madonna mia, so much blood. How could there be so much blood in such a tiny body? The carpet—the carpet had turned another color. I called out to her, she didn't answer. Twice. Madonna mia, help me if you can.

He remembers when he was little and a man from the *vicolo* was sent to prison for stealing who knows what. Then he remembers how his Mamma would divide up their meal, already so small, and set part of it aside for the now fatherless family, just as everyone else in the quarter had done. Still, the children were all forbidden to play with the children of the thief. He'd never let that happen to his own children. Never.

They'd never take him alive. He wouldn't let them take him.

He stopped mincing the salted anchovies, reached his hand down under the counter to check the long, razor-sharp blade of the filleting knife.

Today would be the day. He could feel it in his bones. But they'd never take him alive.

Maione had pulled out his notebook and was reading back over his notes.

"Mamma mia, I can't make sense of any of it, even though I wrote it all myself. That day, Calise didn't see anyone in the morning, so there were only five appointments. She told Petrone that she had to go out to take care of some business of her own. Apparently, that wasn't a common occurrence. Anyway, she was back by lunchtime and she started receiving clients in the early afternoon. I sent for all of them. Perhaps you know some of them, Commissa'? There are people from your part of town. A certain Ridolfi, Pasquale; he can't come in to headquarters, we'll have to go see him. He fell down the stairs as he was leaving Calise's apartment, in fact, that same morning, and now he's at home with his leg in a cast. You remember those stairs, don't you, Commissa'? I almost fell down them myself the last time I was there. Luckily they're so narrow that even if I did fall, I'd've stuck fast between the walls. Then there are the others. The first one to come in was Passarelli, Umberto; he lives in Foria. He's an accountant who works at the Department of Records."

"So what did Petrone tell you about him?"

Maione laughed.

"Ah, Commissa', this story's a rib-tickler. Now then, Passarelli the accountant is sixty years old. He lives with his mother, who's eighty-seven: normal so far. The accountant has been engaged to marry a certain Signorina Liliana, who lives nearby, since he was twenty. A forty-year engagement, Commissa'! And do you know why they never got married? Because Signora Passarelli—the would-be mother-in-law, in other words—was opposed to it. And since she controls every penny, and is old but never seems to die, the two of them are just waiting."

"And why was Passarelli having his cards read by Calise?"

"That's the funny part: to find out when his mamma's going to die! In fact, she's been on her deathbed for twenty years now. Petrone knows the housekeeper of the old woman's doctor; that's how she was able to gather the information Calise needed to read his cards. Unbelievable."

"All right, all right, bring him in. Who's next?"

"A young woman, a certain Colombo. It was only the second time that she'd been to see her, with regard to a matter of the heart, which I'll tell you about later. Our real problem comes with the next woman, a prominent lady from Santa Lucia, Emma Serra di Arpaja. This one's serious business: one of the chief patrons of their little establishment. Petrone couldn't tell me anything about her. That one always met directly with Calise. Maybe there's nothing worth knowing. I wanted to ask you: what should I do? Should I have her summoned along with the rest of them? Or should we approach this one with a bit more discretion? I wouldn't want to kick up too much dust and have the top brass start kicking up a fuss."

Ricciardi snorted in annoyance.

"How many times have I told you that I don't want to hear that kind of talk! If there's an investigation to be done, we do it. Have her summoned along with all the others. Then, if they try to throw a wrench in the works, we'll find a way of kicking them in the head. And the last one?"

"Iodice, a *pizzaiolo* from the Sanità quarter. This one doesn't have to do with the cards; he owed her money. But the promissory note has vanished. I checked. Maybe he paid up and left, and that's why he's in the notebook."

"Or else he murdered her and took the promissory note. We'll see. Bring in Passarelli."

The accountant Umberto Passarelli didn't believe in fate, which was a rather remarkable thing for a man who went to have his cards read. He believed that the course of events was largely determined by the way a man dealt with things. The rest depended on whether the day got off to a good start or a bad one.

And so he paid the greatest possible attention to the things that happened in the first hour after he woke up in the morning, considering them to be unequivocal indicators of the marks that day would leave on his life, and he prepared himself for the remaining twenty-three hours with the appropriate amount of brow-furrowing. Those signs, however, were not always easy to interpret.

That morning, he had awoken to the sound of a number of vigorous knocks on the street door: bad luck. However, he had been the only one to hear them, and Mamma had gone on with her melodious snoring: good luck. Two policemen in uniform: bad luck. But they were polite: good luck. They wanted him to come down to police headquarters that very same morning: bad luck. But they hadn't placed him under arrest, nor were there any charges outstanding against him: good luck. At least, not yet, they had added: bad luck.

And so, Umberto Passarelli, who cautiously entered Ricciardi's office with a courteous "May I come in?" had decided to adjust his usual strategy in accordance with a wait-and-see attitude.

He was a skinny little man, his perennial nervousness betrayed by any number of tics, the most irritating of which consisted of squeezing his left eye shut while simultaneously pulling his lips back on the left side of his face: it looked as if he were winking and starting in fright at the same time. Diminutive gold eyeglasses, stiff collar, shirt cuffs dotted with tiny ink stains.

A careful comb-over had been raked across his otherwise bald pate. The light breeze that came in through the window immediately began toying with it, lifting it now and again. Ricciardi was reminded of the procession on the Feast of Pentecost back home in his village, where the participants acted out the arrival of the Holy Ghost with fluttering strips of cloth on their heads.

After taking down his identifying information, the commissario asked the accountant whether he was aware that the Calise woman had been murdered.

"Yes, of course, I read about it in the newspaper. Such a shame. Quite inconvenient."

"Inconvenient?"

"Why certainly, Commissario. You see, now I—and who knows how many others like me—will need to find someone else who can help us. And it's no easy matter, believe you me," he said, with a wink of his eye, "finding someone you feel you can trust to tell you what to do."

Ricciardi furrowed his brow.

"What do you mean, 'tell you what to do'? Did you do whatever the Calise woman told you?"

The man's left eye quivered.

"Of course I did, Commissario. Otherwise, why would I go to see her? After all, with what I paid . . ."

"And just how long had you been her . . . her client?"

"For a year. I'd go to see her roughly once a week."

"On what pretext? That is to say, what was she giving you advice on?"

The corner of the man's mouth jerked toward his neck.

"Well now, you see, Commissario, I live with my mamma. Don't get me wrong, she's a wonderful woman, an extraordinary person, and she has no one but me. So I have to look after her, and it isn't always easy, because she has serious health problems, she's very old, and she has a bad temper. If you ever heard her yell . . . it's enough to wake up the whole neighborhood."

"I understand. And what does the Calise woman have to do with your mother?"

"Nothing, it's just that I'm a very methodical person. I like to be able to plan my schedule, know what's going on, set dates."

"And so?"

Eye, mouth.

"And so, it would help me to know, that is, more or less, you understand, when my mother will shuffle off this mortal coil. My fiancée—because I'm engaged, in case you weren't aware—a lovely young lady who is infinitely patient, will need some advance notice to prepare her trousseau, and then there's the ceremony—you have no idea how much is involved. I don't want to make you think that I'd like for Mammà to die, heaven forbid. Still, a couple needs to be able to think ahead. There's also the period of mourning to observe, at least two years for a mother. And of course the apartment is full of medicine; she doesn't like the furniture; some changes will need to be made. We'll have to get the nursery ready as well."

Maione, who had done his best to hold himself back throughout the interview, broke in.

"Ah, you have children?"

Comb-over, mouth, eye once, twice.

"No, but both my fiancée and I would like to have a big family."

"And just how old is the young lady?"

Eye, mouth, eye. An instant later, an uncertain tremor in the comb-over.

"She's two years older than I am, sixty-two. But she looks so much younger than her age. For now, I can't even take my pension and retire, until . . . until . . . things are sorted out."

Ricciardi shot Maione a look of reproof.

"And how did the Calise woman seem when you saw her? Did you notice anything unusual about her, was there anything she said . . ."

Passarelli put on a thoughtful air, enlivened by a crescendo of tics.

"No, Commissario, I don't think so. Maybe a little quieter than usual. Not so much as a hello, just the daily update on Mamma's health. But on that she was extraordinary! Just think, she told me the same exact things the doctor had said the day before! I couldn't breathe a word about her to Mamma, but if I could, we could have saved the doctor's fee entirely!"

Ricciardi looked at the heaving shoulders of Maione, who had turned to face the window. The commissario shook his head.

"All right, Passarelli, you can go. Make sure we know how to get in touch with you, though; we might need to talk to you again."

The accountant stood up, sighed, winked, twisted his mouth into a grimace, sketched out a courtly bow, and turned to leave. As he left the office, his comb-over waved good-bye charmingly from a distance.

XXXVI

In front of the church of Santa Maria delle Grazie the sidewalk was crowded with busy people rushing in all directions, the stores were still open, and the air was soft and sweet.

Sitting on the church steps, calm and composed, was Rituccia. She was waiting. If you looked at her closely, you could tell that she wasn't begging for coins. She'd have selected a more strategic location if she were, closer to the church entrance or right by the street. Instead, the little girl sat just outside the cone of light cast by the streetlamp swaying over the middle of the street, where she was unlikely to be seen at all. She'd turned twelve, but she looked younger than she was, and she knew that was an advantage; the less she stood out, the better. That's how it had been ever since her mother had died, when she was still just a little girl, left alone with her father.

Alone with her father.

She felt a long shiver run through her in the already warm air.

She'd given a lot of thought to what had to be done. To how to fix things. For Gaetano and for herself.

The solution would be painful and difficult. It wouldn't be easy to do what was necessary, and the aftermath would be hard as well. Not because she'd be lonely. If anything, that part would come as a welcome change. She sighed.

She saw him hurrying through the crowd, out of breath. His floppy cap covered his swarthy face and his hands were still spattered with mortar, as were the trousers he wore, which ended mid-calf. Thirteen years old already, but Gaetano Russo also looked younger than his years, unless you looked in his eyes.

He sat down next to her, as usual without so much as a hello. Just two children sitting on the church steps, but in their eyes they were a hundred years old between them. She looked at him, and he finally spoke.

"Things have gotten better. They did what you said they would, both the *guappo* and that pig at the place where she works."

She smiled briefly. Simple. Men were all the same.

Tears welled up in Gaetano's eyes.

"She was so beautiful. And now . . . damn them."

She squeezed his hand.

"What about the rest?"

He lifted his head and looked at her. His dark eyes, glistening with rage and tears, glittered in the darkness like the eyes of a wolf.

"Everything just like we said. You're sure? Tomorrow?"

She nodded. Her eyes still, staring straight ahead of her. Mamma, understand what I have to do. If you can see me, I'm sitting on the steps of a church. If you can hear me, you know what's in my heart. And what's on my body, almost every single night. Ever since you went away. I have to do this, Mamma. You understand, don't you?

A gust of wind came up from the sea. Perhaps that was what drew out the solitary tear that rolled down her cheek.

Maione was drying his tears with his handkerchief.

"Commissa', that guy just kills me. Children, he wants children! He's sixty, she's sixty-two, and he wants children! That young lady is out of luck; the mother is going to live another hundred years, plus two years for mourning. She's out of luck, the blushing young fiancée! If you ask me, we'd better keep an eye on Passarelli. Any minute now he's going to put a pillow over Mammà's face and that'll be the end of her. And then the lovebirds can elope!"

Ricciardi shook his head with the half-grimace that on his face constituted a smile.

"People are strange, all right. No one ever seems to see himself the way he really is. All right, who's next?"

Maione tucked his handkerchief away and picked up his notebook.

"We don't know much about this one. The young lady is named Signorina Colombo; another girl accompanied her to the appointment, an old client of Calise's, who hadn't discussed them with Petrone yet. The girl who accompanied her had seen her about a matter of the heart . . . her fiancé was far away . . . then, apparently, she got married. So Petrone assumes the other one came for the same kind of problem. Calise usually spent two or three sessions delving into the matter and then she'd tell the porter woman what she'd found out, and Petrone'd start investigating. On the day of the murder, she was just getting started on this one. Shall I show her in?"

Ricciardi felt a strange sense of uneasiness wash over him. He looked around; his office was no different than usual. He passed his hand over his eyes; maybe he was coming down with a slight fever.

"Yes, have her come in."

And Enrica walked into his office.

When, several months earlier, Ricciardi had found himself face-to-face with this same young woman at the vegetable cart, he had stared at her for a moment. Just a fleeting moment: but in his mind, in his imagination, and in his dreams he had relived that instant countless times.

One of those moments whole lives are built around. One pair of eyes meeting another for the first time.

For normal people. But he knew he had no right to be normal.

After all the time he had spent thinking about that moment, like a man sentenced to life imprisonment or shipwrecked on a desert island, he'd been led to believe that he'd be ready if he ever happened to run into her by chance. Nothing could have been further from the truth.

Enrica was just as petrified as he was. The summons to police headquarters had aroused her curiosity but it hadn't frightened her; she had no reason to be afraid. On her way there, she had run through the events of the past few days in her mind and come to the conclusion that it must have something to do with an episode that she had recently witnessed: four young Blackshirts roughing up an elderly man in the street and calling him a defeatist. Nothing too serious, but these days you could never know what you were dealing with.

And now she was sitting across from the man whose silhouette she glimpsed every night, at the exact same time without fail, the man who haunted all her dreams, her most secret yearnings. Staring once again at those crystal-clear eyes in which her heart seemed to be reflected.

Maione looked up from his notebook and blinked. An unnatural silence had fallen over the office. Even the piazza outside the window was silent. A rare thing at that time of the day.

The springtime went mad with delight. It loved those moments when blood coursed silently through the veins.

The brigadier looked at the two of them as if he were a spectator, waiting for something to happen. Then he let out a cough.

The noise resounded like an explosion. Ricciardi leapt to his feet, his rebellious lock of hair dangling over his forehead, his ears flame red. He opened his mouth, shut it, and opened it again. Finally he said, "Please, have a seat," only the words didn't come out. He cleared his throat, loudly, and repeated the invitation.

She said nothing; it was as if she'd fallen under some kind of spell. She couldn't believe her eyes. She felt like running away but instead she just stood there, with her hands gripping her handbag in front of her chest as if to protect herself, her hat fastened in place by two hatpins, her mid-calf skirt, and her low-heeled shoes. Absurdly, a voice in her head began cursing her for not choosing a different dress, something more modern, and for not wearing makeup.

Ricciardi had remained standing beside his desk, uncertain whether to step forward or back. He also had the impulse to run; he eyed the window appraisingly, seeing as the door was occupied by her. He gazed beseechingly at Maione, who had never seen Ricciardi in such a state.

The brigadier came to his senses and finally intervened, bringing that surreal vignette to life.

"Signorina, *prego*, take a seat. We've just asked you here for some information. This is Commissario Ricciardi. He has some questions he needs to ask you."

XXXVII

Officers Camarda and Cesarano stopped at the corner of the *vicolo*. The former once again consulted the sheet of paper he held in his hand and nodded a confirmation to his fellow officer. They turned onto the narrow lane and walked toward their destination: a pizzeria.

They were relaxed. All they were doing was serving a summons to headquarters for an interview, or possibly to serve as a witness—who could say? It was their last assignment of the day, easy as pie, and then their shift would be over and they could go home.

One of them had two children; the other, three.

Now they were both sitting down. Maione towered over them, like a referee in a boxing ring. The physical impasse had been resolved, but not the psychological one. Ricciardi still made no motion to speak, and Enrica was sitting as if she'd just been embalmed. Maione, with his back to the wall, was forced to intervene yet again.

"Now then: Signorina Colombo, Enrica, residing at Via Santa Teresa degli Scalzi 103. Is that you?"

Enrica slowly turned her face toward the brigadier.

"Buongiorno, Brigadier. The fact that you delivered the summons into my hands and I signed to confirm receipt must mean something. Yes, that's me."

Her tone of voice was a shade icier than she might have liked, but she had every reason to be angry. After waiting all this time for him to approach her, she was stewing over the fact that she was meeting the man of her dreams thanks to a subpoena, a "summons for interview concerning matters referenced," in the words of the document delivered to her that morning.

Maione had run out of formalities with which to fill the time. He looked over at Ricciardi and waited for him to start asking questions, but the commissario showed no sign of wanting to talk. He just sat there, mute. The brigadier was worried, but he couldn't bring himself to ask his superior officer whether he was feeling well.

He coughed again. Ricciardi emerged from his reverie and shot him an indecipherable glance.

It was becoming clear to Maione that he would have to conduct the interview himself, even though he had no idea why that should be the case. It was as if the commissario were in the presence of a ghost.

"Signorina, do you know a certain Carmela Calise: a tarot card reader by profession?"

So that was the reason for the summons. Enrica had heard about the murder from her girlfriend and it had horrified her. That poor unfortunate woman. She'd seen her just the day before she was murdered; and what a horrible way to die. But this thought was immediately followed by the feeling that she'd been caught in the act, along with a scalding sense of shame: then, he knew! He knew that she had consulted a tarot card reader; perhaps he thought she was a stupid ignoramus or, even worse, a blasphemous disbeliever, who'd turned to a witch to help her solve her problems.

She tensed her lips, eyes flashing lightning from behind her tortoiseshell eyeglasses.

"Yes, certainly. I heard about the . . . unfortunate thing that happened. I'd seen her the day before. What of that? Is it illegal?"

Maione blinked at this unexpectedly aggressive tone.

"No, of course not. We just wanted to know whether there was anything that, I don't know, might have struck you as odd. In the way that Calise behaved; was she any different than usual?"

Different than usual! As if she were a regular customer, a habitual visitor to that squalid, foul-smelling apartment. She had no intention of sitting there and allowing herself to be insulted.

"Look, Brigadier, I'd only been there one other time, when a girlfriend accompanied me. So I have no idea what Calise was usually like. I can tell you that she asked me a lot more questions than I asked her, about . . . about a matter that is my own personal business. But I didn't notice anything strange."

Maione shifted his weight from one foot to the other.

"And when you entered the apartment, or as you were leaving, did you notice anything in particular?"

Enrica felt like dying: because of what Ricciardi must be thinking; because he refused to speak to a word to her; because she was being made to look like a perfect fool; because of her damned eyeglasses, and because she hadn't worn any makeup. All she knew was that she felt like bursting into tears.

"No, Brigadier, just that the porter woman greeted us with a total lack of discretion, staring at me right in the face as if she were trying to remember who I was. Now, if you don't mind, I'd rather go. I don't feel very well."

Maione, who couldn't think of anything else to ask, looked at the stone reproduction of Ricciardi sitting at his desk, and waved her to the door with one hand.

Enrica stood up and headed toward the exit. Of course, that's when the miracle took place: the pillar of salt suddenly came to life and leapt to its feet, reaching its hand out in Enrica's direction.

"Signorina, Signorina, wait! I have a question I need to ask you, please, wait!"

Ricciardi's tone of voice made the hair on the back of Maione's neck stand on end. He'd never heard the commissario so muddled, and he never wanted to hear it again. Enrica stopped mid-step and turned around slowly. She spoke in a low and faintly trembling voice.

"Go ahead and ask."

Ricciardi ran his tongue over his dry lips.

"Were you . . . did you . . . what exactly did you ask Calise? What were you trying to find out? Please, what was it?"

Maione started at Ricciardi in astonishment. He thought the commissario was about to explode. But Enrica, though shaken by that heartfelt plea, was unwilling to make a deal with fate.

"I don't believe that's any of your business. Good day."

"But I beg you, I implore you . . . I have to know!"

I beg you? I implore you? Had he lost his mind? Maione would have gagged the commissario, if he'd been able. Enrica looked at him and felt a surge of tenderness fill her heart. She resolved the situation in the way that woman often decide to resolve awkward matters, when they don't know where else to turn. She lied.

"A health problem."

And she walked out, with a faint nod.

Enrica's exit was followed by an extremely awkward moment for Maione. He didn't have the courage to ask Ricciardi what exactly had just happened, nor could he pretend that that stunning spectacle had gone entirely unnoticed.

The commissario had fallen back into his chair, eyes wide open, staring into space, his hands limp on the desktop, his face as white as chalk.

Maione took a half-step forward, coughed gently, said something about having to use the latrine, and left the room, head down.

Ricciardi couldn't believe it. He'd fantasized endlessly about the possibility of their actually meeting, even though the idea terrified him. How could have acted like such an idiot? He, a man accustomed to routinely gazing upon scenes of death and mayhem, had been incapable of carrying on a normal conversation for a couple of minutes. And now she was gone, offended, furious, thinking the absolute worst of him.

He was despondent.

Enrica was walking at a good clip, going back up Via Toledo toward Via Santa Teresa. The aromatic air blew against her, as if mocking her pain.

She was despondent.

She might have expected anything from that interview, but not that she'd come face-to-face with him, of all people. So, he was a police commissario. But now how could she make him understand that she wasn't the aggressive person she had seemed in his office? What a fool she'd been, what a fool. She'd allowed herself to be swept away by her anger at being caught red-handed, and, what's worse, dressed like a member of the women's army auxiliary corps out of a book by Carolina Invernizio.

She hadn't been capable of giving him a smile, a kind world, a pretext for an invitation. And what was worse, she'd been unable to think up anything better than a health problem in her attempt to avoid coming off as a gullible romantic. Now he'd think he was dealing with an invalid, a consumptive perhaps, and that would be the end of his nightly appearances at the window. Oh, what a fool.

In the wind, with the promise of flowers wafting down from the forest, Enrica walked, tears running down her face.

XXXVIII

When he came back into the office, Maione found the usual Ricciardi waiting for him. Inscrutable, composed, lost in thought. Though perhaps just a bit more downcast.

"All right, Maione, let's move on. This day is proving tougher than I would have expected. Who do we have now?"

The brigadier consulted his notebook.

"Now then: next is Antonio Iodice—a *pizzaiolo* from the Sanità, a client of the loan-sharking branch of the operation. Here's the story: Iodice used to have a pushcart, one of those carts where you yourself often stop for lunch, and he was doing reasonably well; our boy's a hard worker, always cheerful, always out working, even in the worst weather. Then he opened a sit-down restaurant of his own, taking over the place from a blacksmith who closed shop, borrowing the money from Calise. But things didn't go all that well, and according to Petrone he'd already asked for an extension on his loan terms twice, and that night he was going to have to '*pavare*'—that is, pay up."

The commissario seemed to be having difficulty focusing.

"And did he pay? Did you check the papers in the biscuit tin?"

Maione nodded his head yes.

"Yes, Commissa', I checked it again, and as I think I already told you, there's nothing under his name. Forgive me, Commissa', but if you don't mind my asking, are you sure you're feeling well? No, it's just that, it's not like you ever have that much color in your face, but right now you're so pale you look like a corpse. If you'd like, we can just leave off here for to the day and start over again tomorrow. After all, Calise is in no hurry."

"I look like a corpse, do I? No, trust me; it takes a lot more than this to look like a dead man. Take a look and see if this Iodice has come in. Let's keep going."

He spotted the policemen at the end of the street from his spot on the balcony, where he was leaning on the railing, trying to figure out the right thing to do, how to react. He saw them advancing toward him, like a pair of gray insects in the midst of the colorful crowd of strolling vendors, women, and children walking down Via Santa Lucia in search of the year's first sea breezes.

He immediately knew why they had come. They'd come for him. Somehow, they'd uncovered tracks that in his naïve foolishness he'd surely left behind. He smiled at the irony of fate. A rank beginner. The most famous criminal lawyer in the city, a professor at the most prestigious university in Italy for jurisprudence, every magistrate's greatest fear, known as "the fox" in court—only to be caught red-handed. And for what? For love.

Because, say what you will about Ruggero Serra di Arpaja, you couldn't accuse him of lying to himself. He knew that what had driven him to that situation hadn't been an attempt to protect his good name, his prominent position, or his social standing. No; it had been love for his wife. The same woman who for a long time now had barely spoken to him, indifferent to his feelings, their home, and the reputation attached to the name she bore. A woman who shamelessly flaunted her own adulterous affair.

And yet he loved her still. With all his heart. Her smiling

face appeared before his eyes, the silvery sound of her laughter echoed in his ears, and he decided that it had been worth going all in if it meant he might be able to hold on to her.

The two policemen had come to a halt in front of the palazzo's street door and were speaking with the doorman, whose livery was even more spectacular than their uniforms. Ruggero watched as they handed him an envelope and then turned to go. What could this be about? He summoned the housemaid with her perennially frightened expression and told her to hurry downstairs to retrieve the document.

A minute later, he was turning over in his hands a summons to police headquarters addressed to Signora Emma Serra di Arpaja.

For the first time in many months, a meager smile appeared on his lips. Perhaps all was not lost.

Given the delay on the part of the patrol that had been sent to fetch the *pizzaiolo*, Ricciardi had informed Maione that he preferred to head out immediately to the home of Ridolfi, the invalid. He lived not far from headquarters, in one of those aristocratic palazzi on Via Toledo, which had been subdivided into apartments a few years earlier due to the economic misfortunes afflicting the venerable family that had once owned it.

Even though Ricciardi had little regard for the city's aristocracy, he still felt a certain discomfort at seeing the interiors of those venerable residences so brutally gutted; it gave him the unpleasant impression of a huge dead animal, its carcass apparently intact and the viscera teeming with hundreds of parasites.

As he walked the short distance together with Maione, he tried to rid his mind of the powerful emotions that he had just experienced: meeting Enrica, speaking to her, looking into her eyes. Dreams he'd nurtured for months, realized in a way that was at such sharp variance with how he'd imagined them.

The doorman did nothing to conceal his open hostility; yes, Professor Ridolfi was at home. He'd hurt his leg. Yes, they could go up and no, there was no elevator. Top floor, apartment twenty-one.

Huffing and puffing, Maione recounted to the commissario everything the Petrone had told him: Ridolfi taught Latin at the high school. He'd been going to see Calise for a year, give or take. He'd been widowed because of an accident: his wife had been using a powerful solvent and had died in a fire that had broken out. He was talking to Calise because he wanted to know whether he'd succeed in tracking down a bundle of family memorabilia, items of no intrinsic worth but great sentimental value, which had gone missing after their downfall. He was convinced, and the Calise and Petrone partnership was glad to agree, that he would find out where it was from his late wife, who would speak to him through the old woman's tarot cards.

The porter woman had told Maione that every time Ridolfi came to see Calise, he had a good hard cry, and that, in her opinion, he'd fallen because he'd been unable to see the steps through the tears in his eyes. He was a wonderful person, an authentic gentleman. It had thrown a real scare into the two women; he had tumbled down an entire flight of stairs, head over heels, that morning.

They knocked on the door, which had been left ajar, loudly asking permission as they stepped inside. They found themselves in a small parlor, clean and nicely furnished. Ridolfi was sitting in an armchair upholstered in green satin, with his left leg bandaged and splinted, propped up on a footstool. He held a book in his hands.

"*Prego*, come right in. Forgive me if I don't get up. To what do I owe this pleasure?"

He had noticed Maione's uniform, but his face showed no signs of worry. Ricciardi had no trouble cataloguing him: fifty years old, neatly dressed and groomed, but not dandyish, with a black tie, a stiff collar, and a well worn-in smoking jacket. A face with regular features, melancholy eyes, black eyeglasses somewhat the worse for wear. Not someone who'd stand out in a crowd.

"*Buon pomeriggio*, Professor; good afternoon. Sorry to bother you, but we have a few questions to ask concerning Carmela Calise."

"Oh, yes, I read about it. What a terrible thing. I was there just the day before. In fact, it was there that I fell down the stairs. A bad sprain; at the hospital they told me they'll remove the bandages a month from now. It's inconvenient, and if it weren't for the help I get from the doorman's wife . . . Of course, it's an extra expense. But compared to certain terrible misfortunes, you come to think of yourself as being lucky. Isn't that right, Signor . . ."

Maione intervened, politely. He liked this man; he struck him as a decent person.

"Commissario Ricciardi and Brigadier Maione of the Mobile Squad, at your service, Professo'. Tell me, what was the reason for your visit to Calise the other day?"

Ridolfi sighed and shook his head.

"Brigadie', old age is a miserable thing. And loneliness is even worse. Since my wife passed away a year ago, I haven't thought about anything else: only her. We never had children; it was just the two of us, and now I'm all alone. Unfortunately, she knew where all our memorabilia were stored, and I haven't been able to find them. They're little things, objects worthless to anyone else, but it would mean a lot to me to have them."

As he went on talking, the man's eyes welled up with tears that slowly dissolved on his face. His voice remained even and low in tone; there were no sobs or sighs, just tears.

"That's why I went to see Calise. At first, just because; it was almost a game, something to get me out of the house. Then

. . . then she started reading things in those cards that only my Olga and I knew. And I started to think that, just maybe, there might really be a way to talk to her again. To meet again in this world, before being reunited in the next."

Ricciardi looked at this man. There was something about him that stirred a sense of uneasiness in the commissario. He couldn't put his finger on it exactly, but he didn't detect the notes of genuine grief in his words. Perhaps it was the fact that he never varied his tone of voice as he spoke, as if he were reciting a litany he was well acquainted with. Perhaps it was his hands, which weren't trembling at all. Or perhaps it was that silent stream of tears. Suddenly, Ricciardi felt parched.

"Professor, could I bother you for a glass of water?"

"But of course, commissario. You'll have to get it yourself, though; my leg prevents me from being the hospitable master of the house I ought to be. Make yourself at home; the kitchen is through that door. The drinking glasses are by the sink."

Maione started to get to his feet to fetch him a drink, but Ricciardi gestured to him to stop. He walked into the kitchen.

He was running the water when he glimpsed something moving out of the corner of his eye. Sitting in a corner, clearly visible in the shaft of sunlight filtering in through the window, was Ridolfi's late wife.

More than a year and he could see her clearly. She hadn't faded a bit, and there were still plumes of smoke curling lazily off her scorched flesh. The emotion she felt in her final moments must have been extremely powerful. The skeleton was covered with tattered flesh, and there was no sign of her clothing except for a strip of fabric dangling from her shoulder. Her cranium glistened, the color of roast almonds. One eye socket had been left empty when the eyeball popped from the heat; the other eye, still intact, rolled crazily. The charred lips revealed a cloister of teeth that almost seemed to glow against the blackness, they were so white. To one side, a gold premolar tooth emitted a faint sparkle in the afternoon sunlight.

The head turned to face Ricciardi and stared at him with its one remaining eye; the hands folded in her lap, the legs reduced to a pair of charred sticks of wood, folded with a strange, bloodcurdling gracefulness. They looked at each other, the corpse and the commissario, the latter still holding the glass under the stream of water as it overflowed, running over his hand.

"You're a whoremonger," the woman said, "a filthy bastard and a whoremonger. You can cry on command. You tell me that she's your true love and I'm the angel of the hearth. Well, when you get home tonight, you'll find a nice hot fire waiting for you. You wanted my mother's jewelry, but it's at the bottom of the sea. You wanted the jewelry, but what you'll get is a nice hot fire, tonight, you and your whore."

The blackened skeleton threw its skull back and laughed. The woman had died laughing, devoured by flames. The angel of the hearth and she had set herself ablaze. Ricciardi noticed a shock of blonde hair at the back of the ravaged neck. He turned off the faucet, set down the glass without drinking from it, and went back into the parlor.

Ridolfi was talking.

"No, Brigadier, I didn't notice anything out of the ordinary about Calise. Perhaps she was a little distracted. But maybe that was just an impression I had. *Prego*, Commissario, did you find the glass? Please, make yourself comfortable."

Ricciardi remained standing, both hands in his pockets.

"Just how did your wife die, Professor? What happened?"

There was a moment of awkward silence. Maione couldn't imagine Ricciardi's reason for so indelicately reminding this man of a tragedy that still tormented him.

After a long sigh, with tears welling up in his eyes again, Ridolfi answered.

"She was cleaning the kitchen, and she was using benzene—who knows why. I was at school. By the time I got home, it was too late. Luckily, a woman from work was with me, and she was very helpful. That was the end of Olga's life and, in some ways, the end of mine."

In some ways, Ricciardi thought to himself.

"Well, we have to go now, Professor. Thanks for your cooperation. I have just one piece of advice to offer: whatever it is you're looking for, stop. I have a feeling you're never going to find it."

XXXIX

When they got back to headquarters, they found the officer on duty at the front door waiting for them in the middle of the courtyard. They realized that something serious had happened.

"Brigadier, Commissario, forgive me. We got a phone call from Pellegrini Hospital; Camarda and Cesarano are there. Someone's been seriously wounded. A knife wound. They said that if possible, you should hurry over right away."

The two men looked at each other and took off at a run.

The awkwardness that had lingered in the air between them after the interview with Enrica was completely swept away. Now their thoughts were focused entirely on Camarda and Cesarano, on their children and their mothers.

When they arrived in the hospital courtyard and found both men standing before them, they felt an enormous surge of relief. Maione, expansive as always, actually rushed forward and threw his arms around them. Ricciardi in contrast stared intently at two women, one young, the other older, standing in a corner, shaded from the afternoon sun. They were so pale and grief-stricken that it was as if the Deed were showing him two souls that had committed suicide over the loss of some loved one, the very picture of sorrow. The young woman was pressing a tear-soaked handkerchief to her mouth, while the older woman seemed to be carved out of marble, her gaze lost in the void, one hand clutching the black shawl that covered her head tight to her throat, the fingers of the other hand intertwined with those of the young woman.

"What happened?" he asked Camarda.

"Commissa', we walked into the pizzeria of this Antonio Iodice. We were ready to deliver the summons—here it is, I still have it in my pocket. So anyway, we were laughing and kidding around, because our shift was almost over, which reminds me, my wife must be starting to worry by now. We walk into the restaurant. There wasn't much of a crowd. The lady over there"—and he pointed to the young woman weeping—"that's Iodice's wife; she was serving tables. It smelled good in there . . . it was lunchtime. We walk in, as I was saying, and the lady comes up to us and she asks if we want something to eat. We wish we could, we say to ourselves, then, 'No, Signo', is this the pizzeria of Antonio Iodice?' I barely have time to get the name out of my mouth when the *pizzaiolo*, who turns out to be Antonio Iodice, lets out a horrible shriek."

Cesarano broke in.

"You wouldn't have believed it, Commissa', nice and loud, ringing out in the silence, came this shriek that froze the blood in our veins, as God is my witness. I couldn't really understand what he was saying. It sounded like 'my children,' or something of the sort. I thought he was going to attack us, and I went to grab my revolver."

Back to Camarda.

"I was facing toward him; I saw him pull this long knife out from under the counter, you know the kind I mean, the kind they use to slice meat. Brigadie', I swear to you, with the flames of the pizza oven behind him, he looked like a soul in hell. So then he raises this knife and plunges it into his chest."

Cesarano went on.

"Madonna Santa, it was a horrible thing to see. First he plunges it into his chest, then he drives it in deeper and deeper. Everyone was screaming, running around: it was a madhouse.

We didn't have time to stop him; we tried but we weren't quick enough. He drove it in all the way, right to the handle. He said 'forgive me,' and then he closed his eyes. Camarda, here, got next to him . . ."

"That's right, I got to him first. Cesarano was holding up the signora, his wife, who kept screaming 'my love, oh my love, what have they done to you, Toni',' but he'd done it all himself right in front of everyone. Anyway, I could see that, even with all that blood everywhere, blood coming out of his chest and out of his mouth, he was still breathing. Madonna, Commissa', he was as white as a sheet. So I lifted up one of the tables, me and Cesarano here; we swept pizzas, plates, and glasses onto the floor . . ."

"We got him up on the table and we carried him here to the hospital. And what a procession it was, out on the street, Brigadie'! It looked like a funeral, except everyone was running. They're operating on him right now. We got here just in the nick of time; Doctor Modo was just about to finish his shift."

Ricciardi looked over at the women again; they stood at a certain distance, across the courtyard.

"So the younger woman is his wife, then?"

This time, Camarda replied:

"That's right, Commissa'. The older one is his mother, I think. She came straight to the hospital and so far she hasn't uttered a word."

The rehearsals had been interrupted, to the evident annoyance of the director and lead actor; he would have gone on rehearsing and re-rehearsing the same scene for eternity. A maniacal perfectionist, thought Attilio, or perhaps simply a narcissist.

The female lead, even uglier than usual, had threatened to relieve herself in the middle of the stage unless she was given a break. The whole crew laughed and, bitter pill though it was to him, that overweening buffoon had been forced to give in to her demand. Romor took advantage of the opportunity to get a breath of fresh air and smoke a cigarette in the *vicolo* behind the theater. The playwright's brother joined him.

"So, Atti', what do you say? That good-looking lady with the dark eyes, the one who always sits in the first row of the second balcony? She hasn't been in for a couple of nights. Is she sick or something?"

"No, Peppino. I broke it off. We're going our separate ways."

"Oh, that's a shame! She was so pretty! And she struck me as something of an aristocrat, a woman with money. How did that work out for you, in the end?"

Romor heaved an indifferent sigh, gazing off into the darkness.

"You know, it's just the way I am: I can't stand to have someone breathing down my neck. Sooner or later, they all wind up the same. And that's when I figure it's time to make a change."

The usher stuck a worried face through the door.

"Hurry, come on; it's already the second time he's called for you!"

Exchanging a glance of irritation, the two men threw away their cigarettes and went back inside.

In the half-darkness of Vico del Fico, Filomena was waiting.

She had finished making dinner for Gaetano, who would soon return home from the construction site. She had changed the dressings that covered her wound. She'd had a couple of neighbor women over who had become strangely friendly in the aftermath of the incident. And now, Filomena was waiting. She wasn't waiting for Gaetano to return home— or at least, that wasn't all she was waiting for. She was waiting for Brigadier Maione to pay a call.

She kept telling herself that it might be useful for everyone to see him coming through the neighborhood, both mornings and evenings; that the presence of the corpulent officer might keep some unexpected backlash at bay, strange reactions from someone like, say, Don Luigi Costanzo, and that in any case a little protection was a fine thing for a change, instead of always having to fend for herself, the way she had all her life.

But none of that was the truth. The truth was quite different. Maione hed met Filomena in the aftermath of her disfigurement, and his glances and his voice made her feel like a woman, without the fear that had long accompanied that feeling. This was a new sensation, and she liked it. And so, she was waiting. Doing her best not to think about the ring that she had seen on his left hand.

Sitting in the kitchen, the French windows that led to the balcony left ajar to let in the spring air, Lucia Maione was waiting. This too was something new; or at least, it was a change from the last three years. She'd brushed her hair; she'd even asked a girlfriend what she knew about Linda, the hairdresser who took care of the neighborhood women's hair and skin.

She had rummaged through the chest of drawers in search of a floral dress that she knew her husband liked, and had discovered to her amazement that it was actually a little loose on her now. She had spent the whole afternoon cooking her famous genovese, an onion and meat sauce that filled the house with its aroma for two days but which the family devoured in two minutes.

The children had looked at her in surprise and apprehension. Then they had smiled at each other and for once had decided not to go out into the street to play, but instead gathered in their room, to see what would happen when Papà came home.

And now, sitting in the kitchen, a little bewildered perhaps but determined to win back her rightful territory, Lucia waited.

Enrica, with her heart in her mouth, was waiting.

Since coming home from police headquarters, she had shut herself up in the darkness of her bedroom. Lying face-up on her bed, her pillow wet with tears, she thought about what would happen later that evening. Her mother had knocked repeatedly; she had pretended she didn't feel well, absenting herself from dinner.

What would he do? Would his silhouette appear behind the closed window? Backlit by the yellowish glow of the oil lamp, his brilliant eyes shining in his dark silhouette like the eyes of a cat, eyes that filled her with warmth? And her: would she be able to maintain the same calm and tranquility as any other evening, moving slowly among her objects, the things that gave her a sense of safety? And what would he think, now that he had seen her up close and discovered her shortcomings, the thousand defects that he'd never had a chance to notice before?

Enrica thought about the look in his eyes, astonished, almost frightened; and now perhaps he thought she was ill.

In the desolation of a thousand fears, Enrica waited.

In the hospital courtyard, Concetta waited. Her husband was inside those walls. The man she had always loved, the father of her children, was dying, and might already be dead. She'd never forget the faces of those two policemen, first smiling, then horrified; she'd turned around to see the flash of the red blade by the light of the oven. She'd heard his scream; then the blood, all that blood.

Concetta was waiting to learn whether her life was over. Whether the hope she was clinging to—the only thing keeping her body erect, her heart beating, her lungs drawing in air—would endure. Her eyes puffy with tears, staring fixedly at the closed door behind which Tonino was fighting for life without even knowing it, Concetta went on hoping.

And she waited.

Now that darkness had fallen, Ricciardi decided to approach them. No one had gone home, not even Cesarano and Camarda, even though their shift had been over for hours. The two women's atrocious yet dignified grief and sorrow had nailed everyone to the spot in the courtyard, awaiting reports from the operating room where Doctor Modo was still working on Iodice.

In a departure from custom, no one had showed up to comfort the family members. Something entirely out of the ordinary had happened, and people were waiting to see what had really transpired before running the risk of getting involved.

The commissario decided that what Iodice had done, even though it certainly suggested he was directly involved in the Calise case, did not necessarily amount to a confession. He had learned from many similar occasions in the past that the arrival of a pair of police officers could drive even innocent people to act rashly. Perhaps the *pizzaiolo* had other crimes on his conscience, or maybe he was just afraid. Ricciardi addressed the man's wife.

"Signora, I'm Commissario Ricciardi of the Mobile Squad. I wanted to ask if there's anything you need. What can I do to help you?"

The woman, recoiling to the safety of her mother-in-law, looked at him, wild-eyed. Ricciardi guessed at her facial features, a delicate beauty ravaged by suffering.

"Yes, there is something you can do. I beg of you, try to find out how my husband is, what they're doing to him. They won't tell us anything, and whenever we try to go inside, they kick us out. We have to . . . I have to find out what to tell my children; they're at home waiting for me."

Her voice, broken with tears, struck Ricciardi as the voice of a strong-willed woman, decisive and direct. He nodded and walked inside.

Just as he was approaching to the door to the clinic, it swung open, and out came Doctor Modo.

"That's right. You walk out of a ward full of blood and pain and what's waiting there to greet you? The ugly mug of a policeman. And what a policeman. The happiest cop of them all."

Ricciardi knew Modo well enough to recognize the signs that he was exhausted, one-liners aside. The doctor's face was creased and furrowed, and underneath his blood-spattered lab coat his collar was unbuttoned, his tie loosened, so that his neck, red with effort and strain, was left bare.

"True, but don't worry, I'm not here to arrest you. Not yet, anyway. Well, what can you tell me about Iodice? His mother and his wife are outside. I didn't have the heart to tell them he was in your tender care."

Modo smiled at him wearily.

"Your sense of humor is simply delightful. Have you ever thought of going into vaudeville? You'd be an unequaled comedian. If they take you on, I'll sign up as a cancan dancer in your act. Besides, you already make me dance for free as it is. Do you realize that I never finish a shift at anything like a normal time of day without you or Maione showing up with some little gift for me at the last minute?"

"Okay, fine, I promise that afterward I'll let you cry on my shoulder as long as like. Actually, you know what? I'll treat you to a pizza. Even though, with all the overtime you're taking in thanks to us, you're getting paid three times what I earn. But now, just tell me how Iodice is doing."

"Ah, is that his name, Iodice? Well, I can't say if he'll make it. The knife blade missed the artery by a hair and that's kept him from dying for the moment. But it went right into his lung. Plunged straight in, like the guy meant it, up to the handle. It was a good thing the men who brought him here had the brains not to try pulling it out; that would have done massive damage. It was a long and difficult operation, and he's lost a lot of blood. He's asleep now, and we need him to stay that way for the next twenty-four hours, so forget about trying to talk to him. We'll see how he is tomorrow. That is, if he lives until tomorrow. Now tell me, who stabbed him?"

Ricciardi was trying to guess what could drive a man to do such a thing, if not the certainty that his situation was hopeless.

"He did it himself. Like those Japanese warriors, you know. Those ritual suicides."

Modo shook his head.

"Incredible. The more I work with the dead, the less I understand the living."

XL

Ricciardi went back out into the courtyard. The two women watched him from afar, trying to decipher his expression but lacking the courage to approach him. He walked over to where they were standing.

"Signor Iodice is alive, though he's in very serious condition. The doctor who's caring for him is, believe me, the best there is. If anyone can keep him alive, it's him."

The woman burst into tears. The mother looked like a marble statue. Ricciardi went on talking.

"Now both of you go home to your children. Let him get some rest. They won't let you see him until tomorrow anyway. If there are any developments, I'll make sure they let you know right away. As for me, you can find me in my office tomorrow morning, in case there's anything you want to tell me."

The older woman linked arms with the younger one and, bowing her head, began walking toward the gate.

Ricciardi walked over to the small knot of his fellow policemen, waiting for him off to one side. He gave them what news he had and told Camarda and Cesarano that they could go home now.

Left alone with Maione, he drew a long sigh.

"There's nothing more we can do tonight. Have you heard anything new about that other woman, what's her name, Signora Serra di Arpaja?"

Maione was taken aback.

"But, Commissa', this Iodice . . . he might as well have confessed, don't you think?"

"Maione, I can't believe I'm hearing you talk this way. You have more experience than I do. There's no doubt that Iodice had some reason or another to give in to despair. But it's quite a leap to go from there to the fact that he killed Calise, no? And so we'll continue the investigation and then, if and when Iodice comes to and confesses, we can call this case closed. If not, we don't. Understood?"

The brigadier bowed his head.

"You're right, Commissa'. Forgive me. Anyway, the summons for the Serra woman has been delivered. She should be at headquarters tomorrow morning. Now what do we do, go home?"

"I promised Modo I'd treat him to a pizza. How about you, you want to come with?"

Maione pulled his watch out of his pocket and glanced at it hastily.

"No, Commissa', I'm sorry. They're waiting for me, it's already late."

Ricciardi looked him in the eye. Then he nodded his head.

"All right, you go ahead. I'll see you tomorrow. Have a good night."

They walked together through the bright lights of the Pignasecca market, the doctor trudging wearily and the commissario with the wind in his hair. The doctor pushed his hat back on his head and lit a cigarette.

"Say, haven't you noticed this gentle warm breeze? It's springtime, Mr. Tall, Dark, and Handsome. A joyful soul like you can hardly have missed the fact."

Ricciardi snorted in annoyance.

"Could you tell me what you find so damned funny about the fact that you've just spent hours digging around inside the body of a man who stabbed himself in the heart? Did you know that he has three children? And the whole thing started with the late Calise, who was kicked across the floor of her room. If that's springtime, you can have it, thanks very much."

Modo laughed.

"You kill me! What are you saying, that human lunacy is dictated by the seasons? Why don't you take a look at our government, for example!"

Ricciardi feigned a despairing expression.

"No, I beg you, not politics! I'd rather go home and suffer through Tata Rosa's pasta and chickpeas!"

"Okay, fine, if you're happy giving up your freedom in its entirety, I won't try to change your mind. But the best thing to do is laugh about it, that's what I was trying to tell you. Do you know that it's been three or four years since I last prescribed a purgative, just to avoid being taken for a Fascist?"

Ricciardi shook his head with a smile.

"Look, Bruno, if you keep this up, one of these days I'm going to find an order on my desk to arrest you and ship you off to internal exile on Ventotene. I'm not worried about that so much, but if they ordered me to stay there to keep an eye on you, then suicide wouldn't be drastic enough."

They'd reached the pizzeria. Ricciardi looked around.

"A place like this. Filled with smoke, hot air, the smell of food. Everyone has their own dreams. And this is the dream that Iodice is dying for. Was it worth it?"

Modo played a little with his cigarette.

"You know something, Ricciardi? When I perform an autopsy or a last-ditch operation like the one I did today, I think the same thing every time. There's a moment when a person starts to die. No, I'm not talking about the death itself. What I mean is, there's a moment when an irreversible process is triggered that leads ineluctably to death. Maybe it takes years, but there's no stopping it. A glass of wine, a cigarette.

The proverbial drop that makes the glass overflow. I find tumors, pulmonary lesions, ruptured livers. Or it could even be a word, a glint in the eye. A love affair. A child. Who can say when someone starts dying?"

Ricciardi listened, fascinated in spite of himself.

"Unfortunately, we can never get hold of that moment, never catch it as it passes."

Modo smiled, suddenly looking much, much older.

"No, my friend. And that's a blessing. That's how we can go on living. Can you imagine if each of us were aware of having triggered the irreversible process that eventually leads to death? During the war, I saw the corpses of lots of men, torn to shreds by shrapnel from Austrian mortar shells, and I wondered what they'd been thinking, what dreams they were nurturing when they enlisted. I always found myself wondering whether at the end, in the instant that they realized they were about to die, whether any of them understood that it had been that dream, that ideal that had killed them. And that's why all these lunatics you see strutting around the city, singing about death and war, fill me with pity."

Ricciardi laid a hand on his friend's arm.

"All kidding aside, Bruno. I understand where you're coming from, and maybe, I'm saying just maybe, I'd even be inclined to agree with you. Still, and this is a point you have to concede, I think it's naïve and foolish to open yourself up to a world of trouble, serious trouble, just for the fun of hearing yourself talk. Think of all the people who rely on you, on your work, on your hands."

"You're right. It's not worth it. Let this nation of idiots take it up the ass, if they like it so damned much. Perhaps the moment in which we as a people triggered our own irreversible process has already come and gone."

XLI

The minute he turned onto the *vicolo* he'd caught sight of the woman at her front door, looking in his direction. "Welcome, Brigadie'," she had said. "I was expecting you."

She was expecting him. And it was almost pure chance that he'd come at all.

"You look tired. You must have had a tough day. Come in, sit down. I'll make you something to eat."

"Don't go to any trouble," he had replied. "I'm sure I'll find something to eat at home."

"I know," she had said to him. "But just a little snack."

And the next thing he knew he was sitting at her table, eating a bowl of pasta with tomato sauce, simple, but to him, delicious. And he had told her about his day, about Calise and Iodice, though without naming names. And about Ricciardi, that strange superior officer of his, who worried him as though he were his own son.

Then, without even realizing it, he began talking about Luca, and it dawned on him that that was something he never did. And as he listened to his own words, he felt a sharp stab of familiar pain and he discovered something he already knew: that it was impossible to resign yourself to that loss, and yet life still went on.

Filomena listened to him, her eyes sparkling in the semidarkness of the *basso*, smiling or shaking her head in dismay. It was nice to be able to talk to her, nice to have her listen.

Gaetano came home and Filomena put food on the table for him as well. A dark, silent young man, but well-mannered and intelligent; Maione could tell from the few words he spoke. Gaetano asked him about his work as a policeman and Maione talked to him with a mixture of frankness and melancholy.

Before he knew it, silence had descended on the *vicolo*. He pulled out his old pocket watch and discovered, to his surprise, that it was almost eleven o'clock. He stood up to say his farewells, expressing his thanks and adding, without even realizing what he was saying: See you tomorrow. The smile that he received in return glittered in the darkness of night like the moon.

He started for home, his heart half happy, half sad.

Ricciardi was afraid to go home. This too was an unfamiliar sensation; anxiety had taken the place of the yearning for serenity that drove him to his window every night. It was late. Both Iodice's unexpected act and the pizza he'd eaten with Modo had allowed him to put off this moment. But now that he was climbing uphill toward Via Santa Teresa and toward home, he was afraid that the window across the way would be shuttered. Shutting him out, leaving him in the dark.

He silently cursed the Calise investigation and his job itself for having placed him face-to-face with Enrica and leading him to show her disrespect, however unintentionally. Thus prompting the anger he'd seen in her suddenly compressed lips and the flashing glare behind her eyeglasses. He couldn't get that picture out of his mind: the tension in her shoulders as she turned her back on him and strode out the door.

Last of all, the thought that she might be unwell tormented him. His naturally analytical mind also entertained the hypothesis that it might be a matter of someone else's health: a family member's, a friend's. How he wished he could speak words of reassurance to her.

But, as his steps echoed across the empty street that ran alongside the construction sites inhabited at this hour only by the dead, he realized that he now thought of her as a woman. Before today, Enrica had been a symbol of a world, a creature from an unreachable planet. Now he could revisualize lips, eyes, flesh, shoulders. As well as hands, a pocketbook, shoes. He could still smell on himself the faint scent of lavender that he had greedily breathed in as she left the office. And the tone of her voice, calm but firm. Suddenly, he was overcome with the desire to look out his window. He went up the steps two at a time.

Enrica had emerged from her bedroom after everyone else had finished eating. She said that she felt a little better now and, with her heart in her mouth, careful not to alter a single gesture, a single expression of her regular routine, she kept looking over at the dark window in the building across the way, always just out of the corner of her eye, with a fleeting glance. Then she turned on the table lamp and, taking a seat in her armchair, went to work on her embroidery.

Nine thirty, a quarter to ten, ten. Every time that the pendulum clock in the dining room chimed the hour, her heart clutched a little tighter in her chest and the anxiety constricted her breathing. Ten fifteen, ten thirty. As she embroidered, she counted to sixty and then totted the minutes. A quarter to eleven. One more minute and then I'll get up. Now, just another minute. Never, never once in the past year had he been so late coming home. The window looked like a bottomless abyss.

She began putting away her embroidery long after she'd heard the door of her parents' bedroom click shut for the night. She turned off the table lamp. Her cheeks were wet with tears.

She closed the shutters, reflecting on her own meager solitude as she did.

And that's exactly when the window across the way lit up.

Deputy Chief of Police Angelo Garzo kept a mirror in one of his desk drawers. The functionary did this because he understood the importance of one's image, and had built a substantial part of his career on his own.

Aside from his physical appearance, recently enhanced by a handsome thin mustache of which he was immensely proud, he believed that image depended largely on a certain status: a growing family, two thriving children and one on the way, a beautiful wife who was active in society and whose untarnished morality was absolutely unquestionable; the fact that she was also the niece of the Prefect of Salerno, whose own career was flourishing nicely, didn't hurt. An almost maniacal cultivation of social relationships: there wasn't an event, a performance, or a concert that didn't see the deputy chief of police seated in the second row, beaming and gleaming in attire that was always just right for the occasion. The obsequious court he paid to the chief of police, whom he actually detested with every ounce of his being, and whose position he coveted, with discretion.

But more than anything else, his true strong point was an inborn ability to sense power relationships. He unfailingly chose the winning side of every barricade and emerged triumphant after each battle, but reliably and comfortably just behind the front line, so that he could always do an about-face, should the need arise, without doing harm to his career.

Having checked on the progress of his mustache the way a horticulturist would check on his orchids, he put the mirror away in its drawer and let his gaze roam around his office with a feeling of satisfaction. It looked like the study of a luxury apartment, so different from the other rooms at police headquarters. Furnished with leather-upholstered sofas and armchairs, as well as dark-walnut tables and chairs, bookshelves lined with untouched but handsome bordeaux-colored leather-bound volumes, which were perfectly coordinated with the overall color scheme. The walls lined with framed family pictures and medals, certificates, and diplomas, with photos of the Italian King and Il Duce in the prescribed places of honor.

He was well aware that he was no one's idea of a good policeman, and yet he thought of himself as a useful and necessary link between the enforcers of law and order and the political institutions that he held in such great respect. He'd met many capable and responsible individuals on his way up the ranks, and he knew they were still right where he'd met them, spinning their wheels in the morass of small-time provincial police stations. His chief ability, the only one that was really necessary, was that of knowing how to treat his inferiors: the thornier the personality, the greater the merit in handling it.

With a sigh, he thought of Ricciardi. The finest of his colleagues: young, intelligent, capable. The most skillful when it came to solving mysteries, and the least diplomatic of them all. In the last three years he had often found himself mending rifts with prominent local figures whose toes the introverted commissario had stepped on; far more often, though, he had enjoyed praise for Ricciardi's extraordinary successes. All things considered, they were perfectly suited to each other. All the commissario seemed to care about was investigating crimes and solving cases, whereas what mattered most to Garzo was recognition, reward, and the esteem of his superiors—and the less he was obliged to get the actual guano on his hands, the better.

If only Ricciardi didn't give him such a sense of uneasiness . . . He couldn't make out the personality behind all those silences, the ironic half-smiles, the hands in his pockets even in Garzo's presence. And, most of all, that impenetrable gaze.

Still, he had to admit he was talented. After the Vezzi case was solved, the one about the tenor who had been murdered at the San Carlo opera house, he'd actually received a personal telephone call from Rome. He still trembled at the thought: he had said, "Yes sir, yes Your Excellency," three times in succession and, as switchboard operators and personal secretaries had passed the line up the ladder and he waited to be connected to Him, he had hastily combed his hair and snapped to attention, as if they could see him through the receiver. His name—Angelo Garzo—on the desk of Il Duce himself: his dream was beginning to come true.

Which was exactly why he needed to act prudently, to let Ricciardi go on working according to his instincts, but without rousing any of the sleeping lions in the wealthy neighborhoods, the ones overlooking the sea.

He glanced at his telephone, the receiver still warm. One of those lions had been awakened. And it had just finished roaring.

XLII

The first Sunday of springtime is different.

It begins with the church bells, just like any other Sunday, and just like any other, it's silent in the early morning; but it brings different promises, and it wastes no time in fulfilling them.

It has a new smell, and it imparts its secrets to those few who awaken at dawn, looking down from the balconies on the upper stories. You will see them sniffing at the air like dogs, and smiling to themselves for no reason.

It has a new taste, as anyone can tell you who breakfasts on the fresh milk that a boy will sell you on the street. It's the same boy who was there just yesterday, but the milk has a freshness that regenerates your throat.

And it especially has new sounds. A pagan feast, with rituals and songs; you'll hear it in the cooing of the doves on the rain gutters, even before the sun is up. And you can hear it in the melodies of the washerwomen as they walk toward the fountains, and in the calls of the strolling vendors on their way in from the surrounding countryside. The wares they hawk bear the scent of the season: violets, wheat for ricotta-filled *pastiera* cakes, young rue, or herb-of-grace, and other aromatic herbs. Even the hens scratching at the ground in the *vicoli* cluck with renewed energy.

Nearly a month late, this is the first Sunday of genuine springtime.

That morning, Ricciardi decided to go to the beach. It was something he did from time to time, when Sunday caught him off guard and he had an investigation in full swing.

He would spend time there, though he was a man of the mountains, to regain his equilibrium and his concentration.

He hadn't gotten much sleep, a couple of hours at the most. The thousands of thoughts running through his head were demanding that he establish a bit of order.

He liked to go sit and think on a small out-of-the-way beach at the foot of the Posillipo hill, not far from where the fishermen's wives sat mending nets. They watched him curiously from afar as they worked; but he was safe behind the bulwark of his unfamiliar attire, and no one bothered him. Sitting on small shelves of rock, he waited, silent and calm, for the wind to kick up. No spray, nothing: just the ebb and flow, the respiration of the green water a few feet below him.

A month earlier, like a retreating army, the winter had decided to unleash one last desperate assault. A furious storm had pounded the coast for two full days, incessantly, flooding the beachfront roads. Many of the inhabitants had fled inland in search of shelter.

A fishing boat, driven by hunger and necessity, had ventured out for one last sortie, hoping to get back to harbor in time, and it didn't make it. Once good weather returned, a number of other boats had set out to retrieve the bodies and bring them home to the wives and mothers, but they hadn't found anything at all.

Now, at the same distance but in the opposite direction from the black-clad women stitching up the tears in the long fishing nets, Ricciardi could make out the forms of the three dead fishermen, whose souls had washed up with the incoming tide. Two of them older, one little more than a child. Their clothes in tatters, their flesh gnawed away by fish, the marks of the fractures and contusions that the angry sea had visited on their bodies as it slammed them against the wood of the fishing boat, before carrying them down to the bottom of the abyss. Ricciardi clearly perceived their thoughts, one of them cursing the saints with a deep, hoarse voice, the other one calling on the Madonna's mercy. The boy, with his lips and tongue swollen from suffocation, was still calling his mother's name with all his heart.

Nothing new there, thought Ricciardi. Between the grief of the dead and the work of the living, the commissario decided that he'd have to make sure his own feelings didn't distract him from his investigation into the murder of Carmela Calise. The clear cold state of mind that he needed in order to evaluate the evidence he had in hand must not be destroyed by the thought of the closed shutters of the window across the way. He had to get his priorities straight: the image of the old woman beaten to death was asking him for justice, incessantly repeating an old proverb in the bedroom of the apartment in the Sanità.

He looked at the translucent figure of the dead boy. Mamma, where are you, Mamma, hug me, Mamma, it kept saying through cyanotic lips. I can't do anything to help you, thought Ricciardi. But perhaps he could still do something to ensure a little justice for Carmela Calise.

For no apparent reason, the two Iodice women surfaced in his thoughts.

It wasn't just melancholy she felt now, but concern and furious anger as well. She had waited and waited and waited. She'd fallen asleep at the table set for two, her head lolling on her arm. The sound of a closing shutter from a nearby building had startled her awake. She'd looked up at the clock on the wall: it was eleven.

In the past, a hundred years ago, Raffaele would have let her know if he was going to be late for dinner, one way or another.

A police officer, a street urchin, a phone call to the accountant on the second floor who gave his enormous telephone pride of place at the center of the living room table. But now, not a word of notice. For some reason, it had never occurred to her until now: it had been more than a year since the last time he'd let her know he was running late.

She had put away the bowls and dishes and packed up the food, then she'd gotten undressed and gone to bed; it would have been humiliating to leave evidence of her long wait. A few minutes later, maybe a quarter of an hour, she had heard the key turn in the lock. Pretending to be asleep, she'd listened intently as her husband clumsily stumbled around in the dark. He hadn't gone into the kitchen the way he usually did when work forced him to come home late and hungry; he'd undressed in silence and lain down, doing his best not to cause the mattress to move more than was necessary. A minute later, he was snoring blissfully.

Moving in closer, Lucia sniffed him alertly: she smelled odors of cooked food. Her husband had eaten dinner. But where? And there was another smell, slightly gamy. Possibly a woman.

She turned toward the wall again, and in her heart it began to rain. Had she only smelled a woman's scent, she might have understood. A man had his needs and she'd been distant from him for years now.

But eating at another woman's table? Not that. That was true betrayal.

Ruggero Serra di Arpaja opened the window of his study to let in the Sunday air. For the first time in days, he'd been able to get a few hours' sleep, and he was feeling better.

The summons for Emma had come as a pleasant surprise. He'd been convinced that the two police officers were there to haul him off and pitch him into a black pit of ruin and disgrace, one from which he would never be able to extract himself, no matter the ultimate outcome. But instead, here he was, still able to defend himself.

The air that entered the room came up from the sea; as usual, it carried with it the smell of decay. He thought of Calise, of the powerful, funky must of her apartment. He'd been there twice: the first time to negotiate, the second time to pay; but he'd also seen her the morning she had come looking for him at the university to demand more money still. He remembered the woman's croaking voice, her geriatric shortness of breath. But she was lucid; was she ever. He'd offered her plenty of money and she'd demanded plenty more. He had accepted, in large part just to get out of that horrible place. Greedy and squalid.

When he went back, he knew it would be for the last time. And then, all that blood. Blood everywhere. When he thought back on it, it felt like a nightmare, nothing but a nightmare; but he felt no pity for that old witch.

From the nearby sea came a seagull's cry. The street was silent: only a few women here and there, their heads covered, on their way to Mass.

Just to make sure, and to complete his descent into hell, he'd even gone to see him: the other man. He wanted to get a look at him, read his face, study his eyes. He'd found exactly what he expected, an emptiness inside a shell that was pleasing to the eye. And he'd found a new certainty.

With a sorrowful smile, he closed the window.

Attilio entered the Villa Nazionale from the Torretta, at the end of Viale Regina Elena. He liked to stroll against the current of the crowds, knowing full well that the more customary route went the opposite way, beginning from Piazza Vittoria. The reason was that he liked to pass by couples and families, launching fleeting glances and subtle smiles at married women and unmarried young ladies, taking pleasure in their confusion.

It was an old game he liked to play with himself, and it still amused him: bringing a blush to the cheek of even insignificant women, arousing the frustration of the men walking at their sides—so much less enchanting than this dark, athletic, and well-dressed young man—as well as the ladies' regret at not being alone and able to return his smile. Attilio felt good. He was enjoying his Sunday in the Villa Nazionale, strolling down the broad, sunny path, amid the scent of the flowerbeds and the nearby sea.

And he was luxuriating in the knowledge that in the end, everything would turn out perfectly. Emma was bound to choose him, he was sure of it; even more so now that he'd looked her husband in the face, a defeated, despairing, broken-spirited man. Could there be any doubt? As he inhaled the aroma of the pine trees and holm oaks that lined the wide path, Romor felt invincible.

He planned to stroll the length of the Villa two more times, smiling at the women and doing his best to avoid the wealthy children who raced along excitedly in their horrible little metal-and-wood pedal cars, and then he'd go off for a seafood lunch not far from the church of Piedigrotta. Now that the solution was at hand, there was no longer any point in scrimping. He could afford to indulge in a few minor luxuries. No more depressing Sundays at his mother's house. He was done going there entirely; it only made him sad, and when he felt sad he could feel the rage swelling up inside him.

He shook his head to drive out these unpleasant thoughts and the irritating memory of his mother's voice, with her perennial admonishments; today was the first Sunday of spring and he wanted no clouds darkening his radiant horizon. He crossed paths with a family, an elderly couple, a young woman with a small child, and a few adolescents; in their midst was a tall young miss, not quite striking but still appealing. He shot her a smoldering gaze, tilting his head to one side and slowing his gait in a way that he knew to be utterly irresistible; she ignored him roundly, preserving a gloomy expression on her face, as if she were nurturing some secret sorrow.

Your loss, thought Attilio, shrugging his shoulders. Go ahead and be gloomy, if you want. As far as I'm concerned, the world is mine and I plan to enjoy it.

XLIII

Sunday surrounded Enrica without touching her. The world left her out of its colors and tones, and she had never felt so lonely in her life.

Like an automaton, she'd taken part in the family rituals: breakfast, Mass at the church of Santa Teresa, the streetcar to Piazza Vittoria. She wasn't talkative by nature, and she'd been able to conceal her melancholy; her father and siblings' excitement about the excursion was something that she and her mother tolerated, certainly not something they shared.

Villa Nazionale, even though it was a place she liked, struck her as noisy and vulgar that day. The carabinieri on horseback in dress uniform rode along the tree-lined path reserved for pedestrians next to the *viale*; the horses were as restless and uneasy as she was. She continued to curse herself for the way she acted during her interview at police headquarters, for having acted so differently from her true self.

Walking one step behind her parents, leading her brothers and sisters by the hand, and preceding her sister and brother-in-law, who in turn were pushing the baby carriage with her little nephew, she thought that she might grow old without having a family and children of her own, as a result of her grumpy disposition; still, hadn't her mother always told her that it was her finest quality? The sun flooded the blossoming trees, the children were playing with their cheerful little pedal cars, and a street organ was playing *Duorme, Carme'*. Sleep, Carmela. How ironic, considering that she hadn't slept a wink.

From beyond the tops of the pine trees came the slow sound of the calm sea. They stopped at a stand selling seeds and nuts; her father, as always, pretended he was giving in to the pleas of her brothers and sisters so that he could buy a few paper twists of nuts for himself. She loved her family, but today they were intolerable to her. She would have liked to return to the darkness of her bedroom. They started up again, walking in the direction of the zoological park's aquarium, another obligatory stop on their Sunday promenade, where they'd look at the starfish, feigning astonishment for the hundredth time; it meant so much to her father.

Passing close by the little temple with the bust of Virgil, absentmindedly listening—for perhaps the hundredth time—to her father's stories about the Roman poet's feats as a sorcerer, she mused bitterly that the sorceress to whom she had turned hadn't been of any help to her: quite the contrary. Then she felt a flush of shame at the thought, as she remembered the woman's atrocious death.

Her eyes fleetingly met the gaze of a man with an idiotic smile on his face; she looked away as quickly as she could. There was no room in her mind for anything other than a solution to her current dilemma.

Still, there was something familiar about that man. Before erasing his image from her mind, she wondered for an instant where she might have seen him before.

Doctor Modo shouldn't have been at the hospital at all, but there he was regardless, as was often the case. The night before Ricciardi, in that distinctively cold yet vibrant way of his, had told him the story of the man who had stabbed himself, a man with whom neither the commissario nor the doctor had ever spoken, and he'd felt the urge to come see how he was doing.

Standing next to his bed, wearing his lab coat, he looked

down at him, pensively running his fingers through his white head of hair. He was reflecting on the power of dreams.

Who says that dreams have no power over reality? the doctor thought to himself. You were fine, until you started dreaming. You'd experienced all sorts of things, many of them good: you had three children; you held them in your arms; you played with them and made them laugh. Working every day and sometimes at night, you always made sure that they had enough to eat and drink.

You held your woman in your arms, in tight, sweet embraces. You made love to her, winning yourself a small patch of heaven. You went out whether it was raining or the sun was shining; you sang, perhaps you wept; you smelled the earliest perfume of the blossoms and of the snow. Your gaze met dark eyes and blue eyes; you saw the sky and the moon. There were times when you were thirsty and no one refused you a cool glass of water. Then, Modo thought, you started to dream. And from that day on your happiness wasn't enough for you anymore. You decided to start climbing the ladder. But tell me this: aside from the sheer difficulty of the climb, how hard you struggled to make the ascent, what ever made you think that you'd be happier at the top of the ladder?

Without changing his expression and without waiting for a reply, the doctor pulled a sheet over the corpse of Antonio Iodice.

The first Sunday of spring was over.

XLIV

As he climbed the stairs of headquarters, Ricciardi ran into Officer Sabatino Ponte. Ponte was a short, nervous-looking man taken on by Deputy Chief of Police Garzo to serve as his doorman and clerk. The position did not appear on any organizational chart, but the little man's brown-nosing, unctuous personality, along with a few shadowy recommendations from people in high places, had helped him to escape regular police duty and win himself a cushy, comfortable job. Maione, who maintained an attitude of polite contempt for the man, grumbled that he was a dog who commanded just as much respect as his master. Which is to say, none at all, he added with a smirk.

The man had a superstitious fear of Ricciardi; to the extent that he was able, he simply avoided him. When he had no choice but to speak to him, he did his best not to look him in the eye, turning and fleeing as soon as the conversation was over. Something serious must be afoot, to find him at the foot of the stairs at this hour of the morning.

"Buongiorno, Commissario. Welcome," he said, staring fixedly first at the ceiling, and then at Ricciardi's shoes.

"Yes, Ponte. What's going on? Have I put my foot in it?"

A nervous smile twitched on Ponte's face, and he focused intently on a little crack in the wall, off to his left.

"No, of course not. And who am I, to criticize a man of your stature? No, it's just that the deputy chief of police wonders if you could stop by his office, when you have a minute."

Ricciardi was annoyed by the little man's darting gaze, which was starting to make his head spin.

"What, you mean the deputy chief of police is already in his office, this early, on a Sunday morning? That strikes me as unusual."

Ponte stared at a patch of floor ten feet away, as if he were following a crawling insect with his eyes.

"No, no, you're quite right; he hasn't come in yet. But he said to make sure you speak with him this morning. Before you take any further action on the Calise murder."

Aha, thought Ricciardi. Maione was right, the sly old fox.

"All right, Ponte. Tell the deputy chief of police that I'll be in his office at ten o'clock. And let me get a look at your eyes; I think there might be something wrong with your vision."

The police officer opened his eyes wide, saluted halfheartedly, and turned and ran up the staircase as fast as he could, taking it three steps at a time.

Waiting for Ricciardi at the entrance to his office was Maione, wearing a disconsolate expression.

"The day's not off to a good start, Commissa'. Doctor Modo called from the hospital. Iodice died last night."

He hung up the phone. It was the third call he'd made. Once again, he'd received ample reassurances.

In the voices of all three of the people he'd spoken with, he could hear compassion; and from what he could tell, though it was hard to judge without being able to see their expressions, all of them knew about Emma and that man. And about him, as well.

Now the important thing was to resolve the matter once and for all; he could deal with mending the damage to his reputation later. He knew from experience that people forget about every scandal sooner or later. And besides, he didn't really think there was any hope of finding a solution.

He heard a cough through the wall: his wife was home this morning. This, too, was good news. Perhaps there were grounds for optimism after all. Ruggero ran the back of his hand over his cheek; he'd better shave and wash up.

So much depended on his image.

Ricciardi, standing by his office window, looked at Maione, who still stood crestfallen in the doorway. Both men could see at a glance that neither of them had slept a wink that night; and both men decided not to mention it.

"I know what you're thinking, Commissa'. Iodice's death, as far as this investigation is concerned, changes nothing. But the fact is that now he can't explain why he did what he did. And this doesn't seem like the time to go bother those two unfortunate women, his mother and his wife. What should we do?"

"Well, first of all I have to say that you hit the nail on the head with regard to Signora Serra di Arpaja. I found your friend Ponte waiting for me right out front this morning, and he told me to come speak with Garzo before getting started on anything else. Obviously, the phone call has already come through. Have you made sure that Iodice's family has been informed, as we promised yesterday?"

Maione nodded quickly.

"They were there at the hospital, Commissa'. They showed up at dawn, mother and wife, but no one had the heart to tell them anything until the doctor came in; even though it wasn't his shift, he wanted to see how Iodice was doing. He broke the news to them."

Ricciardi shook his head.

"What madness. To kill yourself—a father with three children. He really must have lost all hope. But why? It would have made just as much sense to turn himself in if he had killed her. It doesn't gel. Normally, someone who commits a murder with that much rage behind it, the way Calise was killed, doesn't have the sensitive personality that it takes to commit suicide. And anyone who feels enough shame to kill himself doesn't have the rage inside him to kick a person to death."

Maione listened closely.

"To tell you the truth, it doesn't seem all that obvious that Iodice did it to me either. And to see his mamma and especially his wife, the despair on their faces—he must have really been a good man. On the other hand, if it wasn't him, why would he kill himself?"

"Maybe he thought he'd be charged and he'd have no way to defend himself. Maybe he had other problems. Maybe he just snapped. And, of course, maybe he was the killer. Whatever the reason, we have to keep investigating until we find proof, one way or another. A wife's sorrowful expression is not accepted as evidence in a court of law."

Before Maione, who had suddenly blushed bright red, could get out an answer, there was a knock at the office door and Camarda stuck his head in.

"Commissario, Brigadie', forgive the intrusion. The two Signoras Iodice, mother and wife, are waiting in the hall. They would like to speak with you."

The two women walked into the office and Ricciardi and Maione greeted them at the door. The wife was the very picture of unconsolable grieving sorrow: her delicate features were ravaged by twenty-four hours without sleep, filled with uninterrupted weeping; her eyes were swollen, her lips red. The mother, with the same black shawl covering her head, seemed like a figure out of Greek tragedy, her face expressionless, her eyes blank. Only her waxen complexion betrayed the hell she had inside her.

The two policemen were surprised by their visit; by rights, they should have been at the hospital, arranging to have the body transported to the cemetery. Perhaps, it occurred to Ricciardi, they were here to request police authorization, but there was really no need for that; the operation performed the previous day left no doubt about the cause of death, so an autopsy would be pointless. He gestured for them to have a seat, but the two women remained standing. He turned to address the wife.

"Signora, I'm so sorry. I understand your pain and, believe me, we are here for you. If there's anything that we can do, please don't hesitate to ask."

Concetta took a step forward and drew a deep breath.

"Commissa', my mother-in-law and I gave this a lot of thought last night. On one hand, we thought that Tonino . . . my husband, that is, should rest in peace. That there should be no more talk about him, especially not under this roof—forgive me, Commissa'. But then, we thought about my children. There are three of them, and they're young; they have their whole lives ahead of them. And they'll have to bear this name. And this name musn't be tarnished."

Ricciardi and Maione exchanged a glance. Concetta had stopped talking, overwhelmed by emotion. Her mother-in-law, standing one step behind her, laid a bony hand on her shoulder. She heaved a sigh and went on.

"We sometimes say that you can feel things. Things happen, and a person might see them with his own eyes and understand them. Other times someone might tell you about them, so you hear them with your own ears and understand them that way. Then there are other times still when you can see some things and you can't see others, and yet you still understand it all in your head. But sometimes there are things, Commissa', that you can't see and you can't hear, things you can't even think in your head, and yet you know them all the same. That's what happens with people you hold dear in your heart," and with those words she clutched to her breast a hand reddened by hard work and tears, "and you're never wrong. You're never wrong."

Ricciardi stared straight into the woman's face and his green eyes were clear and empty. Concetta stared back unwaveringly from the depths of her certainty, her pupils two dark stars swimming in her reddened eyes.

"My husband never killed anyone, Commissa'. Only himself. I know this, his mother knows this. His children know it too.

"So what we want to do is, what's the word, cooperate. We talked it over between us. You and the brigadier here strike us as two kind and decent men. You've offered us help, and we can see that you're sorry about what happened to my husband. We're poor people, we don't even know how we're going to make ends meet now; we can't hire a lawyer to defend us. All we can give our children is our name, and it must be untarnished."

"Signora," Ricciardi said, "our job is to find out the truth. Whatever that truth might be, whether or not we like it, even if it creates suffering. We're not on anybody's side. We're here for one thing only: to find out what happened. We're glad that you want to cooperate. But if we happened to discover that . . . that your husband were responsible for something bad, something serious, it will only be worse. You understand that, don't you? If we close the case the way things stand now, there might still be a shadow of a doubt. But if we proceed, then there will be no doubts left. Are you sure this is what you want?"

After a quick glance at her mother-in-law, behind her, Concetta answered.

"Yes, Commissa'. That's why we came here to see you, with my dead husband still at the hospital, like a man without any family picked up off the street. Did they tell you what he screamed when . . . when he did this thing? He screamed: my children! And that's what we have to do: what's best for his children. We're sure, Commissa'."

XLV

Ruggero was preparing himself to knock on Emma's door. He was trying to summon the strength. He'd washed, shaved, changed clothes, and considered himself at some length in the mirror. The fact that he'd regained his image, the picture of himself that he was used to, the self that struck fear and respect into others, reassured him and gave him a sense of equilibrium.

But the trial that he had to face was a difficult one: perhaps the hardest of them all.

How long had it been since he'd spoken with his wife? Certainly, brief exchanges of courtesies at the dinner table; simple instructions concerning the management of the domestic help and the running of the house, but real conversation, no. They no longer even looked each other in the eye.

Over time, they had also consolidated their territories. Invisible walls had gone up: the study and the green parlor were his, the bedroom and the boudoir were hers. All they shared were the dining room and their loveless nights. The rest of the rooms were closed off, or else inhabited by the servants.

But now they had to talk. There was no more time for tacit understandings, hidden truths, silences charged with rancor. It was time to talk.

Before everything was irretrievably lost.

Ruggero knocked on Emma's door.

Ricciardi thought something through and then spoke to Concetta Iodice.

"All right then. I have to ask you a few questions. Let's start with your restaurant, the pizzeria. How did your husband get it off the ground? Where did he get the money?"

"Part of it came from our own savings and from the sale of his pushcart. The rest of the money was borrowed. From Carmela Calise."

"What kind of terms was your husband on with Calise?"

"I never went to see her; I don't even know where she lived. A friend of my husband's, Simone the carter, told him about her; he said she was different from . . . from those other people, the ones who come and break your legs and arms if you don't pay back every penny. I'm sure you know all about that here . . . Anyway, he told him that this one was more, how to put it, more human: if you don't have all the money, you can bring the rest later; she gives extensions."

"And did your husband ever have to extend his deadline?"

Concetta looked down at the floor.

"One time. The pizzeria wasn't doing well. And the other day . . . the other day he had gone to see her, to ask for another extension. It had taken him two days to screw up the courage. He thought that I didn't know, but I could see that he wasn't sleeping at night. And so I put two and two together."

"Did he seem desperate to you, at his wits' end?"

"No. But worried, yes. Before . . . before he opened the pizzeria, he used to laugh all the time. Afterward, he stopped laughing. Maybe that's why people weren't coming. Why would you go to eat at a place where no one laughs?"

Ricciardi listened carefully.

"Let's go back to that evening. Did he tell you that he was going to see Calise?"

"No, he didn't tell us. But we knew." She shot a fleeting glance at her mother-in-law, who hadn't taken her arm off her shoulder the entire time, giving her strength. "And he left the pizzeria about nine o'clock, when most of the crowd had gone home. He told me that he had an errand to run, that I should close up and go home. So I closed up, cleaned everything, and waited a little longer just to see if he'd come back. Then I went home, thinking he might be there already. But he wasn't. We fed the children and we put them to bed. He still wasn't back. Then the two of us looked out the window, she and I," and she tilted her head in her mother-in-law's direction, "saying: 'He'll be here any minute.' But it was past midnight when he came home."

"And what was he like?"

Concetta's eyes welled up with tears, and there was a quaver in her voice.

"As if he were drunk, but he didn't smell like wine. He couldn't walk straight; it took him forever to get up the stairs. He said that he was tired and that he didn't feel good. He fell down on the bed with all his clothes on; he had a fever, and he fell straight asleep. I undressed him, the way I do with my children when they fall asleep in their clothes."

She exchanged a glance with her mother-in-law; the older woman nodded her head yes ever so slightly. Then she pulled a folded scrap of paper out of her dress.

"And I found this. It fell out of his jacket."

She handed the sheet of paper to Maione, who unfolded it.

"A promissory note, Commissa'. Eighty lire, payable April fourteenth, signed by Iodice, Antonio. Beneficiary: Calise, Carmela. And . . ."

Ricciardi looked up at Maione.

"And?"

Maione spoke in a low voice, looking at Concetta.

"It's covered with blood, Commissa'."

Emma opened her door just a crack. Her husband glimpsed

part of her face, her hair in disarray. Her eyes were red from weeping, or possibly from sleep.

"What do you want?"

"May I come in? I need to talk to you. It's important."

Emma's voice was full of pain.

"What could be all that important?"

She turned and walked toward the bed, leaving the door half-open. Ruggero entered the room, shutting the door behind him.

The bedroom was a mess. Clothes and undergarments scattered across the floor and furniture, scraps left over from breakfast lying forgotten on the night table, a large, filthy handkerchief spread out on the bed. There was a stale, dank smell in the air.

"You've thrown up. You're not well."

Emma was shaking. She ran a hand through her hair.

"Aren't you sharp. So that's why they call you the Fox. *Prego*, have a seat. Just make yourself at home."

Ruggero ignored the sarcasm. He looked around, still standing. Then he turned his gaze on his wife.

"You've been drinking, too. Look at you: you're a wreck. Aren't you ashamed of yourself?"

Emma let herself flop back on the bed, snickering.

"You want to know if I'm ashamed? Of course I'm ashamed. I'm ashamed I never had the courage to tell my father no when he arranged for me to marry you. I'm ashamed that I didn't have the strength to leave you and this house all the times you treated me like a spoiled child. And I'm ashamed to be here right now, instead of . . ."

Ruggero finished her sentence for her.

". . . instead of with him. With Attilio Romor."

A long silence ensued. Emma struggled to focus on her husband's image through her clouded vision.

"How do you know his name? Damn you! Have you been

following me? Did you hire someone to investigate me? You coward!"

With her lips drawn back in a snarl, showing her gums, her head drawn between her shoulders, her fingers spread like claws, eyes red with fury and wine, her hair a tangled mess, Emma looked like a wild animal. She looked around for something to throw at him.

A bitter smile appeared on Ruggero's lips.

"Investigate you? Spend good money to find out something everyone is eager to tell me, precisely because I don't ask about it? Everyone: my friends, male and female, even the doorman. You didn't deny anyone the sight of you, the spectacle of you playing the stupid slut. And now you're surprised? Spare me your anger and settle for what you've brought down on yourself already."

Emma turned pale. Reaching out with one hand, she groped for her filthy handkerchief and raised it to her lips, fighting back a retching impulse to vomit.

"I've left him, I won't be seeing him again."

"I know."

She lifted her head and looked at him.

"How do you know that? You can't possibly know that."

"It doesn't matter now. We have a more serious problem to deal with. Actually, to be precise, you're the one with the problem. But you're still Signora Serra di Arpaja, to my misfortune, and you need to listen to me, carefully."

Ruggero pulled Emma's summons out of his jacket pocket and started talking.

XLVI

Ricciardi took the promissory note, immediately noticing the bloody fingerprints near where the amount was written in numerals and by the signature. It looked as if Iodice had traced the parts that had been filled in with his finger, stained with Calise's blood, making sure that it was the document he was looking for. He looked up at Concetta.

"He didn't do it," the woman said immediately.

Ricciardi shook his head.

"I know you're convinced of that, Signora. Otherwise, you'd have never given me this note. But you have to admit that it's hard to reconstruct what happened without thinking that your husband might have been the one to kill Calise."

Concetta took a step forward. Her voice broke as she talked.

"I know it: I know it wasn't him. After all, Commissa', tell me this: why would he have kept the note? Wouldn't he just have destroyed it and said he'd paid it in full? Even if his name did come out as one of the people who owed money to Calise. No, you know it yourself that it wasn't him. He found her already dead, he took the promissory note, and he left. You have to find the murderer, Commissa'. Now there're two souls that need to rest in peace."

Ricciardi and Maione looked at each other uncertainly. What Concetta was saying was speculation. Evidence was quite another matter.

Iodice's mother stepped forward out of the shadows. She spoke up in a low voice, roughened by silence and grief. It was clear that she had a hard time expressing herself in a language other than the dialect she was used to speaking.

"Commissario, Brigadier, forgive me. I'm an ignorant woman; I don't know how to speak properly. I've worked hard all my life. That's our fate, to struggle to raise our children. I watched this son of mine grow all his life long, minute by minute. I saw him cry and laugh and then I saw the children he and this fine girl brought into the world, this fine girl who tied her life to his, to ours. I knew him the way only a mamma can know her son, and I can tell you: my son never killed anyone. Much less an old woman, like his mother. Impossible. Believe what my daughter-in-law tells you, believe us both. Don't let a murderer run loose in the streets; don't let our name be stained just because it's easier to stop looking."

Ricciardi gave the woman a searching look.

"Signora, believe me when I tell you that we have no intention of letting the guilty party go free. I promise you: we'll continue the investigation. But I have to tell you, the way things look right now, your son would appear to have committed this murder. You may go now. Maione will see you to the front door. And once again, my condolences."

The women nodded their heads in farewell and walked toward the door. Before they left the room, Tonino Iodice's mother turned back to face the commissario.

"The things a person does, sooner or later they have to pay for them, Commissa'. Or else they get their reward. Remember: *'O Padreterno nun è mercante ca pava 'o sabbato.*" God Almighty's not a shopkeeper who pays His debts on Saturday.

When he returned to the office after seeing the two women out, Maione found Ricciardi staring nonplussed at the door.

"What does that mean?"

"What does what mean, Commissa'?"

"What Iodice's mother said. What did she mean?"

Maione looked at him with concern. This investigation was introducing him to a Ricciardi who was very different from the one he'd come to know.

"The line about God Almighty and Saturday, you mean? Sometimes I forget that you're not Neapolitan. They don't say that where you come from? It's a proverb. It means that when you do something, you don't get your reward or punishment on a set date, like with debts between human beings. But I don't think she was trying to threaten you."

Ricciardi waved his hands briefly in the air, as if dismissing Maione's suspicions.

"No, I know, I know. It's just that I've heard it somewhere before. And I thought it had to do with actual debts and payments. That the saying was literal, in other words."

There was a discreet knock at the door, followed by the pinched little face of Ponte, the clerk of the deputy chief of police. Ponte glanced at the armchair, the wall, and the bookcase in rapid succession, then spoke.

"Commissario, forgive me. The deputy chief of police is expecting you."

As he was climbing the stairs to Garzo's office, accompanied by Maione, Ricciardi reflected on the shift in perspective brought on by his conversation with the two Iodice women. As soon as he'd heard about the suicide he'd thought that the *pizzaiolo* must be the killer; and, rationally, that's what he continued to think. But he had to admit that the emotional impact of what the two women had told him had been powerful, and it had shaken his certainty.

Then there was the matter of the proverb. Ricciardi believed that the murder was somehow connected to Calise's loan-sharking activities, and in fact her last thought, revealed to him by the Deed, seemed to point to the repayment of a debt, which would confirm his hypothesis. But now that he knew that that same proverb could refer to the course of fate, he could see that there were some murky points that needed to be cleared up. Iodice was certainly the most likely suspect for the murder, but he'd have to complete his investigation before he could give in to that belief.

Fate. Once again, there it was: cursed, inscrutable fate. The last refuge from all one's fears, all responsibility: "That's fate"; "Let fate decide"; "Fate will determine the outcome." In songs and in stories. In people's minds.

As if everything were preordained or carved in stone and nothing were left up to the free will of human beings. But that's not the way things work; there's no such thing as fate, Ricciardi mused as he and Maione approached the door to the deputy chief of police's office. All there is in the world is evil, sorrow, and pain.

Garzo came to greet him with a dazzling smile.

"My dear, dear Ricciardi! Life is peculiar, isn't it? We still have to deal with the occasional trivial crime; even if in this brave new era, murders are practically a thing of the past. We live in an age of law and order and prosperity, but if some lunatic decides to buck the system, we're here to set things right. *Prego, prego*, Ricciardi, come in, have a seat."

Ricciardi had listened to this little set piece of political oratory with an ironic smirk on his face. I'd like to send you down to spend just one day in the poorest quarters of this city, you bumptious peacock, he thought. I'd show you law and order and prosperity.

"Dottore, if you have orders . . . I'm in the middle of an investigation, as you mentioned. I don't have a lot of time."

Garzo clenched his fists for a moment. That man really got on his nerves, with his calm and casual way of always showing him disrespect. Still, he did his best to restrain himself, so as not to deviate from the approach he had planned out in advance.

"That's exactly what I wanted to talk to you about. I heard

about this pizza maker, what's his name . . ." He consulted a little sheet of paper before him on his otherwise immaculate desk. "Iodice, that's right. So this Iodice is dead, isn't he? As a result of self-inflicted wounds, according to the report. Therefore, case closed. Another quick and successful conclusion."

Ricciardi expected this line of attack and he was ready for it.

"No, Dottore. You must have been misinformed. There was no confession on Iodice's part."

Garzo looked up from the report he was reading, staring at Ricciardi over the gold rims of his reading glasses.

"But I didn't say anything about a confession. It's the act itself, the taking of his own life: that is a confession. He was the murderer, and his conscience couldn't stand it. There's no doubt about it, as far as I'm concerned."

Ricciardi briefly shook his head.

"No, Dottore. We're not done with our interviews yet. We have another person we still need to talk to, possibly two people, and a couple of places we need to inspect. After that we may be ready to conclude our investigation. Maybe."

With a theatrical gesture, Garzo whipped off his eyeglasses.

"It was precisely this last interview remaining, Ricciardi, that I wanted to speak to you about. I know that you've summoned the wife of a very prominent man for an interview. I assume you realize how important it is to preserve amicable relations with this city's judges and lawyers. I therefore strongly urge you to avoid causing friction."

Ricciardi smiled.

"But, Dottore, it was my understanding that the overriding interest of both judges and lawyers was the pursuit of truth. Can you imagine what a surprise it would be for the press to discover that a subpoena for questioning had been, how should I put this, suppressed by police headquarters? You should know, Dottore, that a certain list of names was found at

Calise's apartment by none other than a reporter, and if it hasn't been published yet it's only because Brigadier Maione here asked the person in question not to disseminate it, so as not to hamper our investigation. But if you really think it's necessary . . ."

Both Maione and Garzo looked at Ricciardi in amazement. Neither man had ever heard him talk that much.

The deputy chief of police recovered from his bewilderment. Among his many fine qualities was his ability to recognize when he'd been defeated and cut his losses.

"If that's how matters stand, please, proceed as planned. And my thanks to you, Brigadier, for your sensitivity and concern for the reputation of the police force and for the people involved. The one thing I would ask, Ricciardi, is that you proceed with the utmost discretion. This means that the . . . person in question will not be coming to your office. Instead, you will conduct your interview at the signora's residence. And you'll go there by car, so that no one sees you arrive on foot. Keep me informed."

XLVII

If there was one thing he hated to do, it was drive a car. Perhaps because it wasn't something his generation had grown up with, or else simply because he'd ridden horses as a boy and in his heart that was still his preferred way of getting around. Whatever the reason, Maione didn't like to drive.

"I don't understand these fixations. Taking the car to go half a mile! It takes two minutes to get there! And they tell us they need it, that they don't want it to be used for police duty. Let them keep it!"

He'd just installed himself in the driver's seat, and he was already drenched with sweat from the agitation. The engine was roaring as it revved. He shifted into gear; the vehicle lurched forward and the engine stalled. A lawyer and a clerk who were standing talking in the courtyard of headquarters took a step back, apprehensively.

"Now look, even the clutch is shot on this, this, this jalopy. I have to ask, though, Commissa', where did you get the idea to bring up this list and this reporter? As if I would talk to a journalist. You know I hate journalists."

Ricciardi, sunk into the upholstery of the backseat, was holding himself steady with both hands on the door handle.

"It was the only thing I could think of. I'm sorry, weren't there any drivers available?"

A wounded expression appeared on Maione's face.

"Listen, Commissa', I'm the best driver out of all the staff at police headquarters! The problem is that this damned vehicle hasn't been maintained properly, that's what it is. Ah, there's the choke, I see."

With a roar, the engine started up again and the car took off. Lawyer and clerk each leapt to opposite sides of the street, running for dear life. Ricciardi's thoughts turned briefly to Enrica, bidding her farewell as he clutched at the door handle to stay upright.

It was, in fact, not much more than half a mile from police headquarters to Via Generale Orsini, where the Serra di Arpajas lived. You just took the new road running along the waterfront, with the monumental buildings of Castelnuovo and the Palazzo Reale on one side, on the other the old buildings of the Italian navy arsenal, the Arsenale della Marina, which would soon be demolished to make way for a park. The city reminded Ricciardi more all the time of one of those houses with a nice parlor for entertaining guests while the rest of the rooms were falling apart.

At the end of the road, just before the broad left-hand curve that would take them to Via Santa Lucia, was the huge construction site for the Galleria della Vittoria, a magnificent tunnel and an undertaking of the Fascist regime. Linking two parts of the city with an underground road. A hole a third of a mile long. Five men had already died in the excavation. Ricciardi could still see two of them, glowing in the darkness of the excavated earth, talking about their families as they were just seconds before the explosion that had blown them to pieces.

These accidents never even came to public attention. First, the authorities carefully covered them up; then they arranged for the surviving families to receive special assistance. Well, that's something, at least, thought Ricciardi, doing his best to hold on tight as they drove through the curve, which Maione had entered by swerving suddenly. A cart piled high with produce and being drawn by an elderly mule lost most of its cargo, and the carter's stream of invective poured out after them like the wake of a speedboat.

"Eh, what's the big deal? That cart was loaded with nothing but garbage, anyway. Now then, Commissa', what's the street number of this palazzo?"

"It's number twenty-four, right here on the right. Start slowing down."

Maione immediately jammed on the brakes, bringing the vehicle to an abrupt halt on the sidewalk. On the exact spot where an austere nanny was walking, with the traditional long white dress, the white lace headpiece, and an enormous wooden baby carriage.

"Is that any way to drive? You almost frightened me to death! And if the child had taken a spill, who'd have told the baronessa? Are you gentlemen mad?"

Maione did his best to placate her wrath.

"Forgive us, Signo', we're engaged in a police operation and I didn't see you. We were in a hurry."

Ricciardi looked down at the toddler, who seemed interested in the commissario's face.

"What's the little boy's name?"

"His name is Giovanni. He's almost two."

Good luck to you, Giovanni, Ricciardi thought to himself. It's not a very nice world, the one you decided to be born into! Even though from this part of town it doesn't look so bad.

The child smiled up at him. He had green eyes, too.

The palazzo's uniformed doorman walked forward to meet Maione and Ricciardi with a soldierly step, inquiring as to who they were and ostentatiously checking a list he had. The brigadier and commissario exchanged a look of annoyance.

"Commissa', would you like to tell the admiral here that

we're members of the police and we're not here on a social call, or shall I? Otherwise, I swear to God, I'm going to shove him aside and break down some doors."

Ricciardi laid a hand on the doorman's arm.

"Listen, please just announce us. They're expecting us."

As they stepped out of the elevator, they found the apartment door wide open and a housemaid curtseying in welcome.

"*Prego*, come in. The professor will see you in just a moment."

Maione shot the commissario a glance.

"But aren't we here to talk with the wife?"

Ricciardi shrugged. He didn't think they had much chance of gaining direct, unmediated access to the signora, but he was determined not to leave without questioning his witness. After a short wait, they were admitted to an austere study lined with antique books. The man walking toward them exuded an air of authority.

"*Prego*, Signori, please have a seat on the sofa; let me order you a cup of tea. I hardly think we need to sit at the desk. You're not here for legal consultation."

He flashed a conspiratorial smile. The policemen let his friendly stare go unanswered and remained standing.

"Professor, we thank you for your hospitality. But we're here to interview the signora and the quicker we can get to it, the better."

"You'll see her, Commissario. She's on her way now. But I will need to be present; that's not up for discussion. As her lawyer, if not as her husband. If you want to see her alone, you'll have to arrest her. That is, if you think you can find a magistrate in this city willing to issue the arrest warrant, of course. So, shall I have her come in?"

Ricciardi thought it over rapidly: it was just a matter of asking a few questions, the answers to which in all likelihood would allow them to close the case definitively. A woman from the better part of town who had indulged in the thrill of having her fortune told by an old tarot card reader.

"All right, Professor. Let's get this out of the way."

XLVIII

Ricciardi observed Signora Emma Serra di Arpaja. He'd imagined her as quite unlike the way she had presented herself.

Pallid, circles under her eyes, hollow cheeks. No makeup except for a hint around her eyes, dressed in gray, hair cut fashionably short and tucked behind her ears, leaving her forehead uncovered. Simple shoes with flat heels, sheer stockings.

She kept her eyes lowered, fixed on the small parlor table, with an undecipherable expression on her face, without any apparent emotion. She had greeted them in a low, flat voice. She seemed to be suffering, but from some dull, recondite, distant pain.

Thus far her husband hadn't looked at her. He was scrutinizing Ricciardi, sizing him up. The tension in the room could have been cut with a knife.

After a long and awkward silence, Ricciardi spoke.

"Signora, please describe your relations with the Signora Calise, Carmela, self-proclaimed fortune teller, found dead in her apartment on April fifteenth."

Emma didn't look at him. She answered in a monotone.

"I'd been to see her a few times. A girlfriend of mine took me there."

"For what purpose?"

"My own amusement."

"What did the two of you talk about?"

Emma shot a rapid glance at her husband, but her tone of voice remained unchanged.

"She read cards. She told me things."

"What sort of things?"

Ruggero broke in, unruffled.

"Commissario, I hardly think the details of my wife's conversations with Calise are pertinent to your investigation. Don't you agree?"

Ricciardi decided that it was time to establish the boundaries of jurisdiction.

"Professor, as far as our investigation is concerned, kindly let us determine what's pertinent and what isn't. Go ahead, please, Signora: what did you talk about?"

When Emma replied, she seemed to be talking about other people in another world.

"I liked her. I didn't have to think; she cleared up all my doubts for me. My life . . . Commissario, we live with so many uncertainties. Should I do this. Or should I do that instead. She didn't have doubts about anything. She moved her cards around, she spat on them, and then she made a decision. And she was never wrong."

Ricciardi looked the woman hard in the face. He had felt a stirring of emotion.

"And lately? Had you been to see her often?"

Ruggero responded, in a decisive tone of voice.

"Commissario, my wife told you that she'd been there a few times. That's an expression that indicates chance visits, and infrequent ones. Under no circumstances can the word be understood to mean 'often.'"

Without taking his eyes off the woman, Ricciardi gestured with one hand to Maione, who pulled Calise's notebook out of his jacket.

"In this notebook," said the brigadier after clearing his throat, "found in Calise's apartment, your wife's name is recorded, either written out or as initials, one hundred and sixteen times over roughly three hundred days of appointments. If you ask me, 'often' is a perfectly reasonable term, don't you think, Professo'?"

Ruggero snorted in annoyance. Emma answered.

"Well, yes, I would go see her. It was a distraction. We all need distractions. Especially when life becomes oppressive."

She'd said something terrible; Ricciardi and Maione realized it immediately. They both glanced over at Ruggero. He didn't react, continuing to stare silently into the void in front of him. The commissario went on.

"And what did Calise talk to you about? Did she ever, I don't know, confide in you, mention any names? Did she ever tell you that she was worried about anything, or did you ever sense that she might be in danger?"

Maione looked over at Ricciardi in surprise. He would have expected the commissario to ask other questions about Signora Serra di Arpaja's troubles, delve deeper into the cracks in their relationship. Instead, he had returned to the topic of Calise.

"No, Commissario. We talked about other things, like I told you. She read my cards. That's all. She told what was going to happen, and she was never wrong."

When the woman had withdrawn from the room, Ruggero saw Maione and Ricciardi to the door.

"You see, Commissario, my wife is like a child. She has her little crazes, her amusements, the silly things she does with her girlfriends. But she was having dinner with me at the home of His Excellency the Prefect the night that Calise was murdered. I read about the mechanics of the murder in the newspaper. Our name is fairly prominent in this city. I'd appreciate it if this conversation was the last we could look forward to. Can I count on that?"

"We want exactly the same thing that you do, Professor: to make sure no innocent person is made to pay for something they didn't do. You can rest assured, you and your wife. We know how to perform our duty."

As they were walking out the front door, under the doorman's resentful glare, Maione reviewed the meeting.

"Commissa', why didn't you delve a little deeper into the matter at hand, so to speak? It seemed to me that the signora was reciting a lesson the professor'd taught her, and then she let slip that she was unhappy. Wouldn't it be worth finding out a little more about that? It wouldn't be that the signora got started killing little old ladies as a way off fending off her boredom, for example?"

Ricciardi stopped Maione, laying a hand on his arm before stepping into the car.

"You have a point. Listen, Maione, there's something I want to tell you before we get back in the car, just in case I don't get out alive: none of this is clear to me. Emma Serra went lots of times to see Calise, who never made use of Nunzia's services for her. That means that someone else was serving as her informer. So I want you to do some digging into the life of Emma Serra di Arpaja, but be very careful how you go about it. I want to know who she sees, where she goes when her husband's not around, the names of her friends, and what the domestics have to say. And as soon as you can. I have a feeling that any minute, we're going to be given a choice: either say Iodice did it, or they'll take us off the case."

"Yessir, Commissa'. But this thing you said about not getting out of the car alive, I don't get it. On the way back you can explain it clearly to me."

XLIX

Teresa watched the two policemen from the kitchen window as they got into the car and departed with a jolt. They'd aroused her curiosity; those crystal green eyes had made a strong impression on her. She'd observed the professor and the signora, too: he, who had gone several days without washing or shaving, more perfectly groomed and elegant than ever; she, who was usually glamorous and dressed in the latest fashions, as modestly clothed as the parish priest's spinster housekeeper back home in her village.

She had served the tea in silence, her eyes riveted to the floor, so she was unable to see their faces, but she'd still sensed all of the tension in the room bearing down on her. Only whispers had escaped through the parlor door; no one had raised their voice. She had taken this opportunity to tidy up the signora's bedroom, scrubbing away the wine and vomit.

Then she had cleaned the professor's study and had noticed the filthy shoes, which she now had there with her, in the little kitchen cabinet.

Teresa raised her gaze to the sea, from which a faint breeze carried a pleasant smell. Spring is really upon us now, she thought.

Having unleashed Maione to follow his trail, Ricciardi returned to his office alone.

Waiting for him at his door, eyes darting to and fro, was none other than Ponte.

Deputy Chief of Police Garzo was beside himself. There was no mistaking his shortness of breath and the red spots on his face. On top of that, he didn't come over to greet Ricciardi when he walked into his office.

"Now then, Ricciardi. As usual, you've ignored my instructions. But this time, I haven't the slightest intention of tolerating this attitude of yours, unless you have a reasonable explanation."

Ricciardi cocked his head to one side, quizzically.

"I don't understand, Dottore. Hadn't we agreed that I would interview Signora Serra di Arpaja? That we were to take the car and drive to their palazzo? That's precisely what we did."

Garzo was snorting like a bull.

"I received a phone call from the professor himself, lodging a complaint about your attitude, which he found anything but deferential; he told me that you treated him like little more than a common criminal. Is it true what he says?"

Ricciardi shrugged.

"Not all of us are at home in the higher spheres of society, Dottore. I've envied you your diplomatic skills more than once. I was careful to stick to the standard questions, not wanting to imply anything. But if I were sitting at your desk, I'd be concerned about this excessively defensive posture: normally, as you surely know from your own vast depth of experience, it's an approach that's used to hide something."

Garzo looked away. Ricciardi felt certain that if he got close to him, he'd hear the whirr and buzz of his brain testing its limits. The bureaucrat in Garzo instinctively shunned arguments with the wealthy and powerful, but the last thing he'd want was to have a murderer on his hands who'd been caught not through careful policework, but rather by chance, knowing that the press would crucify him for his protective attitude toward the professor. It had happened before. And Ricciardi knew it.

"Of course, you have a point. Ricciardi, I don't want to

direct the course of your investigation; perish the thought. But, for the second and I hope the last time, I must advise that you proceed with the utmost caution. If you need to speak with someone in the Serra di Arpaja family, you are to consult with me first. Agreed?"

"Yes, Dottore. Agreed."

Maione was finally doing the work that he loved best: legwork. Collecting information, names, events, insignificant stories that were just fragments of a larger one. The kind of work that allowed him to immerse himself, that took him around the city, into offices and shops, from dark alleyways to grand, tree-lined boulevards. The kind of work that let him get to know new people and see old, familiar faces, and hear the voices of Naples. The kind of work that kept him from other thoughts; that was something he felt the need for, now more than ever. Two nights earlier, he'd filled his lungs with a different kind of air, an air he'd almost forgotten existed: that of a home. He'd felt the caring tenderness of a woman, the smell of food cooked just for him. He even thought he might have detected heartfelt concern in Filomena's eyes for his weariness.

And yet his heart was filled with melancholy. He felt as if he'd been a spectator to someone else's life, the usurper of a throne. He'd felt uneasy and depressed. He'd returned home in silence and had gotten into bed. Only then had he felt he was where he belonged, even though Lucia had doubtless been sleeping for hours, shut off in her world of memories.

These were the thoughts that were running through his mind when he finally saw the doorman leaving the Serra di Arpaja palazzo, changed out of his uniform and on his way home. Maione stepped out of the shadow of the doorway across the street and caught up with the man.

Pretending he'd run into him by chance, he suggested they go get an after-work beer together.

L

While Maione followed his trail made of voices, words, and facial expressions, Ricciardi was working on a different track. He had to find the missing piece that he could no longer hope to acquire through ordinary channels: Antonio Iodice, *pizzaiolo*, suicide.

Walking briskly through the teeming *vicoli* of the evening, he headed straight for the pizzeria that had been the root of both that poor man's dreams and his destruction. He was unwilling to close the books on the case and brand as guilty a man who hadn't even had a chance to confess, though appearances certainly seemed to suggest that he was responsible for the crime. He wanted to live in his world for a little while, listen to his last thoughts, fully comprehend his dying sorrow. Unless the man was still partially conscious when he arrived at the hospital; in that case, he wouldn't find anything other than the smell of death.

It was rare for Ricciardi to go willingly in search of the Deed. Every time he encountered it, he was left with a shard of despair inside him: a fragment of the immense suffering involved in letting go, a sort of infection. He accepted the burden silently, as he always had, shutting himself up in a dark, thorny, internal cell.

But he had no choice: Iodice's wife and mother had talked to him about the man, but the stories they told were distorted by love. He would have to perform his own objective analysis of the expressions of pain and grief. Whether he liked it or not, he alone had this opportunity, and he had to take it.

He found himself standing in front of the usual notice, nailed to the door: the premises had been placed under sequestration by order of the magistrate. He walked into the darkness of the dining room. Overturned chairs, shattered dishes and bowls on the floor, half-eaten food. Flies that had gotten in by way of a slit over the door, through which penetrated a narrow shaft of light.

Everything was arranged just as it had been the moment that Camarda and Cesarano walked through the door, just before the *pizzaiolo* committed his demented final act. As Ricciardi looked around, he thought he could sense the pandemonium, the shouts, the noise. Against the far wall, beyond the tables and chairs, was the counter where the pizzas were made, right in front of the now cold oven. On the other side of the counter, the hearth, with a few saucepans. There were smells in the air: frying, smoke, sweat. Spoiled food. And blood.

Ricciardi's footsteps echoed in the silence and the shadows. He'd closed the door behind him; he didn't need light to see what he'd come here to find. He walked over to the counter; he stopped and stood there, hands in his pants pockets, breathing gently. Then he drew a deeper breath, and walked forward.

Iodice's specter was seated on the floor, its back leaning against the wall, head lolling on its right shoulder. One leg stretched out, the other folded, the shoe kicked off. Spasming muscles prefer to be rid of all constrictions. One arm lying along the side of the body, the palm of its hand flat on the floor, as if his last impulse had been to get up. Vest unbuttoned, shirt wide open, sleeves rolled up. A white apron covered his trousers. The other hand still gripped the handle of the knife, which jutted from his chest like a fractured bone. Gushing from the wound was the black river of blood which the heart had gone on blindly pumping.

As was often the case, the dead man had one eye open and the other shut, and the expression on his face was twisted by pain. His snarling lips revealed his yellowed, bloodstained teeth. The bottom lip was split open by one last furious bite. A reddish froth dripped from his mouth: his lung, thought Ricciardi. You weren't even granted one last deep breath.

Ricciardi had been told that Iodice had called out to his children as he died. But the man's last thought before dissolving into the shadows wasn't for them; Ricciardi could hear it clearly. From his ravaged mouth, Iodice was saying: You know; you know you were already lying dead on the floor.

They looked at each other for a long time, in the darkness, surrounded by broken dishware and stale odors, the dead man and the live one. Then Ricciardi turned on his heel and went back out into the perfume of springtime and all its false promises.

This time, Maione let his feet do the work.

The beers with the Serra di Arpajas' doorman had turned into three: the first to loosen the man up, the second to go with the usual resentful servant's story about his arrogant and oppressive employers, and the third as a token of sympathy and to thank him for the venomous information sprung from his malevolence.

And so by now it was dinnertime, and his conscience had been temporarily silenced. Showing up at Filomena's house at this time of night, again, would clearly push their moments together beyond the bounds of some hypocritical coincidence and establish a routine that he wasn't yet willing to consolidate. Not yet. And so he set off for home with an uncertain step, knowing he'd come to a fork in the road where his feet, of their own accord, without bothering to consult his mind, would decide.

As it turned out, he'd never know which way his feet would turn: the crowd of people that he glimpsed at the mouth of

Vico del Fico made his heart start racing and his breath catch in his throat. He thought that the mysterious author of her disfigurement might have returned to finish the horrible job he'd begun five days earlier, taking advantage, like a coward, of the absence of anyone who could protect Filomena: someone like him, for instance.

As he was hurrying toward the *basso*, making his way through the small crowd, he felt as if he were moving the way you do in those dreams where you're swimming through a mist that makes everything slow down, even your thoughts. And as he ran, he regretted his own hesitancy and the third beer with the Serras' doorman. It wasn't until he came even with the little front door of Filomena's *basso* that he realized that that wasn't the destination of the people of the *vicolo*; rather, it was the *basso* next door. He saw the open front door and the empty room inside, and he mechanically followed the stream of people.

There was a knot of people crowded tightly around the entrance, but as always his uniform opened up a path for him. Inside, surrounded by four or five black-clad weeping professional mourners, sat an ashen-faced little girl, expressionless, carefully dressed, hair neatly combed. Next to her sat Filomena, her shawl pulled up to shield her bandaged wound from sight, the other side of her face streaked with tears.

In the middle of the room, stretched out on the bed, lay a corpse dressed in work clothes, filthy with mortar and dust: a bricklayer, thought Maione. Standing near the bed were a dozen or so men dressed the same way: in their midst, the brigadier recognized Gaetano, Filomena's son.

Even though the body had been arranged as neatly as possible, it was immediately clear to Maione that the man had died from a fall: his spine was bent unnaturally, there were traces of caked blood on his mouth, and the back of his neck didn't leave the impression on the pillow that it should have.

When Filomena saw him, she hurried over to him.

"It's a tragedy, Raffaele! Poor little Rituccia! Her father was the only parent she had left. Her mamma died when she was little; she was a friend of mine. And now her father's dead. What a tragedy. She and Gaetano grew up together. And as fate would have it, Gaetano worked with Salvatore, on the same construction site on Via Toledo. My poor boy actually saw him fall; oh, the horror of it, right before his eyes . . ."

Maione looked at Gaetano, standing off in the shadows, not far from the bed. He heard a few comments, muttered under the breath and behind his back: "Now she's got herself a cop for a friend," "Did you hear that? She called him by name. They're on a first-name basis." For no good reason, he felt a faint flush of shame. And then he felt ashamed of feeling ashamed.

He turned to look at the little girl, who was the target of the noisy wave of compassion emitted by the women of the *vicolo*, and he was hardly surprised to see that her eyes were dry of tears. He knew how common it was for true grief to lack any outward signs. And, as he watched her, he picked up on a glance exchanged between the girl and Gaetano, the boy she'd grown up with. It was over in an instant: just a hint of a smile. It went completely unnoticed by all, save for Maione. It wasn't the smile of a little girl. Gaetano remained expressionless, his faced carved out of some dark hardwood.

The brigadier felt a long shiver run down his spine.

LI

The next morning, on his way to headquarters, Ricciardi carried on his shoulders a heavier burden of sadness than usual. Another day had gone by since Calise's ferocious murder, and bitter experience had taught him that time was his worst adversary.

Just like his own accursed visions, the murderer's footprints were fading away, gradually being erased by the overlay of new ideas, of different emotions. Moreover, the investigators' movements put the guilty parties on notice, allowing them to make counter-moves of their own.

And as if that wasn't bad enough, last night, once again, the shutters across the way had remained shut up tight. Perhaps Enrica had suffered from a relapse of her mysterious illness; that's what his imagination had suggested. Or worse, she was so deeply offended that she no longer even wanted to see his shadow at the window.

He was groping in the dark, and that stirred up a thunderstorm in his thoughts and in his heart, one that he couldn't put to rest.

As usual, he had arrived early, much earlier than the others. The officer at the entrance wasn't catnapping this time, and with a military-style salute, he strode out to meet him.

"Buongiorno, Commissa'. There's a young lady upstairs who wants to talk to you. I let her go up; she's waiting for you in the hall outside your office."

Ricciardi's heart jumped up in his throat at the thought that this could be Enrica. With a nod to the officer, who stared at him, taken aback by the look of fright on the commissario's face, Ricciardi headed toward the broad staircase with his eyes on the floor. Then he looked up, terrified and hopeful at the same time.

It wasn't her.

The girl who sat waiting for him on the small bench in the hallway was very young. She looked vaguely familiar somehow; Ricciardi decided he must have seen her recently, though he couldn't remember where. She was modestly dressed, with a dark overcoat that was too heavy for the now mild temperature, a nondescript hat perched on her upswept hair. In her hand was a bundle wrapped in newspaper pages. When she spotted him coming, she rose to her feet but didn't walk over to meet him. He gave her a quizzical look. She was the first to speak.

"Buongiorno, Commissa'. I have something I wanted to tell you, about the . . . the misfortune that befell Carmela Calise."

That morning, Maione came in early, too. His alcohol-fueled chat with the Serra di Arpajas' doorman had yielded some new pieces of information that he wanted to discuss as soon as possible with the commissario. And besides, lately, work was the only place where he felt relaxed.

He'd stayed by the bedside of the little girl's father for a while the night before, without managing to shake the unpleasant sensation that something there required further explanation, though he couldn't pin down exactly what it was. Perhaps it was Rituccia's composed resignation; she hadn't shed a single tear, and was sitting far away from the bed, probably because she was repelled by the corpse. Or it might be the relative indifference of the dead man's fellow workers, who stood cap in hand, awkwardly shuffling their feet, clearly eager to leave. Or possibly the genuine sympathy that Filomena displayed as she reassured the girl, telling her that from that moment on she would be like a second child to her. Or maybe it was the fact that everyone was staring at him with morbid curiosity, as if he were coming to take on a role of social significance comparable to Filomena's disfigured beauty.

Whatever the reason, the minute he was able to, he'd left to head home, promising the little girl, Gaetano, and Filomena that he'd take care of things, dealing with the contractor that employed the victim to make sure that his daughter was paid the indemnity that was due to her.

When he turned his key in the lock of his apartment door, for once arriving at a reasonable time for dinner, Maione was greeted by the wall of ice erected by Lucia. This wasn't the usual silence made of memories; that much he'd realized immediately. It contained a new kind of fury, reminiscent of the quarrels they'd had during the first few years of marriage. Plates slammed down on the table, no tablecloth, no napkins, cold soup left over from the children's lunch. In response to his one tentatively offered conjecture—whether by chance his wife might not be feeling well—he received a flashing glare and a dry "I'm feeling just fine." Hissing, conclusive. Neither of them had spoken another word, and she'd spent the rest of the evening in the company of her repressed fury, he accompanied by a vague sense of guilt.

When morning rolled around, bringing with it a persistent headache inherited from the night before, he had walked out onto the street with a sense of relief, without realizing that a gaze made of two parts rage to one part affection was following him from the window.

Once he had arrived at headquarters, he went straight to the commissario's office and was shocked to find sitting before him, with a newspaper-wrapped bundle in her hands, the very same person who constituted his principal piece of news.

Both Ricciardi and Maione had seen Teresa the day before;

she had opened the door, shown them inside, and served them tea. With her fine housekeeper's smock and her starched headpiece, she hadn't struck the trained eyes of the two investigators as any more remarkable than the furnishings and ornaments in the front hall. But now, even though she was dressed in a nondescript fashion, she took on a certain personality.

After saluting, Maione signaled to the commissario that he wanted to speak to him. Ricciardi excused himself and left the room with the brigadier.

"Commissa', yesterday I had a long chat with the doorman of the palazzo, and after a beer or two—which I paid for out of my own pocket, of course—he coughed up a lot of interesting information. First of all," he began, counting off the points on his fingers, taking hold of the fingertips one by one with his other hand, "the good signora, so simple and modest, is having herself a nice little affair with a stage actor. Everyone knows about it, and according to the doorman, so does the professor, but he pretends to look the other way." At this point, the limber fingers of his right hand released their grip to make the twin horns of the cuckold, Italian shorthand for a man whose wife is cheating on him. "Next, he told me that he'd heard from the cook that the signora wouldn't do a thing, not a single blessed thing, without the permission of the old fortuneteller—that is, Calise. The chauffeur would have to drive her there as many as three times a day, until she started taking her own vehicle, a red sports car, a brand new Alfa Romeo Brianza, bright and beautiful as the sun. It seems that in the last few days before the Calise was murdered, there was even a fight between them; nobody could understand what they were saying, but they were shouting, and people could hear them out in the street. Last of all, the most interesting piece of news, is what I heard about the signorina sitting in the other room, who's been their maid for the past two years. You want to know what it is?"

Ricciardi shook his head.

"Well, in your opinion, which is it: do I want to know or don't I?"

Maione put on a false air of contrition.

"Then I'll get right to it, Commissa'. The signorina who's sitting in your office has been to see Calise every week for a long time now. She showed the doorman a sheet of paper with that address, along with the name; he was the one who told her which streetcar to take the first time she went."

Ricciardi and Maione went back into the office. Teresa, with the package clutched to her chest, was waiting for them, staring into space. The commissario addressed her politely.

"Tell me, Signorina, what can we do for you?"

The woman spoke in a low voice, little more than a murmur.

"My name is Teresa Scognamiglio, Commissa'. The dead woman was my aunt, my mother's older sister, may her soul rest in peace. I gave it a lot of thought, before coming to see you; I care about my job and I don't want to be sent back to my village in the countryside. And I know that after coming here today I'll never be able to go back to work there. But I couldn't keep quiet. My aunt's spirit in the other world wouldn't leave me alone, it was making me crazy just like my grandmother, God rest her soul."

Her eyes had filled with tears, which began streaking down her cheeks. Ricciardi and Maione exchanged a glance. The brigadier comforted her in a fatherly tone.

"Signorina, tell us what you have to say. We're all ears."

In response, Teresa simply set the newspaper bundle on her lap and started unwrapping it. She pulled out a pair of elegant men's shoes with the soles encrusted and stained. She set them on Ricciardi's desk, side by side, perfectly aligned. Then she looked up.

"I know who it was. I know who killed my aunt."

LII

Teresa's words froze them both in place. The two policemen looked at each other, then they looked at the shoes, and then Teresa. Ricciardi decided to break the spell.

"And . . . ? Who was it?"

In the room, silence. Outside, a truck drove across the piazza, with a festive series of loud, irregular bangs. Maione and Ricciardi knew that Teresa was perched on the edge of the irrevocable. Once she uttered that name, she'd never be able to go back, and nothing would be the way it had been before. She drew a deep breath.

"It was my employer. Ruggero Serra di Arpaja. The professor."

And she began to tell her story.

It all started more than a year ago. Teresa had just arrived from her country village, with a pressboard suitcase full of things that, over time, she'd thrown out, as the family with which she'd found employment "civilized" her, as the signora had put it. She had the right to take the afternoon off once every fifteen days, but for the first few months of her new job she chose to forego it; she didn't want to run the risk of being thought a *lavativa*, a layabout, the worst crime a maid could be accused of.

The first time she left the palazzo, she went to the address that she had for her Aunt Carmela. Her aunt had stood in at her baptism as her godmother, and the family had considered her a disgrace, then a source of pride, and finally a living legend. Carmela had run away from home at a very young age to seek her fortune; she alone had rebelled against the iron law of grueling work and submission that had long subjugated the women of the village. Her name could only be spoken in a whisper, and horrible tales were told about her.

When she finally came face-to-face with that ancient, pain-racked woman, Teresa was at first disappointed, but then, as she sat and listened to her over a cup of hot milk, she discovered that the tales of her village's rustic mythology had actually understated the case. Her aunt had managed to amass a genuine fortune, and what's more, she had done it by reading tarot cards! The kind of thing that back home was the province of quacks and mountebanks at the monthly cattle fair.

And just how had she pulled it off? By exploiting the gullibility of the well-to-do, people like her employers. To her, whose image of the couple she worked for verged on celestial, it seemed unbelievable: those illustrious gentlemen and ladies who held the world in the palms of their hands and did with it as they pleased, who possessed automobiles, fine clothing, jewelry, and even had electric lighting; well then, even they were putty in the hands of the fortuneteller, like so many marionettes made to dance by a puppeteer.

Over the course of that unforgettable afternoon, Carmela revealed the entire organization to her niece, including the help she received from Nunzia, the mother of the little mentally handicapped girl who was sitting there listening, with a vacant smile on her face and a streamer of drool hanging from her mouth. Together they laughed at the stupidity of those people, delivering Carmela's fortune right to her doorstep.

At the end of that afternoon, after telling her aunt about the lives of the Serra di Arpaja family, Teresa bid her aunt good-bye and left with a feeling of contentment, promising to come see her again soon.

That same evening, while she was waiting for the streetcar

that would take her back to the palazzo, and during the rest of the week that followed, an idea took shape in Teresa's mind, eventually transforming itself into a full-fledged plan.

"Putting the Serra di Arpaja family in contact with Carmela Calise," said Ricciardi.

"Yes sir, that's exactly right," Teresa confirmed.

The girl was perceptive and clever, and possessed the gift of being able to go unnoticed, to fade perfectly into the background. By virtue of this talent, she soon managed to penetrate the psychology of the couple she worked for, quickly becoming aware of their incompatibility. The man was old and self-absorbed; the woman was beautiful and emotionally starved.

"At a certain age," she told the two policemen, "a woman must have children, just like a cow. Otherwise, she goes crazy."

"The ideal victims of the award-winning enterprise of Calise and Petrone," Maione put in.

"Yes," Teresa admitted. But that time, for some reason unknown to Teresa, Calise didn't want Petrone involved. She asked the girl to keep her informed of just one thing: when the signora was planning to go to the theater, and which theater she would be going to. That was easy; Emma frequented every theater in town with her girlfriends, and she never missed a show.

And so, one week after another, Teresa gave Carmela the information and Carmela gave Teresa a little money. Teresa sent the money home so she could buy a farm where she could live like a noblewoman when she returned to her village.

Very soon Emma started paying calls on Carmela. The trap had snapped shut. Teresa had no idea how her aunt had pulled it off.

The old woman became an obsession for the signora. She went to see her two or three times a day. The chauffeur complained about having to drive the enormous black automobile through the *vicoli* of the Sanità; then she'd started going there on her own, in her new red convertible. She was so euphoric that she even ventured to talk to Teresa about it, at night, as she was having the maid brush her hair before bed.

Still, there were certain aspects of the operation that the girl had never quite been able to understand: the money, for one. Emma had told her that Carmela refused to take money, and she'd only been able to give a tip now and again to the porter woman. In the signora's opinion, this was clear evidence of the fortune-teller's honesty; she was an honest-to-God missionary. And yet, Teresa was regularly paid the amount they'd agreed upon. So what was her aunt getting out of it? Teresa couldn't puzzle that one out. Nor could she understand why Emma had recently gone from a state of euphoria to one of terrible depression. She described Emma's bedroom for them: filthy, disorderly. She told them about the wine and the vomit.

It had been two weeks since she'd heard, through the door, a violent argument between man and wife; it had been occasioned by her return home at dawn, something that had been happening more and more frequently. That time the professor had been waiting for her, wide awake, sitting in the front hall, and he'd given his wife an open-palm slap in the face. Emma's only response was to spit in his face, just like they did back in her village, Teresa told them. Then she had fled to her bedroom. Ruggero had chased her, and managed to get inside and shut the door behind him.

This was followed by a heated dispute, in the course of which he had forbidden his wife from paying a call on "that old witch" ever again, or else "he'd see to shutting that woman's sewer of a mouth once and for all." Emma replied that "he wasn't a real man" and therefore he'd "be too feeble even to knock on her door." She insulted him for his lack of virility, and her husband fled in tears, passing right by the girl without noticing her. Just as he usually did.

As soon as she could, she'd gone over to warn her aunt; but she had told Teresa not to worry, a smile on her face. She had the situation under control, she'd said. Then, terrified that she might lose her job, Teresa stopped going to see her. Until Emma, her face ravaged by tears, told her she'd learned about the murder from the newspaper.

"But the day before that, Commissa', the professor came home very late at night; it was practically morning. He looked like a lunatic, his hair was standing straight up, he was shaking and sobbing. He was filthy and disheveled, he who was usually as well groomed as a mannequin on Via Toledo. He hurried to his bedroom and shut the door behind him. It was a long time before he came out. When I went in to clean the room, this is what I found," and she pointed to the shoes, neatly lined up on Ricciardi's desk. "If you ask me, that's blood that they're covered in. My aunt's blood. Blood of my blood."

Ricciardi kept his green eyes fixed on the now silent girl's face; she was as calm and still as if she'd just finished reciting a rosary. Then she came to with a start, as though waking up from a dream. He looked at Maione, who was standing beside him, mouth agape.

The brigadier looked back at him.

"Now, who's going to tell Dottor Garzo?"

LIII

It was Ricciardi who told Garzo, the minute Teresa left. She'd been afraid to return home and share a roof with the murderer. But the commissario and Maione made it clear to her that there was no danger until formal charges were filed; in fact if anything, her absence would put the professor on his guard, giving him time to prepare an alibi. Once this whole affair was over, Teresa could take possession of Carmela's apartment or, as an alternative, return to her village.

Maione and Ricciardi went to report to their superior officer, not without a hint of malevolent satisfaction as they savored the thought of the look on the deputy chief of police's face.

On some level, his reaction came as a disappointment. Once they were done relating Teresa's story, and after the professor's shoes had been exhibited by Maione as if he were displaying the ampoule containing the miraculous blood of San Gennaro, Garzo laid his head back on the immaculate head cloth that covered the top of his armchair and shut his eyes. He seemed to be asleep, but there was a worrisome pink spot on his neck, under his now bloodless face.

After a minute or so, he opened his eyes and smiled.

"That doesn't mean it was him."

"What do you mean, it might not have been him, Dotto'? Even though the housemaid told us all the hows and whys and wherefores, and even brought in his bloodstained shoes?"

"Maione, calm down and listen to what I have to say." And, counting off the points on his fingers: "The girl never actually saw the professor kill Calise; nor did she hear him explicitly state his intention to murder her. We also have no confession. Instead, we have an alibi: the Serras were at dinner with none other than His Excellency the Prefect of Naples that night. Last of all, a pair of muddy shoes are certainly not proof of murder. For all we know, that could be the blood of a dead dog, that is, if it's blood at all."

Ricciardi nodded.

"Fair enough, Dottore. You have a point. But you do have to admit that Serra had both the motive, which we can easily verify with testimonies from the other servants, and the opportunity, given that according to Doctor Modo, Calise was killed after 10:00 P.M., by which time the dinner at the prefect's house would have long been over. Moreover, his evasiveness during the interview . . ."

Garzo snorted in annoyance.

"Evasiveness is subject to your interpretation, Ricciardi. Let's not forget that we're talking about a person unaccustomed to being questioned like any common criminal. I don't see any weak spots in the professor's position with respect to Iodice's. On the one hand, we have the accusations of a servant and an angry outburst, while on the other we have a debt that Iodice had been unable to pay and a suicide that is tantamount to a confession. Are you so sure that a court of law would find against Serra?"

Maione let out a muffled roar, like a caged lion. Ricciardi, in contrast, silently went over Garzo's reasoning, which had a certain logic. He needed time. Deep down, he felt sure that given a choice between Iodice and Serra di Arpaja, the latter was more likely to have been the killer; but the way things stood right now, it was no contest.

"Well then, Dottore, how do you intend to proceed?"

Just as the commissario had expected, Garzo's face went pale again.

"Me? What do I have to do with it? You're in charge of the

investigation, aren't you? Why don't you tell me what it is you intend to do."

Checkmate, thought Ricciardi.

"Right, Dottore. Right. Well then, I think that we should go on investigating: check out what Teresa Scognamiglio told us, flesh out the information we already have. Just a few more days, to get a better idea of what happened, and to make sure headquarters is safe from this wretched individual."

Garzo drummed his fingers briefly on the desktop.

"Fine, Ricciardi. I'll give you a day, or actually two, since it's still early morning. But I want charges brought by tomorrow night. The press has started putting pressure on the chief of police, who, as you know, is allergic to pressure."

Ricciardi nodded and left the room, followed by a fuming Maione.

Filomena closed the shutters over the only window in the *basso* on Vico del Fico; a weak light filtered in through the slit over the door. She sat down at the table, smiled at the two people sitting with her, and with a firm hand and slow gestures, she removed her bandages.

Gaetano took a sudden sharp breath and moaned softly, as tears began streaking down his face. Rituccia, her pallor glowing in the darkness, watched calmly, her expression unchanged.

Filomena ran her fingertips over the scar, following its sharp, raised contours. She reached out for the old shard of mirror that she kept for brushing her hair. She looked at her reflection for a long time. Then she laid the mirror down and walked over to her son to give him a kiss. Gaetano took her face in his hands and started to sob.

Rituccia stood up, walked over to the woman, and solemnly kissed her on the slash across her face.

Maione was pacing back and forth in Ricciardi's office, railing against Garzo, while Ricciardi stood silently in front of the window.

"Oh now, did you hear that idiot? We take him for a fool, and just when I think he's fallen asleep, he takes us by surprise and out he comes with all this legal mumbo jumbo, like he's the lawyer's lawyer! I wouldn't believe it if I hadn't seen it myself! And of course, since the professor from Via Santa Lucia is rich, he must be innocent, while poor Iodice, God rest his soul, filthy, weaselly, lower-class *pizzaiolo* without two pennies to rub together, must surely be guilty! And after we got the whole story from Teresa Scognamiglio, who heard everything with her own ears!"

Ricciardi spoke without lifting his gaze from the piazza below.

"As much of a fool as you like, and certainly convinced that it was poor Iodice who did it. Still, what he said wasn't so stupid. The truth is that all we have are clues, in both cases. Both of them had a good motive for murdering Calise. Both of them had an opportunity to murder her. Both of them saw her dead: as we know from Serra di Arpaja's shoes and Iodice's promissory note. But what we don't know for sure is which one of them watched her die."

Maione stopped. He was unwilling to surrender to the evidence of the facts.

"Yes, but Serra can defend himself and Iodice can't, Commissa'. So before we lay the blame on the dead man, we should make sure that the living one is innocent. Am I right?"

Ricciardi stood in silence for a few seconds. He was looking out the window.

"Have you ever thought, Maione, about all the things that you can see out a window? You can see life itself. You can see death. You can see, but you can't do anything about it. So who is he, the man who watches? You know who he is?"

Maione waited, listening. He knew it didn't fall to him to reply.

"The man who watches is the man who isn't living. He can only watch other people's lives go by; he can only live through them. Someone who watches is someone who just can't handle it, who's given up on living."

Maione listened to him. And he understood that Ricciardi was no longer talking about Calise, Garzo, Iodice, or Serra di Arpaja. He was talking about himself.

Even though the brigadier lacked a well-developed sensibility, he did realize that the mood of the commissario, who was already melancholy by nature, had taken a plunge after that interview two days earlier with a witness, a certain Enrica Colombo. And now that he thought about it, this witness resided on Via Santa Teresa, right where Ricciardi lived. Perhaps they knew each other, which would certainly go a long way toward explaining the bizarre direction the interview had taken, the interview that he himself had been forced to conduct because the man who ought by rights to have asked the questions sat in silence. He sat silently and watched.

The brigadier had grown up on the street, and he knew when it was a good idea to keep quiet. There was nothing he could say; he could only sympathize with his superior officer and friend from a distance.

LIV

At the usual small café table at the Gran Caffè Gambrinus, Ricciardi sat waiting.

Garzo hadn't given him much time, far too little in fact, forcing him to gamble somewhat recklessly. Ricciardi liked to plan things out, leaving as little as possible to chance. He know how important strategy was in his line of work. But the time he had now was terribly short.

And so he'd telephoned the Serra di Arpaja residence. It was a desperate, flailing move, a long shot.

But however rarely it happens, even long shots hit their targets every now and then: Teresa herself had answered, and she had told him that yes, the signora was at home, she'd see if the signora was available. He could be sure that the girl wouldn't mention the phone call to Ruggero. And Emma had agreed to meet with him. Luck favors the bold.

Ricciardi, sitting at the café table, looked out through the plate glass window at the wheeled, hooved, and foot-borne traffic that marched over the cobblestones of Via Chiaia; springtime had staged a morning in which the light seemed to surge up from below, the sky was so blue that it hurt your eyes, and the women seemed to be dancing in time to a music that only they could hear. Men smiled and tipped their hats, soldiers walked two-by-two and blew kisses to girls who accelerated their gait, giggling under the brims of their little hats. Near a beggar stretched out on the sidewalk, Ricciardi glimpsed a child badly injured around his pelvis, the unmistakable mark of a carriage wheel: blood was gushing out of his mouth and the upper half of his body was curiously out of alignment with the lower half, as if he were reflected in a fun-house mirror or seen through wet glass. Outside the large plate glass window, Ricciardi could hear his voice, calling, *Il mio canillo, è fuiuto.* My little dog got away. Wearily, he wondered where the puppy had run off to and whether it had found a new master.

"Commissario Ricciardi, if I'm not mistaken."

The purring voice of Emma Serra di Arpaja summoned him back from the dark pit of his soul. He rose from his seat and pulled the other chair out from the table, turning it slightly in a courteous gesture.

He instantly saw the difference between the mousy, reserved person he had interviewed and the confident and brazen woman who was looking at him with amused curiosity. Ricciardi wondered whether it had been her husband's influence that had chastened Emma's personality, or whether she had just been playing a part for the benefit of the two policeman; in any case, he mused, the real Emma was the one standing before him.

He asked what she was having, and she told him a glass of white wine. In the morning, he thought. For himself he ordered the usual: an espresso and a sfogliatella pastry.

The woman laughed. A short, silvery laugh.

"Not worried about your weight, are you, Commissario? A mid-morning sfogliatella. Mio Dio!"

"And you're not worried about getting drunk, first thing in the morning?"

He said it with the full awareness of how rude and provocative he was being. He wanted to let her know in no uncertain terms that he couldn't be intimidated and to verify that the signora liked to tie one on, as Teresa had told him.

Emma reeled from the direct hit: she turned pale, then

blushed and started to her feet. Ricciardi didn't reach out to stop her.

"If you leave now, I'll feel free to disregard your pain."

The woman sat back down in her chair, wide-eyed.

"What pain? I'm in no pain."

Ricciardi shook his head.

"Signora, we both know that what you said yesterday was far from the truth; no one returns obsessively to the same place without a powerful motive. Powerful enough to give you the courage to take on the world; and yet yesterday you didn't take on anyone. You didn't fight; you parroted the lesson you'd been taught, and nothing more. I didn't fall for it, not even for a second. Even before I ask you for the truth, I'm going to ask you why you lied."

Emma looked at Ricciardi, shaking her head. Her hands were gripping the arms of her chair so hard that the skin on her knuckles turned white as wax.

"I . . . I wanted to understand why you'd come to see me. Me in particular. Dozens and dozens of people went to see Calise. I alone must have recommended her to twenty of my girlfriends. So why me, out of all of them?"

Ricciardi didn't want to tip his hand by telling her that hers was just one of the names marked down in the fortune-teller's notebook for that last day. Instead, he decided to go all in.

"Why are you covering for your husband, if you no longer love him?"

Emma opened her eyes wide; then she began to laugh. At first quietly, under her breath, with a look of surprise, and then louder and louder until she threw her head back, tears running down her cheeks. Ricciardi sat waiting, watching her, not saying a word. People sitting at other tables turned to look at them, wondering what on earth that gloomy-looking man had said to that lovely, elegant lady to make her laugh so hard. At last Emma regained her composure.

"Forgive me, Commissario. It's just too funny! My husband? Covering for my husband? That's the last thing I would do. My husband covers for himself; that's how he spends his life, covering for himself. And another thing: what would I be covering for? It's true, he told me what to say yesterday, how to dress, even what tone of voice to use. And what of that? He's a lawyer, one of the best there is. If I was covering anyone, it was myself, to ward off ridiculous suspicions. Not him."

Ricciardi decided that the time had come to spring his trap, and he lied without hesitation.

"All the same, Signora, we have every reason to believe that your husband was in Calise's apartment the night she died. Someone saw him there. Moreover, there were traces of blood on the soles of the shoes he was wearing."

Emma was dumbfounded.

"But wasn't it that *pizzaiolo* that the newspapers have been writing about? The one who killed himself? Why would my husband . . . no, Commissario . . . it's impossible. My husband lacks the courage; he's a very fearful man. He'd never be able to pull off anything of the sort, under any circumstances. He doesn't act. He thinks. He didn't even react when . . . He just doesn't take action, let me assure you."

This was no time to overlook her hesitations, Ricciardi decided.

"He didn't even react when . . . what? This is no time to be less than forthcoming, Signora. Don't make me think that you're concealing something serious, or I'll have no consideration for your well-being. Believe me."

Emma chewed on her lower lip. There was something in Ricciardi's tone of voice that scared her. She thought it over a while. Then she spoke.

"Even when I left him. For good. I wanted to run away, leave our home."

"And you told him this?"

"Yes, I told him. I spewed every ounce of disgust I feel for him right in his face. I told him how I loathed him and how I hated our loveless life together. He begged me not to leave him, and he was crying, an old man with tears in his eyes . . ."

Ricciardi studied the expression on the woman's face; she had flung open the door to her innermost thoughts. This was the moment to push.

"Did he try to change your mind? Did he threaten you? Did he threaten anyone else, say, Calise?"

Emma smiled sadly.

"No. Like I said, he lacks the courage. So when I saw him on his knees at my feet, sobbing convulsively, I just told him."

"Told him what?"

"The truth. That I'm pregnant."

LV

He'd found himself a spot in the shadows. Over time, and with experience, Maione had learned how to blend in. Not like Teresa Scognamiglio, who had a natural gift for escaping notice. He didn't have the build to pull it off, being big, tall, and hairy. Throw the uniform into the mix, and who would be capable of vanishing from sight entirely? Still, over the years, what with the stakeouts, the tailing and pursuit of suspects, he'd learned a thing or two in the way of technique.

The important thing was never to lose sight of the person, so you could stay out of their sight. Filomena walked with her eyes on the ground and never glanced at her reflection. He knew where she worked; she'd told him herself. Now he needed to determine whether Don Matteo De Rosa—the well-known fabric merchant who had inherited the shop from his father-in-law after marrying a woman widely considered to be the richest and ugliest in all of Naples—had really lost his head over Filomena like Bambinella had told him.

Taking refuge in the large entrance hall of an austere palazzo in Via Toledo, he waited for her to finish her shift and to be alone with that man; he wanted to see how he behaved. To get an idea. Just to get an idea. He wasn't obsessed with her, of course. But he didn't like gray areas.

He'd ruled out the *guappo*, Costanzo, immediately. In that city, policemen and camorristi—the Mafiosi of Naples—had learned each other's languages by dint of doing battle with one another. Maione knew that the face-slash carried a specific meaning; it was a mark of betrayal, adultery. No camorrista would hesitate to slash the face of his beloved if he learned that she had been unfaithful to him, but that certainly didn't apply to Don Luigi, who was happily married, and married, moreover, to the daughter of the local capo of the Spanish Quarter. If he'd done anything of the sort, it would have been tantamount to slitting his own throat.

Not him, then. So, who?

The shopkeeper, perhaps. From the limbo of the entrance hall, Maione watched him in the brightly lit store; he was diminutive, pudgy, and effeminate, leaping from one bolt of cloth to another, smiling at the women he served like a halfwit. That man didn't have the strength of body and mind to shave himself, much less slash a woman's face.

Maione waited patiently for the shop to close for lunchtime. Filomena said good-bye to De Rosa, who didn't even bother to look up from the cash register. The brigadier had the distinct impression, even from that distance, that her disfigurement made him uneasy.

Not the shopkeeper.

Then who?

Emma looked out the plate glass window, as if enchanted by the stream of pedestrians, automobiles, and horse-drawn carriages. Once again, the dead child informed Ricciardi that his puppy had run away. In the café, a buzz filled the air around them, while from the next room came the sound of a piano, evoking a May gone by, red roses and cherries.

The news of her pregnancy had opened new vistas to the commissario's eye. It was an irrevocable fact, the kind of thing that could drive men and women to commit unspeakable acts.

"Who else have you told?"

Emma smiled a melancholy smile.

"Just him. And Calise, of course, the second to last time I went to see her. For a change, I told her what fate had in store."

"Why did you tell her?"

"Because I needed her to tell me what to do. I . . . couldn't make any decisions, unless she gave me permission. It was a curse, pure madness. You're welcome to laugh all you like, Commissario, but she had become an obsession for me. I tried to resist the impulse; I told myself that I could do without her. Then an invisible hand would push me out of the house and I'd find myself there, in that foul-smelling waterfront, begging for her to tell me what to do, invoking her command over me. I no longer knew how to live for myself. Or maybe it's just that I've never lived: first my mother, then my husband, and now the fortune-teller."

Ricciardi listened to her every word, his attention riveted.

"And what did she say, when you told her you were pregnant?"

Emma ran her fingers nervously through her hair.

"She asked me who the father was. I was baffled: how could she not know? She, who knew everything about everyone? She knew that I haven't let my husband lay a finger on me for a long time. That there's only one man on earth I love. The man that she denied me."

The commissario leaned forward.

"Denied you?"

Emma began crying as she spoke.

"I met this man at the same time I met Calise. And even though she'd never even laid eyes on him, she urged me day after day to get to know him, to appreciate him, to fall in love with him. And our love grew until it had filled up my whole life. Have you ever been in love, Commissario?"

In his mind, Ricciardi glimpsed a pair of closed shutters, and he felt a fist clutch at his heart with a stab of pain. He blinked, just once.

"Go on."

"I was going to run away with him. Everything was ready: money, a life together, everything. I'm a wealthy woman, Commissario. Independently of my husband. I'd made the arrangements, and then I got the news that I was pregnant. What joy! A child! And I'd stopped hoping for anything like that. A love child, bound to be as beautiful as the father. I rushed to see Calise, I wanted her to be the first to know. But instead . . ."

"But instead?"

"But instead the cards were unequivocal: I'd never see him again. As always, in keeping with her fundamental rule, I couldn't breathe a word of what she told me to another soul, ever, as long as I lived. If I did, terrible misfortunes would rain down on me, him, and the baby. I had her read my cards twice, a third time, ten times. I begged her, I cursed her, I threatened her. It was no good. She said that the cards couldn't be controlled; it was fate, a decision that came from the souls of the dead."

Instinctively, Ricciardi looked out the window for the child who was stubbornly searching for his runaway puppy. He would have liked to tell her that the souls of the dead don't decide a blessed thing. All they do is suffer through every minute they outlive their bodies.

"What about you?"

"I'm not afraid for myself, Commissario. I'd rather die than go back to live that empty life. And a single instant with him would have been worth all the suffering. He could have made his own decision. And after all, he had always told me that he doesn't believe in fate. But the child didn't ask me to be born. I'd never thought about having a child; I thought I just wasn't born to be a mother. But now that I have it inside me," and she held her belly tight with one hand, briefly, as if to make contact, "it becomes more important every day. It's mine, Commissario. Nothing has ever been mine in quite this way."

Ricciardi nodded.

"So then, what did you do?"

"I did what I had to, Commissario. I did what Calise told me to do."

LVI

When Ricciardi got back to police headquarters, he was still confused.

Emma's revelations had settled some questions, but they'd stirred up others. A new figure had appeared on the scene: her lover. Now it was easier to explain the involvement of the distinguished professor, seeing as his reputation ultimately depended on what Calise told his wife.

Even Emma had earned herself a place on the list of possible murderers: her absolute dependency, the limitations placed on her freedom could both be excellent motives for murder, even if the brutality and the violence both seemed to point to a man rather than a woman. But he'd seen them before, too many of them in fact: merciless killings at the hands of a woman.

He continued to be of the opinion that the professor was the most likely intended recipient of Calise's proverb, that obscure malediction concerning the recompense that fate would surely visit upon her killer. In his view, Iodice was innocent; but that didn't mean he could prove it. What's more, he'd learned at his own expense how the Deed tended to steer one away from the truth far more often than it led one to the solution. On the verge of death, people dig up a surprising array of emotions.

Maione joined him, a little short of breath, begging his pardon in a fluster for not having been in the office when he returned. Ricciardi was worried about him, as he had been increasingly as of late. But if Maione didn't ask him for advice, he certainly couldn't barge into his affairs. And so he limited himself to reporting on his meeting with Emma.

"Yes, Commissa', I can see what the professor's problem was," and he made the sign of the cuckold's horns with extended pinky and forefinger, "losing his wife and his reputation in a single blow. But if Calise had forced Emma Serra to break things off with her lover, then why would the professor kill her? After all, they both wanted the same thing, didn't they?"

Ricciardi swept his rebellious bangs out of his eyes.

"Not necessarily. Maybe Ruggero Serra paid Calise to give that response, but when it came time to pay up, they quarreled and he murdered her. It could also be that he didn't learn of Emma's intention not to leave him until after he'd already killed Calise. Or that he simply wanted to take revenge on the old woman for having pushed his wife into her lover's arms. Or perhaps it was Emma who did it, because she wanted to free herself from her state of subjugation to the fortune-teller. It could be anything. Or the opposite of anything."

Maione swung his arms open wide in bafflement.

"So what do we do now, Commissa'? We can't just let the blame be laid on poor Iodice, can we? And we don't have much time, not even a whole day. What's the next step?"

Ricciardi stared pensively at the paperweight made from a fragment of mortar shell sitting on his desk.

"Listen, do you happen to have the name of Signora Serra's lover? I think he's an actor, right? A stage actor."

"Yes, exactly, that's what the Serras' doorman told me. I don't know the name, but I can find out. Everyone knows about it."

Ricciardi nodded.

"Fine, and be quick about it. If you ask me, we're going to the theater tonight."

Filomena was selecting pea pods from the vegetable man's pushcart in the Pignasecca marketplace. It was no simple matter: if they were too hard, they could be unripe and not add enough flavor to the soup, while the soft ones might be shriveled and lacking in nutrition.

She was rediscovering the pleasure of cooking dinner; Gaetano ate like a wolf, ravenously consuming whatever she set before him. Rituccia, who had come to stay at their house, never touched her food. But these days, Filomena thought with an inward smile, someone else came around at dinnertime; someone who clearly showed his pleasure at receiving a woman's attentions.

And she still felt like a woman; in fact, she felt like a woman for the first time since her husband died. She thought of him as a sort of gift, given in exchange for the slash on her face; the loss of the beauty that had been her cross to bear, in exchange for the warm eyes of a man who looked inside her instead of stopping at the surface. In a way she'd never experienced. Smiling, Filomena wondered what kind of fruit Raffaele liked best.

Lucia hadn't gotten out of bed. She hadn't even opened the shutters. She'd just lain there, stretched out on her back, staring at the ceiling.

The children didn't know what to think; they walked back and forth and looked in from the doorway with worried faces, to make sure that she wasn't ill. After a while, the littlest girl asked: "Mamma, are you all right?" She told her yes with a tense smile. But was she all right? That she couldn't say.

She missed Luca, of course. But she missed her husband, too, she missed him so much that she felt intense pain, a physical pain, in her chest, a pain that left her breathless. And she missed her other children, watching them from the other side of the glass wall she'd built around herself over the years, unable to touch them. She even missed herself: Lucia, the woman who laughed, sang, and made love, looking life right in the eye. She felt as though she were already dead, as if she were a ghost observing the world from the beyond.

She would have liked to sleep and dream of Luca, hear him laughing, in that completely unique way of his, telling her: "Mamma, c'mon, get up and take your life into your own hands, like you've always done. You're still the prettiest girl in the neighborhood, you're still my best girl; are you trying to put me to shame?" Instead, her sleep was fitful, sorrowful, and dreamless, and she woke up wearier than she was when she went to sleep.

From the balcony she could hear street noises, the songs of the washerwomen, vendors hawking their wares. Through the closed shutters she could feel the light gusting push of new spring air, heavy with the perfumes of the farmlands of Vomero. Springtime, she thought. Another springtime.

Lucia got up from the bed and threw the shutters open wide. The light hurt her eyes. She looked down, four stories high. Solid, ancient stone; the marks of a century of horses' hooves.

She saw the daughter of Assuntina, wife of Carmine the carter, go by hand-in-hand with a dark-skinned lad wearing a brown cap. Madonna, she thought. It seems like just yesterday that that girl was born, and her mamma was selling sulphur mineral water on the street with the child hanging from her neck; and now there she is strolling with a boy, and tomorrow she'll be married, and before you know it she'll have children of her own.

And Lucia Maione decided that she was alive after all. She turned around and went back inside, because her blood, and the blood of her blood, was still flowing.

And with that another minor, unnoticed miracle of the springtime of nineteen thirty-one was complete.

LVII

The pizza from the pushcart that passed through Piazza Municipio made him think of Iodice and his dream. Ricciardi's solitary lunch generally featured this solution as an alternative to his sfogliatella pastry and espresso, and he gobbled it down, thinking about other things. Work, Garzo, his current case. Enrica.

But this time, as he watched the agile hands of the itinerant pizza chef, the commissario tried to imagine the suicide's thoughts and words, when, not yet a prisoner to his dream, he wandered carefree and happy through the streets of the city. The doctor was right: there is a precise moment in which a person decides his own death. That moment can always be avoided. Fate doesn't preordain; it has no will of its own. There's no such thing as fate.

The piping hot mouthful slithered down into his belly, silencing its savage clamoring for more. Pizza was good, all right. Poor Iodice, his poor children, his poor wife. And his poor mother, who, judging by the proverb she'd uttered as she'd left his office—a proverb that had opened new avenues of investigation—really believed in fate.

He strolled along Via Toledo for a ways. The street's two very different faces were on view: the large, venerable old palazzi with their high windows and broad balconies, the austere entrances guarded by liveried doormen. Illustrious names and heraldic crests; centuries of history having passed by in the shadows of those walls, year after year. Palazzo Della Porta,

Palazzo Zevallos Stigliano, Palazzo Cavalcanti, Palazzo Capece Galeota: severe, majestic edifices, constituting the city's formal drawing room. Behind them swarmed the anthill of the Spanish Quarter, nameless *vicoli* bubbling over with passions and crime: the dark narrow lanes that the Fascist regime wanted to erase through reclamation projects, as if a new piazza and a façade here and there could change people's souls.

Children were getting out of school, a few factory workers and laborers and the city's credentialed professionals were heading home. Nearly all the shops were closed; lunchtime was about to come to an end. The air was steeped in springtime.

Ricciardi caught a gamy whiff of love. Calise worked with money and emotions, the roots underlying every crime. But this time he could feel it: love was the killer.

As he walked, he skirted the construction sites, empty at this hour. The heavy white blocks used in the new constructions, the rickety, precarious wooden scaffoldings. Standing vigil, by now little more than fading shadows, were two dead men, killed in accidents a few months earlier. Distractedly, Ricciardi noticed a new one: *Rachele, my Rachele, I'm coming to join you, they pushed me to join you.* Sighing, he did his best not to dwell on those words, knowing he'd hear them again many times. Who was Rachele? A wife? A sister? And that poor soul in need of her company? Had he fallen or had he jumped? Who could say? And what did it matter now?

A short distance farther on, he saw a couple coming toward him, the man hobbling along on a pair of crutches, his left leg bandaged from knee to foot. He suddenly recognized Ridolfi, the unhappy widower of the woman who had set herself on fire and loyal client of Calise. He was talking excitedly with an insignificant woman who looked to be about his same age, her head lowered beneath a small hat trimmed with a veil.

Before the man's eyes met his, Ricciardi had a chance to overhear: "I looked there too, I tell you. Who knows where she put them, damn her. May she burn in hell the way she burned to death."

His voice was throbbing with rage. When he saw Ricciardi, his face transformed itself into the usual mask of grief demanding compassion; with a comical, awkward gesture, he lurched to a precarious halt, balancing on a single crutch, and removed his hat.

The commissario, offering no response to this greeting other than an expressionless gaze, thought to himself that a crutch was as good a murder weapon as any; and if you could stroll along Via Toledo with a sprained ankle, then you could also get to an apartment in the Sanità.

Still, despicable hypocrite though he was, even Professor Ridolfi needed a motive to commit a murder.

He turned around and retraced his steps; time was short and there was still a great deal of work to be done.

Maione was waiting for the commissario just outside of his office door.

"Commissario, buona sera. Have you eaten? The usual pizza, eh? Lucky you, you must have a cast-iron stomach. If I eat a fried pizza, I have to go straight to the hospital to see Doctor Modo. So I have that name. This city is just incredible; a person does something good, like, I don't know, catching a dangerous criminal, and nobody ever finds out about it; but sleep with a married woman and pretty soon the newspaper boys are shouting it out on the street. Anyway, the man's name is Attilio Romor, and they say he's a good-looking young man. He has a part in a play by that famous guy, what's his name . . . well, you know who I mean, right around here, at the Teatro dei Fiorentini. The show starts at eight. It'll be easy for us to get there, so you tell me. And just in the nick of time: I hear that tomorrow is the last show before the troupe heads for Rome."

Ricciardi thought it over.

"The last show. Tomorrow. Here's what we'll do: let's meet at the theater at eight o'clock. Now let's go home and get some rest; it's going to be a late night."

But Maione didn't go home. He had another place to visit, and he was in a hurry: he needed to clear something up, once and for all.

In his strong, simple heart, there was no room for messiness. He had spent his whole life dealing with direct and unequivocal feelings and emotions; he was incapable of coping with doubt.

The sun had just set when he arrived at Vico del Fico. Filomena was surprised to see him, but she didn't hold back a happy smile. She hastily pulled the shawl up over her face to hide her scar; she'd removed the bandages.

"Raffaele, what a surprise. I didn't think you'd be here so early. I wanted to make you something to eat."

Maione waved his hand, as if telling her not to bother.

"No, Filome', don't go to any trouble on my account. If you don't mind, I was hoping to have a little talk with you. Can we go inside?"

A shadow of worry flitted over the woman's beautiful face; Maione's expression was different from the one she was accustomed to. He looked grim, determined, as if he were struggling with some mute sorrow or being tormented by a thought.

In that ground floor room, steeped in darkness as always, sat Rituccia, intently shelling peas at the table. Maione observed her serene, distant expression. A little old lady who had just turned twelve.

Filomena told her that they wanted to talk privately. The girl nodded a silent good-bye and left the room.

"She's a good girl, but unfortunate. She's suffered so, first losing her mamma, and now her father. Gaetano and I have decided to keep her here with us, at least until her mother's relatives turn up. So far, we haven't seen anyone. Shall I make you an ersatz coffee? It'll just take me a couple of minutes."

Maione sat down, setting his cap down on the table in front of him.

"No, Filome', don't worry about it. Sit down here for a second. I need to talk to you."

The woman took a seat, drying her hands on her apron. In her deep dark eyes there glittered a light of concern and apprehension. As she sat down, she removed the shawl from her head. Maione smiled at her.

"This place, this home, and you, have done something important for me in these last few days. Knowing that you're here, knowing the road to come here, have given me back the desire to get to the end of the day. You've become a good, dear friend to me. You smile at me, and I'm proud to make you smile. But Filome', I'm a policeman. It's not just a matter of the uniform; that's just a shell, a box. I'm a policeman deep down. I can't live with the thought that something's been left unresolved; and also with the thought that you might be in danger. Whoever committed this . . . crime," and here he waved vaguely in the direction of her face, "could come back with even worse intentions."

Filomena gently shook her head, smiling.

"You see, Raffaele, you're something new for me, in my life. You see me for who I am. I uncovered my face, with the wound showing, and you never so much as glanced at it. No one looks at me the way they used to. Not even my son. But you look me in the eye without looking away. We're friends, you said; so why can't we just pretend we met under different circumstances, not these?"

Now it was Maione's turn to shake his head.

"No, Filomena. Between friends, people who have come to care about each other, people who talk and are happy to see each other, things cannot be left unsaid. I have to know, Filome'. With this shadow between us, there can be no friendship."

Tears welled up in Filomena's eyes. She glimpsed a determination in Maione's face that she'd never seen in him before.

Outside in the *vicolo*, the children were playing with a bundle of rags that was serving as a makeshift soccer ball. A woman called her son for dinner. Over the fire, the pot was coming to a boil.

The woman lifted her hand to the scar on her face and traced its contour, with a gesture that was becoming habitual.

"All right, Raffaele. I don't want to lose your friendship, and I want to be able to talk to my friend. But this thing doesn't leave this house, the place where it happened. Do I have your word on that?"

Maione nodded. Filomena hadn't once shifted her gaze away from his eyes.

"It was my son."

LVIII

Tata Rosa was surprised to see him home so early. Out in the street, the last rays of sunlight were still illuminating the highest stories of the apartment buildings. She had imperiously demanded to check his temperature, laying her calloused hand across his forehead.

Ricciardi wasted no time arguing; he knew from his own sad experience that Tata Rosa was unstoppable. He explained that he felt just fine but had come home early to rest since he'd be out late that night for work. He thus managed to sidestep the usual jeremiad on woolen undershirts and the perils of weather during the changing of the seasons, but not an egg frittata with macaroni left over from last night's dinner.

Once he had finished his snack, already bracing himself for the first burning stabs of stomach pain, he went to his window. In the Colombo apartment—he now knew the last name of the family across the way—preparations were underway for dinner. He saw Enrica go by. He was relieved to see that she looked healthy, but at the same time, he was disheartened by her expression, which was sad, preoccupied.

If only he could, he would tell her how important it was to him to be able to watch her movements, day after day, to imagine the words he couldn't hear, her serene, left-handed motions. If he could, he would have erased their awkward meeting at police headquarters. It never occurred to him that Enrica's state of mind might be roughly analogous to his own.

In that reflected life, he'd learned how to live, he who was a prisoner of his own curse.

He remembered that about a year ago, on the floor above the one where Enrica's family lived, something terrible had happened: a young bride, abandoned by her husband, had hanged herself. Lost love, shame, humiliation: it was hard to imagine the hell to which she'd been condemned. The same home that had seen her arrive overjoyed, carried over the threshold in the arms of one man, saw her leave in the arms of four, asleep now and forever. Since then, the shutters had been shut tight.

In the two months until the ghost vanished, Ricciardi watched the same double vignette every night: on the floor below, the peaceful, smiling warmth of a large family celebrating the life of an ordinary day; on the floor above, in the black empty eye socket of an unlighted window, the swaying corpse of the dead bride. The two faces of love: the two extremes of the same emotion.

And while his sweet Enrica went on with her left-handed embroidering, her head tilted over her right shoulder, in the cone of soft light from the table lamp, the dead woman—her neck unnaturally elongated from the rope, her eyes bugging out, her swollen tongue lolling out her open mouth—cursed the unfaithful bastard who had killed her without laying a finger on her.

His arms crossed, hidden from her sight by the fading light of sunset, the commissario mused that a man who bore the perennially bleeding wound of the deaths of others had no right to dream of a life like other people's; like the life he could see out his window. The man who watches may not be able to live, but he can still try to set things right.

'O Padreterno nun è mercante ca pava 'o sabbato, Iodice's mother and Carmela Calise had both said. God Almighty's not a shopkeeper who pays His debts on Saturday. But sooner or later, He pays them.

Reluctantly, he pulled himself away from the window and grabbed his jacket.

The muffled noises from the *vicolo* filtered in through the dim light of the *basso*. The words that Filomena had just uttered had landed between them like a live bomb, but the woman's calm, straightforward tone of voice had made it clear to Maione that this was a statement of fact, not an accusation.

"But why? Your son, Gaetano . . . why would he do such a thing?"

Filomena smiled, and in that moment she resembled a Madonna painted by Raphael. Her gentle voice was that of a woman who was finally at peace.

"I grew up on a farm in Vomero. We were a big family, poor but happy, even if we didn't really know it. Life on a farm is hard work, at every hour of the day and night. If you don't work, you don't eat, and if you don't eat, you die. Everything's simple. But nothing's ever easy.

"Once, when I was a little girl, maybe seven, maybe eight, our hens started going missing. We'd find feathers, blood. We never heard a sound. Could be a fox, maybe a weasel, my father said.

"He set out a trap, one of those wire traps that snap tight to capture the animal. The next morning we found a small paw dangling from the wire. Just the paw: coal black. You could see the gnaw marks of sharp teeth and there was blood all over the ground. That fox had chewed it off, little by little, without crying out. We slept right next to the henhouse, and we hadn't heard a thing.

"My father explained to me what had happened, Raffae': that animal, that fox, had been forced to make a choice. Either live without that paw or be caught. And it made that choice.

"I've lived my whole life with my paw in a trap, Raffae'. And I never realized that I had the ability to choose freedom.

Even when my husband was alive, the minute I was alone someone would approach me, using their hands or using their words. That's no way to live, believe me. It's no way to live.

"And for all the time we've been alone, Gaetano and I, things have been intolerable: my boss was threatening to fire me, another miserable wretch threatened to take it out on the boy.

"We talked it over again and again; we couldn't come up with a solution. Then, one evening, Gaetano came in, hand in hand with Rituccia, the girl you saw, and said to me: 'Mamma, maybe we've thought of something.' And while we were talking I remembered that little black paw dangling from the henhouse door and my father shaking his head. That's when I made up my mind. But I never could have done it myself. Four times I raised the knife, and four times I set it down again. I looked over at Gaetano; I didn't say a word to him. I was crying, he was crying: only Rituccia's eyes were dry. But she was pale as a sheet and she didn't move a muscle. She looked at Gaetano too, and he got to his feet; he picked up the knife. And he freed me. And he freed us. He did what I wanted to do myself, Raffae'. I left my paw dangling behind me."

The silence that followed her words closed in like a fog. Maione thought he could hear his heart pounding; he felt a crushing pity for Filomena, for Gaetano, for Rituccia. And for himself, too.

Then his thoughts went to Lucia. He imagined her locked in a cramped cell, a prison made of memories; hanging from a trap by her paw, ever since that accursed evening three years earlier. And he thought: What am I doing here?

He got to his feet, gazing into her magnificent eyes, the eyes of a stranger, glistening with tears, and that beautiful, Madonna-like smile. And he realized that he loved Lucia, even more than he loved her when he glimpsed her at the fountain at the age of sixteen, washing a sheet and singing, that he'd never seen anything lovelier since then, and if he were to die someday he wanted it to be with that face before his eyes.

He said good-bye to Filomena. The word he used was *arrivederci*, until we meet again, but what he meant was *addio*, good-bye forever, may God be with you. She told him *addio*, hoping it meant *arrivederci*. Maione walked out into the street and turned his footsteps toward police headquarters.

LIX

Only a couple of hours had gone by, but when they met again in Ricciardi's office, they were two different men than they had been when they'd left it.

The commissario was morose, with a fixed glare, and a crease of sorrow furrowing his brow. The brigadier, in contrast, seemed as if he had untied a knot that had been preventing him from breathing. He seemed to be at peace now, untroubled, though there was a faint hint of sadness in his eyes. He had entrusted a boy he'd met in the *vicoli*, a friend of one of his sons, with the task of letting Lucia know that he'd be working late. An old tradition to be revived; but he had emphasized that the messenger was to remember, as he made him repeat several times, that he wouldn't eat before he came home. He missed his home; he hungered for it.

The window was open and the salt air was blowing in from outside. Needless to say, Ricciardi was looking out of it.

"I want to know who killed her, Calise. I want to know who and I want to know why. Work aside, I mean. I want to know whether it was for money or for passion."

Behind Ricciardi's back, Maione nodded. And he chipped in a thought of his own.

"I want to know too, Commissa'. Because she was a poor old woman and someone killed her and then kicked her dead body all around the room. Because, even if she was a loanshark and cheated people out of their money with tarot cards, she still had the right to go on breathing. And because I'm a cop."

Ricciardi turned around and looked Maione in the eye.

"That's right, Maione. We're cops. Let's go see what this actor has to say for himself."

As they walked the short distance, they explored the issues at hand.

"Just for the sake of discussion, Commissa', just thinking out loud here. Let's say that the professor can't stand the idea of his wife leaving him and losing all that money of hers, which really is a lot of money, after all. Let's say he goes to Calise and pays her to tell the signora to get rid of the actor. Then let's say that when he goes to settle up, they get into a fight and the professor loses his head. Or better yet, Calise wants to make more money off him and she blackmails him with what she knows about his private affairs."

Ricciardi nodded as he walked.

"Or let's say that Iodice can't pay her what he owes and is on the verge of desperation. Let's say Calise threatens him, intent on ruining him, making him lose his pizzeria, everything he owns. That she's going to take the bread out of his children's mouths."

Maione shook his head.

"No, Commissa', no. A father with a family would think it over before risking that kind of ruin. Because if he doesn't kill her, he can still always find a way of putting bread on the table, even if he does lose the pizzeria. But if he flies out of control, then his children not only don't eat, they lose their good name, the family honor. It wasn't Iodice, I'm sure of it. If you want to know the truth, I'm more inclined to think it was the signora, so emotional, so desperate to sweep aside the one obstacle to her great love affair."

"Sure. And it could just as easily have been our friend Passarelli, the funny little man with the ninety-year-old mamma and the sixty-year-old fiancée, who might not have wanted another old woman around. Or Ridolfi, who could have just pretended to fall down the stairs. It could have been anyone, and that's the truth. We're still completely at sea here."

Maione smiled.

"True, but my top candidate is still the professor; let's not forget Teresa and the shoes. If you ask me, it was him."

Ricciardi shrugged.

"Still, I wouldn't overlook the ladies entirely. Remember: the doctor said that a young woman, or a very strong one, could have done just as much damage as a man. And I for one wouldn't want to go up against Petrone or Signora Serra, with their lovely little tempers."

They had reached the theater, where the crowd was bigger than they'd expected. The play had been running for quite a while, and it was a weekday, but the playwright's reputation was growing; word of mouth was evidently very effective. What's more, this was the next to last performance before the production relocated to Rome. In short, the atmosphere was one of festive anticipation.

Ricciardi and Maione identified themselves and had an usher accompany them to the stage door. Inside, in the narrow hallway that ran along the dressing room doors, they brushed past actors and actresses already dressed in costume, with pre-show jitters showing in their faces. The actors were talking excitedly but silence fell when one of the doors opened and a face poked out. Maione recognized the playwright and chief actor from his picture in the paper.

The man's face was white with powder and there were two spots of pink rouge on his cheeks, his collar turned up in a fashion popular ten years earlier, a wide, colorful tie, and a jacket with a conspicuous patch on the side. In sharp contrast with his ridiculous getup, his expression was dour: a thin mustache and thin lips, arched eyebrows, a broad forehead with a single vertical crease running down the middle. The brigadier had read that he was just thirty, but now, up close, he struck him as a much older man.

As he stared at them, the playwright spoke to a shorter, cheerful-looking man who vaguely resembled him.

"Are these gentlemen friends of yours? Have you decided to start letting strangers backstage, along with everything else? What have you got in mind now, one of your floating card games in the dressing rooms?"

Spreading his arms wide in a show of helplessness and speaking to a small crowd of actors standing not far off, the shorter man looked heavenward with a smile as he replied.

"Of course, put the blame on Peppino. It's Peppino's fault, even if it just starts raining. No, I don't know these gentlemen. I've never seen them before. But if it's an order, I'll start a floating card game. That'd be more fun than standing here listening to you whine about everything."

The tension became palpable and the playwright slammed his dressing room door shut. Peppino, as he had identified himself, shrugged, snorted, and addressed the two policemen.

"Forgive us. When our governess was giving lessons on good manners, my brother was always sick in bed. Tell me, can I help you with something?"

Maione opened his mouth to speak, but Ricciardi laid a hand on his arm.

"We're . . . friends of Signor Romor, Attilio Romor. Could you tell us where we can find him?"

Peppino laughed heartily.

"Ah, that's a new one on me! Romor has friends who don't wear skirts! In that case, he must owe you money. *Prego*, you'll find him in the dressing room at the end of the hall. The one farthest from my brother."

Shaking his head, he headed off toward the stage door.

Ricciardi and Maione walked in the opposite direction.

Romor had just finished getting into costume.

He was a tall young man, the kind who is aware of his appeal to women. Two girls loaded down with costumes elbowed each other and whispered among themselves as they walked past his dressing room door.

The man appeared not to notice, or perhaps he was just used to it. He courteously ushered them in.

He didn't seem particularly surprised to learn who they were; his open, sincere gaze didn't betray concern of any kind. Maione did the questioning.

"Signor Romor, we're aware of your . . . close friendship with a married lady. We're investigating a misfortune that occurred a few days ago, and we'd like to ask you a few questions."

Romor smiled, revealing a perfect set of teeth. He looked them in the eye and seemed to be completely at ease.

"Yes, the signora is a friend of mine, Commissario. A very dear friend. We were even thinking of going away to set up house together. I heard about the . . . misfortune; I know all about the poor fortune-teller because Emma mentioned her frequently. I've never seen her, but I know that Emma was very attached to her. I'm at your complete disposal."

Maione and Ricciardi exchanged a quick glance.

"Thinking of going away to set up house together? But the signora told us that she had decided not to leave her husband."

The actor smiled politely.

"Brigadier, my Emma is a very sentimental person and, as such, she's subject to other people's influence. On the verge of such a momentous decision, it's only natural that she should feel some degree of uncertainty. Her husband came to see me, a few nights ago. He waited for me outside the stage door and he offered me money in exchange for breaking it off with Emma. Of course, I refused. I'm not the sort of man who can be bought. I care nothing about the money; I have my profession. Then he threatened me: he told me that he would ruin me, that all he had to do was drop a word or two with the director of the troupe. But, and if you've seen the show you already know this, there's nothing he could do to make the director hate me more than he does already. I already know that when my contract expires I'll have to look for another company. Luckily, however, this is a good time for the theater and there's plenty of work. I'll find something."

"And how did you respond to Serra's threats?"

Romor threw his head back and laughed with gusto.

"That's how: I laughed in his face. There's no way to persuade me. I assure you that she can't stay away from me. I'll let you in on a secret: we're expecting a baby. And a baby, Commissario, is an important, irrevocable step. Having a child brings a couple together forever, and that's the way it's going to be between Emma and me."

"Would you be willing to repeat what you just said in the presence of the Serras?"

The Serras. An institutionalized couple: a family. Ricciardi appreciated the way that Maione was maneuvering to provoke a reaction from Romor; if the man felt he was being cut out, that he had no chance of winning back his relationship, then he would show concern and be less than forthcoming. Instead he smiled, without looking away from the commissario's gaze, even as he responded to Maione's question.

"Brigadier, that's something that I already intended to do. I know my Emma, marvelous, sensitive woman that she is. I'm sure that once she sees me, she'll get over any doubts and choose love over the arid social conventions that are presently holding her prisoner. I feel sure I'll be able to give you proof of this in short order. We had decided to leave together after the last performance in Naples, which is going to be tomorrow night. I haven't yet lost all hope that, now that she's had time to think it over, Emma will show up as we had agreed, that she'll come for me here at the theater."

Ricciardi looked the actor in the eye, and Romor looked back, unwavering.

"Tell me one last thing, Romor: who do you think murdered Calise?"

A sad expression appeared on the man's face.

"Who can say, Commissario? I didn't know her. But I'd have to guess that a woman who makes a living by deceiving people and, according to what I read, loan-sharking as well, should expect to wind up that way. I remember that Emma was a slave to her obsession with the old woman; she couldn't breathe unless Calise told her how with one of her proverbs. But I will say that when Emma's husband came to threaten me, he really did seem willing to stop at nothing. If I had to say a name . . ."

As they headed back to police headquarters, Maione thought out loud.

"That guy strikes me as a genuine idiot. He likes women, he knows that they like him, and he thinks that's how it will be for the rest of his life. If you ask me, he would have been better off taking the professor's money, because he won't be getting anything else out of his relationship with Emma."

Ricciardi was wrapped up in his thoughts.

"Don't forget about the baby, though. The professor would be happy to acknowledge the child as his own—that is, if he even knows his wife is pregnant. But would she be willing? She seems deeply involved. In any case, none of this concerns us. What I'd like to know is who had a motive to kill Calise. And we're running out of time. But I just had an idea."

"What is it, Commissa'?"

"The idea that tomorrow evening Signora Serra will be unable to resist the temptation to go to the theater, to enjoy the play she loves so well, for one last time. Why don't you take a walk over to see your friend the doorman in the afternoon and find out if anyone's planning to take a car or a driver to go to the theater."

Maione seemed perplexed.

"The Serras? Aren't we supposed to check in first with that idiot Garzo?"

Ricciardi smiled.

"No. He told me that I'm in charge of the case and I can do what I want. Anyway, it's the last day. You watch, if we don't come up with anything, they'll put the blame on poor Iodice and good night, nurse. Let's see if we can flush the professor out into the open."

Attilio, now alone, smiled into his dressing room mirror. Things were moving in the right direction; he would make Emma face her responsibilities.

He felt certain that, with her back to the wall and no proprieties left to safeguard, she would opt for love. On the other hand, why would the husband have done so much to convince him to leave her? Because the husband knew that Emma loved him. He'd never misread a woman, and he was pretty sure he wasn't wrong now, either.

He hoped that his mamma would come to the theater too, the following night. To enjoy his last performance. His triumphant last performance.

You walk home, kept company by your work, thoughts of the current investigation, thoughts studded with faces, sensations, tones of voice. You walk, cobblestones underfoot, and you smell the fresh air wafting down from the distant woods. And you think about the words you've heard, words you now need to put in order.

You walk among the few living human beings who are heading home, skirting close to the walls, and the occasional dead soul watching you go by, oozing grief from its wounds. You walk and you don't look; you pass through the world like a stranger. You climb the stairs, you open the door, you hear the tired breathing of your elderly Tata sleeping serenely. You undress, you and the night become a single thing. You tell yourself, no, not tonight, you won't go to the window. You'll stretch out and slip into sleep, or rather sleep will come envelop you, dragging you off for a few hours to a land of illusory peace.

Instead, you do go over to the window. Perhaps she'll be there, embroidering, as if to greet you unconsciously, to gently ferry you off to your dreamless slumber.

Instead, your gaze runs square into a pair of darkened shutters. No one speaks to you at all.

You step forward into the night and you know that your eyes will search for peace in the darkness but in vain. You were hoping for rest. But that's not what you got.

He climbs uphill along the *vicolo*, his step slow and heavy. The weight of the day bears down on his shoulders, the weight of the week, of life. He climbs the *vicolo* and he feels lonelier than ever, thinking of all these people looking for love and finding hatred, resentment, fury. He climbs the *vicolo* looking straight ahead; perhaps not even a scream would make him stop this time. Tonight it costs too much to walk. Tonight he wants nothing but peace.

Sea air accompanies him, caresses his shoulders, helps him in the uphill climb. It brings a promise of summer, a promise it may even keep. But who knows how many more deaths, in the meanwhile.

Tomorrow, there will be a guilty man, a man who tonight is still unaware, sleeping peacefully, or perhaps fast asleep deep underground. Perhaps victim and executioner are dancing together in the moonlight, in some enchanted clearing, along with the other dead souls. Perhaps victim and executioner have traded roles: that's permissible in the world of sleep.

Anguish, loneliness. In the rooms that were once filled with her smile, now all is deserted.

Remembering her, her smile reborn, her hand, her caress, her forgotten touch. Imagining his hand, trembling, as it brushes her face, her blue eyes, the same eyes he saw at the fountain when she was sixteen.

Dinner, him trying to talk, and her upraised finger laid across his lips. And then her hand, leading him to bed. And her opening the door of her body and soul to him. Perhaps a dream, a gift of the night, of the moon, motionless, over the souls of the world. Perhaps the air will keep its promise; perhaps he is being reborn in that perfume.

He falls asleep with his life wrapped in his arms: his life, snuggled against his chest. That breathing at once unknown and familiar.

LX

The light of dawn found Ricciardi and Maione well aware that this day would be a decisive one. For the memory of Tonino Iodice and for the honor of his children; for the peace of Carmela Calise's soul; for the reputation of the Serra di Arpaja family; for the welfare and perhaps for the career of Attilio Romor, an actor with a bright future and a challenging present; for the surname and fate of Emma's child.

And for the knowledge that they had solved a mystery in a world where, by official royal decree, there could be no more mysteries, nor blood, nor murder victims.

Maione, on Ricciardi's orders, went to the Serras' building just before lunchtime. He waited for the doorman to withdraw into his glass-fronted cubby and then went in after him, moving cautiously in the shadows to make sure no one noticed him from the balconies on the upper stories.

He learned that the signora would be going out to the theater, and without her chauffeur. She had told the doorman to get her new car ready, the odd one with a red finish, and to top off the fuel in the tank. As always, the man had gone into a litany of complaint about how he always had to take care of everything himself, and Maione nodded along patiently, inwardly detesting him. Then, however, he learned another tidbit that struck him as particularly interesting: the professor had also asked the doorman whether he knew the signora's plans for the evening, and then he had instructed him to alert the chauffeur; he'd be going out that evening as well. To attend the theater, he had added. Wasn't that ridiculously wasteful? Just two people, the same night, the same theater. In two different automobiles.

When Maione informed him, Ricciardi smirked in amusement. The theater. Once again, real and fictional passions would mingle and blend. Who could say which would make the most noise?

The theater. That was destined to be the place where the mystery would be untangled. All right then. The theater. And we'll be there, he thought. He told Maione to put together a small team of plainclothes officers: four men in all, to be positioned at various points in the auditorium and at the exits. One man would need to sit next to the professor, incognito, to forestall any sudden moves.

"What about you, Commissa'? What are you going to do?"

Unexpectedly, Ricciardi half-smiled and brushed the lock of hair away from his forehead with a sharp sweep of his hand. His eyes glittered in the low light of the setting sun.

"I'm going to pick up a young lady. I'll be attending the theater with company this evening. Arrange to have two tickets for me at the box office."

Nunzia Petrone couldn't believe her own ears. She was mistrustful by nature, and especially so with policemen. It struck her as a ridiculous request, practically a joke, but there wasn't a trace of humor in the commissario's eyes.

"Antonietta? But why? What do you need her for?"

Ricciardi, standing with both hands in his overcoat pockets, his shock of hair dangling over his forehead, looked her in the eye.

"Because she may have been present, when Calise was killed. You told me yourself that she stayed upstairs with her another hour the night that she was murdered. And if the murderer had happened to notice she was there, he probably would have killed her, too. Perhaps, if she looked someone in the face, she might be able to help us identify the killer. Perhaps."

Petrone looked around her with her small eyes, as if appealing to the cheap objects in her kitchen for help.

"But Antonietta doesn't understand a thing, Commissa'. She just talks to herself, as if she could see people that we can't, other children she can play with in her imagination. She's . . . simpleminded, you can see that for yourself. What could you possibly expect from her, the poor little thing?"

Ricciardi shrugged.

"It's a shot. Just a shot. But I promise you that nothing will happen to her. I'll stay close to her the whole time. And I'll bring her back to you, safe and sound. And she might even have fun. An evening at the theater."

So Ricciardi found himself strolling downhill from the Sanità toward the Teatro dei Fiorentini, walking alongside the girl, who dragged her feet and held her right hand near her mouth, continuing to murmur her singsong. As they went by, people stopped talking and stepped aside.

The shadows of night were gradually swallowing up the street, and the streetlights had not yet flickered on. This was the hour in which dreams materialize.

At the beginning of Via Toledo, Ricciardi cast his usual sidelong glance at the dead. Antonietta smiled and waved at them.

The commissario shuddered when the girl stopped to caress the ghost of a child with its head crushed in, perhaps the result of a streetcar accident, the bloody, naked skin on its chest grooved by the twine suspenders holding up its trousers. Oddly enough, the cap was still perched on top of the child's head, at least on the half that was intact, while on the other side the cap rested on a shard of white skull and bare, rotting brain matter.

Passersby saw the girl reach her hand out into the empty air and thought nothing of it. Ricciardi on the other hand saw her caress an arm shaking with the final spasms of death, and heard the child's desperate wail for help that issued from its broken teeth.

"Help me, Mamma," Antonietta repeated, dreamily. Ricciardi put his hand on her back and gently pushed her along. She began walking again and didn't look back.

Farther on, when they got to the construction sites of the new white buildings, one by one, in and among the clerks on their way home and the women returning from grocery shopping, dead construction workers who had died on the job began to appear. Ricciardi kept his head down, while Antonietta cheerfully waved her chubby hand, making no distinction between the living and the dead, although neither one nor the other paid her any attention. But maybe the two of them, invisible to one and all, were the real phantoms.

Antonietta blew a kiss to the boy and the old man who had died together; but when they came face-to-face with a more recently dead man, the one who kept calling the name of a certain Rachele, telling her that they had pushed him to join her, the girl started in fright and hid behind Ricciardi's back. What did you sense, this time? he wondered. What other emotion? You must be able to sense even more than I do, then. In that moment, he felt a surge of infinite pity for the young girl, and he caressed her face. She smiled at him, and went on walking.

But she kept turning around to look behind her, trembling slightly.

LXI

Sitting at his desk, Ruggero Serra di Arpaja looked out at the springtime through the glass doors of his balcony. The silk curtains reached toward him, then sank back into place as if the breeze were playfully beckoning him to come outside. The air smelled of salt water and fresh blossoms.

The rays from the sun sinking behind the hill of Posillipo filled the room with sparkling light, hurting the man's tired eyes. Another sleepless night. Another day of waiting.

Unfamiliar emotions, encountered after a lifetime spent speeding along rails determined by his social status, had taken command of his every decision. Lately, he'd done things that he could never have even imagined, and he'd discovered a part of himself that he hadn't known existed.

In that final moment, that morning, he had done his best to maintain appearances: his dark suit, his perfectly ironed shirt, his face clean-shaven, his hair combed and brushed. Only his eyes, behind his gold-rimmed spectacles, betrayed the torment of his soul. The news that Emma was pregnant, which she had told him after a long night of reciprocal insults and accusations, bore the mark of redemption and irrevocability. No matter what, after that piece of news, nothing could ever be the same again.

The morning sun had brought him a new and extraordinary awareness: he loved his wife and without her, life meant nothing to him. Let the police come arrest him, let them denigrate him, let them blacken his reputation, let them toss it to the tender mercies of his so-called friends; if Emma left him, none of this would mean anything to him anymore.

Without taking his eyes off the indifferent springtime, he pulled open his desk drawer and took out the revolver. He'd already checked to make sure it was loaded. Not another loveless night. Not another loveless springtime.

He put on his overcoat. Let's go to the theater, he thought. For the last performance.

Sitting before her mirror, Emma tried to cover the weariness of her sleepless night with face powder. She couldn't stand the idea of Attilio seeing her looking any less beautiful than usual.

She knew that by going to the theater, she was violating Calise's iron rules; but could a woman who hadn't even foreseen her own death really determine the fate of others? And what if the old woman had been wrong from the very beginning? What if she'd condemned her to misery by mistake?

She tried to steer her thoughts elsewhere, anticipating the flood of emotion she usually felt when she saw Attilio: the echo of his love, the passion and the tenderness that she'd come to depend on.

She'd had the car made ready, but she hadn't yet packed her bags; just a few hours to go until their meeting, she still hadn't decided what she'd do. She'd never made a decision for herself in her life, and now she was being asked to make the most important one of all, all alone, without help.

A new feeling, perhaps an impulse to protect her womb, dominated her and roiled her in confusion. All the selfishness that had driven her life till now, her relationship with Attilio, her intolerance for the world she had always lived in, had dissolved. She was going to be a mother. It was as if her entire life had been leading up to this one thing; she found herself experiencing everything in a radically different way than she had imagined, and she felt so distant from and so unlike her girl-friends, who had limited themselves to bearing children only to entrust them, as mere necessary annoyances, to hordes of nannies and governesses.

She felt a vague feeling of compassion for Ruggero, in whose overwrought eyes she'd detected genuine pain; but she had convinced herself that he was Calise's murderer and, for the good of her child, she would have to separate herself from him and his grim fate.

She'd listen to her heart, she decided. She'd make up her mind when she saw Attilio walk on stage with that kingly gait she knew so well. To the theater, then.

For the last performance.

Ricciardi and Antonietta were in the orchestra seats, a little off to the side but still up front, close to the stage. The commissario wanted to make sure the girl could clearly see the faces of both Romor and the Serras; he just hoped that Ruggero had arranged to sit near his wife who, as always, had reserved the box in the first row, the one closest to the stage.

He didn't really know what he was expecting: a false move, an off-key reaction. He had identified the guilty party, beyond the shadow of a doubt, but the clues he had amassed were just that: clues, not proof.

He was pinning everything on a misstep by the killer, or else solid identification by the only possible eyewitness, Antonietta, even though he was well aware that her mentally impaired status meant she'd never be allowed to testify at trial. But it could be enough to unhinge the killer's confidence. He'd seen it happen before.

Hunching his head down between his shoulders, he did his best to blend into the dim light of the orchestra seating. As he had entered the auditorium, he had spotted Camarda, Cesarano, and Ardisio, three men from Maione's team, in plainclothes and strategically deployed. The brigadier himself had taken a second-row seat right below the stage, concealed by the upturned lapel of his overcoat and the brim of his hat. Ricciardi looked up at the box just as Emma was taking her seat, more beautiful than ever, but with eyes that betrayed uncertainty, grief, and weariness. She was alone.

After a few minutes, the commissario glimpsed an indistinct figure standing in the shadows behind her. The professor, he decided. Maione locked eyes with Camarda and darted a glance in that direction; the plainclothesman nodded and left the auditorium. Ricciardi understood that the brigadier was sending him to keep an eye on the door of the box, so he could be in place if things started moving quickly. He knew what he was doing, good old Maione. He really knew what he was doing.

The house lights went down and a round of applause rose up. All the actors were on their marks, both the ones behind the curtain and those in the auditorium. Everyone was ready.

For the last performance.

The play began with an opening monologue by the lead actor. Ricciardi recognized the man who had spoken so rudely to his brother the night before. Even if his attention was focused elsewhere, the commissario perceived the sheer magnetism that the actor emanated, immediately captivating the audience. Antonietta looked straight ahead, continuing to mumble meaningless strings of words. The stage lights lit up the front rows, giving Ricciardi a clear view of both Emma and Ruggero. The woman was gripping the balustrade, her hands white, her face tensed in clear expectation of something; her husband's face looked like a mask, with the expressionless features of a mannequin.

When the monologue was over, the lead actress made her entrance, an extraordinarily ugly woman of equally remarkable talent. Ricciardi guessed that she must be the lead actor's sister, given the resemblance between them, and he absentmindedly thought that it must be quite a savings, to have a family-run theater troupe. The audience was delighted: the duet was brilliant, the pace was good and quick, the jokes were dry and salacious; everyone was laughing except for Signor and Signora Serra, the policemen, and Antonietta, dreamily chasing after who knew what visions.

After a while, hard on the heels of the exchange of banter, Romor made his entrance. The main character greeted him with a sarcastic phrase, prompting the audience to break into a thunderous burst of laughter. Ricciardi remembered the actor mentioning how much the man disliked him, and he now saw that he wasn't overstating the case. In the row in front of him, three young women, showing no regard for their dates, whispered something among themselves and giggled nervously; the man had a following. When silence returned, the actor took a step forward, ready to speak his line; and then something unexpected happened.

Even from backstage, as he was awaiting the moment to make his entrance, Attilio had realized that the front-row box was occupied once again. That box had been empty for many nights now, and he had grown accustomed to the resulting feelings of uncertainty, doubt, and loneliness. Like a lamb to the slaughter, night after night, he had been forced to submit to the damned lead actor's mockery, without a chance to fight back, without any hope of revenge.

But tonight, the last night of all, Emma had returned. He'd seen her, and she was alone, no longer shielded by a girlfriend. That could only mean one thing: that she had decided to live up to her word, to meet him there so they could run away and start a new life together, in defiance of fears and social conventions. He was radiant as he strode on stage. Let that conceited mountebank take his last sadistic pleasure; he was beyond caring now.

When Attilio made his entrance, Emma practically leaned out over the balustrade of the box. She was looking at the stage, but to an even greater extent, she was looking inside herself. She searched for the echo of the passion that she thought she could feel just fifteen minutes earlier. But she felt nothing. The man she had once loved more than anyone in the world suddenly seemed like a perfect stranger. She clearly understood that he no longer meant a thing to her, and in a flash she realized that their affair was well and truly over. She wondered whether this was what Calise had seen in her tarot cards that last séance; and, just as she was thinking of Calise, she heard the old woman's voice down in the orchestra seats. Behind her, Ruggero took a step forward, raising his hand to his overcoat pocket.

At first, Ricciardi thought he was having a vision. Not wanting to miss Emma's reactions or even the slightest movement from Ruggero, he had turned his attention away from the stage and the orchestra seating. In complete silence, the audience was waiting for the next line, while the performers acted out a moment of discomfiture following Romor's entrance. Suddenly, the stillness was broken by a loud voice that he instantly recognized as the voice of Calise's ghost. He turned like a shot and a bloodcurdling image met his eyes.

Antonietta had risen to her feet. Hunched over, she'd shrunken in size: her legs were slightly bowed, her head tilted to one side at an almost unnatural angle; her left hand was dangling motionless at her side, while her right hand sketched out an uncertain, flailing gesture, almost as if she were trying to drive someone away or ward something off. Her normally obtuse expression had taken on a melancholy air, so that she seemed in thrall to some terrible memory.

A hoarse sound issued from her throat; even Ricciardi, a man accustomed to horrors of all kinds, would never forget the words that emerged, loud and clear, from the deformed mouth of that girl who had never spoken in her life.

"*'O Padreterno nun è mercante ca pava 'o sabbato.*"

God Almighty's not a shopkeeper who pays His debts on Saturday.

All the spectators had turned to look in her direction. There was even a small ripple of applause from people who thought that this was some new element of the play itself. The actors on stage exchanged startled glances.

Romor took a step forward, squinting and shading his eyes with one hand against the glare of the spotlights as he peered into the orchestra seating. He said: "Mamma? Is that you?"

Ricciardi stared, petrified, at the ghost of the old woman, reproduced to perfection by Antonietta. He felt something clamp down on his lungs, expelling the air out through his mouth and leaving him breathless.

There was a violent shout, like the voice of an outraged child. Attilio lunged off the stage and into the audience, eyes bugging out of their sockets, upper lip curled back in a snarl to reveal teeth like those of a ravenous wolf.

"Damn you, you're not my mother!"

Maione leapt up from his seat with surprising agility and seized the actor's legs, bringing him down face-first. But in spite of the brigadier's considerable weight, the man continued to claw his way toward the girl, with his fingers curled like talons and a roar issuing from deep in his chest and out his twisted mouth. Antonietta for her part stared at him, repeating Calise's last words over and over. It was not until Ardisio and Cesarano had piled on as well that Attilio stopped struggling and burst into tears.

LXII

Don't try to tell me that's my mother. Damned witch, filthy whore. Don't tell me that she's blood of my blood.

I remember my mother perfectly. She might have been older than the mothers of the other children in the poorhouse; but she was also smarter. She used to tell me, I have to work, you can't stay with me. But I'll give you everything, much more than the other children who have just a single outfit, a single pencil, a single notebook. Not me . . . My mamma showered me with things. And you know why? Because I'm handsome.

The nuns like me, the schoolteacher likes me. To hell with my classmates, who locked me in the bathroom that one time and covered me with bruises, kicking and punching me on the body but not the face, knowing that otherwise the bruises would show and they'd get in trouble. To hell with them.

The bigger I got and the handsomer I became, the more things my mamma gave me. She used to tell me that I was all she had in the world, that she had to make sure I had everything I wanted. And everything is exactly what I wanted, because a person gets used to having fine things. And if I wanted it, Mamma would get it for me. She told me that I was born by accident; not even she knew exactly how it happened. One day, my father would be a sailor who had left us; another day, if I'd been a good boy, he'd be a nobleman; and on yet another day, if I'd made her mad at me, he'd be a stinking drunk. Now that's my mamma.

Now I'm grown up and I want to be an actor. Because I'm handsome, did I mention that? Plus I can sing and dance. And if they say I can't, it's because they're jealous, because they're not as good as I am. Mamma tells me that I can't let anyone know that I'm her son, otherwise the people won't pay, and she won't be able to give me the money. And I go to see her secretly, at night, so she can tell me what it is I need to do. The money—who knows where it comes from? Mamma tells me that the porter woman, the idiot girl's mamma, is putting her money in the bank for the idiot girl. And she told that lady that they're equal partners, each one for her own child. But that lady didn't understand; maybe she's just as much of an idiot as her idiot daughter. Not me. I'm handsome, Mamma looks at me and smiles. And she tells me what to do, what to say.

So don't try and tell me that witch is my mamma.

I remember what my mamma told me. And I do it, word for word. When I can't talk to her, that's when I get mixed up. And I get things wrong.

With Emma, I did everything that my mamma told me to do. She'd been looking for her for such a long time: a suitable lady. Then one day she told me that she had found her, that a cousin of mine I'd never met had brought the lady to her, a cousin who doesn't even know I exist. And Mamma prepared everything, down to the last detail, the way she always did. And she told me where I was supposed to wait and what I was supposed to say. And that I should be even more careful than usual, because Emma could never knew who I was—that I was my mamma's son, in other words. Because, as you know, we only have one mamma; if you need help, she's the one you turn to. Otherwise, what are mammas for?

So then I become Emma's lover. That's something I know how to do; it's something that comes natural to me. Every night I go to Mamma's place. She leaves the door open for me, I climb the stairs after the porter woman has doused the lamp, which I can see from the street. And she tells me what to do next. Emma falls in love with me. She can't live without me anymore. I make love to her; that's something I like. Mamma makes the other arrangements, making sure Emma takes care of the money and her stupid old husband, too: we'll take everything but his underpants, Mamma tells me. We'll be the winners of this card game. And we'll take all their money and run, Mamma says.

Emma is a man-woman, Mamma says. She drives and she smokes; she could easily get into an accident in that red car she drives. For now, let's just get the money and get out of here. We'll see about that accident later.

Mamma laughs and caresses me. I like it when she laughs. It means everything's okay.

Then one night Emma comes to the theater, all puffy from crying. That's it, she says, it's over, I can never see you again. I hardly know what to say to her; it's the kind of thing Mamma usually explains to me. I need to go see her, but then I can't because the porter woman doesn't turn out the lamp. That idiot daughter of hers must have gone to sleep late. I tell myself I'll go the next day and ask Mamma what's happening. She'll explain, wait and see, that mamma of mine is so smart. That's just how we are, the two of us: perfect. I'm handsome, she's smart.

But when I get there, who do I find? This old witch. She looks just like my mamma, true, but it can't be her because instead of talking about me, her son, she starts talking about Emma's baby. She says that where she was unable to succeed with me, she can make it work with the baby, make sure he lives a rich life with an important last name. And I say to Mamma, to this witch, I say: But why? Are you saying I can't have an important last name? That I can't become rich and famous? And she tells me no, that fate pays you back sooner or later. Those who do evil sooner or later are paid back for it, by God.

And she tells me, me of all people, that the baby is more important, that my father told her so in a dream. You understand? My father! In a dream! And now you have the nerve to try to tell me that that was my mother? The woman who gave me a different surname so that I could grow up to be famous? Never! That's not my mother!

And I ask her what I'm going to get out of it. This time, nothing, she answers. And she's weeping as she says it. Maybe another day. Maybe we'll find another one like Emma. After all, Naples is full of bored wealthy women looking for a lover to keep. God Almighty, she tells me, isn't a merchant who pays His debts on Saturday.

And I kicked her out, kicked that witch right out, out from inside my mother. I split her head open, to let the evil out. And I kicked her all around the room. The damned witch. That blood, all that blood: not the blood of my blood. My mother always thought only of me. That couldn't be her, not if she now preferred an unborn bastard to me. Now I'm waiting. You'll see, sooner or later my mamma will come back and make everything right. That's right, she really is blood of my blood.

LXIII

It took a good long time to make Garzo understand what had happened. They found him out of breath in the courtyard of headquarters, accompanied by his clerk, Ponte, with an even more anguished look on his face than usual. He'd hurried downstairs to find out more about Romor's arrest, news of which had beaten them back there. And Garzo wasn't alone; a small crowd had gathered in the street, in front of the entrance, to get a glimpse of the actor and murderer who had brought the play at the Teatro dei Fiorentini to a halt.

The deputy chief of police displayed a level of theatrical skill that Ricciardi would never have suspected: he shifted in a few seconds from worry to relief, and then to astonishment at the sight of the Serra di Arpajas, who had followed the police patrol in the same car, and finally to anger with the look he shot at the commissario.

Maione did a brilliant job straightening things out, even as he was dusting off his trousers following the struggle with the killer.

"Everything's fine, Dotto'. This gentleman here is the murderer in the Calise case. We owe a debt of thanks to the professor and the signora, who went to the theater tonight expressly to corner him."

Garzo went through one last lightning-fast change of expression, now displaying a look of authoritative satisfaction. With a slight and still circumspect bow to the Serras, he turned and addressed the two policemen.

"If you please, in my office, Ricciardi and Maione. Then I'll bid Signore and Signora Serra di Arpaja a good night, if they'd be so kind as to wait just a few minutes."

Perfect manners, as always, thought Ricciardi with a twinge of admiration. The beginning of the conversation was stormy: Garzo wanted to know why, after he had given explicit orders that all contact with the Serra di Arpaja family was to take place only and exclusively through him, he found them in the courtyard of police headquarters so late at night. Involved in a police operation, what's more! What if the professor or, worse, the signora had been hurt?

Ricciardi, with an Olympian show of calm, replied that every detail had been planned out in advance, and that the plan had been designed to clear the professor's name once and for all. That he had come to an understanding with the professor that laying the blame on Iodice would have lent support to theories of the family's involvement in Calise's murder, which is how the press would see it as well. A suicide, after all, was not the same as a confession; and the dead woman's most assiduous visitor had still been the Signora Serra di Arpaja, as everyone knew. And since Ricciardi had come to the conclusion, as the result of an interview, that Emma's lover, Romor, knew more than he was admitting, they had decided that if they subjected him to a state of particular tension, he might well betray himself. Which is exactly what had happened.

Maione and Ricciardi had concocted this whole song and dance that morning, as the early morning sun illuminated the piazza beneath the office window and the factory workers headed for the buses that would take them to work in Bagnoli. They had no backup plan. Their only hope was that this first one would succeed.

And just what had this Romor said, during the interview? What exactly, Garzo asked, had made Ricciardi suspect him?

The commissario described with honesty his conversation

with Attilio the night before. The fact that he knew that Calise had been murdered at night, something that the press had never reported. And Calise's propensity for speaking in proverbs, despite the fact that Emma had never told him about it. And how had he, Ricciardi, come to know these things?

In his mind's eye, the commissario once again saw the broken neck, the crushed cranium, the streak of blood. But it was the memory of Antonietta's voice that made him shiver. Petrone had told him everything, he said. He felt a sharp glance from Maione on the back of his neck and hoped that the brigadier wouldn't ask him for an explanation afterward.

Garzo was finally placated. He smiled and said: Nice job. We did it again. Meritorious action. If it hadn't been for the deadline I imposed on the case, we'd still be here frittering time away thinking that Serra di Arpaja was the killer. You're talented, no question about it, but you need direction.

Without looking at him, Ricciardi was able to forestall Maione's vehement and indignant reaction by laying a hand on his arm and asking permission to head back to his office so he could collect and transcribe Romor's full confession. Garzo got to his feet gleefully and, amid the scent of fresh flowers, which he always made sure to have on his desk, he went to welcome the Serra di Arpaja family.

"Commissa', I bring you the best wishes of the two Iodice women. They were in the crowd outside, but I know you don't like that sort of thing. I told them they should go home rather than sticking around, that you'd be working late. The wife said that you're a saint, that her husband's soul sends you benedictions from the afterlife and so on and so forth—the usual things, in other words. The mother sends her wishes for your well-being; she said that in her opinion you're unwell or perhaps you have some inner pain, that God Almighty helps people like you, if they're willing to let themselves be helped."

Ricciardi grimaced, without looking away from his office window.

"Thank you for sparing me another lecture. I think we've had quite enough fate for one evening, don't you agree? Listen to me: fate doesn't exist. What exists are men and women and the sheer courage it takes to go on living or choose to quit this life, the way Iodice did. And those who live in a sort of dream state, letting the currents carry them where they will. That's what exists."

Maione shook his head.

"What a shame, though, Commissa', to hear you talk like that. Not even solving a case and sending a stinking lunatic to the criminal asylum is enough to bring a smile to your face, is it?"

Ricciardi didn't turn around.

"Do you know the one thing you can take away from a man who lives on what he sees when he looks out the window? The only thing you can take away from him?"

"No, Commissa'. What's the one thing?"

A brief sigh.

"The window, Raffaele. You can take away his window."

Garzo was relieved, and more than just a little, by the demeanor of the professor and his wife. They looked tired, tested by the experience. Witnessing such a violent scene had probably proved to be more harrowing than expected, the deputy chief of police thought to himself. But they'd soon get over it.

Actually, what Garzo wanted first and foremost was to be sure that the influential academic wouldn't be lodging any complaints with the authorities that he regularly had dealings with. If complaints were likely to ensue, then Garzo would distance himself from Ricciardi's initiative; otherwise he'd make it his own and take full credit for it himself.

All that Serra di Arpaja wanted, for his part, was to get out of there as quickly as possible and begin forgetting. His wife, in the face of Romor's violent outburst, had stepped backward into the darkness of the box and she had bumped against him as he stepped forward to protect her. She'd stood alongside him and squeezed his hand. It wasn't much: just a beginning. He had used the handkerchief that he was pulling out of his pocket to dry her tears.

The same pocket in which he was carrying both his pistol and the weight of the decision he'd come to: if Emma did decide to run away with Romor, he would shoot himself in the head, right in front of her. And then they'd see how easy it was to build a new life together, a life built on the foundation of his blood. This was the desperate last act he'd planned, for when all other avenues had been exhausted and he had nowhere else to turn. He remembered his visit to Calise, to try to persuade her to free Emma from her obsession. He remembered the open door, all the blood spread across the floor, his headlong flight, hoping that no one had seen him go in; the certainty that it was all over now, that there was no more hope.

But now he and Emma were going to have a child; perhaps, for the good of the baby, she'd once again begin to appreciate the security that only he, and their lawful matrimony, could provide her.

His wife's thoughts were far, far away, mulling over the days she'd spent believing that she couldn't live without a man who had revealed himself to be a criminal lunatic. She doubted herself, and her judgment. Calise and her son had taught her, with their tragedy, just how much sheer damage motherhood can inflict.

She brushed her belly with one hand, while that idiot functionary whose name she couldn't even remember yammered on with her husband about some uninteresting acquaintance they had in common. But what if the child inherited its father's defects? And had the grandmother's actions been acts of love or extreme selfishness?

She saw it all in a flash. Emma suddenly understood that the old woman's blood, spilled with such brutal fury, was the same blood as that of the child she now carried in her womb. In a certain sense, blood of her blood.

Perhaps, she mused, her unanswered questions were her punishment, the price she'd have to pay. A life sentence.

LXIV

Once he'd concluded an investigation, a sense of emptiness always lingered in Ricciardi's heart. For days the thought of the murder, the grief-stricken indignation of the murdered soul, the various possible solutions to the case invaded his thoughts, his every breath. The commissario, without realizing it, never gave up, not even when he was eating or sleeping or washing or having a bowel movement. It was a noise that became the background of one's very existence, like the wheels of a train or the rhythm of a horse's hooves; after a while you can't even hear them anymore.

When the enigma was solved, it left a crater behind, a crater that he circled warily, having lost the thing that allowed him to distract himself from his solitude. That was when he took refuge at the window, watching the everyday miracle of a left-handed embroidery stitch, or that same left hand preparing dinner; dreaming of a different life, fantasizing about a different self, a self that might have waved or even chatted through the open window.

Petrone had come to collect her daughter, a smile on her face, her wits once again dulled, her eyes flat and listless, the customary streamer of drool hanging from her half-open mouth, hand gripping her mother, feet dragging on the sidewalk. He had envied the girl as he watched her go, unaware as she was of the curse that afflicted her. To her eyes, the living and the dead all lived together in one single extraordinary world.

The solution. For the man who watches there is no solution.

As for the case of the fortune-teller, he knew when the solution had come to him. It was when the Petrone told him what Calise had said when she asked what she did with her money: You and I, she'd said to the porter woman who was saving for her daughter's future, we aren't so different after all. She too had a child. A message for Ricciardi, delivered through the mouth of her business partner.

As he looked out his office window, trying not to think about the mountain of forms he was going to have to fill out, his thoughts turned to his mother. To the dream he'd had of her, her illness, her incurable nervous condition. What was your disease, Mamma? What did you see out there, in the fields, on the streets? Why did you live locked up in your room, bedridden? What was in your blood, Mamma? What else did you leave me besides these eyes that look like glass?

Ricciardi shuddered in the cool air, a thoughtful gift from the budding spring.

Blood of my blood, he thought to himself.

Maione felt light as air. Which, when you're a side of beef tipping the scales at 220 pounds, is pretty good. But he'd been given half a day off as a reward, the way he was every time a case was closed with positive results. He felt pretty sure that this half-day would be a very nice one.

Whenever he concluded an investigation, a weight lifted from his soul. Once again, he could face the world head on. There was no longer a crime to be avenged, a wrong to right. And his hands, his chest, and his head were still full to overflowing with the gift of that spring night that Lucia had given him, smiling without uttering a word. She was right, as usual, he decided. A time for caresses.

But now he wanted to talk to her. And when he arrived home in the light of afternoon instead of the dark of night, he embraced his wife and children and changed into civilian attire, which in his case consisted of an old shirt made of unfinished cotton, a pair of timeworn suspenders holding up a pair of canvas trousers, and the down-at-the-heel work boots he'd never be able to bring himself to get rid of. He played with the boys, who were giddily disoriented by the new air that circulated in their home. He napped for a while, then he took a seat in the kitchen to contemplate the wonderful sight of his wife, the most beautiful woman in the universe, shelling beans and breaking macaroni.

She smiled without looking up and handed him a small mountain of bean pods: Why don't you do something useful for a change, she said. He smiled back and set to work, shelling beans into a bowl with his thumb.

Lucia stopped, looked at him, and said: Tell me about it.

So he told her.

Ricciardi finished filling out the mountain of forms that marked the end of the investigation. He set down his pen, and he closed the lid of the inkwell. The night had taken dominion. The cone of light cast by the lamp illuminated a deserted desk. The task is complete, he thought. It's time.

He took one last look around, listened to the silence outside the door. He was the last one there. He ought to leave.

He walked out of his office, closed the door behind him. He headed for the stairs. *They're not putting me back in there*, the image of the dead thief with a gun in his hand and his brains oozing out of the bullet hole informed him. Then don't let them, he thought resentfully.

He found himself back out in the open air. The weather was perfect. The springtime was prancing around him, doing its best to catch his attention. But the man who watches and sees the dead couldn't see or hear it.

And now home. Without so much as the right to dream of you, my love.

And Maione told her, in a way he hadn't in years, with his heart and with his head.

Lucia found herself in the presence, first, of a poor old woman, brutally murdered, and then of a beautiful woman whose face had been slashed, and she recoiled in pity and horror. Then she saw an odd little man with a comb-over, with a sixty-year-old fiancée and an immortal mother, and she laughed until tears came to her eyes; and she imagined a woman, noble, rich, and starved for love, and felt compassion for her; and an older husband, well respected and heartbroken, and she felt pity for him as well.

Then she was introduced to a fat woman with small eyes, who had decided to become a con artist after a lifetime of honesty, and she shook her head in disapproval; but then she learned that the woman had a mentally handicapped little girl, who had witnessed who could say what horrors, and she pitied her. She followed the meanderings of a conceited actor's deranged mind and once again she was horrified; she saw a pale little girl with the large eyes of an old woman, a child without a mamma and now without a papà, and she wept for her. She shook her head grimly at the sight of a menacing *guappo* and a slimy shopkeeper, both of them blood-poisoned by beauty.

And she studied her husband's eyes carefully when he spoke to her about the woman who had decided to chew off her paw, snared in a trap, so that she could once again become mistress of her own and her son's lives; because she had sensed the stirring of a deep old chord in him, a harmony that she believed she alone had ever heard. But he smiled at her and caressed her face. And he said to her: "Madonna, you're so beautiful."

She made the acquaintance of a cheerful, happy *pizzaiolo*; she saw the blood gushing out of his chest, along with his love for his children and his pride, and she wept for him and those three little ones. She fought alongside his wife and mother to save his name, and she triumphed at their side.

She understood once again just what children are: sons who slash their mother's faces, who kick their mothers to death, who wait for their mothers to die so they can marry; and mothers who lie, steal, and con for them. Mothers who give up love, life, beauty, and dreams.

Last of all, she observed the man who looks out the window, and who then has his window taken from him. She heard the story of that chink in his armor, of the discovery of the forlorn love afflicting the commissario, the man who had tracked down the criminal who had murdered her Luca. She remembered him, through the mists of grief, at her son's funeral: his green, vitreous eyes, and in those eyes, the same suffering and grief as her own.

She decided that fate moves in mysterious ways, often bringing catastrophes with it, but that it can sometimes reserve happy surprises. And that sometimes, fate can use a helping hand.

She compressed her lips. And then she smiled at the love of her life, the father of her children, both living and dead.

In the darkness of her room, Enrica did her best to regain her peace of mind. She couldn't seem to stop crying. Humiliated, offended, angry. These were new emotions to her, and having never experienced them before, she didn't know how to fight them. She hated herself wholeheartedly.

Her family didn't even try to chip away at her loneliness. The girl's wall of reserve was a barrier no one dared to knock down.

She was terrified of the kitchen window, but it was terrible being away from it: she missed those green eyes in the darkness more and more with each passing day.

She heard someone knock softly on her door. She replied by saying that she wasn't hungry.

But her mother's voice persisted:

"There's someone at the door. They insist on talking with you. They say it's important."

She went to the door. There stood an attractive woman she didn't know: blonde, sky-blue eyes. A black shawl, but underneath it, a nice flower-print dress. The woman smiled at her and looked at her eyes, puffy from crying. She said: "Signorina, buona sera. My name is Lucia Maione."

Commissario Luigi Alfredo Ricciardi had eaten practically nothing. He hadn't even responded to the worried questions of his Tata Rosa. Crushed by a sense of sadness, he had listened to the music that came over the airwaves from faraway auditoriums; but tonight there were no dancing couples, and the music was playing for no one.

It was late, but he lacked the courage to withdraw into his dark cell, where he'd be more alone than he had ever been before.

He took off his clothes and dressed for bed. Every gesture mechanical. He could have been a hundred years old, or never even have been born.

He couldn't keep himself from looking before he turned out the lamp. And his heart leapt up, overflowing with love.

In the window across the street, a young woman, her eyes wet with tears and an embroidery frame in her hand, was looking back at him.

High above, perched on the roof, springtime twirled and laughed.

ACKNOWLEDGEMENTS

If Ricciardi exists at all, it's thanks to Francesco Pinto and Domenico Procacci, who supported the idea of him.

But the commissario also owes a great deal to the expertise of Manuela Maddamma and Marinella Di Rosa, the flashes of inspiration and instincts of Antonio, and the encouragement of Michele; to Doctor Giulio Di Mizio and his gaze on death, at once clinical and sympathetic. And to Giovanni and Roberto, the cheerful bedrock of all his sad stories.

The author, in his turn, must once again wholeheartedly thank none but the gentle sweet mistress of his very impulse to write: Paola.

About the Author

Maurizio de Giovanni lives and works in Naples. His Commissario Ricciardi novels, including *I Will Have Vengeance* (Europa 2013), *Blood Curse* (Europa 2013), and *Everyone in Their Place* (Europa 2013), are bestsellers in Italy and have been published to great acclaim in French, Spanish, and German, in addition to English. He is also the author of *The Crocodile* (Europa 2013), a noir thriller set in contemporary Naples.

1